The Savannah Stories

Number Ten

The Savannah Stories

Number Ten

J.L. Lemon

ISBN-13: 978-0-9909589-4-9

Published 2015

For Dad and Mom

Guess how much I love you

It's hard to wake up from a nightmare if you're not even asleep.

Author Unknown

1

May 24

Year 1

Norcross Maximum Security Prison

I sit in a seventy-seven square foot prison cell, a book propped open across my lap. I have carefully printed my name on the title page so it reads:

Killer Instinct

Belongs to Jeffrey T. Holland

I am drawn to the words of the open book. They are written by an author who, over the years, has penned several novels. Her face and name are renowned in Atlanta but I am one of the few who have seen her at her most vulnerable – naked, trembling at my touch, her heartfelt pleas spilling from her lips. Her name is Georgia Prince Rutherford but she publishes under her tried and true Georgia Prince. Her picture on the book jacket reminds me of Rita Hayworth in her heyday. In the picture Georgia's shoulder-length brown hair falls in gentle waves, her features are soft like her skin, friendly like her laugh and cheerful enough to charm any man.

She is beautiful but she is not who I want. The picture on the book jacket is all I have to remind me of the woman I truly yearn for. Georgia and her younger sister Savannah favor greatly and when I see the elder's smiling face, I imagine her sister smiling back at me. It is Savannah that I want. I long to touch her again, to feel her warm, damp flesh beneath my fingertips. I can almost feel the tendons in her sleek, graceful neck straining as my scalpel parts her skin like butter. Her back arches in agony as the blade sinks deeper, her muscles straining against the bonds holding her. Her long legs struggle to hold her trembling five-nine frame upright yet she refuses to surrender. Then she pleads for mercy. But this last image – of her pleading – is a flight of fancy, the reverie of a creative mind because our first encounter did not go the way I intended. I spent days preparing for her yet when I had her, I heard no pleas for mercy, saw no sign of weakness. Her body and spirit are incredibly strong. I admit to underestimating her but never again. When I am finally released from prison – and I will be – I will come for Savannah, this time with a perfect plan.

O O O

July 5

Year 1

Despite my incarceration, I celebrate a modicum of freedom with a new friend. Her name is Tonya. She is eager to please me so a few days ago I asked for a favor. I wanted a picture of Savannah. My request was met with reluctance. Won't the mail be opened and checked, she asked. Yes, I replied, but I barter medical advice for favors in the mailroom. My guard friend will open the mail but send it through with no questions or censoring. That assurance convinced her to grant my favor. Tonya left the prison with a promise to send me pictures of my iron-willed beauty.

Since our last meeting, Savannah has given birth to a baby. The little girl is still too young to know what happened, the past her mother and I share. She only cares about sleep, being cradled in Mommy's loving arms and suckling from her breasts. It has been months since I've seen Savannah. Her hips were still slim, her breasts just beginning to swell. Her face appeared slightly fuller, her skin porcelain and flawless. At that point only the trained eye would have noticed her pregnancy but a person always notices differences in the ones most important to them. And I noticed.

A small TV sits in the corner of my cell. I watch every police news conference she attends, tune into every publicity engagement her sister Georgia gives to promote her book Killer Instinct. After one long month my diligence pays off. Georgia finally reveals the name of Savannah's baby. Lily. Pretty little Lily. Mommy's angel. I spend endless hours pondering Lily's features. Does she bat her pretty blue eyes at Mommy, or does she have her father's dark eyes? I wonder if Lily's hair will be Mommy's color, the rich, silky cocoa flowing in loose waves below her shoulders. So many questions and only my new friend can answer them with a simple photograph.

When I'm not reading or learning the intricacies of computers and the internet, I spend my time exercising. My cell barely accommodates my six-two frame. Only a few paces back and forth, that's the extent of my space. This cold, gray crypt makes it difficult to have a fitness routine but I manage a regimen of pushups and sit-ups. They give me one hour in the exercise yard and I use it to lift weights. I have to maintain my physique for my Southern darling because she isn't merely mentally strong, she is physically strong. Her spirit will not break until her body does so I must be stronger, more patient with her next time.

I hear the sound of letters being sorted. The mail has arrived. I glance eagerly at the narrow slot, waiting to see if Tonya fulfilled her promise. The metal slot finally opens. They use it for everything. Mail, food, medication. When I leave the cell I'm forced to stand hands behind me while they handcuff me through that slot. It is the portal to everything in my life now.

Three letters drop to the floor. I wait, not wanting to appear too anxious. My heart punches against my ribs as I glance down at the mail. I recognize Tonya's handwriting.

I scoop up the letters, discard the others. The only one I want is the gem in my hand. My guard friend has opened it as per prison rules and regulations so when I peek in the envelope, I notice he kept his promise as well. I see the edge of a photograph. No, wait. Four *photographs! Tonya has surprised me with such lavish gifts. Perhaps, like Savannah, I have underestimated her too…*

I set the enclosed letter aside for later. I've waited far too long for Savannah. Far too long to see her and her baby. The first picture steals my breath. My detective is lovely as always. I trace the line of her jaw. She still carries a few extra pounds from giving birth but her fuller cheeks and rounder hips do not detract from her beauty.

The first photo shows her standing outside with her family. She cradles her precious one in her arms. I see love and adoration in Mommy's eyes. The depth of her happiness surprises me. This is a different Savannah from last year when the prospect of motherhood seemed improbable. Back then she focused only on her job, not having children, but the sparkle in her blue eyes reveals another aspect of this remarkable woman that I overlooked. Her delight in her new role as a mother.

From what I see, Baby Lily favors Mommy as I predicted. In the first photo, I can't tell the color of her eyes. But the hair is Savannah's genetic contribution. Swaddled in a bright pink blanket, Lily sleeps soundly while Savannah beams down at her girl. The next two photos reveal Tonya is a sneaky one. She found a way to snap photos of a family get-together in the park. I recognize Savannah, her husband Ennis, then Georgia and her husband (Ennis's brother) and I'm guessing the other couple is Savannah's brother and his family. They all congregate close to get a glimpse of the newest addition to the Prince family.

I marvel at Savannah's relaxed demeanor. When we are together,

her expression transforms from calm to anxious. The fear rises inside her, her pulse feverishly drums in her neck. She is different around me. The woman in the photos is at ease. The woman I know is protective of her emotions, shielding me from seeing or sensing her true feelings.

The joy of motherhood shines as does the pride in her smile. Someday Baby Lily will be a heartbreaker like her mother and probably just as stubborn. The next photo shows the child awake and alert, her blue eyes assessing her surroundings. Yes, I see defiance in those sapphire pools. I see Savannah in those eyes and I know that Lily Rutherford will grow up to become quite a challenge to the male population, just as her mother is to me.

O O O

December 23

Year 4

Tonya is getting on my nerves. While still a viable outlet to Savannah, she's taking liberties I don't approve of. We've grown closer via mail and she now visits on occasion when her surgeon husband is on call at the hospital. She is a lovely woman, though sickeningly desperate to please and has developed a deep affection toward me. The latter makes me uncomfortable. Touching my hand, stroking my arm. Yearning for a woman's touch is foreign to me. I do not care to feel it yet I bear it for one simple reason. The more I allow Tonya to display her affection, the more productive she is and my personal Santa delivered bountiful gifts this Christmas.

Her latest photos show Savannah's second child, Anna Rose, has her mother's charming smile but mostly takes after her father. Lily Christine is approaching four and is a mirror image of her mother.

The Rutherford family celebrates Christmas in full style. The photos show not only the girls wearing festive sweaters but their mother as well. That's a new one. Savannah never struck me as the holiday type. The pictures reveal her and Ennis hanging Christmas lights along the eaves of their house and wrapping them around the porch posts. I am fascinated at the plain-spoken career-minded woman gently clasping Lily's hand in hers while half a dozen shopping bags weigh down her other.

Quite possibly the best photo is Lily visiting Santa Claus at the mall. With joy lighting her expression, Savannah lifts the child into "Santa's" lap. Next photo is Lily crying, reaching for Mommy, her face cherry red and tear-streaked. Third photo is Savannah shrugging apologetically to the jolly old elf. I miss these priceless moments being behind bars but some day I will again see this happy mother – and her daughters too.

O   O   O

Year 5

February 20

I have bided my time and it has paid off. For the last few years I've been a model prisoner, given no trouble, and worked in the library. I have used my time wisely while on the internet. I've kept in touch with Tonya who keeps me supplied with photos of my lovely detective and her girls. In this time my lawyer (slow as he is) managed to stumble on a priceless nugget. Most people, including me, do not understand the legal system. I know the basics however my clever, yet slothful, attorney slogged away, searching for a small, yet significant key. The key to my freedom. It revolves around improper jury instructions. He is working to have me released, if even for a retrial. I'll gladly accept a retrial because by that time Savannah and I will be reunited and I so look forward to that. Soon, I hope to be free of this stuffy, dank cell. Free to walk the streets of historic Atlanta, smell the freshly mowed grass and taste the sweetness of peach pie. I have a undeniable craving for peach pie and I've read the pies are exceptionally delicious at Pie In The Sky. I will make a note to stop there first thing...

2

Year 5

May 6

Pie In The Sky started out as a whim. An idea between two friends, Georgia and fellow church member Jacob Evans. They tossed around the idea of opening a bake shop after several church bake sales raked in double what was estimated. People clamored for Georgia's goods with a couple of members virtually losing their religion to snag three of her pies. After the dust settled, Georgia promised to make the extra pies for the good of their Baptist mission and Jacob and Georgia shook hands on their new venture together – Pie In The Sky.

They chose a location populated by other eateries and found a quaint little store fitting their needs. It sat nestled in a row of restaurants (between a barbecue joint and a hamburger place) frequented by employees of nearby businesses and plenty of hungry tourists. While Jacob handled the arrangements for equipment, Georgia tackled the finishing touches regarding décor, furnishings and the menu.

She decided on a vintage theme with a black and white striped awning with "Pie In The Sky" printed across the front. For color she placed ceramic urns filled with bright colored flowers flanking each side of the door. She chose beige for the walls and tan colored floor tiles for a warm atmosphere and for contrast, black tables and chairs.

When Pie In The Sky opened, the two entrepreneurs found themselves shorthanded on funds and help so Savannah volunteered to work on her days off when possible. Soon the bakery brought in enough money to hire regular employees but Savannah continued pitching in on Saturdays when she wasn't scheduled to work. She brought Lily (sometimes both girls) because her daughter's charm far outweighed her own and as a result the register collected more sales.

Savannah and the girls arrived at nine thirty. They'd stay for the usual three hours then go home for her to begin chores around the house. Helping out at the Pie in The Sky during some free time provided her and Georgia more quality time together. Plus four year-old Lily and two year-old Anna loved spending time with Aunt Georgia.

Savannah placed a fresh peach pie in the display between the pineapple cream cheese and apple crumb pies. God blessed her sister with a creative soul. Georgia penned successful mystery novels since the age of twenty, plus she could cook or bake any chef to shame. Once a person tasted her talents, more times than not they'd become regular patrons of the store. The primarily Southern menu ran the gamut from apple bourbon pie to cherry cheesecake, toasted coconut banana and sweet potato pie. Georgia prepared different pies on different days except for the best sellers which she always kept on hand.

The antique bell over the door jingled, announcing more customers. Savannah looked at the clock on the wall. Eleven thirty on the dot. Savannah smiled with knowledge of who their new customer might be. Every Saturday at that time Mr. Peter Thompson, a kind, elderly gentleman treated himself to a big slice of Georgia's peach pie, complete with a dollop of vanilla ice cream on the side. With it he ordered a cup of black coffee with a "drop" of cream "to lighten his mood."

She glanced around the corner to see Mr. Thompson, hunched over his walking cane, shuffling to his regular perch by the plate glass window. He'd brought his brother that day she noticed. Bob Thompson lived in Murrayville, a city ninety miles north of Atlanta. When he visited his older brother, he made it a point to join his brother for a slice of pie – almost always on a Saturday.

At first Savannah felt nervous around Bob, even out of place since Bob was deaf and only communicated via sign language. Peter waved it off, saying it was easy to learn, that all she needed to know was the signs for chess pie, coffee and ice cold milk. Over the months, however, she picked up more than those words. She learned how to converse with Bob in a decent fashion, albeit a few flubs on her part.

Peter shrugged from his tan sweater. He wore khakis and a burgundy pullover – dressy for an outing at a simple bake shop but Peter Thompson never skimped on his appearance. The man in this early eighties arrived dressed sharp, freshly shaven and smelling of Old Spice, the latter reminding Savannah of her father.

Bob was the hippie of the two. A veritable Woodstock refugee who believed in comfortable jeans, faded Grateful Dead t-shirts and the legalization of marijuana because "it would end more wars than nukes." Today Bob slouched in with jeans ragging at the cuffs, a Jimi Hendrix t-shirt stretched across his ample chest and his toes peeking out of his sandals.

Savannah retied her black apron with pink Pie In The Sky emblem, telling Georgia, "The two Mr. Thompsons are here."

Georgia chuckled as she weaved latticework atop a cherry pie, "I'd swear Peter's got a crush on you. Always on Saturday when he knows you're here and if you notice, he gets brusque with Bob when he comes along."

She rolled her eyes, "You've got a vivid imagination. He's just lonely and he likes the girls."

Georgia shrugged, unconvinced, "Whatever you say. There's a fresh peach pie on the counter and I made another chess pie in case Bob came with him."

Savannah stayed with routine. She headed out to the two brothers, greeted Peter with the customary *Mr. Thompson* then signed *Hi Bob.*

Peter smiled, "I'll bet money you're the prettiest girl in the state of Georgia. And you're always so cheerful."

Savannah heard a little laugh from the kitchen. Georgia. So what an older man thought she was pretty? That's what older men did, right? They were friendly, they complimented women. That didn't mean he wanted to ask her for a date.

"You know, young lady," he continued, "I've said it before. You favor Rita Hayworth, especially when you smile."

This was routine. He volleyed a Rita Hayworth comment and she returned with a one about another famous individual, "Thank you, Mr. Thompson, and may I say you remind me of a gentleman who won five Open Championships in golf. His name was also Peter Thomson." She never mentioned the golfing Peter's last name was spelled differently. She suspected he already knew it.

Bob, bored with their exchange, signed *get a room*. Savannah laughed, speaking as she signed *someone's grumpy*.

He frowned – *Late night. Need extra sugar and big piece of pie.*

She nodded – *Right away.* Then turned to Peter, "Your usual?"

"Please." He glanced past her, "Where are your girls?"

"Entranced by Aunt Georgia's pie making abilities. As if Mama never bakes."

Peter leaned forward in his seat, waved her closer, "Why don't you ditch the cop job and work here? I'd come in every day and I could even entertain your babies. I got lots of stories I could tell them. I'd teach 'em old time games, not this silliness on the internet."

Peter's request came as no surprise. On occasion he mentioned her working full time at the bakery – with the incentive of them both spending more time with the girls. If it paid better, she would have debated his idea. Until then, she only committed to saying, "I'll consider it."

He extended his hand, "Deal?"

She slid her hand in his warm soft one and gently shook, "Deal."

He held on a little longer, a wistful expression shadowing his exuberance, "How you remind me of my daughter. She was so beautiful and kind. Lost her to cancer at forty."

Sadness washed over her. That was partly why he visited. He missed his little girl. Savannah covered his hand with hers, "I'm so sorry, Mr. Thompson."

"Take care of yourself, Savannah. Leaving those sweet girls without a mother would destroy a part of them. They need you."

She smiled then kissed his cheek, "I'll do my best–"

Bob rapped the table with his knuckles, pointed to his watch and signed *while I'm young, please.*

Peter's mouth thinned, "Y'know the extra sugar he wants? Give him two lumps – on the head."

Bob swatted his brother's arm, signing *I can read lips too.*

Savannah teased, "Bob's got topnotch vision, Mr. Thompson. No secrets around him."

Peter harrumphed, "No peace you mean."

She chuckled, "I'll be right back." She turned to see Lily waving at Mr. Thompson whose face took on a much younger vibrancy. The girl ran toward him, "Mr. Thompson!"

He opened his arms, enfolded her in a hug, "There's that angel. Say, what's today?"

Savannah heard her daughter's enthusiastic, "Saturday!"

"It's also the day darling little girls get a treat," he said. He held her hand palm up, covered it with his own then curled her fingers into a fist, enclosing the gift in her hand.

Peter normally gifted the girls with enough money to cover a slice of pie and milk.   Lily opened her hand, her jaw dropping, "I'm rich!" She threw her arms around his neck, "Thank you, Mr. Thompson!"

Savannah couldn't tell how much money he gave Lily but her daughter's zeal cautioned her to check. When Lily said the word *rich*, that meant more than two dollars and Savannah knew the Thompson brothers weren't exactly Donald Trump wealthy.

Peter's eyes sparkled as he returned the embrace, "Tell your mama you want a treat as sweet as you."

Lily took time to wave at Bob who signed *hello*. Peter asked, "Do you remember how to sign the word *hi*?"

Lily worked her small hand into a fist, first pointing her index and middle fingers together like a finger gun. The *H*. Then she swiveled her fist upright and extended her pinkie finger up. The *I*.

Peter applauded, "Very good, Lily." He reached in his pocket again but Savannah, busy pouring his coffee, held a hand up with a shake of her head. He'd already given Lily too much as evidenced by her beaming daughter.

He pointed the girl to her mother, "Go get your treat, sweetie. Mama's waiting."

Savannah slanted Peter a *you-shouldn't-have* frown but he was such a dear man and so good to her and her kids. Lily raced to her, wagging a five dollar bill and asking for a slice of peach pie.

Savannah nearly swallowed her tongue. Peter gave the child far too much money. A quarter, sure. A dollar, maybe. But five? No way. "Settle down, sweetheart. Let me serve the two Mr. Thompsons first."

She scooped a slice of peach pie onto a plate, a piece of chess pie on another. Before pouring Bob's milk and coffee, she went to her purse, withdrew some cash.

Georgia saw her open the register, "What are you doing?"

"Paying for the Thompsons' order. Peter gave Lily five dollars."

The older sister's eyes popped wide, "For what?"

"'Cause he likes her and he's lonely for his daughter. That's why he warmed up to me. He said I remind him of her." She poured the drinks, making sure to add extra sugar on Bob's saucer. She added the scoop of ice cream to Peter's order.

She headed out with the tray, giving the Thompson brothers a wink as she approached, "Freshest pies in the place. And," she signed to Bob, "your extra sugar, my liege."

Bob's mouth curved into a smile – *Thanks.*

She nodded. He was old and cantankerous but Bob was generally nice. Peter snorted, "He'll be human again once he eats." He reached for his wallet but she shook her head, "It's on the house, Mr. Thompson."

"Young lady," he said good-naturedly, "how many times have I said call me Peter?"

"As many times as Bob bangs the table for his food. And I'm not as young as you think and plenty of folks would dispute the *lady* part too," she ended on a quiet chuckle.

He opened his wallet, "I still pay my bills though I appreciate the offer."

She put a gentle hand to his, "You gave Lily five dollars. That was too much. Let me give it back to you. You can spend it on something you need or want."

"But I want to give it to Lily. Don't deny an old man, Savannah. I never get to spoil anyone. Let me spoil your girls."

She considered his request. He looked hurt that she might refuse him. She sighed, "Five dollars just this once but you'll let me buy your pie and drinks today because *I* want to. Deal?" She extended her hand.

He pursed his lips, slid his hand in hers, "You *are* like my daughter. Hardheaded as a mule. Now," he pulled a couple of ones from his wallet, "This is for Anna."

She nudged his hand away, "No, sir. The five will be fine for both. Lily's learning to share these days. She's good about it." *Well, half the time she is...* "But thank you." She pointed to his plate, hinting, "Your ice cream is melting."

Peter put the money away, putting up a light fuss about stubborn girls. "You'll be here next Saturday?" he asked.

"As long as I have the day off, yes."

Satisfied, he sank his spoon into the peach pie, "It's a date."

Savannah bid the brothers farewell, headed to another table

occupied by a young woman texting on her phone. Red hair cascaded down her shoulders and that, along with her posture and attire of jade green silk blouse and black slacks, gave her a graceful appearance. She crossed her legs at the knee, the right one swinging leisurely back and forth.

When Savannah approached, the woman's chin lifted. The second their gaze met, a vague spark of recognition dawned on her. She'd seen this woman before but couldn't place where. "What can I get you today?" she asked.

"The peach pie is delicious," Peter offered from a few tables away.

The woman ignored him. She briefly appraised Savannah from head to toe as if sizing her up and decided upon an unfavorable result. "Chocolate pecan pie, please."

Savannah wondered what the sneer was about. The stranger raked her top to bottom the way a fashion snob judged a homeless person. "Okay. Anything to drink?"

"Coffee. Black."

"Got it," Savannah walked to the back, still confused why the woman took a dislike to her. Dishing up the pie, she searched the recesses of her brain to remember where the two might have met and more importantly, crossed swords.

She poured the coffee, slanting the female a covert glance. Savannah stopped upon seeing the woman's phone pointed at her, snapping a picture. Okay, her jaw tightened. The highbrow crap was one thing. So was being scrutinized like a rat in a maze but cloak-and-dagger pictures were another matter altogether.

Their eyes met. The woman's aloof demeanor shattered into a flustered, frantic attempt to conceal the invasive deed. She stuffed the phone in her purse, scrambling to collect the payment and, Savannah guessed, leave the store.

She hurried to deliver the order. Setting the coffee and pie on the table, she struck up a casual conversation, "I haven't seen you in here before." She extended her hand, "I'm Savannah."

The woman hesitated, stared wide-eyed at the offered hand. She eased hers around Savannah's, "Tonya."

"You look familiar. I don't recall where but have we met before?"

She swiveled to stand, "No."

In a nonchalant move, Savannah stepped around, blocking her, "Are you sure because you act like you know me. Where do you work?"

"I don't. My husband is a surgeon."

"What hospital is he affiliated with?"

Tonya grew antsy with the questions, "Atlanta Medical and Emory."

"My sister-in-law is a nurse at Grady. Thought maybe they worked togeth–"

"How much do I owe?"

"I'll get right on that." She busied herself scribbling the total for the order, "I noticed you taking pictures with your phone."

Tonya fidgeted, her green eyes flitting around the store like a cornered animal searching for an escape. "I like the décor," she said as an afterthought.

"Then why were you taking *my* photo?"

Savannah's blunt inquiry rattled her, "I don't recall taking your picture. I wanted the decor." Again she dug into the small jeweled handbag for money, laid it on the table, "I need to go. I forgot I have an appointment."

"I'll get your change."

Tonya rose to her feet. With the high heels, she stood Savannah's height, "Keep it."

"I'll get this ready to go for you then."

"No thanks." She rushed to the door, threw it open hard enough to jar the bell into a frenzy.

Savannah watched her race from the store and climb into a silver Volvo across the street.

Bob rapped his knuckles on their table. She glanced at the brothers who seemed as bewildered as she was. From the corner of her eye, she saw Tonya speed off as if she'd just robbed the place. *That was weird*, Bob signed.

"*She* was weird," Peter added.

"Yeah," she agreed. "And I know I've seen her before. Why wouldn't she admit it?"

3

Year 5

May 10

I run my hand along my smooth cheek and jaw. The disposable razor takes years off me, giving me a softer, innocuous appearance. My dark curly hair is cut shorter than years earlier. Savannah remembers my hair with noticeable curl, my jaw shadowed with stubble. Before our meeting I will return to my former self, for old times' sake.

I am pleased with my features. I favor my father who lured women with the ease of a master fisherman angling for a prize winning bass. I suppose I inherited a small amount of his charisma and good looks because women have fawned over me since I hit puberty. Once I earned my medical degree, they found me increasingly more attractive. Being a surgeon in a busy hospital, scouting out my next number became a matter of a smile, a dash of charm and a wink. Until I landed Number Ten. Savannah Prince required no pretense, no charm, no line of bullshit. She was and is immune.

Since my lawyer is convinced that freedom is around the corner, I've spent time planning, making mental notes. I need easy access to Savannah away from her children if possible. If not, I'm sure I can make use of her cubs. I also require a quick method of subduing her. I've fought with her before and frankly I'd rather be tarred and feathered before doing it again. First things first, I tell myself. First, what I really need is Tonya. To keep her happy. And that seems simplest of all…

I turn to begin my daily regimen of push-ups and sit-ups. It's not long until breakfast arrives. Rubbery pancakes and a bowl of grits. The food alone in this place is incentive enough to prevent crime early on, if only it were served in schools.

Over the years I've cultivated a few friendships with other prisoners and a couple of guards. My inmate colleagues and I trade food from the commissary. This is what makes the usual gruel tolerable. My guard friends allow me a few extra minutes in the yard for my weight training, another works in the mailroom. This is the real benefit. He allows my mail through without censoring it. The most he does is slit them open to make things appear official – if he reads the letters, he never lets on.

Until the mail arrives I spend time reading about computers and the internet. One of my inmate buddies is a programming expert and all around guru so I learn from him, for when I'm eventually released.

Two cells down I hear the door slot clang shut. Mail. My heartbeat quickens when the slot next door slams. I'm next. What will come today? More fan mail or a letter from Tonya? For the last five years she and I have grown closer. She provides me with news of my lovely detective and I give her what she desires. My attention. Her visits are more frequent now, probably because her hubby is gone so much. This is when I ask her for more "favors". A photo of Savannah alone or her with her children. Tonya has yet to disappoint me with my requests however I see jealousy burning in her green eyes when we are together. I have made my intentions quite clear over the years. Savannah is the only woman I want, the one who keeps me awake at night, the one who invades my every thought. She keeps me alive, knowing we'll meet again. In the meantime Tonya fires every weapon in her female arsenal to entice me, to convince me she is who I want, not Savannah.

The door slot opens and two envelopes drop to the floor. One is heavier than the other. It gives me hope. I scoop them up, discarding the lighter one. It is another female admirer. My attention rivets to the weighty envelope with the sender's name – Tonya Thatcher.

Judging from the thickness of the correspondence she included several pictures. I rip into my gift, set the letter aside and opt for the bevy of photos wrapped inside it.

My greedy vision focuses on the first one. Tonya snapped a gorgeous moment of Savannah twirling four year-old Lily in her arms, the detective's smile spreads contagiously to my lips. What a stunning photo.

The next one was taken at Georgia's pie shop. Savannah wears a black and pink apron around her slim hips, in her hands she carries a tray with pie, coffee and milk. The next picture shows her hugging an older man. *Who is he, I wonder, that she feels comfortable enough to embrace him. In the following photo, Lily stands in front of him, her little hands gesturing somehow. The older man seems impressed. Savannah's hand rests on her girl's shoulder, obvious pride brightening her features. Some women change upon the birth of their child. I see subtle differences in Savannah physically and also by her interactions in these photos. There is contentment in her expression now. Without a close-up shot of her, I can still sense that sparkle in her eyes, that undeniable joy motherhood brings. My detective has changed during our time apart however I expect one aspect remains the same. Her fear of me.*

Breezing over Tonya's letter, I notice she mentioned how polite Lily was, saying please and thank you and helping her mother clear tables. My friend lingered outside the shop a while, she said, observing Savannah and Lily before venturing in. It unnerved her, she wrote, when Savannah began asking questions about her – if they'd met before, where did her husband work, etc...

I glare at the letter. Mental note. Tell Mrs. Scaredy Cat that detectives are naturally curious beings and Tonya, don't, under any circumstances, screw this up for me. Relax, I'll tell her. Like a bear, Savannah is harmless unless threatened. And, I'll add, be careful about photographing the kids. Savannah, I'm quite sure, protects those girls with lethal force, the way any normal mother would.

I turn back to the photos. Taken at Savannah's house, it shows her and her husband Ennis leaning against the fender of her Charger. Ennis's arm cradles her waist, holding her close. They smile while their two daughters play in the front yard. She wears jeans and a short sleeve pullover blouse matching the color of her eyes. A brilliant azure. Her beautiful eyes always betray her thoughts, her moods. I remember that. Their usual friendliness can plunge a person into frostbite in an instant. My first encounter with her was at the hospital after her radiation treatment for breast cancer. We literally ran into each other and her blue eyes flew wide in surprise. I can only imagine her surprise upon seeing me again...

O   O   O

Year 5

June 8

My lawyer finally came through with my release. My new trial will be scheduled for a later date – much later I hope. I have numerous items on my itinerary before I see Savannah and must get busy. For now, I bask in my freedom from the small stuffy prison cell, the mealy pancakes, the Nutriloaf that could be used as building material – and I'm free from the slot. I can walk the street, eat my choice of cuisine, decide when and where I sleep.

Tonya picks me up in her silver Volvo, drives me to the mall for new clothes then to her house where she prepares a tasty lasagna. Always the helpful girl, she withdraws ten thousand dollars for me as a starter bank account. It has been years since I've seen money of that amount. In the meantime, she invites me to stay with her while her husband is away doing charity work for Doctors Without Borders so I feel comfortable saying yes. The house is enormous. I estimate the value at over a million dollars. Mr. Tonya Thatcher has done well for himself.

Located in a suburb of Atlanta where everything shouts extravagance and money, the driveways are long and flanked with lush, sweeping lawns. Tonya's house is perfect, the neighborhood quiet with copious amounts of space and tree between properties.

The five bedroom mansion is furnished with expensive furniture, paintings and sculptures. Nothing but the best for Mr. Thatcher and his bride. The sheer amount of money invested within these four walls stupefies me.

Tonya insists on a tour of the eight thousand square foot palace and considering I'll be staying here, I sign up so I won't get lost in the maze of hallways and rooms.

The entry alone is twice the size of my prison cell. Hardwood floors give the living room a comfortable feel as well as the beige colored walls trimmed in white. I've never seen so many windows in my life. Sunlight beams through every room, brightening them to nearly a hurtful degree.

The kitchen is spacious and classy with granite counters and new, state of the art appliances. The master bedroom holds most of my interest. Heavy dark wood contrasts the lighter "khaki" colored walls, as Tonya calls them. There is a queen size bed with a black metal filigree headboard and cherry wood nightstands on either side. Across the room is a comfy love seat with ottoman for watching the fancy flat screen TV above the stone fireplace. This house is large, breathtaking, and absolutely perfect. I feel the way Goldilocks did. This place is "just right".

The view from the back porch deck is breathtaking. Towering trees surround the property save for one section measuring around twenty feet. Beyond the confines of the trees is Lake Windward. The water sparkles like diamonds in the sun. It is a peaceful, beautiful place.

After dinner, I make a suggestion. To celebrate my release, let's plan a trip. A cruise perhaps. A long, leisure cruise, just the two of us. My suggestion is met with surprising excitement. Since her hubby is gone anyway, she jumps at the chance. She begins calling the maid service and other services, putting them on hold until our return. "Don't forget the mail and paper," I wink. Tonya calls, suspending them both beginning the day after tomorrow. We're all set, according to her. Later that evening we'll scout out last minute deals on cruises.

Her eagerness regarding the trip relocates to her libido, apparently, and she begins touching, kissing me. Her fingers thread through my hair, drawing my lips to hers. I kiss her, hoping to back her off somehow. I'm not a novice at sex but I'm very choosy about my partners. I try to imagine it's Savannah's fingers in my hair, her lips caressing mine, her tongue sliding against mine. I'd rarely entertained having sex with Savannah. My erections resulted from memories of her pain, her screams. But I must keep Tonya happy for now. If I picture *my pretty detective while I screw Mrs. Thatcher, so be it.*

My fantasy flies apart when I feel Tonya's hand at my crotch. I push her offending appendage away knowing Savannah would not be so aggressive, so bold. I retain my temper, just barely, and stress, "Not yet."

This confuses Tonya. She eases her hand to my shoulder. Her compliance gives me an idea. I dive in for another kiss, my hand closes over right breast and I descend into my fantasy again. The soft, warmth in my palm inspires memories of Savannah. The way she reacted to my touch on her breast, the defiance in her eyes when I thumbed her nipple.

I pull away slowly, whispering, "Bedroom. Now."

"Take your clothes off," I tell her upon crossing the threshold.

She's taken aback at the gruff command. She doesn't move. I repeat myself – something I despise doing. Savannah understands this, Tonya does not. Not yet. "Take them off and lie on the bed."

Now she seems hurt. I try to smooth it over, "It's been five years, Tonya. I want to watch a beautiful woman undress for me while I watch."

She's back in the game. A smile curves her lips. She thinks she's gained the upper hand. Yet another thing Savannah would never do. Broadcast her assumptions through facial expressions. Oh sure, she gave me plenty of drop dead glares, and the go-to-hell scowl was my personal favorite. But while in my company she never assumed she had the upper hand.

Tonya strips down to reveal a sleek, trim figure belonging in Playboy. Her breasts are larger than Savannah's, considerably so. She moves with feline gracefulness upon the bed, no doubt to seduce me. Oh, I'm impressed, alright. Those breasts of hers would entice almost any man with a pulse and drive a hormonal teenage boy insane. No, Savannah does not compare with Tonya Thatcher in that respect however I measure a woman by different criteria these days. Breasts do not make the woman any more than tires make the car. A car is a sum of its parts. By that standard, Savannah is a racer. A Lamborghini Veneno – rare, complex, provides high quality performance and can be dangerous if not handled correctly. Tonya, on the other hand, is a run of the mill Chevy. Reliable, comfortable and a good standby.

She eases back on the mattress, gives me a come hither smile. I go to the closet, remove a leather belt from her husband's collection. Tonya sees it, withdraws from me. She eyes the belt warily, "What are you doing?"

I advance on her. "This is how I like sex," I lie. "I like to be in charge, the one who does the touching. If you want me, that's how it will be. Do you want me, Tonya?"

She nods, the action more certain than her expression. I see a twinkle of misgiving in her eyes. Do I trust him – do I know him well enough to trust him, they seem to ask. The tennis match continues in her head – do I or don't I – while I point to the bed, "Then relax. Five years we've known each other. Why are you afraid of me?"

My gentle admonition causes a surge of guilt in her, as if she's been silly and finally realizes it. She completely eases onto her back. I motion for her to cross her wrists above her head. She does. I loop the belt around them, cinch it down tight until she whimpers. I feel her pulling back but force them to the iron filigreed headboard and tie the belt securely. I go back to the closet, take my time choosing two more belts. Tonya pulls at her wrists and I wag my finger at her, smiling, "If you lie still, you'll be in for a surprise."

Reluctantly she settles down. I come back, loop a belt around her left ankle. She again pulls against me and I bear down to the bone, "Tonya, do you want to have sex or not?"

She's not sure now. The furrow in her brow says fear is taking over. I tickle her foot, bring a giggle from her. "Does that feel so bad?" I ask.

She shakes her head and relaxes. I tie her ankle to the footboard, and make short work of the right foot. Now she is spread out before me, expecting more of me than I will give her. I'm saving my energy for one woman. "I'll be right back. Be a good girl and don't move."

I go to the garage. The hot weather and heat from the car's engine warms the room until I break a sweat – or perhaps it is anticipation. I search shelves and drawers until I find what I need. Duct tape. I head to the kitchen. I go through the drawers, then spy a cutlery set on the cabinet. I test one with a seven inch blade. Sharp as a razor. Perfect.

When I step in the bedroom doorway, I smile at Tonya. The knife and duct tape are behind my back. "I have a question for you, Mrs. Thatcher."

She's worked herself into a sweat already, waiting for me to climb atop her and make love to her. "What question is that?"

I slowly step into the room, my voice not betraying my intent, "Aren't you the slightest bit curious why I'm interested in Savannah Prince?"

Her lip curls a degree. She tries not to show her jealousy. "Not really, no."

"Aren't you curious what I want to do to her? It's very special, what I have planned. No other woman in the world will ever know except you, if you want to know."

"Why are you so obsessed with her?" The green-eyed monster awakens. "I've seen her, I've met her and she's average, Jeff. Simply av-er-age. She's not that pretty, and she's certainly not loyal like I am. I've been there for you five years while she's ignored you."

"That's part of her allure," I explain. "To me she is what the near-mint Honus Wagner baseball card is to a collector or what the Gutenberg Bible is to a Christian."

She still doesn't get the analogy so I put it into terms she can understand, "In your world, the Hope Diamond, perhaps. The rarest, most valuable of all. The most coveted and revered. Savannah is my Hope Diamond. She is Number Ten and we all know there's only one Number Ten."

"But what about me? Why don't you want me?"

Whiny little girl. A whiny, little rich girl that can't have her way – or maybe she can... "But I do want you. And I'm giving you the opportunity to experience that. Would you like to experience how I feel *about Savannah? How much she means to me?"*

She gets groovy again, gives me a sanctimonious shrug, "If you want to."

My smile broadens, "Oh, I want to, Tonya. I really want to." I near the bed and swing the duct tape into her view. Her eyes widen and I hurriedly rip off a strip of tape, slap it over her mouth. I hold my hand there, feel my erection stiffen. The vibration of her shaking fear, the sounds of her whimpers and muffled screams beneath my hand. It is all coming back now. I'm home again. My breath quickens. The power I wield over this woman, a woman I envision to be Savannah, causes my heart to leap in my chest with anticipation.

Tonya Thatcher writhes on the bed until I nestle the sharp blade against her tight nipple. She stills, just like Savannah did years ago. Tries to control her breathing, her panic. Just like Savannah. Her terror-filled eyes meet my heavy-lidded ones – the excitement is nearly overwhelming after such a long dry spell. Beneath the silver tape, she pleads with me. Her whimpers sound familiar. She's bargaining with me, if I'll only remove the tape and negotiate. When I don't, her pleading dwindles to capitulation. She knows she's defeated even before I've done a thing to her and that is not just like Savannah. My detective has tenacity and pure determination to outlast me. To fight to the end. To win. My detective is stubborn, strong, lovely in every way. This woman on the bed, she is a means to an end. And her time is up…

4

June 9

Savannah groaned out of bed before daylight. The week tested her patience beyond common decency. The case they worked hit so many twists and turns she decided it wasn't a murder investigation but a Grand Prix in the south of France. No one cooperated with her or Ennis, and the nuggets of information they mined from precious few turned out to be dead-ends.

Saturday mornings at the bakery still classified as work but it fell into the category of light and pleasant. After brushing her teeth and running a comb through her hair, she went outside for the newspaper.

A wispy breeze cooled the summer air, promising a nice morning but questionable afternoon. Nothing tamed Atlanta heat and humidity. If a person wasn't born and raised there, they broiled in the hot sun from May to early September. At least that morning presented a temperate climate for residents and birds alike, the latter singing their melodic songs somewhere off in the distance.

At that hour the neighbors still slept, the houses cloaked in quiet darkness. She was the only brave (or stupid, depending on one's opinion) soul roaming about. Paper in hand, she climbed the porch steps, making a mental note to water her flowerbeds after returning home from work that afternoon. Savannah battled the daily heat to save her pretty hibiscus. She'd worked too hard to plant them and nurture them into a healthy, beautiful display only to let the sun wilt the blooms. The heat was hardest to cope with by evening when Lily wanted her golf lessons. Several times a week (sometimes every night), Savannah and Lily stood in the back yard, the youngster toiling over her swing. After seeing Savannah's trophies (an accident of cleaning out a closet), their oldest took a shine to the game. Lily demonstrated signs of natural talent, a fact that thrilled Savannah. Eager to improve quickly, the four year-old often asked for her mother's advice but Savannah refused to complicate the game yet. Play to have fun, she told Lily. If her interest persisted with age, then she planned more in-depth instructions on form and posture.

She pulled out a dining chair and sat down, opened the paper. The warm and fuzzy notions of Lily someday playing the LPGA circuit vacated the premises, leaving only the words in bold black print to fill her immediate thoughts.

Above the fold read "Woman Found Decapitated in Ravine". The word *ravine* struck a nerve. Memories of tortured women appeared, their breasts cut away with a scalpel, genitals mutilated, and their blood drained while they were still alive. Jeffrey Holland took his time prolonging their deaths (one woman lasted days) while he tortured them and beat them with a cane, then began slicing them to bits. Before removing the breasts, before disfiguring the genitals, Jeffrey carved a number into his victims with a scalpel. Savannah's was exactly one and a half inches below her right collarbone. Being a surgeon, he incised a perfectly straight line for the number one and the zero, though not as deep or obvious, was the size of a hen egg and just as oval.

A quick glance at the clock warned that Lily and Ennis would soon drag themselves from bed and expect breakfast. She read the article closer while she had time. The killer chopped off the victim's head, hands and feet. DNA analysis took weeks so if the woman had no distinguishable scars or tattoos, the killer probably had no real worries of her immediate identification.

Reading further, a sudden intense chill scraped down her back. The woman's breasts had been removed. Sliced away with surgical precision, the article said.

A rumbling set her stomach on edge, a twinge in her back reminded her of the brutal beating from Jeffrey's rattan cane, the blood that seeped from her numerous wounds and the sheer pain that reverberated through every nerve in her body.

Alpharetta was a short twelve miles from Dunwoody where she and Ennis lived. Jeffrey sat behind bars but misguided females all over the country penned letters to him – and possibly men as well. It took very little to instruct a deranged idiot on the finer points of torture and murder, especially if that deranged idiot wanted to impress Mr. Holland.

"Mama, are you okay?" Lily inquired.

Savannah snapped to attention, meeting her daughter's gaze.

Lily's vision focused on her mother's right shoulder. Savannah realized she'd been rubbing the scar beneath her collarbone. She tried to sound convincing, "Yes, honey, I'm fine."

Lily joined her at the table, reached toward Savannah's shoulder, massaged it with her hand. The girl had never seen the scar and Savannah vowed she wouldn't until she was considerably older. Until she understood someone tried to kill her mother.

Touched by her daughter's sentiment, Savannah covered her hand with her own, held it, "Thank you, little one. It's all better now."

"Not hurting anymore?"

"No," she kissed her cheek, "you made it well."

Lily may have physically favored her mother but she inherited her daddy's compassion. Always concerned for others and willing to help whenever needed. For the moment, however, the paper in Savannah's hand caught Lily's attention, "Whatcha readin'?"

Savannah folded the paper in a nonchalant manner, "Nothing important." Lily, while helpful, also hit the age of insatiable curiosity. If she suspected the article bothered Savannah, she'd nose into it and see words and pictures not meant for young eyes.

Lily's interest shifted to her mother's hair. The dark tresses draping past Savannah's shoulders needed a trim but with the hectic schedule at work, one or the other temporarily had to give.

Lily gathered the loose waves in one hand, "Can I make your ponytail today?"

She appreciated the offer but, "Better let me do it today. You can do it tomorrow after church." Her girl worked hard to perfect the ponytail except for one problem. It sat atop Savannah's head, giving her more of a Pebbles Flintstone appearance rather than her preferred Savannah Rutherford look.

Lily combed the mane with her fingers, "I want hair like this. It's pretty and shiny. I want *your* hair."

"I kinda need it right now, sweetheart. Besides, yours has the same color and texture so you *do* have my hair." *Just minus the silver strands I've noticed sneaking in the last few years.* Amazing how her girl either hadn't noticed them or just chose to ignore them – but Savannah hadn't. The malicious little threads crept up on a person like the small lines she noticed at the corners of her eyes. She dreaded to see herself in ten more years – especially if she never had time for a damn haircut. Shaking free of that disturbing image, she continued, "Give yours time to grow longer and you'll see the waves better."

"Are you sure?"

"Have I lied to you yet?"

"No, Mama," she said with absolute certainty. "You don't lie to me."

"That's right, I don't." She rose from the seat, sat the paper aside, "What's my baby want for breakfast?"

"Cocoa Puffs!"

Savannah smiled at the exuberant answer. During her pregnancy with Lily, Savannah craved Cocoa Puffs day and night, eating metro Atlanta out of box after box. Breakfast, lunch and, on occasion, supper.

It drove Ennis to distraction enough he questioned her sanity.   At least Daddy hadn't thought twice about his baby wolfing down the cereal. "One order of Cocoa Puffs coming right up."

Ennis emerged from the bedroom in jeans and a navy blue Dallas Cowboys polo shirt. Her husband was nothing if not loyal to a team that disappointed him with great regularity. Of course the same could be said of herself and the Falcons who insisted on not only disappointing but disgracing their fan base almost every week. There should be a support group for Falcons fans, she'd told Georgia not long ago.

Ennis hefted Anna on his hip, "Another world heard from. She wants her usual for breakfast."

The morning routine both eased her mind but also slightly irritated her. She wanted privacy to call the Alpharetta police for details on the decapitated woman. Well, she sighed, the best way to get privacy was get busy and feed the brood, "Does Daddy want scrambled eggs like Anna?"

He nodded, sat down with his youngest in his lap. Reaching for the paper, she noticed he paused after seeing the headlines. He glanced at her, she at him. There were just enough similarities to Jeffrey to make *him* nervous too.

He flipped the headline face down again, lifted his hand to his ear, motioning he would make a phone call. He eased Anna into her booster seat then disappeared into the bedroom, closed the door.

Lily offered to pour her Cocoa Puffs.   Savannah more than welcomed the help since it relieved her of one task. She fetched the box, a bowl and spoon then the milk. Both hands clasping the box, Lily tilted it to the bowl. Cereal cascaded into the bowl until it overflowed and spilled onto the dining table.

"Uh-oh," Anna said then giggled.

Lily found it less humorous, "Shut up. I didn't mean to."

"Lily," Savannah scolded lightly, "don't tell your sister to shut up. It's not nice."

Lily huffed up, "But–"

"And Anna, don't laugh at Lily. Someday you'll do the same thing and won't mean to either."

The admonition to Anna settled Lily down, "Then can I laugh at *her*?"

Savannah supposed it was in the DNA of youngsters to pick on siblings. She remembered her and Georgia arguing, leaving their mother to play referee between them. Now it was her turn to broker peace between her own kids, "I'd appreciate it if you didn't." She poured milk on Lily's cereal then used a dish cloth to scoop the loose bits of cereal into her hand, "See? No problem."

She poured the eggs in the hot skillet while her mind wandered to a darker time when fear, pain and Jeffrey Holland commandeered her thoughts day and night, fettering her mind as completely as his chains restrained her body.

She blinked out of the memories, forced herself to focus on her husband and daughter's meal. *Keep your mind off Jeffrey. He's in prison and you have a wonderful life now.*

Two arms slid around her waist from behind, startling her. "Calm down, babe," Ennis swept her hair aside, kissed her nape.

"Daddy, stop it," Lily wrinkled her nose. "That's gross."

A tiny smile curved Savannah's lips, "Daddy's not being gross with me, sweetheart. He's telling me a secret."

"I wanna know!" she jumped down from her seat only for Ennis to stab a finger at the chair, demanding, "Stay put."

Lily cowered at the tone retreated back to her seat. Savannah tried to soothe the child's hurt feelings, "Honey, it's a secret only adults need to know. Daddy's not mad."

Maybe not but Lily was. She harrumphed, crossed her arms and pouted while Savannah whispered to Ennis, "Well?"

"I wouldn't worry about it. The detectives told me the only similarities are the ravine and breast removal. The rest is new." Ennis kissed her ear, tickled her side.

Savannah wormed in his hold. She arched a brow, teasing, "Keep that up and you'll be *wearing* breakfast. I don't tickle well if you recall."

"Oh, I recall, alright," he swatted her backside. "You kick like a mustang."

Lily's eyes got big, "Why'd you spank Mama?"

Ennis joked, "Because she threatened to throw breakfast at me." An evil laugh emerged as he advanced on his oldest daughter, "Why all the questions, little girl? You know what little girls get for being nosy?" He wiggled his fingers at her, "A visit from the tickle monster!"

Lily's frenzied laughter filled the house as his tickling hands worked her over. Savannah relaxed with Ennis's information. In her haze of anxiety, she realized she'd overlooked one important fact. If Jeffrey recruited a nut job to kill her, he knew exactly where to find her.

5

June 10

I watch Savannah, memorize her routine. Tonya laid out a detailed schedule a month before my release. I want to ensure it hasn't changed. So far so good. It seems that Saturday is Savannah's day to work at the bake shop but just for a couple of hours.

I sit in Tonya's Volvo, across the street from Pie In The Sky. Aromas of juicy char-broiled hamburgers and spicy barbecue from nearby eateries mingle with the delectable smells drifting from Georgia's bake shop. According to the website, Georgia co-owns the place with a man who, in my opinion, has a very forgettable name. I see her personality in the exterior and interior, thanks to Tonya's photos. The striped awning gives the place a classy air like traveling back in time. Tonya's photos of the interior inspire thoughts of comfy cafes in Paris that promise a leisure, pleasurable experience. Several mouthwatering pies fill large display cases, tempting customers to take a moment to sit and sate their appetites but my attention is drawn to the sign in the window. Help Wanted, it reads. This gives me an idea.

Savannah arrived shortly before ten o'clock with both her girls in tow. Lily on her left – holding her hand, and Anna riding on her right hip. The toddler's position tells me Savannah is not armed, that she left her trusty .38 at home or elsewhere. I do have to assume a weapon is kept close by. Savannah is still a cop and cops suspect everyone. And Georgia, well, no one should underestimate her. However, she's got a quiet strength that tempts a soul to try. A person who underestimates either woman is a fool.

It's eleven o'clock. The two older men in Tonya's photos shuffle into the shop, take a seat by one of the large plate glass windows. There is another table open down the way so I decide now is the time to try Georgia's peach pie.

From the passenger seat I retrieve a shopping bag from Toys "R" Us. I've come bearing gifts, hoping to see the sparkle in Lily's eyes. Anna's too if I see her. I ensure Savannah is out of sight before pushing the door open and taking a seat two tables down from the old men. I wear jeans, a black t-shirt (instead of my favorite white) and to conceal my identity temporarily, a Braves baseball cap. I want to see my beautiful obsession in her natural relaxed frame of mind before I reveal myself.

The shop smells like heaven. My stomach grumbles for instant gratification. The sweet smell of various fruits and coffees blend into a fragrant concoction that reveals why this place is packed with people.

Savannah rounds the corner with a tray balanced in her right hand. She smiles at the two men, "Good morning to the two Mr. Thompsons."

The one with short silver hair returns the smile, "Good morning to the young Rita Hayworth."

The other man moves his hands in a familiar fashion I've seen before but never learned. Sign language. Savannah, however, sets the tray down and signs back. Now I am more intrigued than ever. She never ceases to surprise me.

"So," she doles out the contents of the tray. The silver haired man ordered peach pie and coffee. "Been golfing lately, Mr. Thompson?" she asks.

"How I wish," he replies wistfully. "I'd take you and Lily with me even though I know you both would score better than I could."

Savannah laughs, "Mr. Thompson, Lily could outscore us both as hard as she's been practicing."

Her laugh is infectious. It brings a smile to the old man's face and my lips as well.

"Mr. Thompson!" a child cries with joy. The sound of small feet pounding the tile floor draws my attention to Lily who throws her arms around the chatty Mr. Thompson.

He embraces her, whispers in her ear and she gasps with delight, "Mama, he's got a present for me."

A good-natured frown crinkles Savannah's brow, "What have I said about giving her gifts?"

"And I always ask – who am I going to spoil but your children. Here you are, Lily," he reaches his closed fist out to her. She cups her palms beneath it and when he opens his hand, her childlike enthusiasm

reaches fever pitch.   She bounces up and down, even without seeing the contents of her hand. Mr. Thompson explains, "This is special, Lily. This is something you keep for many years. Every time you see it, I want you to think of me. Will you do that?"

She nods, too excited to really grasp his words.   I watch Savannah. She's growing uneasy with the situation. Her mouth opens to protest but the older man lifts a finger to hush her. His vision switches between the two, "It's been in my family for generations. It's small but worth many, many slices of the delicious pie your mama and aunt make." He pointedly looks to Savannah, "I consider your girls like grandchildren. My daughter died before she had kids. So please let me give this to Lily and the other to Anna."

Savannah crosses her arms, her mouth a thin line. She is somewhat upset, but not willing to challenge her elder, at least too much. "Let me see what it is first."

The other Mr. Thompson, watching the scene unfold, signs to her. She sighs, repeating the man's statement aloud, "'Don't argue, just take 'em, huh?"

His hands move with solid purpose, and a little too much vigor as he signs again. Savannah replies, employing equal inflection with her hand gestures, "Bob, you two mean a lot to us too but whatever that is should be given to family."

His lips purse – now he was growing impatient. He answers then raps the table with his fist hard enough silverware clatters. The deaf Thompson evidently got rough with her.

Savannah's vision lowers, her eyes close. When she looks back up, I see tears gleaming as she simultaneously speaks and signs, "You're like family to me too."

Lily looks up at her mother, her voice quiet, "Mama, can I look now?"

She nods, wiping a stray tear, "Go ahead."

The girl opens her hand and a gold coin sat in her palm. Silver haired Thompson explains, "It's very old, Lily. Older than me. Now don't go spending it. Let Mama and Daddy keep it for you right now, okay?" He reaches his hand out to Savannah.

Guilt. I see guilt in her expression. And uneasiness. She's not used to accepting gifts from others, even on behalf of her children. When she extends her hand and he drops Anna's coin in her palm, she leans toward him and kisses his cheek, "Peter, you're a very generous man and we are blessed to know you. Anna thanks you, and I thank you."

"Thank you, Mr. Thompson," Lily hugs him.

"You're all very welcome. And you know what?" he asks Lily. "Your mama finally called me Peter after all this time. It's a fine, fine day."

The waitress comes for my order. I speak softly – even the span of five years doesn't erase a person's memory. Savannah would hear and recognize my voice and I am not finished observing or reacquainting myself with her mannerisms and disposition. I notice the vast change in my detective. She is happier, her nature seems lighter. Marriage and children agree with her – however I detect the Savannah of old lurking beneath the surface. The rough edges, sharp tongue and hellacious temper.

When it arrives, the slice of peach pie is huge and smells delicious. Georgia's talent for baking equals her flair for writing. My mouth waters with the flaky crust and sweet peaches. My stomach wants more. For the first time I'm happy Georgia survived my attack. The world is a much more appetizing place with her pies. I wave the waitress down, request another slice, this time with ice cream. This woman, a brunette in her early twenties, looks at me as if I dropped from outer space. "Hungry, aren't you?" she asks.

I slant a sly smile, my vision settling on Savannah who enters the room again, "Famished."

I take my time with the second piece, savoring the texture and flavors. Just like I will with Savannah when we are together. I watch her work the room, freely conversing with customers, joking with others.

The waitress is back, "Another peach pie?"

I shake my head, wrap my hand around my coffee cup, "So what do I owe you?"

She hands me the bill and I pay with a twenty, "Keep the change." I point to Lily, "Cute kid."

"She's the owner's niece."

I get the feeling Brunette doesn't appreciate tiny humans being under foot. I say, "She seems friendly enough."

"Yeah, well, she's spoiled if you ask me. Thanks for the tip."

She walks away and strangely I dislike this woman for disparaging

Lily – and Savannah's rearing abilities. Lily appears well adjusted and what good parent didn't coddle and pamper their kids?

I'm about to discover how friendly Lily Rutherford is. I catch her eye and smile. She smiles back. I give her a playful wave and she reciprocates. Mr. Peter Thompson watches our interaction with amusement. I motion for Lily to come closer. She does.

"Hi," I grin.

She toes the floor, bashful with the stranger before her, "Hi."

"You're Savannah's daughter Lily, aren't you?"

Her blue eyes lift to mine in wonder. How could I know such a thing, they seem to ask. She barely nods.

"Your mother and I are old friends. My name is Jeffrey." I wink, "You know, you look a lot like Savannah. You've got that gorgeous hair, and that pretty smile of hers."

Bulls-eye. Young Lily beams, "I really do?"

I point to the chair across from me as an invitation to join me, "Are you kidding? You're her spitting image, just shorter."

My words widen her grin. It's obvious she adores Savannah, wants to be just like her. Lily climbs into the seat and I notice Peter Thompson keeps a close eye on us. Me, in particular. This man is tremendously protective of Savannah and her children.

He sees me looking at him and speaks – cordial but cautious, "Say, how do you know Savannah?"

I'm not nervous about the old guy. He wants to check me out, fine, "We go back five years. Met at the hospital when she had radiation treatments."

This is news to Peter, "Radiation?"

Since Lily is present I discreetly indicate the breast, "Cancer."

The man's face drains of color and I'm curious why. He swivels in his seat, regards Savannah briefly, "She never told me about that."

"I'm sure it's a matter of time before she does. It was years ago anyway." I pull the shopping bag from beneath the table, "Hey, Lily, take a look in this bag for me, will you?"

Her eyes light up at the sight. She recognizes the store's logo and tears into the gift, "Wow! I love it!" She withdraws the twelve inch stuffed palomino pony, her face glowing with joy. "I love ponies!" She jumps down to hug me around the neck, "Thank you!"

I enjoy the feeling of Savannah's girl hugging me. Her little arms feel snug as I return the embrace, "You're so welcome."

O O O

"Who is Lily talking to?" Georgia asked, standing by the cash register.

Savannah turned, followed her sister's pointing finger. Lily stood at a table close to the door. Sitting at the table was a man dressed in new sneakers, faded jeans, and a tight black t-shirt stretched across his well-muscled chest. The cop inside her quickly assessed him. She estimated his height at around six feet tall (about Ennis's height) and his age, judging by his build and athletic appearance, she guessed mid to late thirties. The man kept the Braves baseball cap pulled low enough to obscure his face from a distance and that tweaked her concern. She grabbed a nearby dishtowel, wiped her hands, "I don't know but I'm about to find out."

She wound her way through the tables of dining patrons, her vision trained on the stranger now smiling at something her oldest daughter said. At four, Lily still showed the innocence of youth, trusting people openly and that worried Savannah, especially since Lily was the social butterfly of the two girls.

Savannah's biggest problem resided with the visitor talking with Lily. Being a cop, alarms still rang when a stranger befriended a little girl, especially *her* little girl. And the closer she got to the table, the lower his head tilted to hide his features. At this rate, it was not going to be a pleasant encounter.

She approached the table, called Lily's name. The child wheeled to face her mother, a look of surprise crossed her darling face. Lily wasn't normally this chatty to total strangers. What had this guy said to make her daughter so at ease with him so quickly? Then she saw the stuffed pony in Lily's hands. It was all the rage with young girls now, and Lily was no stranger to the desire of equine friends. She had a couple of others at home but this one was new – and given by someone Savannah didn't readily recognize as yet.

She put a hand to her daughter's shoulder, "Who are you talking to, sweetheart?"

"Him. He gave me this pony, Mama. See?" She lifted the stuffed horse like a trophy. Savannah gave it a cursory glance to appease her then subtly reminded, "What have I said about taking gifts from strangers?"

Her daughter perfected one trait to razor sharp precision. Guilt. She lowered her head in shame, her bottom lip puffed out, "But he said you know him. He's not a stranger."

Savannah gave her shoulder a gentle squeeze, "We'll talk about this later." Her attention switched to the man who'd befriended Lily. He hadn't glanced up since she'd approached the table so she eased into the seat across from him, pulled Lily into her lap.

The detective felt a distance to him. He kept his head down and already she knew the pony had to go – which would lower her stock with her enthusiastic daughter – and after the impending lecture about strangers, her stock would plummet to hell. This man was not a friend because friends smiled, extended their hands in greeting or drew the person into a hug. This guy put space between Savannah and himself. "It helps if you look at me so we can converse." She said it with a forced smile. Her gut warned this guy might either be – or have – a real problem, since he refused to make eye contact.

"It's been a long five years, Savannah. I've missed you."

She paled, feeling the blood rush from her brain to her feet. A chill swept over her, headed straight for her core until she shuddered. Noises drifted to the background, while her heartbeat raced, thundering in her chest. Fight or flight. She wanted to do both – fight Jeffrey Holland and kill him *and* run for her life like she had years ago.

Jeffrey lifted his chin, two deep black holes stared back at her.

Then he smiled, "We've got unfinished business, Detective."

Fight or flight or not, her mother's instinct kicked in and she slid Lily to the floor, commanding, "Go to Aunt Georgia."

"But Mama–"

"*Now*, Lily. Go to Aunt Georgia now." She reached back for the horse, "And give me that pony."

"No!" she argued loud enough to startle the diners.

Savannah stretched, grasped Lily's arm, and urged her closer, whispering, "Lily, give me the pony. This man lied to you. He's not a friend and if you want the horse that bad, I'll get you one but you're not keeping this one."

Her beet red face stared back at her mother, "You promise?"

"I promise," and held out her hand, hoping the authoritative tone she used convinced Lily to comply. The girl slammed the little horse into her mother's waiting palm. Savannah wanted to bring her into her arms and explain why Mama was so abrupt but her oldest daughter gifted her with an angry tearful expression that refused consolation. The four year-old equivalent to *I'll never forgive you.* Savannah recognized the look as one she'd given her mother countless times. Lily at least let her hold her hand a moment, "Be a good girl and go see Aunt Georgia."

She pulled her hand free, mumbling an "okay" and trudged toward the kitchen.

"Anything we can do, Savannah?" Peter Thompson offered.

Without looking back, she shook her head, "Thank you, Mr. Thompson. I've got this." She and Jeffrey maintained steady eye contact. The gleam in his eyes set off warning bells in her brain. *He wants my girl and he'll take her – just to hurt me.* Her parental instincts kicked into overdrive and she positioned herself between his line of vision and her daughter.

Jeffrey's smile widened, "She favors you, Savannah. Like mother, like daughter. Gorgeous dark hair, beautiful eyes. I see she's got that fiery temper of yours too."

"What are you doing here? You're supposed to be in prison for another ten years at least." She couldn't imagine why the system released such a monster but nothing surprised her anymore. Her chief complaint – why hadn't the prison system and state notified her of his release? They were suppose to let victims know when they released evil on the masses again but her years as a police officer taught her never to assume or expect things to go right.

He shrugged as if to say *c'est la vie*, "Improper jury instructions. I can see why law enforcement doesn't trust the justice system. Hasn't helped *you* at all, has it? You testified, thought I was safely tucked away only for some moron to screw it up. I'm getting a new trial so you and I will square off together again. Who will win this time? You or me?"

"I will, one way or another. Get out and don't come back."

His smile turned wily, "I don't think so. I may be out of prison but I'm also out of work. Lucky for me Georgia needs help. I'd like an application please."

"You're kidding." The meeting quickly descended into total absurdity. "We're not hiring."

Until Jeffrey's smile vanished, "There's a sign in the window."

She leaned closer, enunciating, "I'll be more specific. We're not hiring *you.*"

"Why not? I'm a hard worker. I'm good at serving people, giving them their just desserts, so to speak." He looked around, "So is this Georgia's baby? Surprising. She's not that adventurous, as I recall. Very cautious with her life so I would assume the same for her money."

She let his comment hang without replying. The bastard remembered too much about her and her sister. Her back began aching and her shoulder instinctively tightened. That hadn't happened in a long time. Now her body reverted to its old habits regarding Jeffrey. She tried to casually roll her shoulder without drawing his attention to it. It didn't work.

He noticed the motion, stared at her right shoulder, making it ache worse. She asked, "What's your point to this visit, Jeffrey? To harass me and Georgia?"

His dark eyes shifted to her blue ones, "I told you. I need a job."

The man was nuts. "First of all, no one wants you here. Second, do you honestly think *any* restaurant or bake shop will hire you? You like sharp objects too much. Leave before I shoot you." She tossed the pony onto the table with less care than Lily handed it to her. "And shove this where the sun doesn't shine."

Mr. Thompson came to his feet. She'd spoken louder than she expected. He toddled over with his cane, Bob followed behind him. "This young man doesn't know manners," Peter admonished. "When a lady asks you to leave, you leave. Or else."

"Shut up, old man," Jeffrey snapped. "She and I have a past you wouldn't understand." Then the smile returned, "Or maybe I *should* enlighten your older friend to our past together."

Savannah's jaw clenched, "My gun is in the back, Jeffrey. Just try me."

"You wouldn't shoot me in front of Lily or Anna. You'd shoot me in front of Georgia but not your kids." Jeffrey leaned closer, his voice deepening to a threat, "I'm not going anywhere."

His intent was clear. To intimidate her, put her on edge. He assumed his presence and tone stirred the same crippling fear from years ago. It did but now she had children. She felt more protective of them than of herself. She would take matters into her own hands for her own safety, but mostly for her babies. She met his menacing tone with her own, "Did you happen to forget I plugged your stepbrother? I just wounded him, but I'll finish you off."

"I don't think either of us has forgotten anything about the other. I remember the scar on your breast from cancer surgery. The tiger tattoo at the small of your back."

"Shut up and get out," she warned, cutting her vision to the side. Unfortunately Mr. Thompson heard the killer's every word.

Jeffrey continued, "The long, thin scars crisscrossing your back and bottom. I remember your strength, your stubbornness. I remember your screams and your tears. And the number I gave you." He pointed to her right shoulder, "Is it still there or do I need my scalpel again, just to freshen it up?"

"Mama?" Lily's voice shattered the nightmare Jeffrey plunged Savannah's mind into.

When she turned to her daughter, Lily stared at Jeffrey Holland with the same fright she herself felt five years ago. Savannah swallowed but her mouth had gone dry. Not only Mr. Thompson heard Jeffrey's spiel but her daughter probably had too.

Lily's fingers curled around hers and tugged, "Mama, Aunt Georgia wants you."

Savannah drew her closer, unwilling to let Jeffrey make eye contact with her child. Lily didn't need to know the evil that invaded their world. Savannah had hoped to spare her the knowledge but here he was, her living nightmare had returned.

She lifted Lily into her arms. The girl's legs circled Mama's hips, her arms hugging around her neck. Savannah knew Lily felt the frantic throbbing of her heart, sensed her fear. Her daughter held tight and she found herself doing the same.

Savannah turned and stared straight at Jeffrey. He would not win. He got into her head that day but she would fight to the death before allowing it again. "Don't come back," she warned Jeffrey.

His vision switched from her to Lily then back. The unwavering stare dared her to look away. The emptiness in that dark abyss threatened to consume her in a world of misery she thought she left behind.

He suddenly smiled with a reminder, "Aunt Georgia wants you."

She turned and in a brisk walk (not too brisk or he might mistake it for fleeing) and started toward the kitchen. She saw Georgia observing from the counter, her right hand below the customers' line of sight – where they stowed the .38.

Jeffrey summoned Savannah by name but she refused to stop. In a tone laced with an ominous undercurrent only she and her sister recognized, he finished, "Remember *I* want you too."

For Lily's sake, she struggled to curb the crippling terror coursing through her. Her daughter would feel the trembling, hear the short, ragged breaths, perhaps even sense the horrific memories haunting her.

Halfway to the kitchen, Lily looked at her, "Mama?"

Her tone indicated Savannah failed in her efforts. With one word her daughter asked the question. Are you okay?

Inhaling a slow deep breath, she answered with more confidence than she felt, "Everything's okay, baby. Don't worry. Everything will be fine."

She passed Georgia who waited for Jeffrey to exit the shop. When he did, she sat the gun aside, "I was two shakes from calling 911 if he didn't leave."

Savannah eased Lily to the floor but she clung to her mother, refusing to let go.

Lily tightened her hug. Her little girl wanted to help and she'd found the best way possible. A big ol' bear hug from one's child gave even the most harried or frightened parent a moment of solace.

Savannah sidled closer to Georgia, "He's not going anywhere.

Says he wants a job here."

"What?" Georgia reacted as if her sister threatened to burn the place down. "*Here?* What makes him think we'd hire him?"

"I know. Besides the obvious, we all know dishwashers handle knives of all sizes and handymen need tools. Blunt instruments like hammers, long pointy things like screwdrivers and power tools like drills and saws. *And they use duct tape.* We must look stupid to him." She stopped a second. An idea – one as crazy as Jeffrey's notion of employment – sprouted in her mischievous brain. "Or…"

"Or what?"

"Or, we could agree to a job interview after hours then I can shoot the jerk and drag his corpse to the Dumpster. *That* would cure our problem."

"Mama's gonna shoot somebody!" Lily exclaimed.

Georgia crossed her arms, aimed a frown at her sister, "Mama's not going to *shoot anyone.*"

Savannah mirrored Georgia's crossed arms stance, "She's not?"

"Savannah," was the admonishment. "Your children are hearing this."

Both youngsters stared owl-eyed at the adults then Lily giggled to Anna, "Aunt Georgia's scoldin' Mama."

"That's right," Savannah agreed. "And all Mama's doin' is trying to help."

6

June 10

Those blue eyes, once so sure of themselves, now hold a glint of doubt. The terror thriving inside her, the frantic pulse drumming against her neck. The hint of wild panic she tries to hide with bravado, clever comebacks, false confidence.

I saw the glimmer of a little girl today. Her dark hair shining like polished chestnut, the waves as loose as gentle rolling hills. Her blue eyes gorgeous as an early afternoon sky. That little girl blinked, tipped her hand and let me know that yes, indeed, I am the man with her day and night. That I am always there to remind her – she is mine.

O   O   O

June 14

Her name is Amber Martin. A beautiful girl of perhaps twenty but no older than twenty-two. Long golden tresses flow down her back, accentuating a svelte, curvy figure. She has a cherubic youth to her face with her pert little nose and peaches and cream complexion but it is her firm breasts that draw my attention. They are large enough to hold in my palms, generous enough to make my groin tight upon sight of them. Despite their allure, her breasts are not what I'm interested in. It's her innocence and ignorance. Innocent enough to accept my offers of assistance and ignorance of what transpired between me and my lovely detective years ago.

She works evenings at Pie In The Sky, stays after closing to clean up the place. Amber sweeps, gives the cabinets a good wipe down, sanitizes everything in sight and up until three days ago, carried out the garbage. I watched her one evening, lugging the bags to the Dumpster, when an idea struck me. I offered – for nothing more than a slice or two of leftover pie – to unburden the girl with the task. A woman as pretty as Amber shouldn't be relegated to carrying trash. Such a dirty job for an exquisite woman and, I add, I always stroll by Pie In The Sky every evening at this time. It is on my way home. I extended my hand, gave hers a gentle shake while introducing myself. My name was Tom, I said, and it would be my pleasure to help.

For the last few days, I've hauled out garbage for her, getting to know her. Through her, I also learn tidbits about Georgia and Savannah. Details of their lives, their schedules, and routines. It is a windfall of information because Amber has taken a liking to me. She thinks I'm friendly – even attractive – or so she says, so I use it to my advantage.

I linger at the corner of the alley, waiting for Georgia's Tahoe to drive away before I approach the back door which remains locked as per Georgia and Savannah's orders. As late as last week they left it unlocked – this according to Amber. Now both women demand utmost security.

I rap on the back door with my special knock. The old Shave and a Haircut. I tap out the first part and Amber finishes with the last two knocks, the Two Bits. The door opens to a smiling young lady. Ah, how I used to salivate over such a tantalizing morsel of female flesh. Images from days of old still prowl my mind. The sight of a woman straining against the chains binding her. The warm blood rising to the surface when the scalpel parted the skin, sinking into tissue and muscle. The sound of a woman's scream... Oh, the fun I could have with cheerful, naïve Amber Martin…

I snap back to the present, smile at Amber. I'm harmless, my grin promises, and just here to help. "What's the damage today?" I ask, searching the kitchen area for brimming trash bags.

She laughs at my joke a little too long. A facet of her gleaming smile reminds me of Savannah's, only my detective's dazzling pearly whites are rarely revealed with such joy. Mostly with her children, Ennis and Georgia. Otherwise, her serious nature and law enforcement guardedness take over, leaving the unskilled at a loss to her thoughts. I feel privileged to be among the few who can read her mind, her body language. In our brief time together, I have a mental catalog of Savannah and her rainbow of expressions, her abundance of tells and signs. I know when she is scheming, when she's close to releasing her anger or tears. I know her as well as her husband yet I've never been intimate with her, at *least not in the Biblical way.*

Amber's deepening blush tells me she's trying to impress me, laughing at my one-liners. "Those bags by the door. That's all for tonight," she says.

I grab one of the plastic trash bags and nearly throw the lightweight thing over my head by accident. "What's in it? Feathers?" I ask.

"Dunno but that's all your work for the night. There's some leftover French Silk Chocolate Pie if you want it. That and Mississippi Mud. Or I could pay you for your trouble."

"Nonsense. What have I told you? As long as there is a pie in this place, I'm happy to be paid by the slice. Let me run this outside right quick." I wink at her, "Be right back." That little gesture produces a girlish giggle from my new friend. If she'd seen the photographs of other ladies I'd winked at, she'd run faster than a babysitter's boyfriend when the parents' car pulled up.

I sling the bag over my shoulder and heft the heavier one into my other hand. I lug them both to the Dumpster and toss them. I'm about to show Amber I'm a proficient helper in many ways. I leap the two concrete stairs in a single bound and enter the kitchen, closing the door behind me and lock it as per Georgia's edict. I'm ready for more work, "What's next?"

Surprised at my eagerness, Amber stares at me. I ease her concern, "Surely there's more I can do. These muscles aren't here solely for hoisting garbage bags into a Dumpster. Something needs tidying or cleaning, doesn't it?"

She scans the kitchen. She's done most of the work herself. The longer she remains at a loss, the more nervous I become so I search for my own work, "How about the pantry? I can straighten it up. When Georgia comes in tomorrow, the mere perfection will blow her away."

There was Amber's bubbling laughter again. Bingo. She nodded, "Go ahead if you think you can improve on it. She's fastidious about the pantry so enter at your own risk."

I would bet Miss Georgia was religiously fastidious about every part of her life. The woman verged on militaristic from what I could tell. Watching her work tired me and the meticulousness understandably nettled Savannah on occasion. What inspired a smile in me – Amber's adorable caution of entering at my own risk. If the girl only knew…

I head to the pantry door. The interior drops my jaw. I'd seen operating rooms that failed to measure up to this degree of efficiency or cleanliness. No, there was nothing I could do to improve the pantry but I glanced around anyway to give a good impression. Large storage bins sat in rows. I see two bins of flour – wheat and white – each one I guess holds about seventy-five pounds each. Another row holds sugar – one each of granulated, brown and powdered – those I estimate at fifty pounds apiece.

There are other storage containers, these smaller and lined up on shelves. They have labels reading molasses, vanilla beans, espresso powder, coconut, raisins and more. Closer to the back are containers with various chocolates, white, milk, semi-sweet and bittersweet and another shelf dedicated to liquors such as rum, amaretto, triple sec and more. Georgia is one squared away female in all areas of her life, especially business.

What catches my attention isn't the booze she stowed away in the room. It is a little key hanging just inside the door. A key with a label dangling from it. It reads "Back Door". I lift it off the hook, palming it into my slacks. I will have it back in place within the hour, just as soon as I have one cut for myself.

The smile on my face broadens as I turn to face Amber, "You're right. Georgia's arrangement is ideal."

7

June 17

After the arduous, slow progress at work that week, Savannah welcomed
Saturday with open arms. Friendly faces awaited her, along with cheerful
patrons with carefree laughter and plentiful conversation. Saturdays at
the bake shop made up for the lack of success she sometimes felt at her
paying job. The hours at Pie In The Sky cleared her mind, brightened
her mood. And after the long week behind her desk, she could use it.

She'd spent hours at her desk staring at the computer or talking
on the phone, searching for answers from the Georgia Bureau of Prisons.
In usual bureaucratic fashion, no one had answers but offered plenty of
other numbers she could call. The only piece of information they
actually provided was his release date. Jeffrey walked free for eight days
already, two of them before he walked into the bake shop. Other than
that no one knew anything. Each person offered the same empty, tired
"I'm sorry". She fought the urge to fire back, "It's not your ass Holland
wants. It's mine and because of your laziness, he'll probably get it."
Before she blurted that gem, she ended the call, deciding a heart attack

just didn't fit into her schedule that day.

She came home tired and frustrated each evening. The only bright spots were her family and a birthday party everyone put together for her the night before. She dreaded her birthday since she approached forty. No woman – hell, *no one* in their right mind – greeted forty with a smile. They went kicking and screaming and next year represented her jumping off point. Between Ennis and the girls, Georgia, Dane, and Seth and Leah and their kids, the occasion resulted in a happier one than she expected. Georgia baked a Triple Chocolate Cake and the presents ranged from blouses and a robe to an apron with a mother bird and three babies sitting in a nest. The girls put their crayons to use, Lily's picture depicting the family all in a row, standing in front of the house. Anna settled for an Impressionist approach by slashing different colors across the page then adding a few squiggles for good measure. This was one aspect of her current life that dissatisfied Savannah. The inability to spend more time with her girls, to see the little changes in them, to stay home and raise her children as her mother had. There was a comfort in a child's presence, a song in their laughter and when they were separated, she pined for her babies.

The job gave her a different purpose, a way to right some wrongs in the world but with her children she felt whole. She'd missed so much, her conscience prodded, and soon Lily would start preschool. The years and milestones flew by and while Savannah still loved her job, the longing to be with her girls steadily intensified.

Georgia kept the girls the days she stayed home from the bakery, and Dane took over on the others. The two tried so hard to have children that keeping Lily and Anna became a balm to ease their lack of success, at least according to Georgia. Savannah prayed her sister got pregnant soon. Georgia was born to be a mom, she told Ennis, and she'd be the best besides their mother.

Savannah poured milk over Lily's customary bowl of Cocoa Puffs. Lily, dressed in jeans and a plum colored shirt, climbed into the dining chair and bowed her head. Savannah watched her whisper a prayer then a stern *Amen* before plunging her spoon into the bowl.

Two spoonfuls later Lily inquired, "Mama, how old are you?"

Savannah winced. To Georgia's credit, in place of numerical candles, she'd opted for single candles to represent the thirty-nine. It helped the birthday digest easier with Savannah and she thanked her sister for the consideration. Still, Mama thought, Lily sure picked a hell of a time to exercise her inquisitive side. "I'll put it this way. I'm not over the hill yet but I have a great view."

Lily stopped chewing, met her gaze. "Huh?"

No way would Savannah admit to her actual age. Having her daughter fall over faint left a bad impression and hit the ego wrong. Thirty-nine was too close to forty to say without recoiling in dread. So how could she say *actually, in dogs years I'm dead*? She opted for, "Honey, I'll smile forever if you say I'm twenty-nine."

Lily nodded, accepting the reply. Another disaster averted, Savannah hoped. At a point birthdays became redundant and unnecessary. People realized another year passed, why rub it in?

"Can I have a Pop Tart too?" her daughter magically (and mercifully) changed the subject.

"My goodness, you're hungry this morning. What happened?"

Lily shrugged, continued eating, "It's Saturday. I'm workin' and I want to show Aunt Georgia my new pony."

The pony sat beside Lily on the table. The same kind Jeffrey gave her a week earlier, and the same kind that drew battle lines between Lily and her mother for most of that last Saturday.

Savannah fought off a grin, reminiscing when Lily pronounced the day *Saturnday,* not Saturday. She still had troubles with particular words and names such as restaurant (she said restronaut) and Abraham Lincoln (April Ham Lincun). With age she got the hang of their last name instead of saying *Rufferford,* but still couldn't quite tackle the name Savannah – it emerged *Sabannah* – but all the books promised in another year or two the "v" sounds would make their arrival.

Instead of a laugh, Savannah adopted an innocent inflection, "And you need Cocoa Puffs *and* a Pop Tart for all this work you'll be doing?"

Lily answered with an earnest nod.

Mama knew Lily's "lots of work" encompassed being the social butterfly of the place, flitting here and there, but mostly chatting with Peter Thompson. "Well, one time won't hurt. What'll it be? Strawberry?"

Lily nodded with a *thank you.* Ennis trudged from Anna's bedroom, holding their youngest astride his hip. Both looked drowsy and disheveled. Wisps of dark hair curled in wayward directions on both father and daughter. Anna looked slightly more conscious with her coffee brown eyes sparkling at the sight of Lily and Savannah. Her tiny hands reached out to Mama who relieved the semi-awake male of the extra weight.

"They never sleep at that age, or ours don't," Ennis grumbled. "Heard her rattling the crib so I got up."

Savannah smoothed Anna's hair then Ennis's, "You're such a good daddy to interrupt your beauty sleep for your baby."

Ennis found little humor in the statement, "I'm shaving then grabbing a shower. See you for breakfast," he pecked a kiss to Savannah's lips, headed to the bathroom.

She tickled Anna's belly, delighting in the resulting laugh, "You want eggs for breakfast?"

Anna reached toward Lily's bowl and Savannah took it as a hint while easing her into high chair. Soon they'd try her at the table. Another milestone she both anticipated and dreaded. Her babies were growing up too fast. "You mind sharing your Cocoa Puffs?" she asked Lily.

The girl shook her head. While Savannah worked on Pop Tarts and Cocoa Puffs, she handed Anna her favorite picture book.

"When can I help Aunt Georgia?" Lily wanted to know.

"Help her what?"

"Make pies."

Her mouth quirked with humor, "When you get older, I guess.

She won't even let *me* help with the pies so I'm not old enough to help either."

"But you're," the child thought hard a moment before remembering, "twenty-nine."

As promised, Savannah smiled when she mentioned the magic age, "Maybe I'm nearly the right age to help her but I'd rather serve people and visit with them."

"Me too," Lily agreed. "I like Mr. Thompson best."

A thoughtful smile surfaced, "I do too." Savannah removed the Pop Tart from the toaster, placed the warm pastry on a saucer next to Lily's bowl.

Anna turned a page of her picture book, pressed her finger to the page, "Kitty-cat."

Savannah glanced at the book, proud of her daughter's progress, "That's great, Anna. What's on the other page?"

"Kitty-cat," she repeated, still tapping the calico's picture.

"Very good, honey." She pointed to the opposite page where Fido the dog stood wagging his shaggy tail. "Now what's this?"

Ignoring her mother's hint, little Anna tapped harder at Kitty, "Anna want."

Anna want but Anna won't get, Savannah thought. We have enough chaos around here without a pet.

"She likes Mr. Meowgi," Lily volunteered. "She plays with him when we stay next door."

Wonderful. Katherine Collins, the next door neighbor, had an overly friendly tabby cat named Mr. Meowgi. Savannah saw her youngest playing with the cat on occasion but silly-like, hadn't expected a request for her own.

"*Anna want kitty-cat,*" the youngest insisted.

Savannah worked faster with the cereal. The quicker she fed Anna, perhaps the child might engross herself in eating, not soliciting for a pet. "Not right now, honey," Mama said in a gentle voice.

Anna stabbed her tiny index finger onto Kitty's nose, "Anna want kitty-cat."

"Mama said no," Lily reinforced with less diplomacy.

Anna met her sister's gaze with a pouty glare, "Shut up."

"*You* shut up," Lily fired back.

"Both of you hush," Savannah ordered. The argument grated on her that early in the morning. The two exchanged barbs the way tennis players volleyed the ball back and forth. Quick and with serious punch. The spat escalated when Anna blurted *moron* at her sister.

"Hey," Savannah admonished sharply. Both girls snapped to attention as she continued, "No name calling. Hear me?"

The bathroom door flew open and Ennis bounded out wearing half a shaving cream beard, "What's the yelling?"

She put hands to hips, "I told you this would happen. Our youngest pride and joy has adopted your favorite word during football season."

He stood, innocent and clueless, as if a golden halo glowed above his head. It frustrated Savannah when he freely uttered words such as *moron* during a game. Eventually their girls would pick up on it, she'd said, and sure enough one had.

"Moron," Anna repeated, out-and-out ignoring her mother's caution.

Savannah's brow lifted as if asking her husband *remember now?* Ennis approached Anna, his face ripening to bright red with exasperation and probably a tad of embarrassment over getting chastised for his language.

Ennis leaned eye to eye with their youngest girl who giggled at his foamy white half-beard. She reached forward, smeared a finger across his cheek with a giggle. Ennis wiped her finger clean while trying to retain a serious face and firm tone – or firm as Ennis could, "That's a bad word, Anna. I'll stop using it and I don't want you to say it again."

"There's another development this morning." Savannah barely finished the comment before Anna pointed to the book again, repeating, "Anna want kitty-cat."

"And there it is," she sighed. "I've already said ix-nay on the at-cay so it's your turn. I've got to get dressed for work." She headed to the bedroom, Lily trailing behind, as Ennis tried diverting Anna's attention. Savannah heard him flip page after page until, "Tell Daddy what that is."

"*Kitty-cat,*" the child maintained.

"Honey, that's a horse. Can you say horse?"

Yes, Savannah rolled her eyes, and she can say *Anna want horse* which is entirely more complicated than wanting a cat.

Before having children, she considered her job the biggest

challenge. Once Lily arrived, life expressed in grand detail how wrong she'd been. Corralling the bad guys paled in comparison to raising a baby. Her job had guidelines and rules. Babies and toddlers wrote their *own* rulebook and – depending on the situation – changed them every so often to ensure their parents remained confused, panicked, or on the verge of filing Chapter 11 on the precious commodity *patience.*

The cat issue embedded in her baby daughter's brain deep enough to take root for at least two days – or longer if Mr. Meowgi had the audacity to show his face anytime soon. Savannah liked cats and dogs however the thought of caring for a pet, two children and retaining her job stretched her past the limit. Something had to give and it was not going to be her sanity.

The master bedroom remained a sanctuary from children's toys, at least for the most part. Anna deposited toys like Easter eggs on the cherry wood nightstands or the queen size bed, probably thinking how dull and drab Mama and Daddy's room was without a lime green toaster or slice of plastic pepperoni pizza. Day before yesterday Savannah found the toy toaster from Anna's Grow-With-Me kitchen sitting on the nightstand. Weeks ago, Ennis found the toy fork the hard way with his bare foot. He'd outlawed toys in their bedroom ever since. Like *that* would actually happen, she thought.

Anna slipped in a surprise once in a while though. Today was one on those days. Savannah found the plastic spatula sitting on her nightstand. She picked it up, intent on returning it to Anna's room. She turned then stopped short when she saw Lily directly behind her.

"Why is Anna mean to me?" the girl asked.

Savannah bent to one knee upon witnessing Lily's pouting frown. She swept her daughter's dark hair back, saw tears gleaming in her eyes, "Baby, she's too young to understand how hurtful words can be. I'm afraid being the older sister you're the target of the younger sister's temper. I was mean to Aunt Georgia at that age but now we're best friends. I have a feeling you and Anna will be just as close later on. Give her some time."

"I'm not a moron," she sulked, the words quivering like the tears in her eyes.

"No, you're not. You're my sweet baby who'll come to the bakery with me today – but only if you dry those tears and straighten that pretty face."

Lily drew the back of her hand across each cheek, wiping away the tears.

Savannah winked, "There's my girl. Go finish your breakfast so we can go help Aunt Georgia."

Ennis appeared at the doorway, shoulders slumped. He looked comical given his posture and white partial (and finger-striped) Barbasol beard. He shook his head in what Savannah figured was despair.

"I. Give. Up," he declared. "The kid's got an obstinate streak worse than yours. You won't believe what's falling out of her mouth now."

Oh, yes I can, she mused grimly. It neighs, wears a saddle and one went by Mr. Ed. To placate him she went ahead and inquired, "And that is?"

Neither to her shock nor surprise, he replied on a sigh, "A horse."

o   o   o

June 17

Something is awry in the Rutherford household. The couple went their separate ways this morning since Savannah works at the bakery today. Lily paired off with her mother while Ennis left with Anna. There were no harsh words exchanged, no frigid embraces or half-hearted kisses. Husband and wife acted their usual, amorous selves however it seems little Anna stirred a controversy with her kinfolk – over a "kitty-cat".

The family exited their abode to a rendition every parent dreads from a two year-old. The broken record stage. Little Anna, with her dark brown hair and eyes to match, favors Ennis more than Savannah. But her ability to focus on the important things (important to her, at least) reveals her resemblance to her mother. The stubborn side. The child has a head and demeanor as hard as granite, a trait Savannah surely recognizes and probably regrets that particular genetic contribution to her youngest.

Anna chanted, "Kitty-cat, kitty-cat, Anna want kitty-cat" to her father who unlocked his Dodge Ram and proceeded to buckle the child into her car seat.

Savannah and Lily headed to the blue Charger where mother

secured daughter into the back seat booster while Lily shouted, "Mama said no!"

Savannah winced but kept her composure, instructing the girl not to yell in her ear. She finished it with, "Daddy said no too and don't," *she emphasized, "shout that at her either. I'm deaf enough."*

With the children secured, husband and wife turned to each other, their nerves frayed and ragged. They exchanged a brief yet passionate kiss before parting ways.

So Anna want kitty-cat, does she? Well... Maybe "Uncle Jeffrey" can help...

8

June 19

A comedian once said having children was like living in a frat house. *Nobody sleeps, everything's broken and there's a lot of throwing up.* They surpassed most of that, thankfully, but surveying their living room, Savannah decided the place resembled a toy store explosion instead of a fraternity house. Anna scattered her lovelies in all directions. Some on the couch, others in the dining room and hallway. Once Savannah found a baby doll wrapped in one of her blouses that previously resided in the dirty clothes hamper.

Besides being the resident toy wrangler, Savannah discovered being a mother encompassed many roles such as referee at the park. What started as a recreational trip turned upside down when Anna tried crawling up the slide when Lily wanted to come down at the same time. *Let your sister slide down,* Savannah told her youngest, *and stop trying to climb up the thing.*

Motherhood entailed plenty of apologizing too, she learned. Lily taught her that years ago. *She skipped her nap* was a favorite excuse when normally sweet Lily Christine exercised her temper tantrum in public. With Anna, she shortened it to *she's tired.*

Even during the most trying times when their patience bottomed out, they felt bone tired and questioned their ever-loving common sense for having the little urchins, mothers smiled because their directionally challenged, temperamental toddler announces to anyone within earshot, "Mama is my friend."

Mama was her friend but Mama planned to buckle down and teach Anna the importance of tidiness, or at least keeping the toys to a bare minimum in the living area.

Dressed in her usual cleaning attire of jeans and gray Atlanta Police t-shirt, Savannah prepared herself for the spelunking expedition ahead. There was a living room in there somewhere, she just had to find it. While Katherine Collins babysat the girls for the morning, Savannah decided to tackle the toy task.

She picked up the colored wooden blocks that strangely seemed to spell *cat* if one used a liberal eye. Or perhaps it fell into the coincidence category but knowing her kid, she'd done it on purpose. Savannah moved along, gathering the five stuffed animals strewn across the room. Two teddy bears, a turtle, a dog and a cat. Cat. Again. Nope, not a coincidence.

Ten minutes later she stood, reveling in her progress. Checking the clock, she figured another twenty minutes and she'd call the girls in to eat. It would also give Katherine a chance to feed her husband Edward when he arrived home on his lunch hour.

She washed her hands then went to the fridge to collect sandwich makings. Peanut butter and jelly for Anna and ham and cheese for Lily. Savannah smiled. Chalk another one up for genetics, she thought. Lily was just like her – ham, ham, ham. The more the better. And Anna was Daddy's little girl wanting her usual PB & J. No frills, no extras, or else.

The shrill screech of tires followed by a sickening crunch stopped her cold. Her first thought: the kids. She raced from the kitchen, flung open the front door, searching for her girls. Their yard stood empty. Both girls were gone.

Their house sat far back from the street, their yard was big enough to accommodate two towering oaks. Oaks the girls should have been playing beneath, shaded by the long, leafy outstretched arms.

She searched for Katherine but saw no sign of her either. The commotion lay beyond the hedges lining the front sidewalk. A sports car crashed into the light standard across the street. The red Nissan convertible sat askew, half on and half off the curb, both bumper and fender crunched beyond recognition. She saw no kids, no Katherine. Only chaos in the street.

No, no, no, she panicked. *Not my babies.* "Lily! Anna!" she cried, legs pumping hard and fast down the driveway toward the crowd of gathering neighbors, her body fueled by adrenaline and chaste fear.

She found Katherine standing at the curb. A wave of relief washed over her upon sight of Lily standing beside her neighbor. Her daughter's owl-eyed stare turned toward the street and that plunged the panic deeper. "Where's Anna?" Savannah shouted to combat the heated arguing between her neighbors and the Nissan's hostile driver.

Her chest ached from her pounding heart causing her to briefly wonder if she verged on a heart attack. Besides losing Ennis, the thought of losing either child would destroy her. Through the din of her neighbor's voices, she heard the word police and ambulance.

"*Where is Anna*!?" Lord, she prayed, let my child be safe, and not injured or killed by this Justin Bieber clone.

Katherine stepped off the curb, "I'm sorry, Savannah. I looked away for one second and she was gone. I started searching for her when I heard the car–"

"Stay with Lily," Savannah waved her back. *I want to know at least one of my kids is safe.* She rounded the sporty Roadster but did not see Anna. Thankfully the child wasn't sprawled on the pavement, her body broken and bloodied. But she was *missing*.

"The girl *was* right there," a neighbor pointed toward the curb next to the car's wreckage. Savannah recognized him as Michael McCann, a retired principal of a nearby private school. The stocky bull of a man with soft, affable features kept close watch on the area since leaving his job. Probably a little *too* close sometimes but today Savannah was grateful for his attentiveness. He joined Savannah when she ran across the street, looking in every direction for her girl, calling her name. She thought she heard her baby's voice somewhere nearby but couldn't find her in the throng of people and surrounding trees or shrubs.

Tonya Harris, the neighbor across the street, stood sentry at the edge of her lawn, arms crossed, mere feet from the car's front fender, "I saw a guy grab her before the car could plow over her." She glowered at the driver, jabbed a finger at the street, "Look at those skid marks. You were speeding."

The driver, a mid-twenties yuppie, shoved a hand through his hair, angry at the inconvenience of it all, "I didn't see the kid until the last second, okay? And where are the parents, anyway? They should be watching their kid."

Mike McCann sheepishly pointed at Savannah. The insinuation of negligent parenting soured her mood to the point only violence might improve it. She entertained visions of fetching her .38, thrusting the barrel beneath the driver's chin and cutting loose with the old Dirty Harry spiel. *You gotta ask yourself one question. "Do I feel lucky?"*

As appealing as that fantasy was, the fact remained her .38 sat inside, not only locked up from small hands but detectives prone to sudden homicidal whimsies. Plus, she had bigger issues at hand. "Who took my daughter!?"

Oblivious to the outburst, the cocky driver caught sight of her Atlanta Police Department shirt. "Oh my God," he sank against the bumper, his arrogance expelled with a sigh, "you're a cop?"

"Yes, she is," another voice replied with a sense of pride. A voice Savannah recognized all too well. "And you're lucky I was here. You don't want to suffer *her* wrath."

She snapped around to face Jeffrey Holland standing at the car's front fender, beside Tonya Harris. He smiled.

The breath left her body. Her knees grew weak. Jeffrey held

Anna in his arms. The man in her most horrific nightmares cradled her crying child against his chest. He spoke softly to her to calm her then addressed Savannah, "She's fine, Mama. Just a little scared." He nodded to Tonya Harris, "She's correct. This driver has a lead foot. Why, Anna could have been squashed. We don't want that, do we, Anna?"

The driver swallowed hard, tried to bargain, "Look, Officer, can't we make a deal? I mean the kid is okay–"

"Her title is *Detective*," Jeffrey corrected. "If you are going to kiss her ass, address her properly."

The young man shot him a nasty glare, "What's the problem? You grabbed her in time–"

"Which was a miracle considering your speed," Jeffrey's vision never wavered from Savannah's.

Anna reached for her mother but Jeffrey refused to release her right away. He and Savannah stood staring eye to eye, her tone left no room for misunderstanding, "Give me my daughter."

Anna stretched toward Savannah. She stepped forward, wrapping her arms around the hysterical child. In reclaiming her baby, her hands brushed Jeffrey's rock hard biceps, his muscular chest. Memories of his brutality raked a painful shiver down her neck and back.

Savannah's vision never strayed from his as she soothed Anna, cuddling her close. "Mama's here, baby. It's okay."

Anna pressed her body as close to her mother's as humanly possible. Savannah kissed her, her lips lingering on her baby's warm skin. Her heart calmed in those few seconds. The horror of the moment passed and holding her child was the only remedy for her panic.

Jeffrey watched her snuggle Anna closer. A flicker of the old Jeffrey shone in his eyes. The one taking pleasure in her fear. The visual flare was so subtle and brief no one except Savannah stood a chance of recognizing it.

"Isn't there something you want to say?" he pointedly asked in front of the witnesses.

Besides *go to hell*, not really, she thought. Still, despite the animosity she harbored against him, he had saved Anna. How friggin' ironic, Savannah thought. The man who craves to see a woman's pain and hear her screams as he tortured her, that man actually *saved* a life. Her daughter's life.

The small crowd of neighbors stared at her. They expected what Jeffrey expected. A thank you. Despite sharing a quaint, beautiful neighborhood, none of the neighbors knew the history between Savannah and Jeffrey Holland. Only Katherine was privy to that information. The others saw him as a benevolent bystander who saved a child. Today she'd give him what he deserved. She forced the words, "Thank you for saving Anna."

A tiny smile curled his mouth and she yearned to slap it off. She recognized that little smile and hated it. It meant he had something planned. He began to speak but she cut him off, not caring that the neighbors overheard, "Thank you for saving her but if I see you near my house or kids again, I'll kill you, Jeffrey. I *will* empty my gun into you." From the corner of her eye, she saw the driver's jaw plummet to his chest in complete shock. Yes, she promised to kill Jeffrey and she meant it. Deal with it, she'd say.

She marched back to the house, motioning Lily to her side. The youngster scrambled to obey her mother.

Savannah felt simultaneously faint, enraged and sick. Once inside she'd give the girls a lecture – if she managed to retain consciousness *and* her breakfast.

"Savannah," Jeffrey called from the curb.

Lily hesitated a step upon hearing him call her mother's name. Savannah's hand remained firm on her daughter's, her gait purposeful and steady as she proceeded toward the house. Nothing Jeffrey said would interest her. He'd stalked her children and if she'd had her gun, the neighbors would have witnessed far more than a car accident. They'd have seen the annihilation of evil.

"Savannah," he called again. "You're welcome."

O O O

June 19

Savannah slung her hands for the hundredth time then clasped them tight, hoping to rid them of the persistent tremors. They complicated a minimal, everyday task like opening the front door into a tricky, clumsy effort that left Lily inquiring, "You okay, Mama?"

No, Savannah wanted to reply but nodded instead. No, she was definitely not okay. She'd had several minutes to calm down and still her body rebelled against what had happened and what *nearly* happened.

Savannah pressed a hand to her heart that pounded ever since she discovered Anna missing from their yard. Ever since meeting her oldest daughter's wide-eyed stare then watching it shift to the car rammed into the light standard. Anna was there, the look said. Right there.

A powerful thirst for bourbon taunted her, promised her relief from the stress like it had in the past. A warm balm to settle the rioting within. The old nemesis relentlessly tapped at that part of her brain she assumed was long under control. The urge to drink tucked itself way down for years, not rearing its ugly head – until Jeffrey appeared in her life again. *In her kid's lives.*

The shivering, the raging heartbeat – the terror – would recede, she assured herself, willing away Jack Daniels' siren song. It hung on tight, dug in its claws, refusing to back down. She clenched her jaw, battled harder against the craving. With time, she told herself, not booze. Not booze.

Even if your panic fades, Jack nettled, your kids are still at risk. You're at risk too. You're all vulnerable. One swallow will help, it goaded. Just one. You'll feel so much better...

Her throat worked, her tongue primed for a healthy shot of the magic potion. A quick trip to the package store. Ten minutes at the most. Then sweet relief...

Savannah's gaze shifted to the family portrait hanging on the living room wall. *We all look so happy. No arguments over cats or stuffed ponies, no panic over a killer running loose. Nope, nothing but smiles and laughter on those four faces.* She closed her eyes, inhaled a long, deep breath. *I can do this. I can resist the urge to drink and I will not allow Jeffrey to drive me back to it. My husband and girls need me and they need me sober.*

Savannah peered out the picture window at the light standard. The Nissan rounded out an indentation bigger than a basketball. Black skid marks branded the asphalt, stretching for several feet, their trajectory angling straight for the curb where Jeffrey emerged from behind the clustered trees – holding Anna in his arms.

The police arrived with two patrol units. They split forces, two interviewing witnesses, the other pair plodding to her front door to question her. The cops left after ten minutes, leaving Savannah staring at the clock and wishing Ennis would arrive soon. He'd fought noon traffic for an hour, spending half their phone conversation talking her down from crazy to nervous wreck, the other half cussing a string of obscenities so blistering about Jeffrey it could peel paint off the walls. Savannah was grateful the girls hadn't heard his blue streak – the idea of Anna or Lily cutting loose with the Queen Mother of all expletives brought visions of her falling over in a dead faint from mortification.

Ennis pulled into the driveway as the tow truck loaded the wrecked car on the flatbed and rumbled away. The crowd was the last to disperse, she noticed. They stood around, gabbing and gossiping as though their sleepy little Shangri-la never saw any action.

The instant Ennis walked in the door, she dissolved in tears. The girls stood agape at their mother as if seeing her cry was a foreign experience which until then, was pretty much true.

Ennis consoled her until the tears and shaking subsided. Savannah gathered both girls on the sofa and dispensed a scathing lecture, reiterating the dangers of approaching strangers and of venturing into the street. Then she explained in great detail the consequences if they broke those rules. The worst she threatened them with was a spanking but their horrified expressions suggested she promised to disown them but only after beating them like mules. She supposed the tone of her voice guaranteed that spanking to be quite memorable, at least she hoped it had. Savannah swore to never strike her kids in anger the way R.J. had his children. Raising her hand to her kids meant a swat to the bottom, not a backhand or a fist. She would be a better parent than R.J. Prince and she was – or thought so until that day. Her daddy never caught his kids running into traffic. She had.

It was nine o'clock when Ennis and Savannah prodded Lily to get ready for bed. She changed into her pink pajamas – tonight she wore Cinderella, probably because she felt like an unwanted stepchild after Savannah's dressing-down.

Lily trudged to go brush her teeth, her head hanging low the way a puppy cowered from being yelled at for peeing on the carpet. The girl's silence described in glaring detail her feelings on the day and to punctuate them, she refused to practice her golf lessons.

While Lily brushed her teeth, Savannah checked the room's

windows and curtains.   The pink room brimmed with Disney princess furnishings.   Pink and purple curtains adorned the windows, and on the bed, sheets with all her favorites – Sleeping Beauty, Snow White and Cinderella.

Savannah drew the curtains closer together.   The windows – locked. Curtains – shut. No one could get in or see in. She'd done the same with Anna's room, for caution's sake.

Lily lumbered into her bedroom.   Savannah turned the covers down as part of the nighttime ritual. Next came Lily's kiss goodnight to her, then Ennis.   She would conclude the family routine with her prayers.

Tonight, however, Lily bypassed Savannah to wrap her arms around Ennis's shoulders and kiss his cheek, "'Night, Daddy."

"'Night, sweetheart," he pecked her on the cheek.

She hopped in bed, jerked the sheet from Savannah's grasp, covered up to her chin and closed her eyes.

Savannah stood, at a loss. She glanced at Ennis who shrugged, stunned. He asked, "Lily, aren't you forgetting something?"

She dutifully crawled back out, kneeled beside her bed and clasped her hands. Her eyes closed, she prayed aloud, "Now I lay me down to sleep, I pray the Lord my soul to keep. If I should die before I wake, I pray the Lord my soul to take. Amen." She stood up, climbed between the sheets again. This time she turned on her side, away from Savannah.

A rapid fire prayer. No kiss or *goodnight* for Mama. Only an idiot misinterpreted those signs.

"Lily," Ennis admonished, "give Mama a goodnight kiss."

She laid stone still. She had shut Mama out. Savannah's heart squeezed in her chest. She hadn't laid a hand on the child – either of them – and Lily reacted as if she'd chased them with a whip and a chair.

Ennis's patience dwindled, "Lily."

"Ennis," Savannah shushed him. She supposed Lily still smarted after that afternoon. Replaying it in her mind, she remembered their oldest shrinking into the cushions, crestfallen. In retrospect she'd spoken too harshly to the daughter who obeyed the rules.

She bent down, pressed a kiss to Lily's cheek, "I'm sorry, baby. You did nothing wrong today and I apologize. I was just so scared I'd lost you. I love you, little one. Goodnight."

She walked out, resolving not to let Lily's cold shoulder treatment polish her off. She and Lily rarely argued and in less than two weeks, they'd locked horns twice. Savannah decided to keep a tally. Mama – one. Lily – one and a half, because being ignored by her daughter knifed her to the heart.

Barely able to contain her emotion, Savannah plodded to the master bedroom next door. Fuming, she yanked open the dresser drawer a little too roughly. *Damn it, Jeffrey's got me at odds with my kids now.*

She removed a set of lilac pajamas, put them on. She wanted this day to end. Let's throw it in the crapper and flush, she thought. Hitting the hay this early meant waking up at three or four but another minute of this terrible day would be the death of her. She'd toss and turn most of the night, mulling over the crash, Jeffrey stalking the kids, and the few neighbors that made her feel inadequate and negligent as a parent. *Now* she'd fixate over Lily's snub.

Lily loved Daddy more than Mama that night, Savannah sighed. Daddy hadn't blasted them with a fiery lecture or threatened them with a visit to the woodshed. Nope, he played Switzerland and reaped the benefits while Mama's stock plummeted deeper than the argument about that damn pony Jeffrey brought. A perfect way to end the day. *Thank you, Jeffrey. You bastard.*

She sank down onto the mattress, massaged her temple, debated over a Tylenol. The small headache panged all day, threatening a bigger, longer struggle if she didn't settle down altogether.

"Headache?" Ennis asked, heading to the dresser, shook out a pair of folded blue pajama bottoms.

Savannah nodded, "You could say that. Lily hates me and the neighbors think I'm negligent. Meanwhile Jeffrey goes along merrily wreaking havoc in my life."

He changed for bed then parked himself behind her on the bed. He kissed her shoulder, "She doesn't hate you, babe." He said it as if the notion was utterly preposterous. Of course *he* could, couldn't he? Mr. Favorite Parent could say anything he wanted. His reputation sparkled with their girls.

"Oh?" she replied, incredulous. "She said goodnight to you. She ignored me."

"Her feelings are hurt. She's not used to you getting that upset."

"I'm not used to seeing our child in a serial killer's arms either. She doesn't understand how dangerous he is. I was scared, Ennis. I realize I overreacted with Lily, that's why I apologized."

His warm, soft lips lingered on her shoulder. He tossed in two more kisses before his hands settled on the tense muscles, "She'll be fine. Tomorrow she'll have forgotten about it and will want golf lessons again." His thumbs circled the worst of the tension, coaxing them to loosen. He applied more pressure but she pulled away, wincing. What started as a soothing massage turned medieval in a hurry.

"You get any tighter and your knees'll be up to your ears," he said, seemingly justifying his actions. Then he brushed her hair aside, pressed a kiss to her nape.

She groaned, "Now *that* feels good."

"Here's an idea. How about," he punctuated each word with a warm kiss, "Dane and Georgia babysit tomorrow?" He whispered the rest, "Then you and I can spend the day romping? That'll relax you."

His offer sounded delightful. She let herself savor images of them together, the feel of his hands and lips roaming her body, making her moan with pleasure. "You just want to try for a son," she teased.

After Anna, they agreed to shoot for a boy next time. They shook on the deal unaware of the sacrifice they'd be making on their sex life. According to Ennis's mother, the longer a couple abstained from sex, the better the odds of having a boy. The two ended up crossing off days on a calendar the way prisoners counted down their sentences. Three weeks later, their moods bottomed out, their tempers easily flared and the overwhelming desire for a romp nearly broke them out in hives.

Ennis slid his hand around her waist, angled up to her breast to brush the tight nipple, "I'm ready to try for *anything*, babe. I'm miserable, aren't you?"

She leaned against him, blew out a breath, "I feel like a nun."

"I'll call Dane tomorrow," he promised. "He'll keep close watch on the girls for us and then you won't have to worry or think about you-know-who."

"Right now you're making it difficult to think about anything other than sex." She put a hand to his, stopping him while explaining, "Lily thinks it's gross when you kiss me? She'll flip out if she walks in on the whole kit and kaboodle."

"Your kit *and* kaboodle are exclusively mine tomorrow. For now, promise you won't think about that jerk anymore. Just carry your gun from now on. Plug the bastard if you see him."

She intended to but did he expect her to carry the gun everywhere, even around the house?

"Why not?" he answered, still sprinkling kisses along her nape. "Couldn't hurt."

She wondered if the lack of sex eroded his entire capacity for common sense. "Bet the UPS guy will be surprised if he delivers a package. He'll think I'm holding him up. Of course it'll scare off the Hoover salesman and siding guys so there *is* a positive angle to the idea…"

"You know what I mean."

She glanced back at him, "Yes, sweetheart, I do, but having my .38 on my hip while I bake brownies? C'mon."

"Mama?"

Both turned to see Lily peeking around the door jamb. She sulked, chin to her chest, her blue eyes refusing to make contact with either parent. If a child could act or look more defeated, Savannah didn't know how.

Guilt tapped at Savannah's brain upon seeing her daughter's apprehension.

Mama patted the bed with a gentle, "What is it, baby?"

Head bowed, Lily approached. Instead of climbing aboard the bed, she toed the carpet, "You still mad?"

Savannah drew the girl into her lap, "No, honey, I'm not still mad. I was scared this afternoon. I love you both so much I want to protect you from bad things and bad people. When I scolded you and your sister, I only meant to warn you both not to go near strangers or the street for any reason." She tilted Lily's face to meet her gaze, "I'm sorry if I sounded like I was blaming you for what happened."

The apology helped. Lily finally relaxed in her mother's embrace, "I tried to watch Anna but that man kept calling her."

That man. Lily's code for Jeffrey. To be sure though, she asked, "The man who gave you the pony?"

Lily nodded, "*That* man. I told Anna not to go. I went to Mrs. Collins but then the car crashed and you came out."

She fought the urge to tense for fear Lily might feel it. She stroked her daughter's hair to keep Lily and herself calm. Ennis, on the other hand, fisted his hands.

"What did he do?" Daddy inquired with far less composure than she. His voice developed the edge he reserved exclusively for Mr. Holland. He'd kill Jeffrey for involving their kids – but he'd have to wait in line behind his wife first.

"He said he had a kitty-cat for her. I kept calling Anna back but he held out a orange kitty for her."

The image of Jeffrey crouching to Anna's level, luring her across the street with a cute kitten swelled a rage so volcanic she nearly erupted. *Come here, Anna. Jeffrey's got a present for you. Come on, just a few more steps...* She could hear the sociopath turn on the charm to lure her baby into the busy street – and it pissed Savannah off.

Lily sighed, slumping against her, "You're mad again."

No, *mad* failed to describe this feeling. *Insane* fit better. For Lily's sake, she swallowed the rage, "I'm mad at that man, honey." She kissed her daughter's hair, assuring, "Not at you. We appreciate you telling us this. We needed to know."

"How did Jeffrey know Anna wanted a cat?" Ennis whispered.

Savannah shook her head, mulling over that very question.

He asked Lily, "Have you spoken to that man again after he gave you the pony?"

Her eyes flared wide, "You said not to."

He scrubbed a hand through his hair, "Then he overheard it somewhere which means he's following us." Ennis turned to Savannah,

"He's following *you*. Keep your .38 with you at all times. I don't care if you're baking brownies, out shopping or on the throne, carry it."

What once sounded ridiculous now held merit. Jeffrey skulked around the house, obviously, so she expected to share a more intimate relationship with Mr. Smith & Wesson. The old paranoia slipped in and Savannah saw sleepless nights on the horizon until Jeffrey sat behind bars. He'd focused on their kids and she knew why. They were a conduit to her the way abducting Georgia had been years ago. The solution: remove temptation. She asked Ennis, "How about you schedule vacation time and take the girls to your mother's?"

Mama Rutherford lived on a ranch outside Vega, Texas. Her sons Cal and Jake lived in their own homes on the property. Ennis's oldest brother Cal lived nearest to their mother with his wife and three kids. Jake, still the bachelor of the family, lived "yonder a ways" as Mama once explained, "yonder" being about halfway down the property half a mile or so. Lily loved the horses and gathering hen eggs, plus she enjoyed spending time with her cousins and Ennis's mother – or Granna.

Ennis's jaw dropped, "You've lost your mind. Take the girls and leave you here alone with *him* creeping around?"

She realized how she sounded but, "We need to protect the girls."

"We need to protect you too."

Lily perked up at the suggestion of a trip, "Are we going to see Granna?"

Savannah hugged her, "You might be, we're not sure yet. Gotta convince Daddy to take you first."

"You're not coming?" the girl sulked.

"If we go, we *all* go," Ennis stated as fact. No arguing, no compromise, no ifs, ands, or buts, his frown said.

And just like that, her good idea circled the drain. Her last – and only other option, "I can't go right now so we'd better find an exterminator who specializes in eliminating two-legged polecats."

9

June 20

According to Amber, Savannah said a man lured sweet little Anna into the street with the promise of a cat. Past that tidbit of info, the young lady lacked real recollection abilities. I'm fairly sure Savannah can describe me down to the four inch scar on my left bicep – a result of miscalculating a woman's reach with a steak knife. I trust my detective is so gifted she could sketch my features with more realism than Leonardo da Vinci wielded a paintbrush. Amber, however, struggles to adequately paint a decent depiction of this nefarious fiend who baited Anna.

She begins with general details that fit plenty of men in the city. Despite her valiant efforts to describe the man, her portrayal cheats me out of five whole inches of height. She makes me shorter than my six feet two which should insult me however I'm grateful Amber skewed Savannah's description. It keeps me under the radar of suspicion. My hair is darker than she says and I'd like to think the word "broad" applies to my shoulders, not my waist as she indicates. Had the girl even listened to Savannah?

"Maybe the police will find him soon," I say.   Maybe but probably not. That nugget I keep to myself.

"Hope so. Georgia said Savannah was bringing a picture of him for the bulletin board but I haven't seen it yet," she goes on. "She'll probably bring it tomorrow."

Well, won't Miss Nancy Drew be surprised when she feasts her eyes on that picture? Her old pal Tom is actually Jeffrey Thomas Holland, the man, no doubt, Savannah warned her about. "So she got a picture of him too?" I ask with all sincerity.

Amber reaches in the furthest corner for the broom. She brushes the floor with long languid, strokes, "No, it's a booking photo from the police department. She's met him before, I'm not sure how though. I think he threatened her a while back. All I know is she's gotten really paranoid about him the last few weeks."

I busy myself placing new liners in the trash bins, "Poor woman. She's got to be scared to death."

Amber replies with a cynical snort, "You don't know Savannah. Nothing really scares her."

I glance at the young lady. Methinks she's had an unpleasant run-in with my detective – or she suffers Tonya's malady of jealousy. "Nothing?" I ask in mock amazement.

Amber pauses her sweeping, "She's made of steel. If anything in the universe can scare her, I want to see it."

"It" is standing right in front of you, my dear ignorant friend. I have brought the woman of steel to her knees. I have seen her tears, heard her inconsolable weeping. I have caused her immeasurable pain and yet she hides behind a convincing mask of bravery. Convincing enough you believe she's unconquerable but I've found her Achilles Heel. It took five long years but now Savannah is vulnerable. Her sweet little cubs are the key to my success.

I finish lining the trash bins, "Everyone is scared of something, Amber. I'd bet Savannah is no different. She just doesn't show her fear." Not unless she's with me.

Amber gives me an are-you-nuts stare as though I've declared Elvis is alive and standing behind her. Finally she shrugs, "Whatever you say. If you met her you'd change your tune, believe me. She's nothing like Georgia."

In several ways that was true. Their differences were obvious on the surface. Georgia's easygoing nature conflicted with Savannah's abrupt manner. Georgia's quiet demeanor was the polar opposite of her sister's outgoing one. I want to tell my new young friend, neither Savannah nor Georgia readily displayed fear. However when a mother senses her babies are in danger, Mama raises a shield against that fear, cloaking it and channeling it into defending her young. But the fear is there. And so is the anger.

Hornet's nests, like Savannah's children, are dangerous to toy with. I've awakened a beast in my detective now. A fiercely protective, lethally armed beast.

"Tom?" Amber snaps her fingers, bringing me from my fantasy. She is amused at my lapse.

"Sorry. I was thinking about Georgia's chocolate pecan pie. Is there any left?"

Amber shakes her head, "It sells out pretty quick. There's a slice or two of Crack pie though."

I'm confident I've misheard the young woman, "Did you say Crack *pie?*"

"Not that *kind of Crack,*" she rolls her eyes with a laugh. "It's a salty-sweet pie with an oat cookie crust. Here," she traipses to a lower cabinet, reaches way at the back. It's her secret place that Georgia hasn't discovered yet – a place Amber stows my "payment" each night. She squirrels a few slices back from the deliveries to the homeless shelter where Georgia sends the day's leftovers.

Amber hands me a fork and a saucer, the latter holds a slice of what appears to be chocolate pie with a thick buttery-type filling. Had anyone besides Georgia made the thing, I'd have outright declined. It is not a particularly attractive thing, unlike her other efforts.

I sniff of it first. My brow raises. As usual, Georgia's abilities amaze me. I'm convinced the woman could fry dirt and make it delicious. I take a bite and instantly moan with pleasure. The homely pie is heavenly. After another bite, I admit, "I see the reason for its name. It is addictive."

In the process of leaning the broom in a corner, Amber's hip nudges a few papers off of Georgia's small desk. I set the pie aside to help pick them up.

"What's this?" she asked.

I look over her shoulder to see a photograph in her hand, the person's face hidden by a Post-It note. On the yellow three inch square I see Savannah's elegant cursive. "Call the police if you see this man. DO NOT approach him." Above the note she'd written in capital letters "JEFFREY HOLLAND".

I tense, holding my breath to see what she does. I'm baffled when Amber treats the photo with nonchalance, "I like Savannah but being a cop has made her suspicious of people. From what I heard, the neighbor said the guy saved Anna's life."

I try not to stare at the contents in her hand. "Guess you had to be there," I pause to see if she lifts the Post-It to reveal my image or if careless disregard – and her opinion of Savannah's mental footing – wins out and she ignores the photo.

I wait as Amber deliberates over a decision. Inquisitiveness made most people lift the note to see the face beneath. Why was she hesitating?

Surprisingly, she sets the photo aside, returns it to Georgia's desk. A small rush of relief washes over me, "Not interested in it?"

Amber turns to face me, shrugged one shoulder, "Like I said. She's paranoid."

Maybe, but my gut says that picture is calling to Ms. Martin. Mysteries are meant to be solved, unknowns meant to be identified. I recall the saying "curiosity killed the cat…" If Amber so much as breathes in that photo's direction, nothing, certainly not satisfaction, will bring her back.

She eyes the saucer on the cabinet, "You gonna finish that pie before we leave?"

I nod, feeling my heart's tempo increase when she glances back at the desk. Retrieving the dish, I fork another bite into my mouth. I can no longer concentrate on the delicious flavor for I see Amber lurking too close to that photo. "I see Georgia keeps her desk as tidy as her pantry," I say. "Perhaps you should let her do that." In other words, back off, young lady, and you won't get hurt.

She leans over a notepad, grabs a nearby pen and answers while jotting something down, "I'm just leaving her a note, telling her I found the photo Savannah left."

What a conscientious employee. Leave your helpful note then step away, please.

Amber stops writing, reaches for the photo and lays it beside the note. She stares at the handwritten Post-It with such intensity, I step forward.

"You know what?" she asks.

I move closer, "What?"

"Georgia wanted this on the bulletin board anyway. I think I'll save her the trouble." She plucks the photo from the desk, strips away the note, revealing my likeness.

Her gaze reveals no reaction. When she swallows, it is hard and loud, the way one swallows when a bite of chicken clings in the throat, refusing to budge without a generous drink of water.

"Jeffrey Holland," she says on a tremulous whisper. "But your name is…"

"*Jeffrey Holland,*" *I reply, dropping each syllable like a brick.* "*Jeffrey* Thomas *Holland.*"

Amber releases the photo, lets it drift to the floor. When she turns to me, her vision unveils the terror I've seen many times before. Fear mixed with the innate urge to run.

"*I did more than threaten Savannah, my dear girl,*" *I move closer as her wide eyes dart around her for a weapon or a way out.* "*I left scars, not just physical but emotional ones that will remain until her dying breath. I beat her until her body lay bloody and broken.*" *I reach toward her right shoulder,* "*I used a scalpel to mark her as mine. That's why she never wears a blouse that might reveal those scars. When I had her, she had that same look you have now, only she never begged me for mercy like you will. Because Savannah is strong.*"

Amber dashes toward the back door. As she passes by, I strike fast, launching my fist into her face. A spray of blood flies from her nose, splattering my t-shirt and Georgia's paperwork.

The blow knocks Amber backwards, she careens off the edge of Georgia's desk, scattering the papers – and the photograph – onto the floor. She stumbles into a metal rack. It overturns, crashing stacks of saucers to the floor in thousands of shards and pieces. Amber ends up, her back against the toppled rack, her head thumping the frame.

She lifts her head and a steady stream of blood trickles from her nose. I see a scream poised on her lips so I reach down, close my hand around her throat, cutting off her air. Stunned panic registers in her eyes. She can't believe this is happening. From exchanging easy conversation with her friend Tom to feeling her life slowly ebb in the grasp of a killer named Jeffrey Holland.

Amber shows the spark of courage I expected. The disorienting dizziness has passed, giving way to chaste terror that she is, in fact, losing consciousness and she's doing nothing to stop me. Her hands claw at my face, swatting at me like an angry cat. I dodge the attack, only my neck takes a hit. The slicing sting angers me and I bear down on her throat. "Stop fighting me," I tell her. "You're not dying." At least not yet.

She puts up a decent struggle for such a trim, slight woman but she's no match for my strength, especially after years of weight training in prison. I'm much stronger now than before.

Amber's battle lessens, her attacks lose their potency as her oxygen deprived brain succumbs to my grasp. I smile into her eyes that begin drifting closed, "You thought Savannah was irrational to fear me. Now you'll find out how right she was. After all, just because she's paranoid doesn't mean I'm not out to get her."

10

June 21

A noise drew Savannah from deep, precious slumber. After Anna's close call, Lily's propensity for nightmares escalated. Like clockwork, fifteen minutes after her parents went to bed, with teddy bear clutched to her chest, she tiptoed to Savannah's bedside to whisper if she could sleep with them. Savannah lifted the covers, invited her in. Lily positioned herself snug between her parents, tucked Teddy close and drifted to sleep.

The repetitive noise continued. Somewhere in the dreamy state Savannah had fought hard to achieve, it registered that a phone rang in the distance. Consciousness floated in, bringing with it the realization her daughter commandeered most of her pillow during the night. A neck spasm jarred her wide awake when she raised her head. She slung her arm toward the nightstand, muttered a complaint about pillow hogs. Squinting to read the Caller ID, her blurry vision made out Georgia's name. Hell, she thought, the sun's not even up yet. Glancing at the digital clock on the nightstand, Savannah groaned at the sight. Her sister called at the unholy hour of 5:00 in the morning.

A bolt of anxiety brought her upright in the bed, careful not to disturb the pillow hog beside her. Georgia (Miss Manners reincarnated) never dialed a phone before 8:00 a.m. unless it was extremely important or a flat-out emergency. Forgoing the usual greeting, Savannah answered, "What's wrong?"

"I'm sorry for calling so early but something's happened here at the shop."

Savannah sat up, rubbed her right eye with a balled fist, "What?"

Lily stirred without waking, snuggled closer to Savannah to claim her mother's pillow all for herself.

Savannah heard the concern in her sister's voice, "Amber left the back door unlocked and she left her purse. The place is a wreck."

"Get out of there right now," Savannah demanded. "Get someplace safe." Her heart went from zero to ninety. One minute earlier she struggled to open her eyes, now she battled visions of intruders hiding inside the place and her sister was alone to fend for herself.

Savannah flipped through a mental Rolodex for who was on shift at that hour. Christine Clark took a week's vacation so that left Mathis. "Call the station. Get Mathis out there pronto."

Savannah heard the shop door squeak shut, the lock snap in place. "Savannah," Georgia complained, "he's a homicide detective. Just a uniform will be–"

"Georgia, call him or I will." She tossed the covers back, climbed out of bed. "He can get there faster than I can. I'll get dressed and be there ASAP." She hung up, already opening the closet to grab a pair of jeans and a blouse.

Ennis propped onto his elbow, his voice and features leaden with sleep, "What happened?"

She shucked out of her pajamas, "The back door is unlocked and Amber left her purse at the shop. Georgia said the place is trashed."

After sliding on a pair of jeans and donning a navy blue pullover, she hurried to the bathroom to run a quick brush over her teeth and another through her hair. She grabbed her cell phone, "I'm calling Mathis. He's only a few minutes away. Georgia's there alone." She told Ennis, "I'll let you know what's going on when I find out anything."

o o o

June 21

Anyone strolling by the store later that morning might wonder why Pie In The Sky shut down for the day. Anyone walking by the alley would see why. A police cruiser, detective's sedan and forensics SUV all blocked the back entrance. Joining the hodgepodge of vehicles were Georgia's Tahoe and Savannah's Charger, the latter arriving forty-five minutes after Mathis drove up.

The instant Savannah saw the bakery's kitchen, her mouth dropped open. Pieces of broken saucers littered the floor, the stainless steel table once holding them now overturned in the middle of the kitchen. Papers from Georgia's desk cluttered the floor. Savannah recognized supply orders, rental bills and other mail, once neat and tidy on her sister's desk now lay like a fifty-two card pickup on the tile.

In the midst of surveying the damage, Savannah's vision ran across a forensics tech crouched to the floor, a camera in his hands. The man, clean cut, mid-twenties and dressed in blue Dockers and beige polo shirt greeted her then, "I'm getting photos right now so..."

"Hands off, I understand." Not that she would venture where to begin. She sidestepped the strewn papers, "Where's Georgia?"

"Up front with Mathis." He expelled a loud breath, "He's in a mood. I hate it when he works nights."

"He's a real ray of sunshine, isn't he?" Her cynical remark expressed how *not* sunny John Mathis acted on those long, summer nights at work. The tech's singular raised brow concurred with her.

An odd sight caught her attention amid the flagrant chaos of the room. On a prep counter across from the door sat a saucer and fork, the contents resembled a piece of half-eaten Crack pie. Had Amber indulged in a snack, she wondered, or was it left behind by whatever crazy person destroyed the joint? "Have you dusted for prints yet?"

"Nope. All alone today. Once I'm done with the photos, I'll do the prints. Saucer, fork, door handles..."

He continued on as if she'd questioned his abilities. Mathis wasn't the only sourpuss that morning, she wanted to say but didn't. Instead, she swiped a pair of latex gloves from the tech's toolkit, "I'll give you time to work. That is, unless Detective Sunshine orders me back in here."

She walked to the front of the store where she found Georgia standing at the door, arms folded over her chest. She stared, disheartened, at the "Closed" sign. Savannah put a hand to her shoulder, "Hey, sis."

Georgia turned. Tears shimmered in her eyes, "How did this happen? I mean, what exactly *did* happen last night? I don't know if Amber's okay. She's not answering her phone at the dorm. I'm scared something terrible has happened to her."

She brought Georgia into an embrace. Besides her writing, Pie In The Sky was her baby. She fussed over it, nurtured it into a thriving business. Someone injured her child last night and, in the process, an employee disappeared. Georgia worried about their employees more than any other boss and one was now missing under suspicious circumstances. Judging by the kitchen, one hell of a fight took place the night before and Amber Martin lost the battle.

John Mathis rounded the corner from the bathroom, complete in rumpled suit, a set of bifocals perched on his nose and five o'clock shadow darkening his jaw. He stopped upon sight of his colleague, obviously miffed, "'Bout time you got here."

Savannah parted from the embrace, overlooked his brusque tone, "I've got two kids and my husband doesn't know how to deal with either one. Plus I haven't had a single drop of coffee yet. You're lucky I got here at all. You're extra lucky I'm not snarling like you are."

He harrumphed, "That snarling thing is a natural habit with you, kid." He aimed his ballpoint toward the kitchen, "That girl, Amber

Martin, musta given the guy the what-for.   And don't climb my case about assuming either.   Had to be a guy that did this."

"Okay, a guy did this. Who is he and why'd he choose Amber?" She pursed her lips. It was too early in the morning to argue, especially without the benefit of coffee kick-starting her brain.

He peered over his glasses at her, "What, did your kids break a neighbor's window? That why you're in a bad mood?"

She did a doubletake. *She* was in the bad mood? Oh for God's sake, "No, John. My home life is June Cleaver perfect. What can I do to expedite this so you can go off shift sooner?"

"Good of you to ask." He pointed to the kitchen again, "You can check Amber's cell phone since you know her so well."

"I know her casually," she replied. "We don't share our deepest, darkest secrets. I'll call around and see if anyone's seen her." She put a hand to Georgia's waist, "Sit down. We'll be here a while. There's not much you can do for now."

"Yeah, there is," Mathis countered. "She can walk me through her morning. You get busy with the cell phone."

"Yessir, Detective Mathis, sir," she halfway joked. She decided to play nice with Mr. Sunshine. If she poked too hard at him, the results would not be pretty.

Slipping on the latex gloves, Savannah went back to the kitchen. The tech looked up when she entered the room, "Orders?"

"Orders." She slipped her reading glasses on, "Checking the purse is all. I'm out of your way."

She opened Amber's purse, retrieved a set of car keys (her blue Toyota was parked behind the shop), then Savannah removed the wallet. She counted fifty-one dollars in cash and two credit cards, Discover and Visa. She put the wallet back, retrieved the cell phone. On a lark, she dialed Amber's dorm. Georgia already tried it but one more call couldn't hurt. No one answered. Savannah called the last number dialed. Amber's boyfriend, roused from his early morning slumber in his Georgia Tech dorm, yawned his answer. He'd not seen her since supper the night before.

She waded through the contact list, making early morning calls to every name, asking if they'd seen Amber since seven o'clock the night before. No one had.

The tech put his camera away, "I'll get prints next. You're free to roam over here though."

She thanked him, seeing Mathis round the corner of the kitchen, glasses lower on his nose as he scribbled on a notepad, "And there's nothing missing that you can tell?"

"No," Georgia replied, following behind. She waved her hand across the room, "Everything is in order except the half-eaten pie and the obvious destruction and disarray."

Single-minded Mathis concentrated on the food first. If it involved edible items, he dropped everything. True to form, John lifted the saucer with a gloved hand, appraised the remaining three or so bites with a raised brow.

Savannah watched from the corner of her eye. She'd bet a

hundred bucks he'd sniff it at least twice and if it hadn't been evidence, he'd have sampled it straight from the plate.

Sure enough he took a cursory snort, "Looks funny but smells great. What is it?"

Georgia replied, "Crack pie." Then considered the meaning of his statement, "What do you mean it looks funny?"

Savannah shook her head at Georgia, rolled her eyes, "Yeah, Mathis. How does it look funny? Besides the fact it's a day old, been hacked to pieces and basically smeared all over the saucer."

Mathis griped, "I meant no insult to your sister, Prince. It still smells great." He stared at it long enough it made her nervous and caused Georgia to frown, obviously chafed at his *looks funny* comment.

"That's evidence, John," Savannah reminded, in case his appetite overrode his common sense. "The tech's going to dust it for prints if you'll let him."

"How's he gonna fingerprint a pie, wiseass?" Mathis argued.

First day as a rookie cop, Savannah labeled Detective Mathis an asshole. Loud mouth, gruff personality and cursed with a razor sharp tongue. Years passed and she understood why his wife filed for divorce and it wasn't difficult to fathom why his kids shied from him too. Now, with two kids of her own, Savannah added Mathis as her third child, the one she worked with, and who outnumbered her in age but not in patience. She shook her head, exasperated, "The *fork and saucer*, genius. He's dusting the fork and saucer for prints."

He made a show of setting the saucer down and stepping back, returning to his conversation with Georgia, "So does this Amber have a habit of eating the leftovers?"

The question puzzled her. "Not that I know of. I always send the leftovers to the homeless shelter so I guess she kept that slice for herself."

"What homeless shelter?"

"Safe Haven on Ponce De Leon Northeast."

Savannah inquired, "Don't they send a guy to pick up the leftovers?"

"Yes," Georgia replied. "He comes about an hour after we close."

"And Amber's here at that time too, right?" she asked.

Georgia nodded, "She's the one who lets him in."

Savannah waited for Mathis to finish taking notes then suggested, "I'd go to Safe Haven and find out who they send and ask him if he saw her last night – then check *him* out."

Mathis sneered, "But *you* won't check with them because you're not on shift. *I am*. And you're making work for me, kid. You know I hate that. But I'll do it. Anything to square up with you and your sister about the Crack pie comment."

Savannah stepped around the papers scattered on the floor. Crouching down, she collected each one, sorting them, straightening them for her sister. Two of the orders caught her attention. Small, almost inconspicuous drops of blood speckled them. She separated the envelopes from the others for the forensics tech to bag as evidence and arranged the others in two categories the way Georgia preferred. Business paperwork in one pile, everything else in the other. She sat aside orders for flour, sugar and fruit. Beneath the bloodstained envelopes sat the picture of Jeffrey she'd left the day earlier. Savannah paused on the photo. It was missing the yellow Post-It she stuck on the front.

Savannah stood up, approached the desk while Georgia and Mathis continued their conversation. The Post-It note sat right on top of the desk. Someone peeled it off the photo and stuck it to the desk. For some reason, it struck her as odd. She asked Georgia, "Did you remove the sticky note from Jeffrey's photo?"

Georgia shook her head, "I forgot to pin it on the bulletin board so I haven't touched it. I told Amber about the photo though. Maybe she removed the note."

Savannah placed the papers and photo on the desk where they belonged then headed to the pantry. All seemed in order and nothing disturbed. Even the back door key hung in its proper place. She closed the door.

Her watch read seven fifteen. A peek out the back door revealed clouds filtering the morning sun into a gray shroud. There was barely enough light to see by. She stepped onto the small landing, visually examined the railing, then stooped down for a closer look at the concrete. Another blood drop. "Georgia," she called, "get me the flashlight please."

Her sister appeared seconds later, handed over the MagLite she stored in the desk drawer, "What did you find?"

"Blood." She stepped down again, letting the bright beam of light lead the way. The shaft zeroed in on the spot. Congealed blood.

"Better get Detective Surly out here."

She descended the next step. Another drop of blood appeared then another then another, making a breadcrumb trail down the stairs to the alley, until they abruptly stopped.

John Mathis appeared on the landing, his specs perched on top of his head, "I heard that, you know. Detective Surly? You realize when you were knocked up you weren't exactly a pleasure to be around – not that you normally are."

Yeah, yeah, whatever, "Tell the forensics guy to keep his camera handy."

"Why? What'd you find?"

She pointed to the last red spot, "A blood trail. From here," she swept the flashlight beam to the area in front of the landing, "to there."

"Stupid question but there's no chance it's not blood, is it?" he asked without taking a closer look. "Red food coloring? Icing, maybe? It *is* a bakery."

"You know when you said it was a stupid question?"

His brow sank, "Don't make me mad, Prince."

"Well, *you* said it, I didn't. Look at this place, John. The whole thing is a mess, Georgia's employee is missing and there isn't a woman walking this planet who'd leave their purse behind by choice. Her money and credit cards are still in her wallet. Her car keys are in the purse and her car is parked right there," she pointed to the blue Toyota Corolla. "There are blood drops on the mail and congealed blood leading from the store to the alleyway. I think you were right. A guy did this but he only wanted Amber, not her money or car. Just her."

11

June 22

They say money can't buy happiness. Money can certainly buy my *happiness. In fact it's bought me the finishing touches for my plan.*

Thanks to Tonya's money, I've purchased the last of the equipment and drugs I need. A hospital pharmacy usually hires trustworthy employees. I found the one that employed a particular fellow with a gambling debt. I know about his habit thanks to Tonya who heard it from her husband. I offered a trade upon making his acquaintance. Money for drugs. Not painkillers, I stressed, but a drug comparable to Propofol. Propofol is my preference I tell him then offer a bonus if he comes through. I've used it before and the drug works fast – within seconds of administration – and allows a person to later awaken rapidly and more clear-headed.

I also required an ample amount of syringes and one or two other drugs which I wrote down. I put in my order for a few surgical supplies as well. I need specific items for my time with Savannah that can only be found in a hospital so I use his job to my advantage. If he procures everything on my list (and does so before his shift ends) he will receive enough cash to not only pay his debts but place wagers for at least a month.

By evening I saunter to the car, in my hand I hold a rather sizeable bag and my friend leaves with pockets brimming with Benjamins.

I stop to admire the beauty and breathe in the fresh air only a park can provide. Peace washes over me. I am ready for her. And how symbolic that my new (now richer) friend and I met at Piedmont Park. It is the place I made my first mistake with Savannah.

Sitting in the car, I hold the sedative vial, remembering back. I turn toward a certain hedgerow in the near distance. It has flourished in the five years since I pushed Savannah beneath their burgeoning leafy branches. I remember seeing Georgia and Savannah strolling along the jogging path. I decided Georgia would be my next victim. I based the decision on an encounter at the hospital where I worked as a physician. Georgia's calm in the storm of her emergency convinced me she was a worthier choice than Savannah. I misjudged the detective's boldness and protective nature toward her sister. I labeled her a loose cannon. A woman without restraint. She'd issued commands to nurses and to me. I'd discovered women with loud mouths were naturally weak. They overcompensated for their insecurities. But I was wrong. Savannah's demeanor underscored her strength.

My stepbrother and I used Tasers to bring the sisters down. They both collapsed to the ground but Savannah's struggle against the disabling current impressed me. Her fingers dug into the grass, groping for stability to rise and fight. When the Taser's effects waned, she drew a deep breath, intent on alerting any nearby ears. I clamped my hand over her mouth to muffle the scream. She'd pushed her way almost to her knees before I shoved my left one into her back, bracing her on the ground and replaced my hand with duct tape to silence her. Even then, without the ability to defend herself or her sister, she refused to surrender. I felt her pull beneath me, to crawl free. At that moment, I doubted my decision about taking Georgia. The woman writhing, battling with the ferocity of a cornered wild animal, this was who I searched for. I'd made my decision, however, and –Cole, my stepbrother, already carried Georgia to the car.

I slid the sedative-filled needle into the detective's arm, leaving her behind – but only for a time. The drug took a bit longer to calm her fight but eventually, as I dragged her toward the hedgerow, she succumbed to the sedative. She fell limp in my embrace and I left her there, tucked under the hedge, while I drove away with the wrong woman.

When I did finally acquire my detective, she proved well worth the effort. The feeling was akin to a compulsive gambler (perhaps like my new, richer friend) who bets on the sleekest, prettiest horse only for it to lose. Then, by chance, he tosses his last ten dollars on the long shot, expecting to go home broke. But somehow that horse pulls ahead of all the others, showing its potency, its value and heart by leaving the competition far behind to win the race. The compulsive gambler regains *hope, feeling the exhilarating high return, the success thrumming in his veins. The thrill of winning – this time with an unexpected surprise – a dark horse.*

I blink back to the here and now, place the sedative back in the bag, crank the Volvo to life as a smile crosses my lips. Oh yes. The dark horse. My dark horse. We are getting closer to the finish line…

12

June 23

Savannah finished her shift late that evening around seven-thirty, fed the brood and herself and after a soaking bath, she slid on her soft blue robe and relaxed with her family. She and Ennis put the girls to bed, Anna earlier than Lily who begged for an extra thirty minutes. Savannah was about to sit down with Ennis for quiet time together when the phone rang.

The man on the phone introduced himself as Detective Austin Wallace from Zone 5. Since Zone 5 covered the area of Georgia Tech, she immediately thought of Amber Martin.

Wallace began by apologizing for the late hour – 9:45 – then broached the subject of the missing person's report she'd filed two days earlier on Amber. She allowed herself a glimmer of hope that Amber was safe (despite the obvious signs she probably was not). The job rarely held pleasant surprises but unlike many of her colleagues, the job's constant disappointments hadn't doused all her optimism. Savannah tried to hold out hope on occasion, especially when the case hit so close to home. "Did you find her?" she asked Wallace in a upbeat manner.

She also tried to disguise the weariness in her voice. Her shift was over that day but Wallace was smack in the middle of his. She knew what long days (and nights) were and having a person sigh in their ear wasn't pleasant when the detective was already exhausted.

"I need you at the bridge over Lake Clara Meer now, Detective," his tone still leaning to the apologetic side. "It's important."

Her heart sank. "You found her," she groaned, her hope officially gone. Mathis, honorary president of the Pessimists Club, might have phrased it in his best poetic terms. *It ain't good news. It ain't good at all.*

"I'll fill you in once you're here."

"It'll take about forty minutes to get there."

"I'm not going anywhere."

She hurried to change clothes and gather her phone, gun and badge then began her journey to Piedmont Park.

She drove along Northeast Expressway for ten minutes but it felt longer. The whole trip took twenty-five minutes from Dunwoody to the park. Another couple to hoof it along a pathway to the bridge.

Blinking blue and red cruiser lights blazed a beacon for her in the dark of night. She turned onto the road running through the park, drove until pulling behind a detective's sedan. She put the Charger in Park, switched off the engine and headlights.

She climbed out to warm, sticky night air and the earthy smell of wet soil and fresh mowed grass that brought images of kids at play, laughter and family fun. Tonight however, the swarm of cops, crime scene tape and late night phone call canceled it out, replacing it with the harsh truth. Something tragic occurred beyond that fresh smelling grass. And she dreaded that discovery.

She saw a uniform officer standing sentry at the crime scene tape blocking public access to the bridge. Onlookers crowded the yellow barrier, jockeying for a glimpse of whatever the fuss was about. She flashed her badge to the uniform as he lifted the tape high for her to duck beneath.

Lake Clara Meer measured nearly twelve acres in size. It began as a spring and in 1895 was enlarged to a lake. A few years back the city decided it needed improvement so the area underwent renovation. Two of the big projects were the dilapidated gazebo and to update the granite bridge spanning the width of the lake at its narrowest point. They added fishing piers and installed several sodium pole lights along those piers that bathed the area in an eerie pinkish-orange glow.

The walk to the bridge was less than fifty yards. She glanced at her watch, tilting it toward an overhead light lining the pathway. 10:35. Savannah spent the trip to the park preparing herself for the worst. In her opinion, Amber was a typical college girl. She was full of life, ambition and enjoying a new freedom only college life provided. She seemed nice enough, though maybe a fraction too trusting for Savannah's taste.

At the base of the bridge, she sought out another officer, "Where's Detective Wallace?"

The short, stumpy cop pointed ahead of her, "In the gazebo, ma'am."

She started the walk up the bridge. Water rippled in a lazy tide of liquid black velvet around her. In the near distance a mirror image of the city's skyline floated on the surface, the building lights broken only by the gentle flowing waves.

Officers cordoned off sections on either side of the stone bridge, their flashlight beams sweeping the grass and ground leading to it. From what she saw, few yellow evidence markers dotted the sea of green.

Halfway across the bridge a man in a gray suit exited the gazebo, wiped a hand down his face. The tall, lanky man looked skinny enough a decent wind might inflict whiplash on him and, Savannah reflected, a Texas Panhandle wind would break him clean in half.

She quickened her pace toward Gray. He spoke to a uniform officer who pointed at her as she approached. Detective Wallace turned, his angular features grim, "Detective Prince?"

She gave a nod, "You're Detective Wallace?"

"Yeah. Sorry to call you out here. Wish the news was better." He waved her to follow him.

He led her to the newly restored stone-based gazebo with eight white Roman pillars supporting the roof. The picturesque location served as a favorite for couples exchanging wedding vows but that night a somber mood replaced the usual celebratory one.

At the gazebo's entrance she saw Amber Martin near the far wall, nearest the lake. Savannah's breath left her, taking with it any hope of the young woman's survival. Amber's nude body lay face up and splayed out, her wrists bound above her head with duct tape.

Wallace glanced behind him, "As I've been told, you're familiar with this."

She forced herself to nod. *This*, as he put it, was her worst nightmare come to life. Savannah pushed one foot in front of the other as her brain regressed to the past. She'd not seen *this* in years and it would haunt her until her dying day.

The scope of brutality came to light – literally – under the bridge post lamps funneling in their gloomy, sick glow. Crouching down, she swallowed back the gall rising in her throat as she stared at Amber Martin's chest. A momentary flash appeared, one of Amber dressed in a knitted green Christmas sweater. Savannah remembered the large white snowflakes all over it, two in particular aligned perfectly with the girl's breasts. Breasts that were no longer there. Two round, bloody voids stared back at her, the muscle and tissue sliced away with meticulous precision. Surgical precision.

Wallace retreated behind her, shined his Maglite along the body, "I talked to a Detective Mathis at your station. He said you worked the Ravine case back when."

She nodded again, not trusting herself to say anything without cursing Jeffrey Holland. She searched Amber's face, wondering what on earth Jeffrey said or did to sway and charm her. Of course, he'd done the same to Georgia years ago. Charmed her with his good looks and undivided attention. He'd been an emergency room physician then and she'd been a patient in the throes of a life threatening allergic reaction. She found his sweet personality soothing and attractive but not so much after he was finished with her at the cabin.

Detective Wallace continued, "Mathis also said the fingerprints on the bakery dishes matched Jeffrey Holland. You didn't realize he was working there?"

"He wasn't officially working at the shop," she corrected. "Evidently Amber adopted him, I guess she let him help her clean. She must have compensated Holland herself and this is how he repaid her." She looked back at him, "You got gloves?"

"Sure," he reached in his suit pocket, handed her a pair of latex gloves that she slipped on.

Savannah visually examined the ashen form in front of her. Blood at the juncture of the thighs drew her attention, "Signs of sexual assault?"

Wallace swallowed hard, "Who can tell? Have you seen it down there?"

Her jaw instinctively tightened. More visions from years past roared to the surface. Yes, she'd seen Holland's work below the Mason-Dixon Line, as she called it. It made her sick then and it would now. Jeffrey tortured the women with the scalpel, cutting, slicing, mutilating their privates until they were barely recognizable as human, much less female. Seeing Amber's blood-smeared thighs and butchered chest, she had no doubt who'd killed her and Jeffrey hadn't changed a bit.

Wallace's flashlight beam seemed to instinctively follow her vision when she scanned Amber's legs for bruises and cuts. A dark band circled each ankle. Nothing new there. "Restraint marks," she mumbled to no one in particular then angled for a glimpse between the thighs. What she saw turned her stomach. No, Jeffrey Holland had not changed. She held the back of her hand to her pursed lips, curbing the urge to puke. In the recesses of her mind the animal called fear exposed its teeth in a menacing low growl. It lowered its head, took a step forward. She closed her eyes to mentally stare it down until it stopped and sat on its haunches – but it did not retreat. The trick would work for a while but as always when Jeffrey was involved, that vicious creature would lurk close by, ready to consume her, to tear her life apart if she didn't keep it at bay.

She braced a knee on the stone floor, slid her hands beneath Amber's back and rolled the body partially on its side. "Shine your light on her back," she told Wallace.

A bright beam of light swept across the body, paused at the back. It revealed flawless, smooth skin with a thin tan line where a bikini top blocked the sun's rays. "No cane marks," she said, confused. "That's new."

"Cane marks?"

"Holland beat his victims with a rattan cane."

"That's pretty specific. You're sure it was rattan?"

Savannah tossed a glare over her shoulder, "He gave me my own beating when he abducted me so yes, I'm sure it was rattan."

Wallace shied from her expression, offered an apology, "I transferred from Knoxville last year so I didn't realize your history with this guy. Mathis did say Holland numbered his victims. There's no number on her that we found."

Amber had no number, she replied, because Mr. Holland wouldn't resume numbering his victims until scoring Number Ten first.

"I don't understand. If *he* killed her, why wouldn't she be number ten?"

She looked back at him, made solid eye contact, "Because *I'm* Number Ten. He will kill anyone who prevents or interferes with his goal of killing me. I guess Amber posed a threat somehow."

Shame darkened Wallace's face as he uttered yet another *I'm sorry.*

Finally, she thought. Maybe he understands now. "There's just one more thing," Savannah said, turning Amber's head to the side.

"What are you looking for?"

"A puncture wound from a large gauge needle." Another brief memory clawed its way to the surface. Finding Georgia secured to a makeshift table, a needle inserted in her jugular, the attached IV line draining the blood from her sister's body, drop by drop. "There it is," she pointed. "He drained the blood."

"Yeah, probably to lighten his load. Killers do that."

"No," she dropped the word like a boulder. Rising to her feet, she faced Wallace and stated with authority, "He drained it while she was alive, not after she died. That's what Jeffrey Holland does. Now he's out of prison so he's getting back to work." *And aiming straight for Number Ten.*

Wallace stepped closer, "I know this is personal to you because of the past."

"What he did to those women, to my sister, to me?   Damn straight it's personal."

"Now I understand things better.   Between you and Holland, I mean. It certainly explains this." Again he reached in his suit coat. This time he withdrew an evidence bag. Inside was a note. "This was with the body."

Savannah stripped off the gloves, took the note. She reached in her jacket for her glasses, slipped them on to read the bold block lettering, "Detective Savannah Prince. Amber's death is your fault. A picture is worth a thousand words and one dead college girl. Remember what I always say. Your actions have…"

"Have any idea what he's talking about?" Detective Wallace pushed.

She had a damn good idea, yes. The photo of Jeffrey she brought to the shop. She wanted it posted on the bulletin board for all to see, to be forewarned of the evil lurking around the business. *So shit like this didn't happen*, she gritted her teeth. *So no one died.* But she'd failed in her efforts. Amber lay dead because Savannah fixated on trying to keep her and everyone else safe but what else could she do? Let Jeffrey run amuck? Not friggin' likely. "Consequences," she answered. "That's the word he left off. My actions have consequences." She removed her glasses, pinched the bridge of her nose. What a nightmare this was. All because of "improper jury instructions".

She put away her glasses, explaining the scene at the shop earlier, when she left the photo on Georgia's desk. "That's the reason he referenced the word *picture*."

Wallace's expression left a lot to be desired. If he'd spoken with Mathis, her colleague backed up everything she'd said. Little things triggered Jeffrey, she wanted to tell Mr. Frowny standing in front of her. Little things like not answering a question quickly enough. A simple turn of phrase or look in her eye. And, of course, bringing a photo to the shop to warn the masses a killer walked among them.

Wallace's vision shifted to Amber then back to her. Savannah rubbed a sudden twinge in her neck. It subsided to a prickling sensation that refused to abate. In her mind, the animal's growl deepened when it exposed its set of razor sharp teeth. It rose to its feet again, stalking toward her. Something was wrong. She rubbed harder, consciously trying to chase the beast back. This time, though, it stepped forward once then twice, advancing on her. It was not going away.

Savannah glanced past Wallace to the crowd gathered at the crime scene tape. Her vision skimmed across the faces illuminated in a sick pink-orange glow from the bridge lights. Darkness shrouded most of the inquisitive bystanders in obscurity but she was certain. Certain that, "He's here." She pivoted from the crowd at one end of the blocked pathway to the other. Dozens of people congregated, most only faceless shadows behind several other shadows. All anonymous.

"Why would he hang around here after sending you that message?"

"That's *why* he's here. To see my reaction." *To catch me off-guard then strike...*

o   o   o

She cannot see me yet she senses my presence. Seeing her turn back and forth, searching, lets me see her in action, much like years before. Savannah's blue eyes pass straight across me but I stand in the shadows, behind many others who gather the way they do at a tragedy. People want to see the blood and gore, the pain and suffering – as long as it's not theirs. They are no different from me yet I'm labeled a sociopath. How ironic, I think while remembering an old saying – it takes one to know one.

I notice the male detective scans everyone but not with the laser-like intensity Savannah does. She is focused on ferreting out her nemesis. I can see her determination to find me, as though her life depends on it. She and I both know it does.

The male detective rounds up a group of uniform cops, points all but one in various directions. They disperse, on their way to fulfill their assignments. The single officer speaks with the male detective then with Savannah. He motions her past him, allows her to lead the way across the bridge. Her pace is casual, unhurried. She is headed back to her car – with a watchdog in tow for protection. I move from the congested crowd, ease my way within sight of her Dodge. Yes, indeed, Mr. Male Detective played the right card, at least for her. I, however, had hopes of bringing home a playmate. I console myself with yet another old adage – good things come to those who wait. Well, *I smile,* they do unless your name is Savannah Prince...

13

June 26

Due to Amber's loss, Savannah helped Georgia clean the shop after hours until they hired another employee. Between her day job, taking care of her family then spending extra hours at the shop after shift, Savannah came home each night spent of energy and patience. Things looked up on Thursday, however, when Georgia announced they hired a new employee for clean up duty.

Ennis stayed home with the girls Friday morning while the sisters attended Amber's funeral. Two hours later Savannah pulled into the driveway with an exhausted sigh. The service, while beautiful, depleted a soul in several ways. She spent the time pushing aside images of her mother's funeral and reaping little success for her efforts. When the soloist began "Amazing Grace", she lost the battle to find comfort in Georgia's embrace.

She sat in the car, noticing the street sounded quieter than normal. No kids playing outside, no lawn mowers growling through grass. She climbed out of the Charger and took a moment to appreciate the sounds of happy birds. A cardinal tweeted somewhere in their oak tree, a mockingbird sang a melodious tune reminding Savannah of a song she'd heard on the radio. The biggest commotion came from the blue jays in Katherine Collins's backyard. They squawked and screeched, probably to irritate Katherine's cat, Mr. Meowgi. People needed to appreciate life more, Savannah thought. To relish birds' mellow songs, the feel of a cool breeze blowing across their skin in summertime, the smell of magnolias and the sight of clear blue sky. To simply stop and enjoy.

The front door opened and Ennis leaned out with a confused, "You comin' in?"

She nodded, gathered her purse and headed inside. She'd be glad to shed the hot black dress and heels as well as the memories of the last two hours. A hell of a reason to dress up, she thought. To bury someone.

"You looked preoccupied," Ennis said, closing the door behind her.

She shrugged with a sad smile, "Just taking a minute to unwind, that's all." She hadn't known Amber that well but the funeral reinforced how dangerous Jeffrey was. He murdered an innocent young woman to make a point with Number Ten.

"Was it that bad?" Ennis's brow sank. "I mean, funerals are depressing anyway but…"

"It was that bad. Amber's father was inconsolable. He buried his only daughter…" The sentence trailed to silence.

Ennis wrapped his arms around her, held her. She sat her purse down, held him tight. Amber's father wept throughout the service, his sobs so mournful they made her heart ache. She'd stared at the mahogany casket, her mind drifting to grim thoughts. *What if we lose one of our girls? I couldn't bear that loss. We have to protect our kids. We just have to.*

Tears welled in her eyes. During her career she'd seen parents lose a child, seen their devastation. *Parents shouldn't bury their children and Lord, I pray we never have to.*

"Hey," Ennis pulled back, surprised by her weeping. He wiped her tears, kissed her, "You're home now. *And* I've got news."

She straightened her face, sniffed back her emotion, "What news?"

"Anna learned a new word. It's a biggie too. Spaghetti."

"She did not," she denied, hoping she was wrong. A word like spaghetti? At the tender age of two?

He shrugged, "It comes out *buh-sketti* but that's the word, I'm sure of it."

Most people probably assumed Anna pronounced the word *biscuit* but Savannah suspected Ennis was correct. She smiled, "Lily. She asks for spaghetti all the time. Anna must have picked up on it. Ennis, we have genius children."

He grinned with pride, "Of course we do and our oldest genius requires your help with her golf practice. Mama knows best, apparently. I mean, I tried helping with her swing."

Oh God, she thought. The mere notion of her husband tackling the finer points of a golf swing nearly inspired hysterics. "You didn't. What did you say, swing for the fences?"

His reaction said yes, that's exactly what he did. He harrumphed, "She said I didn't know how to golf."

"Do you?"

"No."

"Then she's right, isn't she?" Savannah pecked a kiss to his lips, "Cheer up, Daddy. You may suck at golf but you're a great father and husband."

"Mama! You're home!" Lily ran straight for her.

Savannah kneeled down and welcomed her daughter's embrace. Lily's arms stayed snug around her neck, "Are you staying home now?"

"Yes, sweetie, I'll be here all day."

Anna toddled in from the living room, reached for Savannah, "Mama, Mama."

Savannah lifted her into her arms, kissed her, "Hello, sweetheart. Were my girls good while I was gone?"

Two angelic nods answered her question. She hugged them both close, "I had no doubts."

Lily grabbed her hand, tugged her toward the back door, "Come help me. Daddy doesn't know golf."

Savannah slanted her husband an empathetic smile to soothe his ego. She stopped Lily long enough to say, "Let me change clothes before we get started, okay? Mama's tired of this dress."

Lily's shoulders slumped, "Okay. But hurry."

Savannah chuckled, saluted the girl, "Yes, ma'am."

o   o   o

In celebration of Anna's new word and Lily's constant yearning for the meal, Savannah prepared spaghetti. For the first time in days they ate a leisure family supper together. Savannah's vision roamed from Anna to Lily then Ennis as they ate. She loved her family but that morning gave her deeper affection for them. She treasured this snapshot in their lives, the simple act of sharing a meal. Yes, on occasion the girls were loud and fussy, sometimes they drove her one step short of insanity. Moments like this erased those frustrations, replacing them with poignancy, reflection. They would only be this age once. Overnight Lily would mature into a beautiful woman, ready for her own family. Anna would be applying for college before Savannah knew it.

Savannah listened to Ennis and Lily converse while she watched Anna feed herself. The girl progressed well despite expected accidents. That night her small hand brought the fork to her mouth without much incident. Savannah cheered her on, causing Anna to giggle at Mama's joy. Lily may have favored her mother but Anna bore a strong resemblance to Ennis. His features shined through in their youngest girl's laugh. Her warm brown eyes smiled along with her lips, encouraging anyone nearby to break into their own grin. And when she pouted, her face puckered with her downturned mouth until she resembled Daddy when his beloved Cowboys laid an egg and lost. She asked Anna, "What bedtime story do you want tonight?"

Anna reached to the table. Savannah took a wild guess and picked up the book Anna carried around for weeks. *Guess How Much I Love You.* "This book?"

Anna nodded, abandoning her fork, choosing instead to use her hands for eating.

Savannah spread her arms wide while quoting the book, "*I love you this much.*"

Anna stretched her spaghetti stained hands out, "Ah wuv you."

"She's nearly got it," Ennis said.

Anna put another bite in her mouth. Two strands dangled out. Her fingers still reached for the book, "Readed book."

The difference in her kids amused Savannah. Anna the quiet one. Lily the social butterfly. Anna loved puzzles, Lily loved golf. And their preference in books at two years old were polar opposites. Anna enjoyed the *Guess How Much* book and Lily fell in love with *Ten Tiny Toes* so much their friend Abel nicknamed Lily "Tiny Toes".

Savannah wiped Anna clean, teasing, "Do you want me or Daddy to read to you?"

Anna's face scrunched in a humorous frown, chanting, "*Ma-ma, Ma-ma.*"

"You know," Ennis interrupted, "a fella could lose an ego in this joint. Neither kid wants me."

Anna giggled. Lily played peacekeeper, "You can read to me,

Daddy."

He leaned to kiss her cheek, "Thank you, darlin'."

His sulking amused Savannah, "Neither kid wants you, huh? Wasn't it Lily who, just lately, asked if she could marry you?"

Ennis's shoulders straightened and Savannah swore his chest swelled along with his head when he replied, "Oh. I do remember that."

Lily volleyed her blue eyes between mother and father, "Can I, Daddy?"

From wounded to flattered in less than six seconds, Savannah noted as Ennis tried to let his girl down easy, "Sorry, sweetheart. 'Fraid I'm spoken for."

Savannah playfully nudged his foot beneath the table, "And I've got you locked in for life, buddy. Remember that too."

Lily took the rejection well, choosing to redirect the conversation to golf, "Mama helped me with my…" Her brow furrowed while she referred to that afternoon's putting lesson.

"Your grip," Mama finished. "You did well too. Just point your thumbs down on the club. Now show Daddy how you keep a balanced swing."

Lily climbed out of her chair, assumed the pose at the swing's completion. Her stance resembled the gold figure atop several of Savannah's trophies. Lily added, "I point my belly button at where I want the ball to go."

Savannah's grin broadened, "That's right. At the end of your swing, you should be pointing your belly button at the target."

Ennis looked at his wife, astounded. "Isn't that advanced for a kid her age?"

Savannah shrugged, "She asked and I kept it as simple as I could. I hope her interest stays with the game but if it doesn't, it doesn't."

Lily sucked a strand of spaghetti into her mouth with a slurp, "I wanna win toe-fees like Mama."

"It's *trophies*, sweetie, and if you keep practicing and you might win lots of 'em," Savannah encouraged. Then admonished good-naturedly, "Mind your manners during meals, kid. Eat that way in front of Aunt Georgia and she'll faint."

14

July 1

If anyone dared place a bet with Savannah, she'd have put money on the fact the underworld had wind chill warnings and possibly a few snowflakes drifting about. She marked her calendar on June 30 as the day Hell froze because Georgia asked for help at the bakery. Actual assistance in preparing and baking pies, not just waiting tables. Savannah felt honored. The sheer joy and anticipation of working with her sister in the kitchen motivated her to rise and shine early.

She was surprised to see Lily bright-eyed, fully dressed and insisting to go too. "It's going to be a long morning," Savannah forewarned. "Sure you don't want to hang with Daddy and Uncle Dane today?"

Lily shook her head, determined to pitch in because, "Aunt Georgia needs our help."

However by six fifteen, Lily curled up asleep in one of the only two booths in the shop. Savannah measured ingredients for the pie dough and kept the mixers running nonstop. She kept the assembly line moving for Georgia who rolled the dough, placed each crust in its pie dish. An hour into their work, Savannah realized why her sister found baking so cathartic. The flaky crusts, sweet fruit fillings and anticipation of creating a beautiful, delicious dessert lifted her spirits. Every slice might bring a smile to a customer, giving their day a moment of tasty respite or a temporary diversion from their troubles.

When Georgia completed the crusts, they began mixing the various fillings. She took the chess pie, and Savannah volunteered for the peach. The older sister cocked a brow, "Why doesn't that surprise me?"

Probably because peach pie was Savannah's favorite, that's why. But that went without saying within the Prince clan. Savannah's ability for sniffing out peach pie verged on magical, the way some people used a tree branch to divine for water.

"Mama," Lily shuffled into the kitchen, rubbing her eyes.

Savannah knew the child's ambition outweighed her four year-old internal clock. There was a reason kids slept past seven, she wanted to tell the youngster. Four o'clock wake-up calls were for adults and then it should only be for an emergency – unless they owned a bakery, of course. "Yes, honey?" She wiped her hands, ready to retrieve her cell phone and call Ennis to pick Lily up.

"I'm going to the bathroom."

Her hand moved from the phone on her belt. Her brow lifted. As sleepy as Lily appeared, Savannah figured home was where she wanted to be. She acknowledged the update and when Lily left, Georgia smirked, "You make her tell you when she's going to pee?"

"Thanks to Jeffrey, yes," she started toward the restroom. "She's only allowed to go alone if we're at home."

Georgia considered that, "Good idea. Listen, you stay here." She dusted the flour off her hands, washed them in the sink. "I think I'll go pee too. There's *my* official notice to Mama."

Savannah chuckled at the fuss. Georgia teased her lightly about her fanaticism but she understood. She listened close for the restroom door to squeak open, a sure sign Georgia was out of earshot. The peach pie filling invited her – no, *seduced* her into sneaking one bite. She eased a drawer open, grabbed a spoon. Her mouth watered to taste the juicy peaches, brown sugar and the bit of nutmeg and cinnamon mixed in. Aiming the spoon toward the bowl of heaven, she gave one last brief listen for her sister. Yes, she thought, the coast is clear...

"Savannah, don't do it," Georgia cautioned from the other room. "I need that for the pies."

Savannah stood, gape-mouthed. How the hell did Georgia *know*? The spoon never touched the filling and she hadn't made a peep or a noise. She wrinkled her nose, annoyed at the fact her sister possessed the ears of an owl and the E.S.P. of a mother.

Still gripping the spoon, Savannah harrumphed, greedily eyeing the peach pie filling. "I'll be good," she lied while dipping the spoon quietly into the bowl to claim the smallest peach, the least bit of sweetened juice she could. Then tossed the morsel into her mouth with perverse glee, amending, *I'll be good after this one bite...*

"Busted."

Savannah wheeled with the spoon still in hand and a euphoric smile adorning her features. Georgia leaned around the corner with a parental frown. Savannah's smile transformed to a sheepish one after swallowing the yummy bite, "Consider that my payment for helping today. Cheap enough, right?"

Her sister returned the grin, "Can you possibly wait until they're *baked* before attacking them?"

Savannah crossed her heart, "I'll try my best."

Georgia resumed her trek to the restroom while Savannah vowed to keep herself from diving head first into the tasty pie – at least until it was ready to eat. To expedite that goal, she poured the mixture into the two waiting crusts, sat the bowl aside. All that was needed was latticework on top. That was Georgia's bailiwick. She could make latticework worthy of a Southern Living magazine cover.

"Mama!"

Lily's scream echoed through the business. Savannah dropped the spoon, stripped off the apron and raced from the kitchen to the restroom. She rounded the corner and slammed on the brakes. She backpedaled to avoid a collision but ended up skidding directly into Jeffrey Holland's firm, muscular chest.

She stepped back, her brain refusing to accept what her eyes saw. He not only stood inside the securely locked business (or what she thought was securely locked) but the killer pulled her daughter against his waist, one hand firmly across her chest. Upon seeing her mother, Lily tugged toward her but Jeffrey warned, "What did I say about disobeying me, Lily? There are…"

Consequences. Savannah gnashed her teeth as her four year-old tried to repeat the new word he'd apparently taught her. Savannah yanked her .38 from its holster at the same instant he withdrew something from behind his back: a syringe partially filled with a milky white substance.

She saw the light glint off the bare needle as he placed it precariously close to her daughter's neck. He preached, "Mama's forgotten that word so I'll remind her. There are consequences, Savannah, and you will decide who suffers them. This sedative is meant for you, not a small child. This will incapacitate you but it will kill Lily. You're responsible for one tragedy, don't make the same mistake twice."

She reinforced her grip on her weapon, aimed straight at his nose, "Let her go."

"No. I have her, she's mine now."

His defiant statement enraged her. Her finger tightened on the trigger.

Jeffrey shook his head, pressed the needle against Lily's skin. The child squirmed, "Mama, help…"

Without breaking eye contact with Savannah, Jeffrey instructed, "Lily, tell your mother to drop the gun. That's the first step in helping you."

"Let my girl go," Savannah ordered.

"Tell her, Lily. Tell her now."

Lily's tears began in earnest, "Mama, please."

Bitter panic and the bite of peach pie filling threatened to climb out of her throat. She had dead aim on the bastard, ready to blast him back to Hell when Lily pleaded with her once again, struggling to say *drop the gun* while in the killer's grasp. Lily's safety – iffy as it was – depended on obeying Jeffrey. No, she thought. Obeying *her little one's* heartfelt request, "Okay, baby. I'm putting the gun down." She lowered the .38, slowly crouching until setting the gun on the floor.

"He hurt Aunt Georgia," Lily wept.

Savannah's hand did not retreat from the .38. Her fingers curled back around the handle, "What did you do to her, Jeffrey?"

He tsk-tsked, "Mama's a slow learner, Lily. Should *you* have to pay for that? Let's ask her – or she could simply *leave the gun alone.*"

Savannah glanced up at him, saying only, "Georgia."

"Aunt Georgia is sleeping. She'll be fine." He pressed the needle enough to rouse Lily's tears once more, "Lily, on the other hand..."

"You hurt her and I will kill you. Let. Her. Go."

"Remember when boys traded baseball cards?"

"*My daughter. Now.*" She kept a close eye on the syringe, shifting her vision from it to Jeffrey then back again.

"Once again Mama thinks she's in control," he taunted. "She thinks she makes the rules even though I could plunge this needle into you and kill you, Lily. You don't want that, do you?"

"No," she cried.

He motioned Savannah to her feet, "And I'm reasonably sure Mama doesn't either. Do you?"

Savannah rose to her feet, "Of course not."

"Then answer my question. Remember when boys traded baseball cards?"

"I remember."

"Each participant had something the other wanted. I believe I have something you want and you have something I want. Let's trade."

The tilt of his chin. The arrogance of his tone. The gleam in his eye. She recalled every aspect of the demon standing across from her, holding her daughter hostage. The shrewd killer who didn't just kill but bargained with his victims knowing he'd win anyway. The needle lingered too close to Lily's skin to chance grabbing her gun. "And you want…" *Me.*

He smiled, each row of teeth gleaming white, "Oh, I think you know." He patted Lily's shoulder to emphasize his point. "Let's call Daddy to pick up Lily and you and I will catch up on old times."

She glanced toward the restroom, "Did you kill Georgia? Tell me the truth."

"I told you. She's sleeping. I don't want her. I want you. But you procrastinate any longer and I'll either slice her throat or drag her along to the party."

She started toward the restroom but Jeffrey stopped her. His head tilted as if daring her to take another step. "I'll allow you to check on her after you set your phone next to your gun."

Savannah slid the phone from her belt, placed it on the floor, "My gun and my phone. Let Lily go."

"No." He nodded to the restroom, "Check on your sister."

She shoved the door open so hard it slammed against the stop. Trying to push back the awful memories from long ago, she called Georgia's name. Two jeans-clad legs protruded from beneath the last stall. Savannah rushed to her side, pressed her fingers to Georgia's neck for a pulse. To her relief a solid heartbeat met her touch. Tears slid down her cheeks and she thanked God Georgia was alive.

"Do we have a deal, Savannah?" Jeffrey asked from behind her.

She turned to see his casual stance with her little girl. Fear registered in Lily's blue eyes, the needle still poised at her neck.

"Show Mama the phone," he told Lily.

The girl extended the cell phone to her mother. Jeffrey continued, "One phone call and your baby goes home unharmed and your sister stays alive. That's my best offer. Hesitate too long and we'll make this a family affair." He patted Lily's shoulder, his voice softening, "She favors you nearly to a tee." He petted her hair, "Same features, this thick dark hair–"

"Stop touching her," Savannah warned.

His fingers eased down her daughter's arm, stroking it, "Oh yes. I can feel the strength there. More than physical strength too. She'll be strong like you."

"*Stop touching her.*" She left no question what would happen if he disregarded her words again.

"You're going to be strong like Mama, aren't you, Lily?" he asked. "Did you know your mother is the strongest woman I've ever met? But

I don't think she's strong enough to lose you. I believe that would destroy her." He glanced at Savannah, "So what'll it be, Mama? Will Lily go home with Daddy or will she be joining us?"

Tears streamed down her little girl's cheeks. Savannah reached for her but Jeffrey tugged her away. She tried to calm Lily down, "It's okay, baby. Don't cry. Everything will be okay. Daddy will be here soon and you go home with him. Until he gets here, stay with Aunt Georgia." She held her hand out, met Jeffrey's vision, "I'll call him."

Her nemesis narrowed his eyes, "I'll be listening. One word about me and..." he cut his eyes downward to Lily. "It will end in seconds. Lily, give the phone to your mother."

When their fingers brushed, Savannah gently squeezed her baby's hand, gave her a smile. She dialed Ennis who answered on the second ring. She kept her voice calm, even, "Can you pick Lily up right now? She'll have more fun with you and Dane today, I think."

"Sure," he said then paused. "You okay? You sound funny."

"I'm fine. You're coming now, right?"

"Be there in a few. Love you, babe."

A swell of emotion caught in her throat. She swallowed it back, tried to steady her voice, "I love you too." She clicked off, held the cell phone out in surrender.

Jeffrey nodded to the floor. She sat the phone down.

He kneeled to face Lily, "Be a good girl and stay here until Daddy arrives. Otherwise your mother will worry herself to death. You don't want that."

Lily's tear-filled vision lifted until meeting her mother's gaze. The girl's arms extended in a silent plea to embrace her, "Mama."

Savannah opened her arms, "Let me hold my baby, Jeffrey. Please."

He mulled over her request. "One wrong move and this reunion is over. And *Mama*, you know the consequences." He released Lily who charged into Savannah's waiting arms, squeezing her tight. Savannah couldn't help but smile. The child exhibited the strength Jeffrey mentioned earlier. Her girl was damn tough and Savannah allowed herself a fanciful notion that Lily took after her in that respect as well. Life could whip a person if they let it. It kicked the legs from under them at times but Lily showed amazing courage in those brief minutes. She would be a force to be reckoned with later in life. A chip off the old block, as Charlene always said.

Savannah kissed her hair, letting her lips linger in the soft tresses as she breathed, committing the smell to memory. She pressed a kiss Lily's warm, soft cheek, thinking how lovely her baby was and what a beautiful woman she would become.

"Mama, I'm scared," Lily's voice trembled.

Savannah stroked the silky hair, shushing her, "It'll be okay. You'll go home with Daddy–"

"Come with me," she hugged Savannah even tighter.

Tears gathered at the heartfelt plea. She never imagined a child might be so devoted to her. For years she refused to have children for fear she'd screw up their raising and warp their young minds. Lily proved she'd been wrong all along. She'd done something right in her life besides marrying Ennis Rutherford. She gave birth to two sweet angels that loved her as much as she loved them. The tears slipped down her cheeks, "I wish I could, baby."

Jeffrey curled a hand around Savannah's arm. "Get up."

She pressed one last kiss to her daughter's cheek, "Be good, little one. Mind Daddy while I'm gone. I love you, Lily."

Jeffrey wrenched her from the embrace, his fingers digging into the flesh until her arm throbbed, his purposeful stride towing her away from her weeping daughter. Lily followed her mother, still begging her to stay.

Jeffrey rounded on the child with a low, threatening tone, "Your mother said stay. If you disobey her, I'll hurt her very badly and it will be your fault."

"Jeffrey, please, she's a *child*," Savannah admonished.

He jerked her to face him hard enough she winced. Eye to eye he stated, "She's old enough to understand consequences."

Lily sobbed uncontrollably. Savannah tried to settle her down, "Don't cry, sweetheart. It's okay. *Nothing* he does is your fault, no matter what he says." Her heart broke for her little girl. She'd be alone at least half an hour, wondering why this man forced her mother from the bakery, wondering why Aunt Georgia wouldn't wake up, and wondering if she'd see her mother again. Maybe, just maybe, she'd luck out again and escape Jeffrey Holland. She'd survived him twice. Surely she was due a third. "Go back to Aunt Georgia, baby. Wait for Daddy."

Savannah's softer tone quelled the river of tears. Lily sniffed them back, wiped her eyes with the backs of her hands, "Yes, Mama." Then she turned and slowly walked away, around the corner toward the restroom. Savannah wanted to bring her into a comforting embrace, tell her everything would be okay and *mean* it.

A hand went to her shoulder. Her eyes closed, squeezing tears from them.

"Hands behind you," was Jeffrey's command.

Savannah looked toward the restroom, hearing her daughter's weeping. The sound consumed her. She always held Lily when she wept, she thought. This time she shed tears without Mama consoling her.

"Savannah," Jeffrey's lips brushed her ear. "Put your hands behind your back. You recall how I repay defiance."

She recoiled at the touch of his warm lips, his hot breath on her skin. His grasp tightened, a sign she'd exhausted his patience. A sudden paralyzing pain traveled up her neck and down her shoulder and arm. Jeffrey bore down on the nerve until she sank to the floor with a sick whimper.

He unleashed his anger, shoving her flat against the floor. She sprawled, nearly slamming her chin on the tile. Jeffrey stabbed his knee across the back of her neck, pressing her cheek and jaw against the floor.

A thin plastic cable tie encircled her wrists. He cinched it tight until she grimaced from the pressure.

She squirmed beneath the pain of his knee which pressed harder until bone ground on bone.

"I thought we had a deal," Jeffrey's anger surfaced. "You are reneging so it looks like Lily comes with us."

Her fight renewed with his threat, "No, Jeffrey, please leave her alone. Don't hurt her."

"Then lie still. One twitch and I'll bring her along."

She barely felt the needle prick in her arm. Instinct implored her to fight, to not surrender so easily. Common sense prevailed, however, when images appeared of Jeffrey torturing mother and daughter equally, each witnessing every swipe of the scalpel inflicted upon the other.

A dizzying rush swept over her, clouding her vision and mind. The drug slowed her heart, robbed her muscles of strength. A warm, thick, liquid blackness covered her. She floated in the black sea, the warmth calming her, stealing her consciousness.

Jeffrey's voice faded in the distance, "Relax and go to sleep. I'll take care of the rest."

15

July 1

My obsession sleeps peacefully upon Tonya's queen size bed. I rarely see Savannah so peaceful, her body slack and boneless. It is odd yet comforting to me.

I'm afraid my temper has tarnished her alter. Tonya's blood saturated the mattress when I cut away her breasts. It bloomed to the surface, oozing over the curve of her ribs to the bed where it pooled beside her. Her persistent jealousy stoked my anger. I'd waited years for my detective and to have her insulted (by a stranger, no less) sent me into a rage. The instant the knife sank into Tonya's carotid artery, brilliant crimson arcs jetted forth, repainting the ceiling, streaking the drapes and a wall or two. Savannah will not meet this fate. I have specific plans for her and they do not include an expedited demise.

My fingers glide over Savannah's velvet soft stomach. Her nude form rests free, without restraint and I marvel at her athletic physique. Five years and two children later, the woman maintained her trim waist, her toned muscles.

I stroke the warmth of her throat, let my fingers linger at the hollow then sweep them up to the languid pulse tapping beneath her ear. My arousal lengthens in my jeans at the memory of this woman's screams. I want time to explore my beautiful prize before she regains consciousness. It will be the only quiet time we share together.

I touch her breast, trace the scar from her cancer surgery. She stirs ever-so-slightly. My hand cups the weighty flesh, caressing the soft skin, then my vision drifts to my previous work. Below her right collarbone is the faint shadow of the number 10. Its five years of healing rendered it basically invisible to me. I'm disappointed that my presence in her life faded to this degree. This time I will ensure the number is prominent and timeless, even if I must sever muscle to accomplish my goal.

Easing my hand down her arm, I feel her strength despite her deep slumber. The muscles beneath my hand wait to tense, to show their power. Her thighs and calves have retained their muscular form, a telltale sign that she still regularly jogs to keep in shape.

She will be waking soon. I scoop her into my arms, her cheek cradled against my chest as I descend the stairs. I have spent long, precious hours preparing for Savannah's arrival. Everything is now perfect. If I've done things correctly, she won't be the only one surprised when consciousness drifts back in…

16

July 1

Georgia touched the soreness on her throat, wincing at the memory of Jeffrey's hand cutting off her air. She battled him as her brother Seth taught her. Jammed her heel into Jeffrey's instep, tried to slam her fist into his face. Even tried clawing at his eyes but he'd proven much stronger. Her only thought as the curtain of black descended over her brain was to protect Lily and Savannah. Lily, busy in the stall two doors down, heard the scuffle and hurried out to see the problem. Georgia remembered the wide-eyed fear on the girl's face. She struggled to speak, to warn Lily to run but Jeffrey pressed harder on her larynx. She shooed Lily toward the door, praying the child broke free of her paralysis to flee and find safety with Savannah.

But Lily stood rooted to the spot. The lights in the room dimmed to black and Georgia barely registered Jeffrey Holland catching her in his arms as Lily screamed for her mother.

"Whatcha thinkin' about?" Lily leaned her elbows onto the dining table.

Georgia blinked out of the memory, tried for a smile, "Oh, a lot of things, sweetheart." She glanced over at Lily's empty bowl. Georgia made the girl her favorite soup – tomato complete with goldfish crackers "because Mama always fixes it that way". It amazed Georgia how her little sister fretted for years over being a good mother. When she finally had Lily, she doted on her daughter, raising her with a gentleness that frankly surprised Georgia. Rarely did Savannah swat Lily and the strength she used made Georgia wonder why she even bothered. Savannah vowed that if she had children, she'd discipline them but never resort to beating them like their father had his kids. She held true to that vow.

Lily tapped the half-full bowl in front of Georgia, "Didn't you like the goldfish?"

She stared down at the six orange fish grinning up at her. She agreed to join Lily for lunch only because the child refused to eat without her, however Georgia's appetite went MIA, "Honey, I loved the goldfish. I'm just not very hungry right now." She rose from her seat, gathered her bowl and reached for Lily's.

The girl claimed her own bowl, started toward the kitchen, "Mama likes it when I pick up my bowl."

Georgia complimented her little niece, and thanked her for the help. She watched the girl disappear around the corner and took time to reflect how Savannah, for all her rough edges, worried for nothing because she raised a sweet, thoughtful daughter.

Georgia sat her bowl in the sink and waited for the girl to set hers on the cabinet. This day was awful, the oldest sister lamented in silence. Jeffrey Holland had Savannah again and this time Georgia doubted she'd survive.

Ennis and his colleague John Mathis sat in her living room, trying to figure out Holland's location. When they weren't talking to each other, they kept the cell phones busy calling their boss Josh Hunter, area hospitals, and anyone they thought might help find Savannah.

Georgia thought about checking on Anna who slept in the downstairs bedroom. The last few times she looked in, the child snoozed soundly. At least someone avoided the stress of the day, she thought grimly.

"Where's Mama?" Lily looked up at her with hopeful azure eyes. "Where'd that man take her?"

"I wish I knew."

"Is she going to be okay? He wasn't nice to her."

Nice wasn't the beginning of it, Georgia wanted to say. Jeffrey came straight from the bowels of Hell. "I know he wasn't nice, honey, and I truly hope she'll be okay." *But I know the truth. Only a miracle, not hope, can save my sister now.* She attempted to change the subject, "You haven't worked on your Lego house in a while. Want to add a room to it today?"

For an instant, Georgia swore she stared at her sister at four years old. Lily frowned, her mouth screwed to the side. The same identical expression still emerged with Savannah on occasion, the one flat-out accusing a person of diverting the conversation. Lily's, though, evolved faster than Savannah's. The girl then shrugged with a tiny smile as she grabbed her aunt's hand, "Okay. You can help me."

Georgia bent to one knee, kissed her cheek, "I sure will, sweetie. Just give me a few minutes and I'll be there. I need to make a phone call right quick."

Lily meandered to the dining room again. Georgia waited until she was safely out of hearing range before dialing Duke Shelton. Years ago, she met Duke through a friend. Being in her early twenties and a new author, she wanted to spice up her writing so she asked to meet the professional dominant for research purposes. Over the course of months, they became close friends to the point he bestowed a special pet name on her – Beauty – and asked her to move in with him. She declined the offer because she was dating a marine whom she later married but she and Duke remained friends.

The man answering the phone, upon hearing the caller's name, patched her through to her long-time friend – an insanely wealthy friend who possessed not just money but the influence and abilities to get things done. Duke also employed several special forces veterans for his own private security – veterans no one wanted to cross, not even Jeffrey Holland whether he knew it or not.

After exchanging pleasantries, Georgia got down to business and told Duke what happened at the bakery.

"Of course I will help," he replied. "I will dispatch my men and see if they can dredge up some information. I am flattered and grateful you called. Your sister means the world to me, as do you, my dear. Call me immediately if you hear anything."

Another hour passed. Georgia worked with Lily on the Lego house then checked back with Duke. The news was disappointing. No leads, no trace of Savannah or Holland anywhere, he said.

A tugging on Georgia's blouse brought her attention to Lily who asked, "Aunt Georgia, I wanna to make my house look like April Ham Lincun's."

The goof inspired a smile. Savannah told her about Lily's grammar mistakes over the last few years. Mama corrected plenty of mispronunciations and written gaffes. The most notable was amending the name Satan to Santa. Savannah nearly fainted upon seeing Lily's letter to the jolly elf addressed to the ruler of the netherworld instead. Today Aunt Georgia assumed the responsibility of rectifying her niece's flubs. "You mean Abraham Lincoln, sweetheart."

Lily listened as Georgia repeated the name. She gave it a shot and fell just short. Georgia tried again and Lily formed the words with careful precision, "A-bra-ham Lincoln."

"That's right but we don't have enough Legos to build the White House, so why don't we finish *your* house first?"

The doorbell rang with the Westminster Chime. Georgia spent a chunk of change for the brass chambered chimes because she'd loved the tune since childhood. It inspired a comforting nostalgia reminding her of the grandfather clock in the entry back home in Augusta.

Today the beautiful tune put her on edge. She expected no one at her door that day. No deliveries, no friends, nothing. Unless... A spark of crazy optimism registered.   Maybe, just maybe Savannah outwitted Jeffrey and got away.   Then reality snuffed the flickering flame of hope, leaving behind the wisp of truth.   This time Jeffrey ensured Savannah would not escape.   In five years, he studied his prior mistakes and learned from them.

The doorbell chimed again.   Lily rushed past Georgia toward the door, "Mama's home!"

Georgia caught the girl, drew her into a hug to stop her, "I don't think it's Mama, sweetheart." *In fact, I'd bet my own life on that.*

Dane eased in front of his wife and niece, shielding them as Ennis and Mathis drew their .38s from their holsters.   The two exchanged a discreet nod then Ennis opened the door.

A young scruffy-faced fellow in old jeans and dirty t-shirt jumped back at the sight of the two guns, "T-t-take it easy, man.   I'm not s-s-selling anything.   I'm j-j-just delivering."

Ennis's expression explained in great detail how he disliked the interruption, "Delivering what? We're not expecting anything."

Especially from the likes of you, Georgia heard unspoken accusation.

The man raised one shaking hand in surrender, eased the other toward Ennis, "I was told to d-d-deliver this to Georgia or Ennis R-R-Rutherford."

Georgia saw a small white envelope poking out between his index and middle fingers.

Ennis did not take the note.   Georgia watched his jaw clench.   He wanted to shoot someone. Anyone. Judging by his expression the disheveled vagabond facing him might do just fine.

Mathis plucked it from the guy's hand, "Who sent you?"

"I-I don't know him," he stuttered back. Georgia figured right about now the guy understood why *he* delivered the note instead of the sender doing it himself. The longer he spoke, the harder the stutter set in, "H-h-he g-g-gave me a h-h-hundred bucks, t-t-two addresses and this envelope."

Mathis holstered his gun to study the sealed envelope, "What's the other address?"

The young man's stare never wavered from Ennis's revolver as he reached in his pocket. He took a split-second to refer to the address then rattled it off just as quick, "4886 T-T-Tilly M-M-Mill Road. He t-t-told me to c-c-come here f-f-first."

"That's our house," Lily said. "Tilly rhymes with Lily." Georgia hugged her close, recalling when the girl struggled to remember their street name. Savannah devised the rhyming trick for learning purposes and before long Lily also memorized the house number. Any time someone needed their address, Lily piped up with *4886 Tilly Mill. Tilly rhymes with Lily.*

Mathis asked for a description of who recruited him. The guy took a long, deep breath, closed his eyes. To calm down, Georgia assumed. Facing a loaded gun held by an enraged man tended to unnerve even the best of people.

"Tall, m-m-muscular guy. White t-t-shirt and faded jeans. Had dark short hair, hadn't sh-shaved in a couple of d-days. K-k-kinda looked like that doctor on a show I've seen where they name everyone McSomething-Or-Other. "

A chill raked down Georgia's back. McSomething-Or-Other. It was, without a doubt, Jeffrey.

Ennis continued the interrogation, "Did he have a woman with him?"

"N-no, he was alone."

"Where'd you meet this guy?" Mathis asked.

"He came to the h-homeless shelter on P-Ponce Northeast."

Ponce De Leon Northeast, Georgia thought. That's where I send the leftover pies.

"Did you see what he drove? A car, truck?"

He shook his head, shrugged. "I'm sorry."

Mathis closed the door, "Yeah, thanks for nothing."

Ennis grabbed the envelope, ripped into it. He withdrew a single piece of paper with a series of numbers and the words, "Enjoy the view. I know I will."

Mathis glanced at the page, "Looks like an I.P. address."

"That's what it is," Ennis looked to Georgia who nodded to her computer.

She waved Dane over, "Would you take Lily upstairs and read to her? I bought her a new book yesterday." She hugged the girl, "Go with Uncle Dane, sweetie. He's going to read that new book to you."

"Who was that man?" Lily wanted to know. "Where's Mama? I

want Mama."

Dane swept her into his arms, "C'mon, squirt. Let's check out your new book."

Georgia reached for the note, "I'm calling Duke. His men can trace this."

Mathis agreed, "You got my vote. You okay with it, Ennis?"

Georgia really didn't care if he was or not. Duke had resources the police didn't. Her hand remained extended, waiting.

Ennis handed it to her with a cautionary frown. No, he wasn't a huge fan of Duke's but the truth was they needed him.

Ennis's pursed lips revealed his bitterness of the dominant. An unreasonable resentment developed after Lily's birth when he accused Savannah of sleeping with Duke. Georgia remembered the time well. Their captain assigned Savannah to an undercover assignment involving the alternative lifestyle. She and Duke spent weeks together with him instructing her on the finer points of submission, lessons required for credibility's sake. Duke composed a carefully written contract stating kissing was allowed but sexual contact remained off-limits – a term Savannah, Ennis and Duke all agreed on. Ennis, however, let his insecurities run rampant upon seeing the two in a convincing lip-lock. The result was explosive and nearly destroyed their marriage. Ennis drove to Georgia and Dane's house stewed to his ears. Besides *Hi, I have to pee*, his first words were *I left Savannah*. When Georgia finally found her voice to ask why, his reply emerged in a soup of nonsensical mush, "Forfor... Forforkinate... For fornicanating... Ah hell," he slurred, "for screwing Duke Shelton."

Georgia had tried to penetrate the fog of booze, "And you saw them…" she used his colorful phrasing against him, "*screwing?*"

"Theytonguekissed. That's one step from fornicat…" He cursed under his breath then amended, "Screwing."

For God's sake, she had thought. "Ennis, she's playing a part. As I recall you read the contract and agreed to it. Savannah said it allowed kissing but specifically said no sexual contact. She said *you read and agreed to it*," she reminded. "I do not believe for a second they slept together."

"Well, you're her sister so I'd expect nothing less. Y'know, she's not as innocent as you think. S'all I gotta say."

Despite her best efforts, Georgia regarded her brother-in-law with a slightly jaundiced eye ever since. Forgiveness was easy to preach but difficult to accomplish sometimes.

Pushing the ugly memory aside, she glanced at her computer. While it booted up, she called Duke and quickly relayed the information to her friend.

Ennis sat at her writing desk, took the note and typed the I.P. address into the computer. His finger hovered over the Enter key. Dread sickened Georgia, dread of what awaited them once they made the connection.

After a deep breath, Ennis pressed the button. The screen blanked white then after what seemed an eternity, a picture appeared. Georgia's stomach revolted at the sight of her naked, unconscious sister. Heavy duty cable ties secured her wrists, elbows and ankles to a sturdy wooden dining chair. Savannah's head bowed to her chest as if praying, her loose tresses draping over her shoulders.

Georgia watched Mathis squirm, look away for modesty's sake since Jeffrey posed his victim legs apart and facing the camera. Mathis concentrated on a picture sitting on the desk. A picture of the Prince siblings as children. Savannah was eleven. "She, uh," Mathis stammered, "she look hurt to you?"

Georgia shook her head, "Not yet but I'm betting Jeffrey's waiting to ensure we're watching first." That's the way Holland worked. He loved sharing the pain.

She surveyed Savannah's surroundings. Jeffrey held her captive in a large house, a mansion, she guessed. Georgia's first thought was Buckhead but Atlanta and the outlying suburbs had dozens of such neighborhoods. A couple of hours lapsed since he abducted Savannah so he could have holed up anywhere within one hundred miles of the city.

The décor looked upscale and expensive, the room spacious with white carpet, beige walls and large floor to ceiling windows with the curtains drawn. Across the room she saw vibrant Impressionist paintings on the wall, each one in thick gold ornate frames.

Georgia's cell phone rang. She hurried to answer it, hoping it was Duke with promising news. It *was* Duke but his news fell short of favorable, "Tracing the I.P. is impossible. He has obviously studied how to bounce the signal or was tutored well on it. My men are trying to find the location via the background and the house. If you think you recognize anything regarding the location, call me. And Beauty, we will use every resource at hand to find Savannah."

Georgia thanked him, clicked off the call. Sounds from the computer speakers caught her attention. Savannah stirred awake. She instinctively pulled at her hands and arms to no avail. Confusion knitted her brow as she ascended from what Georgia assumed was a drug induced sleep. Her sister blinked several times, clearing her vision. Then recognition and panic replaced the confusion. She saw him – Jeffrey lurked somewhere behind the camera.

"Good morning, ladies and gentlemen," his gregarious voice carried into the living room. He sounded akin to a ringmaster welcoming an audience. Except, Georgia narrowed her eyes, his spiel should've been, "*In the center ring we have the victim of a seriously disturbed psychopath...*"

Jeffrey continued, "As you see, the star of our show has finally arrived. Savannah, I've invited your family along for our journey so you won't feel lonely." He stepped forward, entering camera range. He wore his customary jeans and white t-shirt. His killing attire.

He moved behind Savannah. Georgia tensed. She remembered the last time he stood behind her sister. He nearly choked her to death.

This time Jeffrey tenderly swept her hair behind her shoulders then bent down until his chin rested on her left shoulder. He smiled at the camera, "Aren't we a handsome couple? Made for each other."

Mathis, still obviously feeling awkward, cut his vision to the screen.

Georgia gasped when the glint of a scalpel entered the camera's range. Jeffrey swung it to Savannah's vision that widened at the sight. Mathis flinched, "Tell me he's not gonna cut her right now, in front of us."

Jeffrey's smile broadened, "I suggest if her little girls are anywhere nearby, you remove them now. No need to traumatize the innocent." He waited a few moments, toying the scalpel toward Savannah's breast, coming within a whisper of the nipple.

Savannah drew back against the chair, trying to gain space between her breast and the sharp blade. He removed the blade, "Don't worry, I'm saving the best for last. Right now maintenance is required." He repositioned the scalpel in his right hand. Georgia saw him place it against the "1" he'd carved below the collarbone five years earlier.

"Somehow this number faded over the last few years. I want the world to know you're mine," he said sweetly in Savannah's ear. "I've been in your dreams at night, your thoughts in the day, and I'm the man who is always there when you and Ennis make love. He sees this every time he draws your blouse down your arms." Jeffrey lightly skimmed his fingers down her left arm to her hand. "He has seen that another man owns you. I know you better than he does. I know how much pain you can endure. I've seen that fire in you, the one that refuses to die. You refused to beg last time. You denied me what I desired the most and this time I *will* get it."

Georgia, engrossed in his monologue, cringed when her sister screamed. A hand instinctively went to her stomach long before the nausea hit. Her body teetered on the precipice of purging the tomato soup right there in her living room. She turned away upon seeing Jeffrey slowly dragging the blade while pressing it into Savannah's flesh, reopening the wound from years ago.

Mathis, under his breath, muttered the mother of all curses. Ennis sat, silent and stunned. Georgia's brain shifted into a weird kind of neutral, telling herself this wasn't real. It couldn't be real. It couldn't be happening *again* to her baby sister. She dared a glance at the screen. Blood trailed over Savannah's breast, oozing in a thick crimson stream down her belly to the juncture of her thighs. Soft weeping drifted from the speakers, and Georgia covered her ears to block it but still heard Jeffrey when he looked at the camera saying, "See? She's a strong one. There's not a plea in this woman. Yet."

Dane appeared at the top of the stairs, leaned over the railing, "What was that? It sounded like a scream."

Temporarily swallowing the nausea, Georgia waved him back, "Keep Lily busy. *Please.*"

He disappeared, returned to the bedroom, closed the door.

Jeffrey was on his feet now, facing Savannah, the bloody scalpel poised over the "0". Savannah wrenched in the seat, hoping to avoid the inevitable. She made repeated verbal attempts to stop him, but fell short of begging like he wanted.

Georgia saw the pressure on the blade increase. Savannah threw her head back with an agonizing shriek, forcing Georgia to slam her hands over her ears but the cry penetrated to her soul. Georgia squeezed her eyes shut, wishing the sound to stop, for Jeffrey to stop, for the world to stop until she regained her composure. Because as her sister's scream ebbed, Georgia's sanity stretched to a fast unraveling thread.

Uttering the Lord's name in a vicious way, Mathis reached forward, turned the volume down, "That's tearing me up. I'm calling the boss, see if he knows anyone that can help find her."

Ennis's hand locked around his colleague's wrist, "I'm not having this broadcast all over the station, Mathis. She doesn't deserve it."

"What're we supposed to do, just let him kill her?" Mathis wiped a hand down his face, "I'll never get that scream outta my head."

"Georgia's called Shelton already."

Ennis turned his bitterness loose with the comment, as though she committed a cardinal sin by contacting Duke. Grow up, Ennis, she grumped. *As Yoda might say,* "a shit I don't give" *because Duke Shelton cares about Savannah. He will put more effort into finding her than anyone else I can think of.*

"Let me call the boss," John pleaded. "He can put one or two forensics techs to work tracing it – or something."

She crossed her arms, turned to her brother-in-law, prodding, "Ennis?"

He looked as sick as she felt. Finally he gave a nod of approval, "Call him."

Mathis dialed their captain again, "Boss, you ain't gonna believe the jam Prince is in now..."

On the screen, Jeffrey's index finger traced the wounds. The number ten was deep as evidenced not just by the volume and intensity of her scream but by the amount of viscous blood oozing from each wound. The number was no more a shadow of the past.

Savannah whimpered, worming in the chair no doubt trying to ease the aching. Her breaths sounded small, shallow. Sweat surfaced along her body. Georgia yearned to help her sister. She searched the background again. Frustration set in when nothing became evident. Light filtered in through drapes covering floor to ceiling windows to Savannah's left. The front door also sat to her left, perhaps fifteen or twenty feet behind her. Every avenue for a clue seemed shut down. In a city of millions of people, searching for her surpassed a needle in a haystack. Jeffrey Holland made sure it was impossible.

Movement drew her attention back to Jeffrey who dipped his finger in the blood again then wrote one word above Savannah's breasts. *Mine.*

17

July 1

Six hours ago Georgia hugged Savannah hello and thanked her and Lily for helping at the bakery. Before she tired out for her nap, Lily regaled them with a new joke. "Why did the banana go to the doctor?" After both Mama and Aunt Georgia asked why, she burst out with, "Because he wasn't peeling well!"

Bouncing from one subject to another, the youngster quickly displayed her new golf pose, the one Mama taught her just yesterday. What struck Georgia most: Savannah's proud smile. Her love for the game carried over to her daughter who craved Mama's guidance and approval which Savannah freely gave.

Savannah looked especially beautiful that morning, Georgia reflected, and her youthful charm emerged in her carefree laugh and teasing banter, not to mention her swiping a taste of peach pie filling. They all took Georgia back to when they were children playing together. She hadn't seen that side of her sister in weeks. Not since Jeffrey arrived.

She seemed to have fun helping prepare the pies but they'd always enjoyed baking and cooking together. Georgia rarely asked her sister to pitch in at that early hour because of her family and job. Savannah loved the time they shared, she'd said, and offered to help whenever Georgia needed it. Now Georgia wished she'd asked more often.

She heard Lily giggling upstairs. It took the better part of the morning to shift the girl's attention off Savannah even for a minute. It was the first genuine laugh Georgia heard from her since she told the banana joke at the bakery.

While Savannah's girls frolicked with each other, Savannah moaned her misery with each breath, her skin glistening with sweat. On occasion her vision passed across the camera and stopped as if trying to connect with her family watching from afar. She shook her head, imploring them to, "Turn the computer off. Ennis, Georgia, just turn it off. Please stop watching."

Jeffrey circled the chair the way an animal stalked prey, "They'll keep watching. They think they can help you. Probably have enlisted the police department's help too. But they can't find you either. I've made sure of it. Now, where was I? Oh, yes. How to squeeze blood from a turnip, so to speak. In other words, how to make you plead for your life..."

His pacing paused when he brainstormed, "Perhaps I'm going at this all wrong. Perhaps I shouldn't focus on you pleading for *your* life." He leaned down, smiled against her ear, "I'll make you plead for your *children's* lives."

Savannah focused strictly on the camera, telling her family,

"Protect the girls. You know he'll come after them. Protect them from him."

Jeffrey eased the blunt side of the scalpel along her throat, "I will bring your cubs to you. I will hold the blade to their young, precious throats," the pressure hardened, "and I guarantee you will beg me then. You will plead with me not to harm your *little ones*, as you called them. Won't you, Savannah?"

Georgia saw her sister's expression transform through the pain. She mustered the fiercest glare she could, "Leave my girls alone. That was the deal. I come with you, you leave them alone."

Jeffrey rounded the chair again, stood behind her. He crouched, resting his chin on her shoulder, whispering, "You're always pushing your luck. You know what? I can push things too." He placed his index finger on her open wound. "Let me show you." He pressed the finger into the cleaved, bleeding flesh.

Savannah cried out, writhing against the bonds. Her face contorted, the tendons in her neck stood out as she gnashed her teeth with a whimpered, "Stop, *please, stop...*"

"Isn't pushing fun? Don't you want me to keep pushing?" he rammed his finger deeper to rip another shriek from her depths.

"No," was the vicious cry, her body straining so hard every muscle bunched and trembled.

"Then stop pushing *me*, Savannah." He withdrew the finger, wiped the blood on her shoulder. "If I can't control you, your children most certainly can. You refuse to listen to me but as you proved at the bakery, you will obey your kids.   I'm going to need their help."   He reached toward the camera and Georgia watched the screen go blank.

Ennis sat at the computer, brooding silently. Georgia chanced a look at his face. His anger was similar to a bomb. It was armed and ticking but no one knew exactly when it would blow – but the wise cleared the area because it would, at some point, explode.

"I'll chase the bastard to the moon to kill him," he vowed after several minutes. "If she dies, I'll kill him the same way he kills her."

"No luck on tracking the I.P.," Mathis volunteered. "Boss said it's bouncing everywhere. They're still trying though."

Ennis turned in the chair, a shroud of hate clouding his features, "How many people are watching this?"

"Two, Ennis.   He assigned our two best computer guys to it. They're the only ones besides Hunter allowed access."

Georgia jumped at the sound of the doorbell.   Since Jeffrey switched the camera off, she worried he'd make good on his promise to come after the girls.   The men withdrew their guns before approaching the door.

"Georgia," Ennis pointed behind him, "stand by the stairs. If that's Holland, I don't want anyone hurt but him.   Once he tells us where Savannah is, you'd better leave the room cause it's gonna get messy."

She nodded, positioning herself at the base of the stairs. If Jeffrey tried taking the girls, he'd have two cops, her and Dane to get through first. Common sense said Jeffrey was smarter than to barge into a house full of armed people, much less announce his arrival by ringing a doorbell. He was crazy, not stupid, but underestimating a desperate psychopath wasn't prudent either…

Ennis yanked the door open, the gun leveled straight ahead, his finger on the trigger.

Georgia braced for a barrage of gunshots. She heard nothing. Leaning to get a view of the door, she breathed a sigh of relief. Abel and Cyrus, two of Duke Shelton's men stood in dark blue suits, the jackets slung over their forearms. Georgia saw a .45 on Abel's hip, another in Cyrus's shoulder holster. The two hulking black men engulfed the whole front porch and it took Ennis a moment to re-gear from homicidal mode.

Abel noticed Georgia at the stairway, "Boss sent us for protection."

She waved them in. Ennis and John holstered their guns. Abel and Cyrus greeted them then Abel explained, "Boss heard what the man said about the little ones and wants more firepower in case he gets bold."

Dane poked his head over the railing, "Who's here?"

Lily charged past him, excitement bubbling over into giggles, "Is it Mama?"

Halfway down the stairs she stopped cold at the sight of the two black men. She turned, scrambling back to retreat behind Georgia.

Abel crouched, wanting to know, "What're you hiding for, Tiny Toes? You remember Abel, don't you? Why I used to hold you when you was just this big," he indicated halfway up his forearm.

Lily warily peeked one eye around her aunt's thigh. Georgia

chuckled, patted her back, "It's okay, Lily. Abel and Cyrus are friends. It's been a while since you've seen them though."

Abel reached in his pocket, enticed her with a small package of Skittles, "Look what I brought for you, Tiny. Your favorite candy."

Still clinging to her aunt, she ventured another peep. He stepped closer, "Go 'head," he nudged the package closer, "take 'em."

Lily stretched her hand way out to retrieve them. She muttered a quiet *thank you.*

Abel's grin encompassed his whole face, "You're a sweet little lady, just like your mama."

For weeks after meeting Abel, Savannah's nickname for him was Warren Sapp. His resemblance to the football player verged on uncanny, Georgia agreed, and Abel, good-natured as he was, took it in stride. Abel seemed to take everything in stride unless his friend Savannah was threatened.

Georgia turned her attention to clearing the downstairs of kids, "Abel's good at building Lego houses. Why don't you let him help with yours?"

Abel's chest broadened, "I built a Lego castle for my nephew years ago." He spread his arms wide, "It was this big."

Lily's jaw dropped, "Really? That big?"

"Abel knows his Legos, Tiny," he said with utmost certainty.

He presented a convincing argument, so much so Lily's nervousness gave way to youthful excitement. "Make me one! I'll show it to Mama when she comes back."

She grabbed his meaty hand, led him up the stairs, the two chatting about the vast universe of Legos and the best construction plans and layouts.

o   o   o

July 1

With Jeffrey Holland no one except Savannah and Georgia knew how to gauge his anger. He gave the saying *if looks could kill* a legitimacy that made Georgia believe he could actually follow through.

His dark unblinking stare bored through a person but that wasn't the sign one looked for. He had one subtle tell that foretold his imminent rage. A muscle at his jaw. It clenched and released, not repeatedly, but once. When that muscle tightened, the recipient soon discovered why Hell existed – because Jeffrey Holland certainly deserved to roast there.

Her sister could not move two inches one way or the other. So upon seeing the muscle in Jeffrey's jaw clench, Georgia held a hand to her stomach knowing he danced close to the edge of unleashing his most vicious nature.

He leisurely circled the chair, his fingers lightly brushing across Savannah's shoulders, touching her hair, as he passed. He stopped behind her, curled a loose wave behind her ear then leaned closer, "This time I want more from you than begging."

Georgia angled closer to the speaker to hear his faint whisper. The blood still oozed from the earlier wounds. From her sister's movement and expression, her misery level peaked into the dull numbness of pained acceptance. Savannah cringed, "What else could you possibly want?"

Jeffrey smiled against her ear. Georgia closed her eyes, shutting out the sight. She remembered that smile well, the one confirming every child's worst nightmare. The boogeyman does exist, it said, and he's meaner than you think.

"Revenge," he replied with deadly calm.

He stepped beside her, lifted his pant leg to reveal a shiny white scar marring the hairy calf. "Remember your nifty set of golf clubs? I recall every detail of that moment, the driver in your hands. That graceful, sweeping backswing. How your muscles tensed before beginning the follow through. That little noise you uttered when you put all your strength into the downswing. It was an impressive demonstration of your talent at the game. I admire your talent, Savannah. Even though you broke both my tibia *and* fibula when the club slammed into my leg, I still admire your talent."

Her expression conveyed her lack of interest in his admiration, "I aimed for your head next." A pained smile crossed her face, "Nearly made it too."

Georgia's stomach dropped at the proud declaration. "Savannah, no," she pleaded, wishing her sister could hear her, "don't provoke him." Jeffrey's silence unnerved Georgia. Savannah had a knack of spurring the wrong people. Their father and Jeffrey in particular. Georgia knew. When Jeffrey straightened, she saw his jaw muscle twitch a rare second time then he sauntered from the room.

Savannah closed her eyes. Georgia heard her mutter, "Thank God." *You'll need God shortly,* the older sister reflected. *And you'll be begging too. Maybe not Jeffrey but you'll be begging God to intervene, just like last time.*

No one said a word. Georgia swallowed hard because when Jeffrey did return, God only knew what awaited her sister. Ennis stared at the screen, his hands fisted on the desk. Mathis turned away and Georgia heard him grumble, "Told that kid her whole career to watch her mouth."

Seconds later Jeffrey appeared again – still off-camera, "So you think it was funny to shatter my leg, do you? And you were perfectly happy bashing my head in, right?"

Savannah's blue eyes widened, her fight renewed against the cable ties as panic rose in her voice, "No, Jeffrey, don't do it. *Don't...*"

"Not so funny *now* is it?" He stepped into view – in his hand he held a driver, the club head's diameter spanning the size of a giant grapefruit.

Georgia watched Jeffrey take a few practice swings with it, his biceps flexing as he did. A swell of nausea boiled in her stomach. Revenge, he'd said. Jeffrey Holland wanted more than Number Ten. He wanted his pound of revenge before letting her die.

Savannah pulled frantically at the ties that began cutting into her flesh. Her violent thrashing producing a collective groan from the three watching the horror unfold.

Ennis bolted upright, sending the chair backward, nearly into Georgia's knees. He marched past her, Mathis and Abel toward the downstairs bathroom. The door slammed.

"Help me, Savannah," Jeffrey leaned on the club. "I need advice."

On which express train to board to Hell? Georgia could hear those words in her sister's mind. She sensed them because she herself had the same thought.

Savannah wisely remained quiet, her gaze riveted to the driver. Jeffrey swung the club again, the sound slicing the air with a *whoosh*. "I've heard stance, grip and tempo are the keys to executing a good swing."

The word *executing* was not lost on Georgia. Savannah's terrified vision lifted to him.

"Tell me if I'm doing this correctly," he gripped the club. "Left hand over right... Good. Feet apart... There we go. Now, does all my weight go on the back foot during the, what do you call it? The take back?" He demonstrated by swinging the club back.

"Jeffrey, don't do this," her voice trembled. "You at least had a fighting chance against me. I'm tied to a chair."

He ignored her. His concentration appeared consumed with his stance and club positioning. He whispered the steps again as if going through a checklist, "Left hand over right..." Then took another swing, this one harder. Finally he shrugged, "Oh, what the hell.   It doesn't really matter, does it? This is the only time I intend to use one of these monstrosities anyway.   Here goes nothin'."   He stepped in front of Savannah, swung the club back.

Georgia turned away, covered her ears to drown out her sister's impending scream.

18

July 1

Savannah sat rigid in the chair, her muscles taut in a vain effort to prepare for the feel and sound of bone cracking and an excruciating pain she'd never experienced in her life. Time inched by, her body trembling. She prayed in those split seconds. Prayed to God that He find a way to distract, derail and destroy the lunatic with the club clenched in his fists.

Images of disfigured appendages, the agony of bone shattering to bits and slivers drove the terror deeper until she could barely breathe. She felt the club against her leg. A brief shriek burst from her lips. Her brain registered the fact her leg was history, crushed, and at the best she'd be crippled for the rest of her life, however long that might be. Then she waited another split second for the pain to hit. Why wasn't her body convulsing in misery? Why wasn't she writhing in the chair and pleading Jeffrey to stop the pain?

She opened her eyes to see the club head nudged against her calf. It merely bumped the bone with no more than a bothersome pang.

Savannah looked up to see Jeffrey smiling. A humorous smile.

An amusing smile on Jeffrey Holland looked odd, at least odd in the respect no one expected a tiger or bear to grin. He laughed, pleased with himself, "Oh, I'm going to love this. If your reaction is any indication, I am going to savor this moment forever."

As swift as the smile appeared, it vanished, leaving the usual cold, direct Jeffrey in its place. "Nothing can prepare you for this, not even closing your eyes, or *praying* as you so often do around me." He leaned to her ear whispering, "No, my lovely detective. This, I promise, will hurt like hell and if you scream just right, I'll break your other leg too."

He stood up with club in hand and swung it back full force. His vision zeroed in on her left calf. This was it. She squeezed her eyes tight, every muscle tensed. The club sliced the air. She held her breath – how stupid, she thought for a fleeting instant, since that breath would be expelled as a bloodcurdling scream. The time ticked away in slow motion. Her ears began ringing from the panic racing in her veins. She strained at her bonds hoping to snap them and break free – *then* snap Jeffrey's neck with the driver.

"Shit," she heard Jeffrey curse. A distinct thud registered. Something hit the floor – or was dropped. Heavy footfalls stomped past her.

She dared open her eyes, released the shaky pent up breath. He'd dropped the club as the doorbell chimed. The door must have chimed earlier but her mind had focused on battling the new pain of broken bones, a pain thankfully not realized – yet. After a second she realized to her sheer amazement and delight, "Help is here." She finished the tremulous whisper with a sincere thanks to God.

Her mouth opened to scream for help. A hand cradled her jaw from behind, forced her mouth shut as Jeffrey braced her head against his stomach. His other hand slammed over her mouth, his thumb and forefinger clamped her nose shut.

Savannah struggled to suck in a wisp of air past the iron hold but her lungs locked down. She thrashed in the seat, fighting to free herself of his iron grip.

"Do you want to breathe?" Jeffrey inquired with disturbing composure.

Savannah nodded in his hold. *Yes, please,* she tried to communicate. *Please let go.*

"If you want another breath, you must remain quiet. Utter one peep and I'll break every bone in your body with that golf club, do you understand me, Savannah?"

She gave a frantic nod. Anything to get air. *I understand, just let me go...*

Jeffrey removed both hands but stood behind her, ready to act if she even squeaked. She preferred oxygen over screaming for help, however, and closed her eyes while drawing in a long gasp. Before she released the breath, his fingers shoved a cloth in her mouth, nearly jamming it in her throat. She coughed to dislodge it but Jeffrey leaned to her ear, "Spit it out and I'll shove *down* your throat."

He grabbed a roll of duct tape on a side table, stripped off a piece of duct tape and pressed it over her lips, silencing her complaints. He picked up the scalpel, warning, "Not one peep."

The doorbell rang again. Jeffrey headed to the door. It surprised her when he not only opened it but greeted the visitor in a genial manner. She heard the male visitor say he was the neighbor across the street. A package was delivered to the wrong address. Jeffrey answered the man's questions with his usual ease, "She's on vacation. I'm house-sitting while she's gone…"

Savannah glanced back as best she could to see Jeffrey, one hand on the doorknob, the other blocking the visitor's view inside.

"Certainly," Jeffrey's cheery side showed. "I'll be happy to take the package." Then a hiccup in the conversation. "A what?" Jeffrey asked. The man mumbled a reply.

"You're sure she never returned it?" Jeffrey's frustration began to show. After the man answered, Jeffrey said, "I'll look for it. Stay there, I'll be back."

He closed the door behind him, directed his next comment to her, "Remember what I said," then tossed the package on the entry table and grumbled into the kitchen. A few seconds passed when the door opened, "Hey, buddy, don't worry about it. I'll ask for it when she–" the man's jolly tone trailed off to barely finish, "gets… back."

Savannah glanced over her left shoulder. The neighbor stood in the entry, staring at her, she assumed, in complete disbelief. You might want to run now, she thought, because you may stand a chance of staying alive.

But the portly fellow with a comb-over waddled his way to

Savannah, "Lady, are you okay?"

Do I look okay to you? She eased off the sarcasm and for an instant, actually entertained motioning for him to help her. How many opportunities for help would there be anyway?

He reached toward the tape with a shaking hand. His round face and friendly features reminded her of a Norman Rockwell character, only this Rockwell character sported sweat stains and his belly strained against his heather gray polo shirt and bulged over the belt of his black khakis.

A nagging feeling prickled at her neck. The feeling of being watched. Jeffrey tested her, her gut warned. He stood nearby, seeing the neighbor's attempt to free her, waiting for her to break her promise.

Savannah tilted away from the neighbor's hands, tried gesturing for him to leave. *Please get out. Please leave and call for help. Don't let this madman see you or we're both dead...*

He paled at the sight of her wounds, "I'll get help. Just let me get this tape off."

The tape is the least of my worries, mister. Go call for help... Instead, he concentrated on the duct tape on her mouth, picking at it with unsteady fingers. It was no use, she sighed. Mr. Neighborly came over with good intentions. Deliver a package to the rightful owner and to collect a borrowed item. He got the shock of his life upon seeing a woman tied up and bleeding in his friend's house.

Oh yes, now she sensed Jeffrey's definite presence. She stiffened in the chair. She felt him continue watching the neighbor fumble for the tape's edge, trying to peel it away, to merely get a grasp on it.

Jeffrey's dark eyes bored into the back of her skull. He blamed her. He assumed she alerted the guy to her plight and begged for help.

She stared at the little camera positioned on the desk across from her, squirmed in her seat. Her family watched every move, every moment of her nightmare. Except for the neighbor's interruption, Jeffrey planned this flawlessly. Savannah stared at the camera, hoping her family stopped watching soon, if they hadn't already. Misery did not love company, not in this case.

She did not look back for fear of inflaming Jeffrey. She sat still with hopes he realized she had not uttered that peep he warned of earlier.

"I told you to stay outside," Jeffrey stated within arm's length of them.

Savannah tensed, her wide blue eyes lifting to the neighbor's. He stumbled for a reply after meeting Jeffrey's gaze, took a step back toward the door. The sweat stains on his shirt grew a bit larger, smelled more pungent. It was the same terror that coursed through her every time she encountered the killer but she knew what Holland was capable of, Mr. Neighborly did not.

"I... I was helping her..." he backed up a step then another as Jeffrey slowly advanced on him.

Jeffrey's cold hand fell heavy on her aching shoulder, making her jerk then groan from the pain. Goose flesh rose along her body from the chill – and fear. He'll kill me, she convinced herself. He wasn't testing me at all. He believes I broke my promise...

"Did she ask for your help?" Jeffrey bent down, wrapped his free hand around the driver shaft. "Tell me if she gave you any indication she wanted your help. This is important because I specifically told her *not* to make a sound. If she did, well," he dangled the club in front of her face, "I'm afraid I'll have to punish her for that."

She leaned away from the club, silently imploring him to remove the gag. She hadn't lured the guy inside, she tried to convey. She hadn't done a thing.

The guy retreated to the other side of the chair, "Why *wouldn't* she want help?"

"Did she ask for your help!?" Jeffrey's voice carried throughout the house.

"No," the man replied, keeping a keen eye to the golf club.

Jeffrey wielded the driver with ease, swinging it away from Savannah who released a trembling breath. "Good girl, Savannah," he patted her shoulder. "So, Neighbor, that means you're to blame. You want to free this woman, do you?" He gripped the club with both hands and swung it back like a homerun king who eyed the perfect pitch.

The club started forward in what seemed slow motion however Savannah heard the club slice the air at full speed, saw his muscles flex as he amassed all his strength into swinging the driver – right at her noggin.

Seeing the solid black titanium head speed toward her, it occurred to her that her life was about to end. Now, her brain asked, what will we do about that?

At the last instant she ducked. The driver zipped overhead until a sickening crack and scream pierced the air. The neighbor fell behind her.

She dared a glance behind her to see his hand cradling his left shoulder. Jeffrey stalked past her with the club in his fist, seemingly unaware that he nearly launched her head across the room.

Savannah struggled to breathe behind the tape. The cloth worked down closer to her throat, triggering her gag reflex. She fought that and the sickness fueled by hearing the club's thudding against flesh and the snapping of bone.

Her heart raged in her chest, punching like repeated upper cuts into her ribs. If her reflexes had been one second off, her head would've been too. Good job, her brain congratulated her. I didn't want a divorce either.

Jeffrey stared down at the neighbor, "What's your name?"

"Paul Smith," was the whimpering reply. "Look, man, I was only trying–"

"You should understand one thing, Paul Smith. I've waited a long time for this woman. I spent years planning this. You tried to ruin it. I'm not happy about that."

Behind her Savannah heard the club swing again. Another thud, another cracking bone followed by a gut-wrenching wail. Then Jeffrey, "I'm not happy at all." Another thud. A muted yelp and now crying. She may not have begged Jeffrey Holland but Paul Smith spilled words in rapid succession, all pleading with the killer to stop. He spoke so fast she hardly recognized his frantic rambling as words.

Jeffrey ignored him, "No one will take her from me. Not the police, not her family, and certainly not you." The club cleaved the air behind her. A dull thud silenced Smith's pleading. The only sound in the room were Jeffrey's angry breaths.

Movement beside her snapped Savannah to meet Jeffrey's glare. The rage was still there, but not at her. Blood spattered his jeans and white t-shirt. Her vision slid down his body to the club. Blood spattered the shaft, trailing down to the driver's head speckled with bits of pink brain matter.

"Now," he stripped the tape from her mouth in one quick motion that made her cringe. "I'll take care of Mr. Smith's body later. Just pretend he's not there." His brow knitted, "Where were we before he interrupted us?"

Savannah heard a gurgle behind her. Paul was still alive – sort of. A soft moan and a second gurgle emanated from the dying man's throat. She winced in sympathy.

The muscle at Jeffrey's jaw clenched. A flame flickered in his dark eyes, "He's quite distracting, isn't he? Since I want your full, undivided attention, I'll ensure I get it." He snatched the scalpel from the desk beside the camera, marched back to Smith. From the corner of her vision, Savannah watched him crouch beside the man. She turned away to avoid seeing the fatal stroke of the blade. She only knew Paul Smith fell still and quiet.

"I'll be back," Jeffrey walked to the kitchen. The kitchen faucet ran for a good minute while, she assumed, he tidied up his hands and his shiny surgical instrument.

While he was gone, panic from the past minutes waned. Fatigue set in, allowing her mind to concentrate on her own misery once more. Tears and pain dulled her eyesight. The cuts were deep, so much deeper than last time. He sliced into the muscle judging by the ache and numbness setting in, leaving her arm crippled.

Jeffrey emerged from the kitchen holding his precious scalpel and a dish towel. He returned the scalpel to the desk in a delicate, deliberate move, "What will I do with you, detective? The only sign of true emotion came when I threatened your cubs." He lifted the club again. Taking his time, he rubbed it clean with the dish towel, "Second best show of emotion was when I planned payback for my broken leg. Tell me, Savannah, which is more important to you? Your legs or your children?" He nudged the heavy titanium head beneath her chin, pushing her head back to meet his gaze, "Careful how you answer. Remember when you volunteered to take your sister's place at the cabin?"

Yes, he chose Georgia anyway. No one could second guess the bastard. No one. "What do you really want, Jeffrey? For me to beg you? Beg you for what?"

His jaw clenched again. He lifted the driver to her throbbing shoulder, shoved the cold metal against it. Nerves awakened anew, rekindling the fiery pain and making her writhe in the chair.

"You're doing it again," he said. "Keep pushing me and I'll break more than your legs." He pressed harder on the club, "I don't care where your little girls are, I'll find a way to get them. I'll bring them here and cut them to bits with you sitting in the front row." The pain grew unbearable as he continued, "I will kill them both while you watch. Do not patronize me, disrespect me or think you're smarter than I am. Remember who's tied to the chair."

"I'm sorry," she cried, the tears falling freely.

The pressure of the club released as Jeffrey stepped back, leaned on the desk where the camera was. He seemed in awe, "I accept your apology, Savannah. Now I want an answer. What is more important, your legs or your girls?"

She tried to control her weeping however the pain reached insane levels. It reverberated through her arm to her hand, across her chest and back. "You know the answer," she replied between sobs. "You know the answer."

"Such a good mother." He turned to the camera and smiled, "Isn't she, kiddos? She's a good mother, trying to protect you. Too bad it won't work."

19

July 1

Lily sat in Georgia's lap while her aunt read Winnie the Pooh's "Pooh Goes Visiting" out loud. Georgia stopped to survey her audience. She'd been reading stories to Lily for the better part of twenty minutes. After so many pages, she checked her niece to see if a hint of drowsiness drifted in yet because the little girl showed no inkling of relaxing. Lily leaned against her shoulder, tucked her head beneath Georgia's chin but the tension lingered, making her fidget during the story.

"What's wrong, sweetie?" Georgia caught her glancing at Ennis and Savannah's wedding portrait. The room, once Savannah's when she lived with Georgia years ago, still bore mementos of her presence. The older sister hung a collage of photos depicting Savannah's successes at golf. A second collage displayed the ceremonies of her commendations as a police officer and detective. The room brimmed with Savannah, especially to her daughter who sat enthralled by each photo.

"I miss Mama," Lily sulked, her gaze never wavering from the wedding picture.

Georgia closed the book, hugged her close, "I know you do, sweetheart. I miss her too."

"She's pretty there," she pointed.   "Cinderella and Prince Charming."

The smile on her sister's face was the most beautiful Georgia had ever seen – until Savannah gave birth to Lily and Anna. In the photo the newlyweds did resemble a fairy tale couple with Savannah in her flowing white tulle gown and Ennis in his black tuxedo. "Yes," Georgia agreed wistfully. "Cinderella and Prince Charming."

"I'm hungry. Can I eat supper now?"

One glance at the clock convinced Georgia the young girl's belly tuned to meals with Swiss accuracy because it was fifteen minutes of Savannah's preferred time to feed her family supper.

Eleven hours had passed.   Eleven long, excruciating hours Savannah suffered at Jeffrey's hands, with no leads on her location, no way for her to escape.

"Aunt Georgia," Lily prodded.

"Yes, sweetheart, you can eat now. I'll bet your sister is hungry too."

Anna slept in the downstairs bedroom, curled up in her crib. Georgia had heard stories of quiet children – the ones who mostly cried for diaper changes or food – and filed them in the mythical realm of dragons and elves. Parents who swore their children rarely threw temper fits (and seldom cried) were simply lying. Until she met Anna. The child had loud moments and the occasional humdinger tantrum (the kitty fiasco being the latest) but Anna behaved herself better than most two year-olds, at least in Georgia's opinion. Her sister definitely had not stretched the truth or outright lied about her youngest girl's nature.

Georgia spent a minute contemplating how to sneak the girls into the kitchen without them hearing or seeing Savannah and Jeffrey on the computer. The living room sat next to the dining room, so close that any volume level might be heard, especially a child missing their mother's voice.

She eased Lily from her lap, "Stay right here..." She descended the stairs, called Dane.

Her husband appeared almost immediately, his features grim, "Yeah?"

"It's the girls' suppertime. Turn the volume down so they don't hear."

"Sure," he began walking away. "The camera's still off so go ahead and bring Lily down. I'll get Anna."

Before going upstairs, Georgia saw Jeffrey kill the neighbor and nearly decapitate Savannah in the process. The sight sapped Georgia's strength, forcing her to sit down or pass out. Dane shooed her upstairs, telling her to read to Lily, if for nothing else but to clear her mind a moment. She'd had her moment – twenty of them to be exact – now she needed to feed the girls and pretend something was normal in their lives. Because when that camera switched back on, the images would be more graphic and horrific, the screams would grow longer and louder and there was sure to be plenty of suffering on both sides of the camera lens.

Before she headed upstairs to Lily, the group spent several minutes debating over the dead neighbor's name. Was it Bob, Rob, Paul or what exactly? Only the name Smith came across loud and clear and that name was as common as dirt. They couldn't even use the neighbor's name to trace Savannah's location. Fate appeared to be on Jeffrey's side at every single turn.

Georgia pushed the dread of what came next out of her thoughts. The primary goal was feed the girls as soon as possible and ensure they never heard or saw Savannah or Jeffrey.

Georgia turned to the bedroom, held her hand out, "C'mon, sweetheart. Let's go fix supper for you and Anna."

Lily's small hand grasped hers. The two descended the steps slowly with Georgia listening for sounds that the camera was back up and running. What would they do if Jeffrey switched it on while the girls were eating? She'd need lots of help not only hiding the sight of their mother's misery but hearing it as well.

They approached the bottom stair when Lily looked up at her, "Can I have some cake?"

"Yes, but you'll have to eat supper first. Your mother doesn't allow dessert before the meal."

"But Mama's not here," the girl hinted with a lilt. "She won't know."

"But *I'll* know," Georgia sing-songed back with a smile. "Would you like leftover fried chicken for supper?"

Apparently the idea hit the mark. Lily tugged her along, her eyes brightened, "With smashed taters and gravy too?"

"We'll make smashed taters and gravy but you and Anna have to stay in the kitchen with me, okay? I'll need some help." They rounded the corner to the living room. Georgia held her breath. Still no sounds from the computer.

"Anna's too young to help."

"She is right now," Georgia answered, "but later you can show her how to do things. That's a big sister's job, to teach the younger ones."

"You taught Mama?"

"Some things, yes. Grandma Charlene taught her most everything. I just filled in where I needed to – or thought I needed to."

Dane rushed behind her, "Anna's gone. I can't find her. The window's open and she's not in the room."

Ennis raced to the downstairs bedroom with Georgia and the others behind him. Her vision scanned the room in a frantic search for the child. The crib stood empty, the rails still in place. The window yawned wide, the hunter green curtains shoved apart and flapping in the hot evening breeze. Had the girl climbed out? Maybe but a child of two could not possibly reach the window lock. A lock that remained in place at all times while Anna resided in the room. There were only two ways that window would open. Obviously if someone inside unlocked it and the other, more frightening possibility – Jeffrey found a way to pry it open and fulfill his promise.

Georgia stood in mute shock. Savannah's baby was gone. This could not be happening. The room shifted around her, her head feeling full, cloudy and unable to assemble a logical thought past Jeffrey abducting Anna and what he intended to do with the girl. She tightened her hold on Lily's hand, unwilling to release the child for fear she too might vanish. Georgia swallowed hard, bit back tears. How did this happen?

Panicked men scattered in every direction, both inside and outside. How, she asked herself again. How had Jeffrey managed to sneak past everyone to take Anna? Since they arrived, Abel and Cyrus took turns patrolling outside while everyone else remained in the house.

Searching each room, Ennis called for his youngest, his desperation so intense it physically hurt to hear him.

Mathis joined him, asking, "Rutherford, are you sure the kid didn't pull a jailbreak? Has she been climbing out of the crib at home?"

"She's climbed out before but she couldn't open the window. He's got her, I know the bastard's got her." He barely contained his rage, "He's got my wife *and* my daughter."

While Abel and Cyrus scoured the outdoors, Dane stood beside Georgia, seemingly paralyzed with disbelief – until he buried his face in his hands with a groan, "It's my fault. It's all my fault."

Stunned by the admission, Georgia glanced at him, "What do you mean it's your fault?"

Dane shook his head, dropped his hands, reluctantly meeting her gaze, "We always keep the window closed and locked when the kids are here but this morning, before Holland took Peach, I had it open. I closed and locked it afterward. Or I thought I did. I was sure of it."

"Where's Anna?" Lily asked her aunt.

"I..." Georgia stopped herself. *I don't know* didn't cut it. She already felt substandard as a sister, as an aunt. *Protect the girls. You know he'll come after them. Protect them from him.* Savannah's heartfelt plea haunted her. Her failure to do so would likely result in Anna's death. Georgia lost her family one by one, each disappearing into the hands of a killer. "We're looking for her, honey. In the meantime you always stay with one of us. Never go off by yourself."

Lily disapproved, "The bathroom too?"

"The bathroom too." Because the bathroom had a window. A portal to the outside world, to Jeffrey. "I'll go with you." She finally understood her sister's fanaticism about leaving the kids alone. The usual mundane task of going to pee posed a real threat to Lily's life. No, the child would be escorted everywhere beginning now.

The girl whined, "But why?"

"Because I said so," she answered with stern finality.

"Look!" Lily pointed into the small bedroom. She stripped free from Georgia's hold and dashed inside.

"Lily—" Georgia pursed her lips, trapping a harsh scold. She loved playing the fun aunt, the person Lily came to when Mama and Daddy were tired or busy. However if the child disobeyed once again, she'd discover Aunt Georgia's palm landed harder on her bottom than Mama's.

When the girl emerged, she nuzzled a tiny orange and white tabby kitten to her cheek. "He was hiding in a corner," she announced as if she'd saved the kitten from imminent death. "Can we keep him?"

Georgia regarded the cat with a contemptuous frown. She knew who left the kitten behind.

Lily cuddled it closer, pouting her lip, "Mama said we couldn't have a kitten but he could stay with you and Uncle Dane."

"We can't keep it either, sweetie," she replied. That cat, by default, was the last creature she'd consider housing under their roof, just because Jeffrey Holland put it there.

20

July 1

A half-locked window and one eager child. Georgia and her husband will bear the brunt of Ennis's temper for their lack of security. No one need ask who took the child. The kitten suffices as my confession. I can hear the rhythmic chant "kitty-cat, kitty-cat, Anna want kitty-cat" drumming in Ennis's brain the way an annoying song implants itself, tormenting its victim with every redundant refrain. Anna really wanted that kitty-cat, I smile. So much she shushed when I placed a finger to my lips while jimmying the window open.

The frantic search will cease soon, leaving Mr. Rutherford with his impotent rage. He can blame his wife for this unfortunate turn of events. Her inability to control herself forced me to these drastic measures because I truly (in a thousand different ways) despise using children as leverage. To begin with, they are fussy, unpredictable creatures that act out on the slightest whim. Which leads me to their worst trait – tantrums. They don't call them Terrible Twos for nothing,

I discovered that fact as a physician – and a child of two can skillfully unhinge a person's sanity in seconds.

That being said, little Anna surprises me. She is a quiet child which serves me well for my endeavor. At Georgia's, one loud peep and the whole brood would have descended on me before I had Anna in my arms. I poked my head in the open window and asked if she wanted to see Mama. That's all it took. Less than five minutes later, Anna and I were on our way.

The key to my detective's heart sits beside me wearing a purple Tigger shirt and pink pants. She sings the Alphabet Song. I listen to her merry performance over and over (this rates as one of those aforementioned annoying songs), and cringe when she blends the five letters into "elemeno-p" as young children do. She completes the song forty percent of the time. The remaining sixty ends with, "Elemeno-p, now I know my A-B-C's..." Not quite, kid, I think, but you're getting there.

I've told her Mama is in a castle far, far away and that it will take time to get there. Twenty-five minutes later (and twenty-five hundred song repetitions later), we cruise down Windward Parkway then turn onto the long, winding Club House Drive. Houses in the near distance are obscured by tall Georgia pines but once in a while I see a mansion through the thick foliage as we drive. I point out the window, show Anna one of the spacious homes barely visible though the pines, "There's Mama's castle."

She stretches to peer out the side window. Anna is impressed with Mama's new digs and as I veer onto Muirfield Court, she claps her hands chanting, "Mama, Mama..." It is a damn fine reprieve from "elemeno-p".

I hurry to the house, park in the garage and mash the magic button to roll the door down to ensure our privacy. Only then do I gather her from the car. I shush her, telling her we're surprising Mama so she must be quiet. Anna doesn't like it but nods anyway. I hoist her onto my hip, carry her to the inner door. It gives a slight creak upon opening, the silence inside surprises me. I figured Savannah might exercise those lungs in an effort to alert the masses to her plight. Then I remind myself this is no ordinary woman. She is stronger, smarter than the first nine. Number Ten is special. Thus she receives a special gift.

I take a detour with Anna, diverting to the great room instead of the kitchen. I lower her to the floor, whispering that she should stay quiet or she'll ruin Mama's surprise.

Before I left the house, I covered Paul Smith's corpse with a blanket. It hides the worst of the carnage but not all the blood. I don't expect Anna to pay attention to that part of the room anyway, not when her precious mother is present.

I head to the living room where Savannah sits. Her head is bowed as if asleep but I can tell she's awake, just extremely miserable. I switch on the camera, wondering if anyone in Georgia's house is watching or if they're in such a dither they have forgotten the show.

I tip Savannah's head back by the chin. Her eyes open to pained slits. Her face is wet with tears.

"I have good news." I wait for a reaction. The closest I get is an anguished glare. As if it took every ounce of strength to convey her hatred, her shoulders slump, her head hangs down with a groan. She's not surrendering yet but the damage I've done is wearing on her.

Dr. Holland has the perfect prescription to pep her right up. First, however, I check my handiwork. The bleeding has subsided, leaving thick, tacky, coagulating trails down her breast. When I touch the wounds, it brings her alive again with a blue streak curse trapped behind clenched teeth. "Now, now," I scold. "You're going to feel terribly chagrined by those words when you see what I brought for you." Against her angry whimpering protests, I closely inspect the wounds. "I understand you're in pain. I severed some muscle." I touch an area with a knot beneath the skin, "My best advice is to sit still."

She scowls. Sweat glistens on her skin. She's trembling from the pain, "Wouldn't kill you to part with an aspirin, you stingy bastard."

The fire of her temper burns hot even after bearing incredible suffering. "Sorry. Aspirin thins the blood. As you can see, you've lost enough."

Uttering a mild curse, she squeezes more tears from her eyes.

Instead of a pain reliever, I offer something more valuable, "Like to see the gift I brought?"

"What is it?" she asks, her voice hoarse from her earlier screams. "A machete or a whip?"

Her smartass remarks are her defense. I learned this five years ago. Sass is her primary method of coping with helplessness in a situation. I smile easily, "Neither but don't give me ideas or I might use them."

Off to the great room I go, anticipating Savannah's reaction to seeing her baby. Anna wandered a few feet to a display cabinet filled with colorful Hummel figurines. I bend to one knee, put my hands lightly to her shoulders, "Are you ready to see Mama?"

"Yes, please," she says with utmost politeness.

I tell her, "Now Mama's got a boo-boo so let's not touch her, okay? We don't want to hurt her, do we?"

She shakes her head. I take her hand and together we proceed to the living room.

The entry to the living room is to Savannah's right. She will see us from the corner of her eye in a moment. At the doorway, I feel Anna draw back. She senses something. Or perhaps she's confused at her mother's nudity. Maybe she spied the blood staining the carpet – maybe even smells the odd coppery odor. Smith certainly left a pungent bouquet behind as he bled out. That combined with Savannah's contribution probably tweaked the youngster's nose. Or does Anna hear her mother's soft whimpers or her short, labored breaths?

Without her daughter saying a word, Savannah turns her head. Her eyes seem duller, less lively – until she sees Anna. The blue pools sharpen their focus. I see no signs of discomfort in them. It has been abandoned temporarily by disbelief and horror of what awaits her little girl. She shakes her head and in her tone I hear a different anguish. A mother unable to protect her baby except with words, "Dear God, no. Not my girls. Jeffrey, not my girls…"

My hand goes to Anna's shoulder again, "Only one. Couldn't snag Lily. She was probably busy with Aunt Georgia but I brought your youngest cub. She couldn't wait to see Mama."

Now her voice gains considerable strength, "Don't let her see this. You wanted me and you've got me but let my baby go."

I consider her demand – for three whole seconds, "I would except having her here renews your spirit. Why, look at the change in just this last minute. I think I like having Anna around." My hand urges the girl forward, "Go say hi to your mother."

The child pushes against my hand. Her vision stays watchful and wary on Savannah the way a person regards a strange, snarling animal. Her reaction wounds Savannah deeper than any scalpel could. Mama turns from us and I see her shoulders shaking – she's weeping.

"Please," she says between sobs, "take her out of here. Somewhere away from this. Please."

I bend down to Anna, surprised she refuses to approach her mother, the woman who gave her life and literally protected her with her own. I want to know, "Why won't you go to her?"

Anna's wide eyes never waver from Savannah. She pointed, "That's not Mama."

Ouch. I can't imagine the heartbreak of one's child uttering those words. I agree Savannah looks pretty ragged and exhausted after what I've done.   Her eyes are red-rimmed and puffy from incessant crying, her hair falls in loose, sweat-dampened waves.   Her whole body trembles in the chair and her screams have stripped her voice to a hoarse fraction of its normal timbre.

My patience withers along with my semi-convivial mood.   I tighten my hold with a brusque, "That is your mother."

Anna pulls against my grasp, her little face blooms scarlet to her hairline, her protests ramp in volume until they threaten a wailing fit.

I'll have none of this foolishness, I tell her, and forcibly stand her to face Savannah who chances turning back to her.

"My sweet baby," she says, scarcely able to retain control of her tears. "I'm so sorry he brought you here."

Anna yanks free of my hold, runs back to the great room in a storm of screaming squalls.

"Anna!" her mother strains to see her child flee the room but the heartfelt summons ends on a cry when she twists in the seat, stressing her wound.

I am fed up with Anna's petulant attitude.   If she realized what awaits her mother, she'd not only return but climb on her lap and embrace this woman.   I see Anna one of two ways in her later years. Either an older version of this bratty two year-old or a woman filled with regrets stemming from this one singular event.

I pity Savannah and I hate to pity anyone.   Two year-olds aren't renowned for selflessness, I am aware of this.   Nor are they used to facing death at such an early age but I cannot accept this blatant rejection.

I snatch the scalpel from the nearby table. Savannah sees this and goes temporarily insane. Without regard to pain or further injury, she struggles, wrenching against her bonds while screaming "no" at the top of her lungs. She believes I'm going after her baby. Mama Bear is back.

Valiant as her efforts are, I cannot tolerate the screams at this moment. I'm still angry at Anna and unfortunately Savannah suffers my wrath. I backhand her, commanding her to shut up.

The blow knocks her silent. She works her jaw, shakes her head to regain her bearings. "Please don't hurt Anna," she cries to me. "She's just a child. A scared child."

"I'm not hurting her, Savannah," I assure, appraising her condition. Despite her earnest battle moments earlier, she's weak. Probably unable to stand for long. Certainly unable to attack me and do much damage.

I angle the scalpel's blade to her wrist. She draws back but the cable tie holds firm. I see her eyes close tight against the inevitable pain.

I slice the tie binding her to the chair. She dares to peek and is shocked at the sight. Disbelief and confusion cross her features. I have released her right wrist and I busy myself freeing her elbow then move to her left side to finish cutting her loose. She stays quiet, as if mulling over my motive for such drastic measures. The fact her child is hiding and weeping in the other room seems lost on her.

"There are rules to this newfound freedom," I caution. "It is temporary and can be revoked in an instant if you disobey. Do you understand?"

Savannah frantically nods, turning toward the great room, searching for her daughter.

I lean to her right ankle, cut the tie then do the same with her left, "She is the reason I'm allowing this. You were able to say goodbye to Lily. This is your chance to do the same with Anna." I take her by the jaw, bring her vision straight to mine, "Do not betray my trust, Savannah. This is your only warning." I take the scalpel with me – she may be weak but I don't believe she's too weak to swing a sharp object at me. "I'll go get her. Stay in this room. You won't run from me or fight me. Do that and you will pay dearly."

I jaunt to the great room, set the scalpel aside then scoop the bawling brat into my arms. I lift her to meet my gaze, hoping daughter will comprehend my warning as effectively as Mama had, "Be quiet, Anna. You've hurt your mother's feelings. You were mean to her. She loves you and protects you – you're too young to understand the sacrifice she's making for you but one day you'll regret treating her so badly. Tell her you're sorry for being mean." I lecture her all the way into the living room. I see Savannah still seated, her expression unreadable. It seems to waver between offense at my berating and puzzlement as to why I'd bother.

With Anna on my left hip, I curl my free hand around Savannah's arm to bring her to her feet. She sways, forcing me to brace her with an arm around her waist.

She looks at Anna who continues pulling away from her mother. I've had enough, "Say you're sorry."

She shakes her head, hides her eyes. Savannah holds her heartbreak at bay, leans forward to kiss Anna but the child squirms away. With her left arm holding across my back for stability, Mama struggles to lift her injured right arm. She manages to touch Anna's hand and places a kiss on the girl's small fist. I witness the tremendous effort it takes and resulting agony it causes.

"I love you, my sweet girl," the words quiver on a rising torrent of tears. "You and Lily are my heart and soul. I will always love you."

I hear it. The sound of a voice fading, losing its strength. Savannah's weight gradually sinks against my embrace. Quickly, I set Anna down as her mother's knees buckle, sending the mighty detective to the floor.

Anna takes off in a run, of course, anything to escape this courageous woman who dedicated herself to her children. I let Anna have her way while I tend to Savannah. The detective is conscious, just dizzy and weak from shock, pain and likely sorrow of having such an ungrateful child.

I try lifting her without stressing her right arm. I hold her to me, her breasts flush against my chest. I can feel warm, sticky blood soaking my shirt. All the activity and her fall reopened the wounds.

Savannah's left hand clenches in my shirt for a handhold across my back. I notice her firm grasp and know there's still untapped strength left in this woman...

21

July 1

Georgia sought refuge in the master bathroom a few minutes while Abel played Go Fish with Lily in the guest room next door. She had to clear her mind of Anna rejecting her mother and of Savannah's devastation. Jeffrey needed nothing more than a child to break Savannah, at least in a way. By denying her mother, Anna helped accomplish Jeffrey's goal. She'd weakened Savannah's resolve.

Spilling tears, Georgia braced her hands on the vanity, her fingers tightly gripping the marble counter top. She wanted a lull, a temporary breather from the nightmare. Problem was, her sister would not get one so why should she? Guilt and worry sank to the bone. She'd tried everything to find Savannah. Literally everything she knew. So Georgia lifted her vision to her reflection in the mirror, tried bolstering the image staring back. Maybe another prayer. One more prayer couldn't hurt. She'd spent most of the day praying anyway. Prayers of mercy, of rescue, of peace for her sister. She blocked the memory of Savannah's screams and misery from her mind while in prayer with God. *Lord, please help her. Help her find a way to free herself...*

The house phone rang, jarring her from her thoughts. In that instant, she let herself hope that Duke's men managed to track down the video feed's location. Wiping her tears, she hurried to gather herself in case (Lord, please let it be) Duke asking for her.

Someone knocked on the door, "Georgia?"

It was her sister-in-law Leah. With Seth away in the Army National Guard, Leah drove to Macon to visit her parents. When Georgia called to inform her of Savannah's situation, Leah immediately headed back to Atlanta. She arrived shortly after Jeffrey abducted Anna.

Georgia unlocked the door, opened it, "Who called?" *Lord, please....*

Leah sounded confused, "There's a Peter Thompson on the phone. He called Savannah's cell when he noticed neither of you at the bakery today. He wants to know if everything is okay."

Her hopes dashed, Georgia sighed, ran a hand through her hair and tried not to question God's delay on answering her prayers. She trusted God through her mother's cancer, stuck by Him, remained strong in her faith as her mother had. Now, her faith shook just a little more with each passing hour. With each scream, each drop of precious blood her sister shed. Georgia fought to hang on to her beliefs but found herself too often questioning His plans for her sister.

"Georgia," Leah called softly, breaking her from the daze.

Georgia nodded, her mind switching gears to Peter Thompson's call. Wait, did Leah say he called Savannah's *cell* number? Yes, she had. When had Savannah given him that number, Georgia wondered. She assumed they were just casual friends but the fact he called her cell phone defined the depth of their relationship since Savannah vehemently protected that number.

Georgia's shoulders slumped, "This'll break his heart. He and his brother really care about Savannah, they look for her every Saturday." She opted to answer the call downstairs, away from Lily.

Once she picked up the receiver, Peter Thompson apologized for the interruption (and for calling her private residence), "I'd never call unless it was important," he began. "Savannah gave me her cell number in case I ever needed her. Bob and I missed her at the bakery but when neither one of you were at work, I was afraid something happened."

Georgia searched her brain, trying to choose her words carefully. Last thing she wanted was him dropping dead of a coronary. She already felt close to one herself. As she filled him in, Peter fell stone quiet. Half a minute passed until, "How can we help? Whatever Bob and I can do, tell us."

"Pray we find her in time, Mr. Thompson. That's all I know to do."

"Are there any clues where he has her? Anything at all?"

"Unfortunately, no. The police department is trying to trace the video feed."

Mr. Thompson again offered his and his brother's help, ending the conversation with a request for her to keep them informed.

She hung up from the call drained of energy. Returning to the living room, she wrapped her arms around herself in a feeble attempt to calm her nerves.

Upon her arrival from Macon, Leah evaluated Savannah as best she could. Yes, Jeffrey was correct, she said. Unlike the last time, the incisions beneath the collarbone severed muscle. When – or if – they found Savannah alive, she'd need surgery. The amount of blood wasn't dangerous but, she said, it didn't take a large blood loss to feel the effects.

Mathis stepped aside for Georgia, his vision riveted to the computer monitor. Ennis and Leah joined them, staring silently at the movement onscreen. Earlier when Georgia dashed from the room in tears, Anna had just refused her mother's touch, her kiss. Georgia lost her tightly held composure when Savannah fought to retain a brave face at her baby's denial.

Chancing a look at the screen, she stopped, mesmerized by the scene. Jeffrey held Savannah in his arms, his hold snug around her as tender as a lover's embrace. They stood together for a solid minute, her clinging to him with her good arm then whimpering as he gently eased her into the chair. "Stay there and don't move," he instructed in a tone Georgia hadn't heard before. Compassionate. Kind.

He touched Savannah's cheek with a tenderness she hadn't expected – as if he cared about her. As if, strange as it sounded, he *sympathized* with her.

Georgia was about to ask what happened while she was gone when Jeffrey's demeanor transformed, sending a chill along her spine. He stepped back, stripped off his bloody shirt, flung it to the floor, "Anna! Where are you?" He was angry, so raging angry at the child, Georgia feared for Anna's life.

"What are you doing, Jeffrey?" Savannah wanted to know. Demanded to know. Georgia cringed at her sister's throaty voice. She pushed the words out, her voice cracking then catching syllables like a car engine missing a cylinder.

In the distance, Georgia heard Anna's bellowing cries. She could only imagine the toddler's fright. A strange house, a strange man and the promise of seeing Mama but the woman she faced hardly looked or sounded like her mother. Now that strange man shouted her name in a way that promised violence and the woman who was supposed to be Mama could not help her.

Jeffrey ignored Savannah's question, instead striding with purpose – and clenched fists – toward the crying child. He grumbled something unintelligible by the microphone but his words stirred a storm with Savannah who turned, trying to track him from her chair, "Don't, *please*, Jeffrey. Not my baby."

"Anna!" he shouted, making not only Savannah jump but everyone watching the computer feed.

"Leave her alone," Savannah warned, her voice growing stronger. She leaned her left elbow on the chair's arm, levering herself unsteadily to her feet. Using small, measured steps, she labored on wobbly legs to follow Jeffrey. Halfway to the door, her right knee gave, sending her to the floor. "Leave her alone!" she cried while using her legs and left arm to crawl closer to her baby.

Georgia stared at the doorway, dreading the instant Jeffrey saw she not only abandoned the chair but inched toward the other room.

Savannah approached a sturdy wooden table – an entry table – grabbed a thick leg and pulled herself to her knees. She tucked her right arm close, cradling and protecting it from further injury. "Leave my baby alone!" she warned again, finishing with a rare, unflattering reference to his paternal lineage – or lack thereof. "You wanted me, not her! Come after me!"

A mother's instinct, Georgia thought. Protect the baby at all costs, even her own life. "I can't watch this anymore," Georgia swiped at her tears, pushed past the group. She went straight to the kitchen, pressing her hands over her ears.

Seconds passed when a collective groan from everyone brought her back to the doorway. She still heard Anna's wailing screams. Still heard Savannah's threats end on painful whimpers. Still saw her creeping her way to Anna to protect her. Georgia asked, "What happened?"

Mathis shook his head, "She was nearly on her feet, reached onto the table and everything went down in the floor, including her."

Georgia returned to the kitchen. She opened an upper cabinet, dragged out a bottle of brandy, poured herself a healthy glass and downed it. When she turned, she saw Dane sitting at the bar, head in hands. He'd sequestered himself there since Ennis lambasted him over the unlocked window. She hadn't appreciated her brother-in-law's tongue-lashing but understood his hostility. Still, Dane hadn't intended to leave Anna vulnerable and if Jeffrey wanted the child, he would have found a way to get her, Georgia felt certain of it.

"Stop feeling guilty, sweetheart," she said. "No one could have predicted Jeffrey's actions, not you, not me and," she lowered her voice to a whisper, "not Ennis."

"How'm I gonna live with myself if he kills that baby?" He clenched his fists, "How can I look my brother in the eyes if his girl dies because of my stupidity? It's bad enough he may lose Savannah but to lose his *child*?"

Georgia went to him, wrapped him in a hug from behind. Her voice softened, "Please stop doing this to yourself. We'll take this one step at a time. To my knowledge Jeffrey's never killed children."

He turned in her arms, returned the embrace, "I pray he doesn't start now. God, do I pray."

Ennis rushed past, stopped upon sight of her, "You got anything stronger than that brandy?"

She hitched her thumb to the cabinet she'd squirreled into, "Bourbon and scotch. Take your pick."

Leah gasped then, "Sweet Jesus, no."

Both Georgia and Ennis about-faced, returned to the computer. They entered the room to an eerie silence. Anna's cries had magically ceased. Savannah's moans reduced to short, shallow breaths barely perceptible by the microphone. Her objective outlasted her strength.

She'd collapsed flat on the floor, her hand grasping the carpet for a handhold to pull her forward.

Those sights and sounds tugged at Georgia's heart but the sight beside Savannah, the one her younger sister had not seen yet, drew a groan from Georgia. She grabbed Ennis's hand, held tight. She imagined these next few minutes would be her sister's last.

Hands on hips, Jeffrey stood over Savannah who, with her good arm and both legs, rallied enough energy to grope another inch to the doorway where Anna ran earlier.

He bent at the waist, addressing her as a parent scolding a rebellious child, "I told you not to move. Do you remember that?"

"Where's my daughter?" she demanded. "What did you do to her?"

Jeffrey grabbed a fistful of her hair, pulled her head back until she braced onto her left hand to relieve the strain. His voice hardened, "Do you remember me ordering you to remain in that chair?"

Her anger mounted to white-hot rage, "Where is Anna, you son of a bitch?"

Georgia flinched. Savannah would – as Jeffrey vowed – pay dearly, especially for that. She'd pushed him past his limit with the slur.

It was strange how things moved in slow motion at times. Car accidents, train wrecks – and Jeffrey Holland. Georgia's eyes received the information only for her brain to slow it down frame by frame. He released Savannah at the same time his foot swung back. The motion resembled a football player kicking a fifty yard field goal. Only this time the foot buried in a set of ribs, not a ball.

The cry spilling from Savannah made Georgia sick to her stomach. She held a hand to her mouth, heaving. She tried and barely succeeded to force the sickness down.

All eyes turned from the screen. Jeffrey unleashed another kick – Georgia assumed this because of the resulting scream. Georgia jerked with a soft cry as if Jeffrey drove his foot into *her* ribs. That is it, her mind warned. That is all I can tolerate without leaving you completely, it said.

She ran to the kitchen, grabbed the brandy and nearly mowed over Ennis as she bounded up the stairs. She slammed the bathroom door, locking herself inside, away from the brutality and screams. Her hands shook so violently she held the bottle with both to tilt it to her lips. Savannah fast approached her last breath and what was everyone doing? Nothing but watching her die.

She swallowed a gulp of brandy, felt it bounce when hitting bottom. She closed her eyes, held her breath, willing the booze to stay down. A minute passed when she chanced another swallow. Shame suddenly weighed on her. Shame that she'd criticized her sister all those years for drowning herself in bourbon after their mother's death. *You are a hypocrite, Georgia May. Judging Savannah for anesthetizing the painful memories, for trading sobriety for a warm, temporary balm. She wanted a brief respite from the images and sounds of misery and dying.*

Bourbon provided that. And you judged her. Berated her. Made her feel inadequate.

Georgia tilted the bottle to her mouth again. The smooth stinging slid past her tongue, down her throat. It coated her stomach in soothing heat now. She guessed the bourbon had done the same for her sister years ago. She realized how booze encouraged a person to tip that bottle just one more time. It wrapped the tormented mind in a downy soft cocoon, and for Georgia, that meant blurring the visions of Savannah's anguish, dulling her screams.

If she saw her sister alive again, Georgia would apologize for her high and mighty attitude years ago because today she understood the value of a good stiff drink and its therapeutic magic. By God, liquor *did* help. Not much but it did.

Georgia's eyes closed on a prayer. She prayed that God spared her sister one more time, that He provided a way for her to escape. The next part of the prayer was the most difficult. She hadn't prayed this kind of prayer since their mother wasted away in agony from cancer. A prayer for peace. *Lord, if it is Thy will that Savannah does not come back to us, please do not let her suffer at the hands of that monster. Take her quickly, take her home to our mama…*

A knock on the door fueled her anger. Leave me the hell alone, she clenched her teeth until they ached. But before she chewed out the intruder, a young voice inquired, "Aunt Georgia? Are you okay?"

The question brought more tears to the surface. Sweet Lily. "Yes, sweetheart, I'm fine."

"You slammed the door. Me and Abel wanted to check on you."

She could see her sister at that age. Lily's facial features favored Savannah so heavily that Georgia found herself drifting back in time when her sister played hopscotch on the sidewalk outside their home in Augusta. Lily would grow up never fully comprehending the depth of her mother's beauty, not only outside but inside. "Thank you, honey," she answered back, cursing her trembling voice. "I'm fine. You and Abel go play cards."

She wasn't sure how long she stayed in the bathroom. The quiet seemed deafening. The day's horrific images burned through her mind. What had Jeffrey done with Anna? The absence of Anna's wailing cries gave credence to him killing the child – not just to silence her but to destroy Savannah and break her will to live. The tragic reality was Savannah would die not knowing what he'd done to her baby – a baby that battled like a warrior not to be born. Anna resisted nature with fierce tenacity, forcing Savannah into such an extended, ugly labor the doctor considered a forceps or caesarian section just to relieve Savannah of the unnecessary stress. Georgia saw her through the birth – every sweaty, unbearable hour of it until finally one last, exhausting push brought the boisterously protesting Anna Rose into the world. Savannah fought hard giving birth to her youngest and equally as hard to save her from Jeffrey.

Another knock on the door. She assumed it to be Lily again, "Honey, go play cards with Abel."

"It's me." Me, in this case, was Dane.

Georgia unlocked the door and when Dane brought her into his comforting embrace, she clung to him, her self-control shattering, "She's going to die and we can't stop him."

He shushed her, held her close, "Hang in there. We all know Savannah never gives up. She's a fighter."

He sounded more confident than she felt. *Even fighters get defeated when faced with the right opponent.* And Jeffrey planned this for five long years. Only a miracle could help Savannah escape or be rescued. If he killed Anna – which would cement Dane's guilt until *his* last breath – Savannah's will to live might dwindle even the slightest degree. If that happened, Jeffrey would see it and take full advantage of it.

Georgia wavered between wanting an update on Savannah's condition and not wanting it. The brandy called to her – just one more, it sang to her, just one more swallow…

She reached for the bottle. Dane's hand covered hers, his brow sinking. He shook his head, "Another belt of that won't help."

On the contrary, her jaw tightened. Every emotion, every sharp word her sister flung at her years ago hung precariously on her tongue as well. Today she understood Savannah's past indignation upon being preached at. *Do not lecture me,* she'd said. *Do not assume you know what will help and what won't.*

Dane's grasp tightened on hers, "Holland stopped with two kicks."

Georgia pulled away, incredulous, "Two is enough to break ribs, especially as hard as he kicked her. She's probably got a punctured lung." Ghastly images flashed in her mind like a perverse slide show. Ones of her sister trying to fend off Jeffrey's attacks. Reaching her uninjured arm out in a silent plea to stop. Her face contorting when his foot buried in her side and her struggling to curl up to protect herself against the second kick...

Dane caressed Georgia's cheek, dragging her from the memories, "She kept trying to find Anna though. That tells you how tough that girl is. She's not giving up."

She didn't have to give up, she nearly shot back. It wasn't a matter of mental toughness, it was basic knowledge. If the body surrendered before the mind, the person was still just as dead. Savannah almost reached her breaking point the first time Jeffrey abducted her but she had no children then. *They* were her breaking point now. Jeffrey knew it too.

Georgia held her tongue against lecturing her husband. He already suffered his brother's wrath and guilt weighed on him because of Anna. She held Dane close, rested her head against his broad chest, grateful for his love and support, "How's Ennis?"

"It's tearing him up but he refuses to leave the computer. The feed is down for now so maybe I can talk him into a break."

"I'll help you." Before she vacated the bathroom, she confiscated the brandy in case Lily's inquisitive nature kicked in and she stumbled onto it. They had enough hell on their hands without dealing with a drunk four year-old.

On leaden feet and heavy heart, Georgia followed her husband down the stairs. She waited at the bottom stair, listening for sounds from the computer. After expelling a relieved sigh, she rounded the corner into the living room. Ennis sat at the computer, elbows on the desk, his head in his hands, defeated.

Georgia slid her arm across his shoulders, "Get away from this a minute. Dane's got a beer with your name on it. Or we've got the scotch or bourbon."

He shook his head, thumbed away tears, "I can't leave. If she says anything, anything at all to give us a clue and I'm not here to catch it…"

"Ennis, what could she possibly say that one of us in this room wouldn't hear? Please take a break."

His shoulders tightened beneath her touch, his tone cross, "Fact is she would not be going through this if I'd let her kill him. I deserve to watch this, Georgia. By denying her I also sentenced her to this."

"Rutherford," Mathis called from nearby, "she ain't no killer. She couldn't live with herself if she'd offed him."

"She's not going to live through this, John," his voice caught. He swallowed back the emotion to finish, "You saw her and he's not even close to done with her."

The screen blinked on. The blurry picture focused when Jeffrey took two steps back. He wore his trademark jeans and clean white t-shirt, the latter neatly tucked in the former's waist. He adjusted the camera left then a little bit right. "Perfect," Georgia heard him declare. Jeffrey moved aside an inch. He'd moved to a large bedroom. He positioned the camera higher this time, maybe on a dresser. He aimed it facing what she guessed was a bed since she saw the edge of a dark wood headboard past his right shoulder and a taupe wall behind that.

Jeffrey bent toward the camera, close enough his face engulfed the screen. She stared into black eyes that drove a knife of terror through her. She remembered those cold, soulless eyes and what that expression meant.

"Hello, Georgia," he greeted as if he saw her through the screen. She retreated, accidentally bumping into Dane and Leah in the process. Her husband eased his arm around her waist.

"I assume you and Ennis are curious as to little Anna's condition and whereabouts."

She detected the underlying rage in his voice, like distant thunder forewarning of an approaching storm. She swallowed hard as his dark eyes held her gaze.

"Write this down." He gave her time to grab a pen and paper however Mathis supplied it, offered to transcribe for her.

Jeffrey continued, "You can find her at this location..."

Georgia dissected his phrasing. *Her condition and whereabouts. Find her at this location.* Words that could easily mean a dead child, not a living, breathing, *crying* one.

As he relayed the address, Mathis volunteered, "Ain't that a Baptist church on the corner?"

"That's my church," Georgia replied with a hint of hope.

"You can thank Amber for being so loquacious," Jeffrey proceeded. "She told me what church you attended." He stepped out of visual range to reveal Savannah lying unconscious and splayed out on a queen size bed. Voluminous, dried blood stains ran the length of the mattress. Lines of arterial spray arced across the taupe wall behind the bed, like a painter gone wild while slinging paint from his brush. The scene resembled a horror movie.

Instinct forced her vision to her sister's chest that slowly rose and fell with each shallow breath. Thankfully she was only asleep. The blood came from someone else – probably Amber Martin. Georgia imagined the poor, naïve college girl lying there, struggling against Jeffrey and begging for her life only to become another casualty of his cruelty.

Now Savannah occupied the spot, her wrists and ankles spread wide and secured with straps similar to hospital restraints.

Georgia's heart sank. This was it. This was Jeffrey's coup de grâce. She knew from experience what awaited her sister and if they failed to find her in the next few hours, she *would* die.

Jeffrey looked at his watch, "I'll give you thirty minutes to pick up the insolent little brat and be back at your computer." He winked at the camera, "You don't want to miss what comes next."

22

July 1

Savannah floated down a blazing river in a tiny boat. Fiery lava oozed down the walls that seemed to converge on both sides. The smell of brimstone filled the air. Strangely, though, the heat from the river felt icy cold while the flames licking at her boat promised an instant scorching death.

She pulled her elbows snug to her sides only for the flames to erupt higher. Pain swept her from head to toe. Sweat dripping down her face and body caused a frigid shiver that purged a groan from her depths. There was no respite from the swells of misery. It hurt to breathe the stifling air. It hurt to think. It hurt to simply move.

None of it made sense. The walls, the lava and lake of fire all mixed with the glacial feel of the air around her. The inability to draw a full breath without wanting to scream. It had to be a nightmare, her brain concluded. Just a really bad nightmare. She'd had them since childhood and stress crafted some lulus over the years. This morning's rated as the number one crappiest, most realistic of them all.

Savannah willed herself to wake up but something fought against her. A shadowy haze prevented her from ascending to full consciousness as if an invisible weight pushed her beneath the surface into a twilight slumber. The lake and all its confusing peculiarities faded into a mist of obscurity but the pain remained, a steady tide that rose with inhalations and barely ebbed with exhalations. It extended from her navel to her head and she literally felt broken, as if she'd fallen from a cliff onto a pile of jagged rocks hundreds of feet below. This, she surmised, was either a whopper of a nightmare or she'd died and gone straight to hell.

An odd smell penetrated the fog. It wasn't brimstone as in the nightmare. The sharp coppery odor sliced through the murkiness in her mind. The smell was blood.

"Anna," her hoarse voice called. The name surfaced in mostly a whisper but she tried again, tried for her baby's sake, "Anna…" A vague recollection drifted in. One of her chasing after her daughter before Jeffrey harmed her. The gleam in his dark eyes promised punishment for her child – consequences, he always said – and punishment for a screaming, stubborn toddler likely meant…

Savannah snapped awake. Had she saved Anna? Had she reached her before Jeffrey? No, her brain reminded. She tried but Jeffrey left the room (don't move, he warned her) then her daughter's crying abruptly ceased. The sudden silence could only mean one thing. The most excruciating reality for a parent to bear. The loss of a child. Anna Rose, her introverted headstrong baby, the one that battled for hours upon hours to be born, was probably gone. And unlike Amber Martin's father, Savannah would not choose her daughter's casket or attend her funeral. Ennis would choose two caskets, one for his little girl and the other for his wife, if the latter didn't find a way out of this quick.

She raised her head then promptly flopped back down with a loud groan. She pulled at her legs, trying to close them yet they never budged. Tight restraints on her ankles prohibited any movement. One tug on her arms revealed her wrists were stretched out and secured near the bed corners with thick black Velcro straps. That revelation fell by the wayside when a sharp cough blasted from her throat. A soft cry spilled from her lips. A glowing hot poker of pain stabbed through her right side, see-sawed from her shoulder to her legs. The sweat beading on her skin felt alternately hot and cold, a combination she'd experienced one other time. After Jeffrey Holland beat her bloody with that damn rattan cane. An involuntary shiver jarred her from head to toe, bringing forth another surge of torment.

A second cough rattled at the base of her throat. The previous cough compressed her injured ribs and strained muscles that were already pulled taut from the restraints. She cleared her throat hoping to rid herself of the tickle. *God, let this work,* she prayed. *Another cough will kill me.*

She drew a shallow breath then released it on a whimper, squirmed when the pain seemed to flow into her veins, spread throughout her body like acid eating away at her sanity and spirit. There came a time when a person realized death was the only remedy to end their agony. She'd knocked on that door before, at the cabin with Jeffrey and Cole. She begged God to take her and stop her suffering, to bring her home to her mama. She was not quite there yet but Holland would ensure she not only knocked on that door again but kicked it down to get in. For now, though, she focused on evaluating her physical condition after his tirade. She hadn't experienced broken ribs before – and wasn't entirely sure they *were* broken. Maybe they weren't fractured but just bruised, was the internal pep talk. *Yeah, bruised. If they were broken you'd probably cough up blood. You didn't taste blood. Yeah. They're just bruised.*

The throat tickle caught her off-guard, launching her into a violent spasm. She cried out, writhing in the restraints, instinctively pulling to cradle her side. Tears slid from her eyes. Broken. The ribs were broken.

Damn Jeffrey, she cursed. He left no slack in the straps, leaving her to lie in utter misery, her body tearing itself apart with each cough and spasm.

He'd slammed his foot into her ribs twice for disobeying him. Any parent, she reasoned, would have ignored the *don't move* command if they loved their kids and wanted to protect them. She'd crawled her way to a table, tried levering to her feet. When she collapsed, she fumbled for a handhold and accidentally swiped two trinkets and a small package off the table. Paul Smith's good deed hadn't been in vain. It provided her an address – her location – but what was it? She prodded her brain, struggling to visualize the bold, typewritten address on the package. She winced with another breath but kept her focus on what she'd seen before Jeffrey kicked the daylights out of her. One-one-something-something, that was the number. *One-one... Oh dear God, I'm so miserable...* She squeezed her eyes tighter to purge her self-pity. She had business to tend to – no, she had real *hope* – if she could recall the address. *Come on, Savannah, think. One-one... One-one-three-zero!* That was it. One-one-three-zero. Now what was the street name? It was a crazy name, one so odd she'd never heard of it before. Something-field. She concentrated on what she'd seen. *1130 ...field.* Over and over she ran the partial address until a brief word flashed in her mind. Alpharetta. The house was located in Alpharetta, a suburb twenty-six miles north of Atlanta metro. Sandy Springs, where Georgia lived, was a mere thirteen miles from Alpharetta. Dunwoody, where Savannah resided, was separated by a short four miles from Sandy Springs and only twelve from Alpharetta. While holed up in this house in Alpharetta, Jeffrey was a hop, skip and a jump from either sister.

But where was she *now*? Savannah prodded herself to think before allowing the pain's voice to override her focus. Surely they were at the same address which was 1130... Savannah groaned again, this time in frustration. 1130 *Something*-field in Alpharetta. Keep thinking, try to remember before it's too late, she told herself.

She glanced around the large bedroom with taupe walls and heavy wooden furniture. A ceiling fan spun at a dizzying speed above her. The low hum of an air conditioner whirred somewhere in the distance. Across the large room sat a small sofa and sitting on it – Jeffrey Holland, with his feet propped onto the matching ottoman. He was staring at her.

O   O   O

I'd never been to a sex shop or bondage store before. I left that part to my stepbrother who frequented them with the tail-wagging, drooling excitement a dog shows a bone. Me, I've always been more of a Home Depot man, buying chains by the yard, cable ties by the hundred, anchors, eye bolts and an occasional power tool. A utilitarian do-it-yourself soul, not one prone to skulking the aisles of a sex shop. Until a few weeks ago.

After dispatching Tonya, I needed a good, durable set of restraints fast so I dropped by an adult shop (appropriately named Pleasures) to survey their wares. I stepped inside, lost in amazement and intrigue. The variety of inventory entranced me as I envisioned how I might use such items with my detective. I searched shelf after shelf, row after row in meticulous detail, tested various whips and canes. The store, like a hospital pharmacy, represented Christmas to me. So many nice, useful, fun things – all I needed was Savannah to play with.

Seventy dollars and an hour of window shopping later and I invested in a sturdy set of restraints requiring no back-breaking preparation or reinforcement involving drills or eye bolts.

They are called Under the Bed Restraints. They are similar to the same restraints used in hospitals to restrain combative patients, only those are made of leather, mine are Velcro. I chose the basic style due to my familiarity with the hospital setup. In mere minutes I slid the straps beneath the mattress and positioned the four-point restraints to my satisfaction. Just add Savannah, close the Velcro cuffs around wrists and ankles and voila, the ideal gift for Jeffrey.

I positioned my lovely detective spread-eagled across the bed, all four graceful limbs stretched wide. Men fantasized about such long, toned legs as hers. My stepbrother Cole spent weeks salivating over her, yearning to violate and defile her in the most base manner a man could. In every way a man could. I too am attracted to her beauty, but my fascination lies within her. That will of pure determination, to never surrender.

She's been restless despite the sedative. Since my return she's moaned and whimpered in her sleep. She's called for Ennis, her girls, Georgia and even her parents. No calls for God yet. I'll change that. When she summons her Lord, prays to Him, that's my cue she's reaching her limit. She'll quote scripture first, resort to pleading with God later. I am jealous of this invisible entity she worships. I consider putting her faith and hopes in a myth extremely ignorant for such an intelligent woman. She might as well worship a loaf of bread. At least she could see it. How many lives have I saved with my surgical skills, my gloved hands covered in a patient's blood while I clamp an artery? How many have I saved with my scalpel, excising a diseased or failing organ then stitching the wound closed? If anyone is a god, it is me. I have the power and ability to save a life – or end it in any number of ways. If her God is all powerful, why didn't He stop me from killing? She claims her God is *loving and merciful. If He loved the true believer tied to this bed, why hasn't He saved her? Why doesn't He stop me? Seeing her stir awake, I wonder if she's posed those questions to Him. Why, Lord, why don't you rescue me? I am Your good and faithful servant, singing Your praises, sharing Your Word. Why won't You spare me?*

Savannah's eyes drift open from their drug-induced sleep. She's confused as to her surroundings, her mind still clouded from the sedative. She blinks once, twice, clearing her vision. It will be any time now.

I watch her give a tug on her wrist. She repeats the action with a bit more determination. Now it begins dawning on her. The third effort rocks the bed and even with the resulting groan, her sudden burst of strength surprises me. She tests the bondage store purchase with her struggles but to their credit, the straps remain strong and tenacious like her. The futility of her efforts does not discourage her. Racking coughs do. The first one spurs a cry, her body wrenching in the painful spasm. The second produces a louder cry, more useless writhing until finally she falls limp on the bed sighing a groan.

I rise from the small sofa in Tonya's bedroom and go to the bathroom where I draw up a bowl of warm water. I return to see hatred blazing in Savannah's eyes. Her body flushes from head to toe, the anger bringing a soft pink glow to her cheeks and her breasts. Her struggling ebbs when pain from her ribs rolls through. I'm afraid my temper caused a few fractures but I'd forewarned her of dire consequences if she disobeyed me. I hear her pained shallow breaths, the ones that can get a person into serious trouble if they don't force deeper inhalations but my detective won't need to worry about pneumonia. She won't be alive long enough to develop it.

Her hatred subsides when she sees my bowl of water.

Eagerness and hope brighten her eyes, "I'm thirsty." Her throat works at the sight of the drip, drip, drip of precious liquid into the decorative ceramic bowl. Her tongue licks parched lips, her vision fixates on the sponge dribbling a small steady stream into the container. "Could I have a drink?" she asks.

I would grant her wish except, "What's that special word you taught your girls to say? May I have a drink..."

Without hesitation she says please. *I smile, draw water into the sponge, "Open."*

With a cringe, her head raises to meet me and her lips part, eager for a drink of water whether warm, hot or cold. It reminds me of a baby bird begging for food. I give the sponge a gentle squeeze. A narrow stream of water trickles into her mouth and she swallows greedily. She opens again. I do not offer more.

"May I have another drink please?"

"Only one," I reply, impressed by her courtesy. "Too much at once will make you sick and you can't afford that." I dribble more into her waiting mouth, watch her swallow. A stubborn drop lingers at the corner. She quickly sweeps her tongue over her lips, claiming it. For a moment I see bliss in her expression. Instant, yet temporary relief. She wants more. Entranced by the wet sponge, the sparkle of delicious water glistening on my hand. Surprisingly she refrains from soliciting a third

drink. *This appears to be a bargaining chip to me.* "If you're a good girl, I'll give you another drink in a few minutes."

Her focus breaks from the sponge, lifts her gaze to mine. She's measuring my words for a lie. No, I'm not lying. I do not break promises unless I feel cheated. She would be foolish to try a second time as evidenced by the bruise ripening on her right side.

I drop the soft sponge into the pleasantly warm water. What I intend to do next will test her. I expect her anger to resurface and if it doesn't, I will take my plan a step further, pushing her. I will ask How badly do you want that drink, Savannah? Can you, *will you,* behave yourself long enough to earn it?

I dip the sponge in the water, wring it out. Savannah pulls at the restraints, keeping her vision on my hand. I repeat the action then take the damp sponge, place it at the side of her right breast. She grimaces at the pressure, tries to retreat from my touch. I gently admonish, "What have you got against sponge baths?"

"Only that you're giving it."

"That comment is my thanks for giving you two drinks of water?" I shake my head, "Tsk-tsk, Savannah. You must not want a third. Watch yourself or you'll lose that reward for good behavior." *I ease the sponge around the plump flesh, rinse and take up where I left off. Methodically I wash her blood-streaked breast, wringing the blood into the already pink water. The sponge circles beneath and around her breast and I watch her nipple tighten in the cool air. I lay the warm sponge beneath it and lightly rub around it. Savannah alternately squirms and cringes. I can tell she is uncomfortable with my touch, even with a mere sponge in my hand. I want her uncomfortable, on edge but I want to show her that my hands can produce pleasurable sensations, not just pain. So I rinse the sponge again, glide it down her stomach, washing more stain from her. Rinse, wash, rinse. Savannah shivers from the ceiling fan circulating the cold air. The master bath has heated towel racks so I fetch a warm, soft towel to dry her with. Her muscles relax beneath the cozy heat of the fluffy towel and the motion of my hands nearly lulls her eyes closed.*

I head back to the bathroom for a fresh bowl of warm water. I dip the sponge in, then ease it below her navel heading south. Her eyes spring open, center on mine. I glide the wet sponge between her thighs. She pulls at her ankles, telling me to stop.

"No. There is blood here too." I rub then rinse and return to the same area. The pubic hair is neat and trimmed as I remembered from years before. Only now one or two shiny silver strands gleam from the dark hair.

I slip the sponge between the folds of skin, concentrate on rubbing one spot. That magical spot.

Her hips jerk, her lips purse. She tries to wriggle away from the friction but only manages to stir up additional pain in her ribs.

I move the sponge aside, press my thumb between the warm folds of skin until settling on the magic button, circling and rubbing.

She strains in her bonds, "Stop it, Jeffrey." That warning, spoken with a strained, broken voice makes me smile. She's helpless yet anyone who heard those words also heard the violence in them. She hates me touching her but despises that I'm touching her there.

This is new to her, my gentle nature, the intimacy of my touch. Oh, I know how to please a woman. Certain women, that is. The ones I like. And I do like Savannah. "I'm actually pretty good at this. I've had women scream for different reasons other than pain, you know."

"I said stop."

My thumb continues its rhythmic motion while the tips of my index and middle fingers poise at her entrance. All her muscles clench, especially the ones "down there" – her only meager defense against an invasion. I see her left hand roll to a fist, her eyes squeeze tight with sheer determination to prevent me from slipping my fingers inside her. I tease, "Women have complimented my technique but also my long fingers."

"This woman will tell you where to stick your technique and your long fingers and it's not in any orifice of mine."

I slow the motion down, feeling the little nub swell beneath my thumb. Her eyes open then narrow at me. She's angry at me and herself. Her body is betraying her. The reaction is a purely physical response, one she cannot control – but the idea of my touch arousing her is shameful and repulsive. In her mind it is unforgivable.

"Stop. Touching. Me." Evenly spaced words drop like boulders.

If she wasn't restrained I'd heed the tone in her voice. It promised a busted nose, maybe even a black eye or two. If she could reach them, that is.

My thumb still massages her but my fingers remain nestled against her, ready to show her how talented my hands are with other, more pleasurable activities, "If you refuse, you forfeit your drink of water."

"Shove your damn drink. Leave me alone!" *she yells, her hips bucking to displace my hand. The voice cracks but she does not. A soft cry punctuates her flare of temper but the anger remains strong in her expression.*

I withdraw from between her thighs to see her body slacken, an anguished whimper escaping her lips. Her tantrum has deepened the throbbing in her shoulder and ribs. Fresh perspiration glistens on her forehead. Each breath ends in a pitiful childlike mewl.

I place the sponge and bowl on the dresser. She thinks she has won this little battle. I get up, meander to the other side of the bed. I know exactly what I'll do. I sit at her hip, place my hand on her stomach. She stares at me with that deadly glare I'm well accustomed to seeing. My touch skims up to her left breast, palms it, gives it a tender squeeze, "I think you've forgotten one important fact."

"I told you to leave me alone," *she cringes on the words, biting down on her lip at the conclusion. Whatever reserve of endorphins her brain has, she's squandering them by arguing with me, fighting me.*

"And I told you, remember who's tied down and who's not." *Before she voices a complaint, my mouth covers her left breast, sucking gently and raking my tongue in slow strokes across the nipple.*

Savannah's struggle renews, her body writhing to push me away,

*then she stops, again surrendering to her side's protests.   "Get off me,"
she whimpers past the quick, shallow breaths.*

*I don't of course. My teeth close around the nipple. I don't bite
but the threat is there when I pinch as a warning. A different Savannah
emerges, a fearful one, terrified I'll follow through. My hand eases over
her hip, down her thigh. I remember where the scars are from the sharp
raps of my caning five years earlier. I trace them from memory. My
teeth ease their hold on the nipple but I continue sucking and teasing
with my mouth and tongue until she squirms again, straining in earnest.*

*My fingers ease up the inside of her thigh. The muscles go rigid
once more. She tenses while trying to squeeze her legs together to stop
me but she can't. My fingers journey up, up, up toward the hot nether
region. Again they stop at the apex. The coarse pubic hair tickles my
knuckles as I brush against it, "Tell me, Savannah. Are you a moaner or
screamer when you come?"*

23

July 1

Savannah Rutherford is a screamer. No matter her fractured ribs, she is a bona fide banshee. Whether she screams upon climax I would not venture a guess but the woman possesses an earsplitting shriek that collapses an average person's brain inside their skull. She also suffers a debilitating case of the Blue Streak. One threat of sexual violation set off this volcanic eruption. One. Paltry. Threat.

Savannah hurls words at me that would positively mortify her cubs. I assume over the years Ennis experienced a shot or two of the vicious tongue however she's saved the bluest streak for me.

Finally taking enough abuse, I backhand her, stunning her silent. She blinks a few times to regain her bearings while I regain my composure. In our history together, my fingers have entered only one of Savannah's "orifices" as she put it. It was her mouth and I shoved two pills down her throat (at the cabin) and earlier when I silenced her with the handkerchief. Today when I withdrew my mouth from her breast and my hand from her privates (which hadn't dared penetrate the pearly gates), I stood to unbutton my jeans then stopped. Had I been reduced to my stepbrother's base animal desires? To take what I could before claiming the very last part of a person – their life?

I never intended to rape Savannah because it never appealed to me. However after five years of dreaming of this woman, her image filling my mind day and night, her voice caressing me (even with her vilest words), I think I actually care about her. In my mind it is not rape. Neither is it making love because I do not love her. But this new feeling confuses me – why I want to have sex with her. She watches the crotch of my jeans, sees my arousal swell and lengthen. Her eyes narrow with a warning, "Don't you dare."

In a moment of folly, I imagine crawling atop her, aligning my body with hers. I wonder how she might feel, those clenched muscles trying to prevent my entry. I give one solid thrust to breach the fortress and slide to her warm depth. Those same muscles that tried denying me now embrace me tightly inside her. In my mind I look at her face but her eyes are squeezed shut like locked doors, blocking my gaze from hers. There is no intimacy in our union, no sign of pleasure or passion in her features. Instead, she expresses disgust and venomous contempt for my actions, for me, and my degradation of her. Believe it or not I respect Savannah, her strength and courage. Her loyalty and love for her family. I respect her too much to violate her in such a way. My goal isn't to sexually assault this intelligent, headstrong woman (because that's what she considers it). My goal is to kill her. And it is time to proceed with my plan.

I slip on a pair of latex gloves. I cannot work with her wriggling in the restraints or her shouting for help in the silence surrounding us. "No one can hear you," I say. "The house sits on a parcel of land surrounded by trees in every direction."

This, of course, does nothing to dissuade her. My hand itches to backhand her again, this time harder. I reel in my anger because I want her awake, not knocked senseless.

I walk to the dresser and pick up a large bore needle. It is a lengthy, imposing sight to those not familiar with it. Savannah recoils, her wide-eyed stare evolving from raging fury to chaste fear. She knows what's next. So when she draws in a deep breath – even against the pain of those ribs, I realize the resulting scream will be memorable. I set the needle back down and retrieve the sedative again – just as she belts out a scream for help that physically jolts me, jars my concentration. I draw up a minimal dose, enough to relax her without inducing unconsciousness. She struggles in the restraints but I grasp her elbow, immobilizing the arm, locate a vein and slide the needle in. It is disappointing that the sedative is required but it's also expected. Savannah will not go down without a substantial fight.

I watch the clock. I give the sedative two full minutes to take effect. In that time, she slackens to the bed, her fight reduced to a fraction of its previous potency. Her eyelids droop but do not quite shut. She is awake and aware but docile. It is the best I can hope for.

I turn her head aside to expose the right side of her neck. Her carotid artery thrums a steady leisure tempo, not the frenzied pounding prior to the sedation.

Next I swipe an alcohol prep pad from her ear down the length of her neck to her clavicle. I repeat this action in a slow, soothing motion while speaking softly to her. The repetitive stroking is not only meant to calm her but also to stimulate the jugular to the surface. Plus, I want to savor this moment, extending it as long as possible. Savannah shivers and I stroke her arm, assuring her this part will be over soon.

I reach for the IV line, lay it beside her hip. Normally to distend the jugular vein, protocol dictates I should tilt her head fifteen to thirty degrees lower than her feet but I've done this numerous times and my own method has yet to fail me. I press down just above the clavicle to help engorge the jugular. The pressure rouses a whimper from her. The wound I incised below the bone, my beloved number 10, still seeps blood, still radiates pain down her arm and chest.

When she settles, I study her breathing to memorize the timing of the short, rhythmic respirations. Inhalation causes the vein to collapse, so I keep the pressure firm above the clavicle and time my move to correspond with her exhalation. I take the needle in hand, position it over the jugular and wait.

"Jeffrey," she whispers.

It sounds plaintive, almost pleading. Almost. I tenderly shush her, cautioning, "Don't move. This is extremely delicate. Be very still."

"Jeffrey, please. My girls and Ennis..."

She's begun to cry. I keep the pressure steady while talking calmly to her but nothing consoles her. She keeps talking about her kids and Ennis. *Her emotion throws off her breathing and my timing. My frustration mounts. Her sudden meltdown is ruining my ideal image of this procedure. I try for a more authoritarian approach,* "Do not cry, Savannah. You knew this would happen. You knew your fate when you agreed to trade Lily and Georgia for your life so don't cry." *Now the jugular virtually disappears. It is there, I see it, but with her sobbing I cannot insert the needle for fear of missing the vein and perhaps jabbing the carotid by mistake. I refuse to sedate her further. Part of my five year fantasy is for this woman to show me how strong she really is, how much fight she has and how long she will struggle to live. Having her die as she sleeps is not going to happen.* "Stop crying, Savannah," *I demand, pressing harder above the clavicle, imploring the vein to appear long enough I can insert the needle. When I drive my fingertips deeper into the flesh, she shrieks, writhing anew on the bed. I fear she is winding up for a long battle since she seems wide awake – or awake enough to hinder my objective.*

I concentrate on that vein, staring at it while my other hand now strokes it, trying to lure it to the surface. I do this as she drones on about her children growing up without her, how her family means the world to her, and how, if she gets her hands on me, she'll gut me like a fish.

Ah. Now *there's the Savannah I remember. And at that instant, when she sighs upon a sob, I slide the tip of the needle in. The prick startles her. She winces at the twinge. For the moment she lies stunned and I advance the needle deep into the vein, hearing her muted whimper as I do so.* "Do... not... move," *I warn, taking great care to slide the long needle home. A flashback of blood appears in the chamber. Perfect. I reach for the transparent dressing and tape. She lies absolutely still, I assume in complete shock of her situation.*

I secure the IV line with extra strips of tape, ensuring my efforts remain intact no matter how she flails or wrestles around. Then I drape the tubing down into a large, steel stockpot I found in Tonya's kitchen cabinet. The first sign of blood peeks into the tube, hesitates, then ever-so-slowly trickles down, down, down the tube toward the shiny silver pot. Just one more thing and I can sit back and enjoy.

I fetch a syringe and a vial of the anticoagulant Heparin. While drawing up her first dose of blood thinner, I smile down at her, "Five years ago you said two words to me. I obsessed over them day and night, probably because at the time you were right. But now, my lovely detective, I will repay your kindness, so to speak." I lean down but do not whisper the words. I want her family to hear them too. "I win."

I slip the needle into her arm, push the plunger. I hear her continue her spiel about family, but this time it takes on a tone of finality. She is saying goodbye to her husband, daughters and sister.

Savannah pulls against the restraints but not too hard because, in her heart, she knows it's over and I have, at long last, conquered her.

24

July 1

Georgia's eyes closed tight, shutting out the awful sight and memory of being in Savannah's position. She recalled details in frightening clarity even after five long years. The prick of a long needle piercing her flesh, the sensation of it sliding into her neck. The pounding of her heart making her dizzy, the weakness creeping in. The smell of her own blood emptying from her body.

She heard the queen size bed creak when her sister yanked at the restraints. Georgia held a hand to her stomach. Nausea boiled and rumbled inside her all day. Her throat convulsed to hold the growing urge at bay. She wasn't sure how long she could battle the sensation before bolting for the bathroom.

This was not how her sister should die, she told God. Being hunted then murdered by a monster released from prison on a technicality. A monster undeserving to walk the planet with good, decent people. *Especially* not someone who protected others all her adult life the way Savannah had.

Her sister's pleas broke Georgia's daze. Lying there, Savannah mentioned Lily and Anna. She didn't want them growing up without her. Overwrought, her tears flowed in earnest, streaming down her face. Georgia saw defeat in her sister's watery blue eyes when she spoke Anna's name. She assumed her baby girl had met a tragic demise when, in fact, the child was traumatized but very much alive. Savannah continued pouring out her emotions while, in her own way also pleading with Jeffrey. She fell short of actually begging which incensed him. His main goal besides killing her was to hear her beg for her life. Georgia suspected he wanted Savannah to prove all women were alike, that they resorted to tears and pleading at some point. What he could not know was that as a teenager, Savannah stopped pleading for mercy or leniency because their father punished his children for doing so. It extended beatings into fanatical marathons that forced their mother to stop them – if she could. So Jeffrey Holland's efforts would ultimately fail in that regard. An occasional "please" was all he'd get because Savannah trained herself that begging never worked.

Do not cry, Savannah, Jeffrey's voice thundered from the speakers. *You knew your fate when you traded Lily and Georgia for your life so don't cry.*

The declaration stunned Georgia. Her knees weakened until two arms – Dane's – enfolded her, brought her snug against him. She had no idea Savannah saved her by going with Jeffrey. She heard Lily tell Ennis *Mama went with the man and he told me to stay with Aunt Georgia.* She assumed the trade was for Lily only. Today marked the second time

Savannah put herself between Georgia and Jeffrey – and Georgia couldn't even reciprocate by locating her baby sister to save her.

"You didn't know about it," Ennis slurred, directing his statement to Georgia. He still sat at her desk, one hand fisted around the neck of a Jim Beam bottle. He'd not only indulged in the bourbon, he'd soaked himself in it for the last half hour.

"I had no clue," she heard herself say. She savored the comfort Dane's arms provided. A refuge from the raging storm around them. The whole day exhausted her. She'd done everything in her power to help, including calling Duke, all to no avail.

Ennis poured himself another shot of bourbon, tossed it back in one gulp.

Georgia hadn't witnessed that amount of consumption since Savannah's drinking days. Their father downed scotch by the bottle but only Savannah and Ennis knocked back bourbon like water. In the last thirty minutes he'd swilled four shots and truthfully Ennis Rutherford made a lousy drunk. The booze loosened his tongue, muddled his manners and generally produced a testy, slurring grump. Neither her sister nor Ennis tolerated bourbon well. Oh, they held it down fine. Could probably drink plenty of people under the table too. But liquor transformed their personalities in a negative way. Ennis became mouthy, Savannah got mouthy *and* physical.

Georgia looked at the screen to see Jeffrey's hand brace Savannah's head to the side. His other hand held the needle. The long needle that gave Georgia countless nightmares and sleepless nights. She heard her sister cry out *no* as her futile battle continued.

Jeffrey ran out of patience, again ordering her to stop crying. He still pressed just above the collarbone, the fingertips bearing down in the flesh hard enough to illicit a loud whimper. Five years ago he'd done the same to Georgia. She remembered the steady pressure – and the waiting. The long wait while he stared at her, memorizing her breathing pattern for the right moment to slide the needle in.

Savannah's inconsolable crying continued. She said something then ended it with, "If I ever get my hands on you, I'll gut you like a fish." She cringed immediately after. He'd pushed the needle in, cautioned her not to move. Georgia saw the blood before he finished taping the IV in place. Time now began ticking on her sister's life. Jeffrey added the first shot of blood thinner. He proceeded in a taunting, almost mocking tone then ended his spiel on two simple words – *I win* – that were spoken in such a casual manner, he sounded as if he claimed victory at Gin Rummy, not robbed her sister's life drop by precious drop.

As the thick, red liquid slowly inched its way along the clear tube, Georgia wiped away her own tears, looked away.

"You remember this, don't you, Georgia?" Jeffrey called. She turned to see him leaning toward the camera until his face filled her computer screen. She instinctively backed away as he winked, "Too bad you can't tell your sister how it feels for your life to drain from your body. How the weakness sets in, the confusion." She heard perverse glee in his voice, "Your heart starts pumping faster, doesn't it? A fluttering that causes your breathing to increase but you just can't get enough air."

She shuddered at his spot-on description. No, she couldn't warn Savannah what to expect but he had. Her sister heard every word. Jeffrey Holland mastered his psychopathic qualities long ago, torturing women physically but he also refined the art of psychological torture. By divulging those hideous details, he got two for the price of one, taunting them both with the awful memories *and* what was to come.

A hand on Georgia's shoulder nearly shattered her composure. Dane stepped in front of her, blocking Jeffrey's face, and tried to bring her into his embrace. She refused. "Go upstairs with Lily," he pleaded.

But she had to stay just in case she saw a way to find her sister. Walking away meant giving up and she would never give up on Savannah.

Jeffrey glanced into a stainless steel stockpot collecting Savannah's blood. His voice was eerily soft, "Don't worry, Savannah. You're not dying anytime soon." He drew the blunt edge of the scalpel around her right breast, "We have a few other things to do before that happens."

A sharp pain in her hand snapped Georgia from the screen. Tiny lines of blood oozed to the surface of her palm. She clenched her fist so tight, the nails sank into the flesh. She stripped a tissue from a Kleenex box on her desk and held it to the wounds. She, Ennis, Mathis, and Leah all stared at the screen. Georgia shook her head, her frustration escalating, "I don't see anything that could identify where the house is."

"All we heard," Mathis said, "was the house is on a section of land with trees around it on every side. That could be anywhere."

"I never got this far with your sister," Jeffrey told Savannah. "You managed to save her before the good part even began. Isn't it ironic she's watching this, unable to return the favor?"

Georgia wrote stories upon stories about people who slashed throats, fatally shot others, knifed and even dismembered their victims. She'd experienced homicidal feelings before – when Toby Jackson tried to rape Savannah then again when her own ex-husband Matthew broke down her front door and rampaged through her house. But neither seemed to compare to this burning desire to end Jeffrey Holland's life.

The blade of Jeffrey's scalpel nudged against Savannah's right nipple. He toyed with her, applying pressure then backing off. Her sister's cheeks already lost their rosiness, not from lack of blood but from stark terror.

Georgia's vision rose from Jeffrey's hand to her sister who seemed to look squarely at her through the camera. Savannah began saying her goodbyes to Ennis, the girls, the rest of her family. Her whole body shivered and her mouth was dry, forcing her to work her throat and tongue for moisture, "Georgia, tell Peter and Bob I'll miss them. Tell Bob I appreciate everything he's done for me."

"Bob?" Ennis questioned, setting the Jim Beam down. Confusion knitted his brow. "Isn't he the sorehead customer who slams his fist on the table?"

Georgia wiped a tear, "Evidently they grew closer than I thought."

Ennis pushed to his feet, wobbled then steadied himself with a hand on the heavy mahogany desk. "Well," he spoke with bleary-eyed gloom, "I managed to fail my wife twice. I coulda prevented this years ago an' let her bash his head in but stupid-like," he shrugged, "I didn't." He tossed back another belt of Jim then stepped past Georgia on unsteady legs. He turned to her with tear-filled, bloodshot eyes, "I'm so sorry, Georgia."

"Ennis, it's not your fault–"

"I can do a lot but this," he pointed to the screen, his emotions unraveling, "*this* is too much." He shook his head, trudged toward the downstairs bedroom.

She watched him stagger off, shaking his head. She wondered if he'd given up on Savannah. Sure, leaving was easier. She'd also taken time away from the horror – but only to regroup. She came back to support her sister whether Savannah felt her presence or not. She was *there.* Maybe she judged him too harshly because of the past but Ennis walked away with a drunken determination that, in her opinion, said he was not returning.

His actions surprised her but mostly they just plain hurt and that hurt quickly yielded to anger. She bowed up but pursed her lips tight to trap the scathing lecture building since the day he'd accused Savannah of sleeping with Duke Shelton.

Ennis assumed Savannah and their father possessed the hottest tempers but he'd soon discover the Prince temper was more than inherited. Sometimes it became a badge of honor and a damn efficient weapon.

"You're giving up on her?" Dane accused, verbalizing her thoughts.

Ennis stopped. Leah retreated beside Georgia and out of the way of the oncoming storm while Cyrus stepped forward, shielding the women and preparing to intervene between the brothers. Oh, they'd definitely need some intervening, Georgia thought. Anyone who saw the Rutherford boys argue realized they did so physically. They used words too but only as a garnish to the whole smorgasbord of raw power they all embodied. And Georgia sensed a hell of a fight brewing between Dane and Ennis, especially when Ennis swiveled on one foot with a glare that sent even *her* back a step.

Ennis's eyes narrowed to slits, "Wha'd you say to me?"

"You heard me." Dane stabbed a finger at him, "You're giving up on Savannah. You're quitting on your wife and our daddy is rolling over in his grave at the shame of it."

Ennis bulled toward his brother in a lumbering, stumbling gait that appeared half-comical. His nostrils flared as he drew his fist to his shoulder, "I'll lay you out for accusin' me of quittin'."

Dane met him face to face, not backing down, "Then tell me your word for walking away. I remember a girl shoving a gun under a guy's chin – her finger on the trigger – because he shot and nearly killed you. *She* didn't give up on *you*."

Ennis threw a feeble punch. Dane shooed it aside. Georgia and Cyrus stepped between them, their backs together, Georgia facing Dane, Cyrus facing Ennis.

"Let's all calm down," she said.   Then leaned to her husband whispering, "He's sloshed and you'll never get through to him."

Dane glared at his brother, "Drunk ain't no excuse for abandoning his wife."

Ennis bucked against Cyrus, "You think it's easy for me to watch that? To see her dying in front of me?"

Dane shot back, "Do you think it's easy for Georgia to watch it? For *any* of us?"

"Settle down, both of you." Cyrus's deep voice warned and with his sheer size, Ennis would have been foolish to ignore it.

Ennis shouted past Cyrus's shoulder, his speech suddenly clearing somewhat as he carefully enunciated, "I know what she did for me when I was shot! I'd blow Holland's brains out *if I knew where they were!* I can't even *find* her to *help* her. She's the love of my life and she's dying alone, wondering where the hell I am. I've got so many regrets. I regret I didn't kill him myself. I regret I accused her of sleeping with Shelton." He thrust a finger at the computer, "I regret I can't save my wife from that bastard."

"Runnin' off ain't helping her either." Dane drew Georgia into his embrace, "You're supposed to stay with her, even now. Especially now. She knows you love her so be there for her when she needs you the most. Don't let her die alone."

"I'm not leaving her but I need a few minutes away from this." He angrily swiped his tears with the back of his hand. "You've all had your time so why can't I?"

"Rutherford," Mathis called from the computer, "pull it together and tell me what the hell she's doing." He pointed to the screen. Specifically at her left hand.

Leah and Georgia leaned closer, watched as Savannah stared at the camera, her hand shifting in shaky, erratic movements. She made a fist then lifted her index finger once then twice, then extended her thumb, index and middle fingers then she made a fist.

"What the hell *is* she doing?" Ennis rubbed his temple, sounding close to losing his mind. "Anyone know what all that is?"

A glimmer of hope parted Georgia's desperation. She smiled, "I *do* know what that is. And that's why she specifically mentioned Bob." She ran to call Duke Shelton. While waiting for someone to answer, she glanced back at the screen. Savannah's fingers curled into a loose fist like she gripped a golf ball in her palm. Then turned her fist up, extended two fingers upward. "Please pick up," she whispered impatiently in the receiver. "C'mon, Duke, pick up. I know what she's doing. I can finally help her."

Mathis mimicked the movements, his brow furrowing.

Savannah closed her hand, extended her pinky finger. Again Mathis aped the motion, still confused.

"That's an *I*," Lily exclaimed, sending everyone in the room into wide-eyed alarm. The child stood two steps from the base of the stairs and held to a baluster to aid in her descent.

Everyone converged toward her but Mathis caught her first, propped her on his hip, started back up the stairs with her, "Hey, kid, where's your buddy Lego Man?"

The upstairs bathroom door creaked open and Abel rushed down the stairs to reclaim the child. Mathis frowned at him, "You had one job. One lousy job. Keep the kid upstairs..."

Abel returned a more intimidating frown than Mathis could ever muster, "Nature called." He put on a smile for Lily, "Come here, Tiny. Let's go back–"

"Mr. Mathis," Lily interrupted, "here's how you say *hi*. I showed Abel how to do it too. Watch." She curled her hand into a tiny fist then stuck out the index and middle fingers as if pointing across the room, "That's the *H*". Then she repeated John's attempt at the *I*. "That's the *I*. See? It's easy!"

"Yes, sign language," Duke concurred when Georgia called. "Aurora learned it as a child because her mother was deaf."

Duke was a systematic being, intent on one goal at a time. Despite his questionable lifestyle, Duke Shelton was a financial genius who took a sizable inheritance and multiplied it until he was, without a doubt, one of the state's richest residents. His wisdom and aggressive, almost predatory, choices in investments paid off in mountains of money. He had a razor sharp focus for business and pleasure, an unrelenting desire to have his way and make things happen. He hadn't risen to the top by being weak or indecisive. This conversation with Mr. Shelton took on a different tone than the others with him that day. He had enough answers to put a plan in action, "Savannah is signing an address. My men are on their way now."

Just let her live, she prayed. Lord, just let Savannah live. She cupped her hand around the phone's mouthpiece, whispering, "What's the address?"

"It's at Lake Windward in Alpharetta. One of the upscale subdivisions with acreage around the homes."

Frowning, she said, "That's not an address, Duke."

"No, Beauty, it is *not* an address," he confirmed with a tone cautioning *and do not ask for it either.* "I refuse to disclose that information for fear the whole Prince/Rutherford clan might converge on Holland and exterminate the animal. Not to mention what her colleagues will do to him."

Her brain booted Insanely Happy Georgia out the door and slammed it. Really Pissed Off Georgia took her place, "Don't you think he deserves that?"

"Of course he does," Duke replied with his usual calm. "But don't *you* think it prudent that Lily and Anna have at least a few blood relatives on this side of the prison bars? They need parents and if Savannah survives, it would be nice if conjugal visits weren't required to conceive a third child, am I correct?"

Don't bother me with common sense. I want revenge for my sister. "Jeffrey deserves more than being thrown in prison. You see what happened this time. Five short years for murdering nine women–"

"Beauty, if my men get their hands on Holland, he will not leave that residence alive. That is a promise."

Oh. Well, that certainly sounded more appropriate. Georgia

agreed that the whole family would be in jail if they found Jeffrey. Better to let Duke's men handle the situation and end the bastard once and for all. "Okay, but at least give me the street name. I swear I won't tell a soul."

"The street is Muirfield Court. You can deduce the house number from Savannah's signing."

"Thank you, Duke."

"My pleasure. I am grateful she is resourceful. It may have saved her life. I've dispatched an ambulance to the address. They will take her to Kaiser-Lee."

25

July 4

Lord, let her live. Georgia repeatedly prayed since her phone conversation with Duke. *Lord, let her live.* In retrospect, she should have prayed *Lord, let her live and be whole again...*

The hospital room brimmed with family. Except for Dane and the girls (who were at home), everyone claimed their personal perch – chairs, the sofa or the window ledge. Those who didn't flirt with napping either stared out the window or stared at Savannah lying in the bed. The sight, while miraculous, also hurt to see. She lay unconscious and dependant on a ventilator. They waited days for her to regain consciousness and every passing minute eroded a tiny bit of hope, dug the uncertainty deeper.

Georgia yearned to write in her journal. Typing served more than putting words on a screen. She poured her thoughts and feelings into the machine. The thing was better than a shrink. In the past, one hour with her computer describing sights, sounds, and memories helped relieve some tension. She hoped it worked so effortlessly again but doubted it would considering the gravity of the situation.

Georgia waited for the laptop's background to appear. When it did, an immediate swell of emotion forced her to swallow hard. The family photo taken last Christmas showed a happy little crowd. Georgia and Dane, R.J., Seth and his family, and Savannah, Ennis and the girls. Lily and Anna claimed a parent apiece, Lily with Mama, Anna with Daddy. Georgia temporarily forgot the photo served as her computer's background image. Now she fought back tears, praying no one in the room noticed.

She clicked on the blue *W* icon accessing the portal to her journal. Her last entry had been two days before the whole nightmare began.

Once Word loaded, she selected the correct document then waited. Scrolling down, she stopped at the final sentence of the last entry. *I can't wait to tell Savannah.* The thrill of telling her sister she might finally, at long last, be pregnant was too exciting to delay but she had. With Amber Martin's murder, Georgia felt the timing was inappropriate. She recalled her excitement of picking up the pregnancy test. The anticipation of waiting to use it. She waited on that too, just so her joy would carry over when she called her sister with the good news. *I can't wait to tell Savannah...*

Unfortunately there was nothing to tell her sister. The night before Jeffrey abducted Savannah, nature dealt Georgia the first of many cruel blows that weekend. She went to bed with her period, not a baby in her belly.

Georgia rested her fingers on the keyboard. The *Home Row.*
She closed her eyes, shored up the courage to plunge into a portion of the
living hell they'd experienced. She took a deep breath and let her fingers
lead the way:

Tuesday
July 4th
8:30 P.M.

While the city celebrates Independence Day with picnics,
family reunions and fireworks, the six of us (me, Ennis,
Daddy, Seth, Leah, and Mama Rutherford) sit in this quiet
hospital room listening to the rhythmic drone of a ventilator.
The last few days have tested our family. A person discovers
the depth of their physical and emotional strength during
their most difficult times. Not to mention the depth of their
faith in God. To be honest mine is shaken. Not broken –
yet – but shaken to its absolute foundation because of the
images on the computer, Savannah's screams, her suffering…
My sister did not deserve this, I stormed at God. She did
not deserve it once, much less twice and unequivocally not
three times.

   The minutes pressed on to hours, the hours stretched past
six, eight, ten then eighteen. Eighteen long, excruciating
hours she suffered at Jeffrey Holland's hands.

As believers we go to church, we read the Good Book. We pray for protection and peace for our loved ones. We depend on God. We live on faith that is tested on occasion, sometimes with simple problems, others with tragic events. My faith in God wavered that day and as I look at her now – her eyes closed with no response to voice or touch – my faith continues to reel, to find balance again. *She did not deserve this, Lord. Hasn't she been tested enough?* Savannah lost her faith when our mother died. After my sister and Ennis married, he helped her regain a foothold on the subject of God. I'm grateful to him for that. They joined the Dunwoody Baptist Church shortly after Lily's birth. Unless their job schedule conflicts, they are regular Sunday churchgoers now. I fear the last few days might destroy Savannah's faith as our mother's passing did. I fear my sister will resort to drinking again as she had long before Mama drew her last breath. My biggest fear is that this latest encounter with Jeffrey will change her forever and the loving, devoted sister I grew up with will no longer exist. And all this depends on whether she regains consciousness.

I'll never write about what I witnessed on my computer Saturday. It breaks my heart to revisit it in any respect. Flashes of that day sneak in during quiet times, mostly at night when the hospital's noises subside and voices lull in the hallways. I try to block the memories but they are too fresh.

It will take time for their sharp edges to soften and fade. Years. Maybe never.

Losing my mother to cancer, a devious, malicious disease that stole her life by agonizing degrees, was the worst time in my life. Sunday morning is now its indisputable equal. Ennis, Leah and I arrived at Kaiser-Lee at one fifteen that morning. Paramedics wheeled a gurney through the emergency entrance and we three watched them sprint past us as if they ran a race and were losing. Two saline bags hung on a metal hook above Savannah, the intravenous lines leading to two IV needles, one in each of her hands. The most disturbing image, however, was the third paramedic utilizing the manual resuscitator.

I trailed the paramedics, begging them for answers they never gave. They concentrated on keeping Savannah alive – a task that looked iffy judging by Savannah's pale. I remember calling her name as they passed by. I remember being distraught. I also remember Leah's sudden, gentle embrace to comfort me. She told me to have faith that Savannah would be okay. At that point, I ran hot and cold about God. I went ahead with a prayer for Him to save her – and hoped He heard me because I wasn't so sure He'd listened during the last eighteen hours. I mainly concentrated on my sister, to send her one clear, specific message. *Don't you dare give up, Savannah Charlene.*

You've got so many people who love you and are rooting for you. Don't you dare give up.

From the emergency room they transferred her to surgery. I don't recall how long Savannah remained in the ER while they fought to stabilize her. I only recall the ten hour gap from seeing her on the gurney to seeing her in ICU. The operation to repair her shoulder and arm turned out successful, the surgeon said. He added her ribs were fractured but not in danger of puncturing a lung. He also told us she'd be in ICU – then he dropped the bomb. Due to the severe blood loss, Savannah suffered a heart attack. They planned to schedule more tests in the following days to determine the extent of the damage.

He neglected to forewarn us that Savannah was on a ventilator so when Ennis and I rounded the corner in ICU, my knees went weak upon sight of her. Ennis steadied me with an arm around my waist. The whole weekend seemed surreal but the shock of seeing her so helpless and dependent on a machine devastated me. Lord, I prayed, let her live and be whole again.

I wasn't sure how much more I could bear. I'd watched her tortured, seen her near death and to me, the ventilator signified another obstacle for her to overcome. Most importantly, I wasn't sure how much more *she* could bear before giving up. *Stay strong*, I told her, *rest and heal your mind and your body. We're right here waiting for you when you're ready. We will always be here for you.* I wanted to ease her concern about little Anna so I explained her baby girl was fine and she and Lily also waited for Mama's return.

I stayed until the tears got the best of me. I left the ICU before Savannah heard them in my voice. I wanted her to fight for herself like she'd fought for Anna at that house. To claw her way back to life the way she'd crawled to that table and, by chance, knocked a package to the floor and memorized the address. Duke said that's how she discovered her location. His men found the package (the one delivered by the neighbor) and some whatnots on the floor. I believe that was the avenue God provided to save her. It is unfortunate the neighbor wasn't so lucky. If only he'd left sooner and called the police, perhaps he'd have lived and Savannah might have been spared some of Jeffrey's cruelty. It doesn't pay to entertain the "what-if" scenarios though. It happened and thankfully she has survived Jeffrey once more. So far, that is.

The hospital finally moved her to a private room where we all gathered at her bedside. This is no ordinary hospital nor is her room typical of other facilities. As per Duke Shelton's orders, Savannah was transported to Kaiser-Lee, a hospital with the highest and best security in the area. It also provided patients and their family with plush, comfortable surroundings.   It resembles a high dollar hotel suite, complete with wood paneled walls, a separate queen size bed for relatives to spend the night, a big screen TV, sofa, refrigerator and microwave oven.   The menu is vast and varied from health food to comfort food and meals are catered for patients and families.   Kaiser-Lee is insanely expensive, but Savannah holds a special place in Duke's life. Besides working undercover with him, years ago she exonerated him of murder charges. The two have been good friends ever since.

Mama Rutherford arrived on the redeye Sunday morning and has been by Savannah's bedside along with the rest of us. Our mother-in-law rivals any heroine, real or fictional. On the surface she reminds Savannah and me of Ellie Ewing, the steadfast yet soft-spoken matriarch of the Ewing clan on Dallas. Beneath that layer is a woman who has faced life's toughest challenge – losing her true love. Mama's presence comforts not only me but her son who, thank God, still has *his* true love.   On some level it also comforts Savannah because I know she can hear us, and Mama Rutherford is very similar to our own mother. She is considerably more extroverted than our mama (and wields quite a thick Texas accent), but she shares that same Southern steel backbone and deep-rooted religious faith. She is, like our mama would be,   a   constant   source   of   support   and   words   of encouragement.

By yesterday afternoon, friends and colleagues converged on the hospital. I can't remember a moment when her room was devoid of visitors. Besides family, several others dropped by including police officers, John Mathis and her captain Josh Hunter. Members of Dunwoody Baptist brought flowers and prayed with us. The two Mr. Thompsons – as Savannah calls them – stopped in for a brief visit. Peter toddled to her bedside with cane in hand then bent down, patting Savannah's hand and spent a good deal of time speaking to her. He is a sweet gentleman a lot like our Grandpa Prince and I wonder if that's why Savannah feels so close to him. She and Grandpa always hung out together talking golf. While Peter spoke to Savannah, his brother Bob, usually a fussy and temperamental man, stayed near the door, his head bowed in what looked like prayer.

When Duke Shelton arrived that same afternoon, I noticed his trepidation (a rare reaction with Duke). To my surprise his uneasiness wasn't due to the family crowding the room but the sight of his friend in the bed, fighting for her life. He stared at Savannah with stoic sadness but made an effort to stir her by talking to her a while. Duke hadn't stayed long but I made a point to thank him for his help, including the private ambulance and her admittance to Kaiser-Lee. Despite his controversial lifestyle he is a good man.

When Duke's men charged into the house, Jeffrey Holland was gone. He left my sister to die, struggling to breathe and stay alive until help arrived. Meanwhile Jeffrey fled into the night like a coward. Coward or not, he lurks out there, waiting. In my heart I feel he knows Savannah survived and he still wants Number Ten.

As a precaution, Josh Hunter assigned two officers outside her door for protection. Along with the two uniforms, Duke arranged for Abel and Cyrus to take shifts inside the room for a second line defense. If Jeffrey attempts to breach this fortress, either hospital security, the cops or Duke's men will end it before it begins.

Today saw fewer visitors except Duke, the Thompsons, Josh and close family. We are all exhausted but holding tight to hope. If anyone is blessed with nine lives, it's Savannah. She's survived Holland three times, a breast cancer diagnosis, that bastard Toby Jackson and God only knows how many other situations she never told me about.

Since Sunday we have all taken shifts babysitting the girls. Dane is with them tonight while Ennis, Mama Rutherford, Leah, Seth, Daddy and I stay at the hospital, right by Savannah's side. Seth made it back from his army duties during Savannah's surgery. Daddy drove from Augusta and arrived at three thirty Sunday morning. For the first time I can remember, he was sober upon walking into a hospital.

So now we wait. Wait for my sister to return from whatever otherworldly journey she's taking and join us once more if she can. To join her family who treasures her wholly, reveres her strength, admires her fight and prays to hear her voice and feel her arms around us again...

Georgia closed the laptop, sat it aside. She swiped away a tear, once again appraising her little sister. The cardiac monitor continued its soft, slow cadence, the ventilator droned on. No change.

Georgia watched Mama stroke Savannah's hand, heard her words of encouragement, "C'mon, darlin'. You've had a long nap, it's time to wake up now. Your little angels are anxious to see you. We all are."

Georgia listened until Mama rose from her chair, vacating her spot and waved for Georgia to take her place.

As the hours dragged on without a change, the group grew quieter. When he spoke, Ennis vigorously exercised his self-reproach about not killing Holland years ago. For days he'd done this and Georgia retreated into her memories to block him out. She remembered Savannah the tomboy who slugged Mikey Meadors for kissing her in third grade. She wanted Caleb Young, not Mikey to kiss her. Georgia recalled the young girl who utilized her smile and charm to wheedle an extra Coke from Grandpa Prince while working in the orchards. Then the young woman who, in the course of growing up, charmed Roy Carlson into a lifetime of loving her, temper and all. And finally, the beautiful bride with her bashful smile, walking down the aisle to exchange vows with a big ol' Texas boy who, like Roy, also fell in love at first sight.

A tired sadness passed over Georgia's features, a lump lingered in her throat at the image of Savannah in her wedding gown.

She eased into the chair, lifted Savannah's warm hand, stroked it, trying to draw her from slumber.   She looked so fragile, Georgia thought.   So different than what people normally associated with her. The woman of steel proved even steel bends under enough pressure. A bruise darkened her right cheek, a bandage covered the right side of her neck, another protected the incision below her collarbone and a sling cradled her right arm.

Savannah aged gracefully over the years, she noted.   She developed a few tiny lines at the eyes – laugh lines their mama called them. Georgia touched her sister's hair. The baby of the family stood at the threshold of forty as evidenced by sporadic silver strands gleaming from the wealth of dark chestnut. Georgia wondered why she hadn't noticed them before. The silver hairs glinted in the room's light, each one reinforcing how time slipped by, and how much Savannah matured from a vivacious child to a loving, caring mother.

In her mind, Georgia always saw her little sister skipping down the driveway humming a tune or kneeling by her bed at night, hands clasped in prayer. Forever young...

Georgia smoothed the silver laced hair back, praying that child still existed inside her sister. Savannah saved that carefree, girlish demeanor for family, especially her children. Turn her loose with her girls and one would swear there were three children at play, laughing and frolicking with each other.

Those images inspired Georgia to smile. She relayed those memories when speaking to Savannah. The special moments at birthdays, Christmas, and all the "firsts" awaiting her with her girls. If anything might rouse her, the babies would. "Wake up, little one," she told Savannah, hoping the longtime nickname might stir her awake. As kids Georgia referred to her sister as "the little one", later abbreviated to "little one". She rarely used the term anymore but noticed Savannah since bestowed the name onto Lily. "We miss you and want you back," she finished.

Georgia thought she heard the cardiac monitor speed up a beat or two. She glanced at the faces around her. Judging by their somber features, they hadn't heard a change. Great, she groused, now I'm imagining things...

R.J. touched Savannah's feet, gave them a little squeeze through the blanket. He glanced at the clock, "Savannah, you take any longer and I'm going after my scotch."

Georgia got the impression he said it for an incentive to awaken his youngest rather than an actual threat to leave and get smashed. They all hated for him to drink, and quite frankly, Georgia marveled that he stayed sober for the time he'd been there. When a hospital was involved, their father usually hit the package store hard.

R.J. rubbed the back of his neck, sighing, "What the hell's going on? She should be awake by now."

She detected a thread of fear in their father's voice. Fear that his daughter might never open her eyes. Fear that during his life he'd bury not only his wife but a child as well.

Normally the voice of confidence, Leah addressed R.J.'s statement with reservations, "No one can really predict when a person will regain consciousness, not in these circumstances. It all took a toll. The trauma then the surgery and anesthesia."

Ennis touched his wife's cheek, kissed her forehead, whispered in her ear. Georgia heard him apologize to Savannah for the hundredth time. He harbored an incredible amount of guilt about Jeffrey and about his assumptions regarding his wife and Duke Shelton. For the first time since he and Savannah reconciled, Georgia felt her heart truly go out to him. Perhaps, sometimes, it took a dire situation to forgive a person, she wasn't sure but she knew her bitterness toward Ennis Rutherford diminished the last four days.

A natural introvert in such circumstances, Seth stepped forward to stroke Savannah's ankle and volunteered his own contribution, "C'mon, sis. You gotta wake up. We need you. The girls need you." His tone turned brusque as if bolstering a fellow soldier, "Don't let that bastard win. You're stronger than he is, you've proven it."

R.J. moved to the window, stared outside, "Your mama's passin' 'bout killed me but if my baby goes, I won't make it."

Seth bristled, "Pops, watch what you say. She can hear you. She can hear us all."

"She can, can she?" R.J. argued. "Then why the hell ain't she awake yet? She not *heard* us frettin' over her?"

"Daddy, please," Georgia swallowed back the urge to cry. This was hard enough without him stating the obvious.

Mama Rutherford chimed in, "She's just taking a long rest but she'll be back. She wants to be with her family again."

R.J. stared at her, his scowl leaving no doubt to his thoughts but in case the older woman misunderstood, he lashed out, "So did my Charlene but she died anyway."

"Pops, that was different," Seth said.

Feeling ganged up on, R.J. aimed his narrowed vision at his son, "You seem to know everything, don't ya, boy?" He faced the whole group, put hands to hips, "I'll tell ya one thing *I know*. The only way I ever got through to that kid was to quote chapter and verse to her. She needs a swift kick in the ass, that's all."

Georgia and Seth glanced at each other. In their youth *chapter and verse* meant a beating. How many times had R.J. advanced on them with willow branch in hand with the ominous, "It's time I quoted chapter and verse to you..." Georgia realized the improbability of it meaning the same thing today especially in Savannah's condition, but the threat still sent shivers down her spine when she heard it.

The declaration, however, spurred Ennis's temper. He knew what the phrase signified, "Didn't she have enough abuse with Holland?"

R.J. maintained, "I'm tellin' ya, she needs an old fashioned kick in the..."

The monitor's tempo picked up slightly then settled back to the slower rhythm. Georgia looked at Ennis, "Did you hear that?"

He nodded, bent closer to Savannah, kissed her forehead, "Come on, babe. Open those beautiful blue eyes for us. We've missed you and want you back. Wake up."

They waited, listening, watching. The rhythm remained steady, slow. Georgia's shoulders slumped. Seth sighed.

R.J. stepped around Georgia, "Let me over there. I'll take care of this."

Ennis blocked his way, squared his shoulders, "Watch what you do and say to my wife."

R.J. pushed past him, "She's *my* daughter. I'll say what I damn well please." He took Savannah's hand in his, leaned to her ear.

Georgia strained to hear their father's whispers but couldn't. He gently squeezed Savannah's hand, emphasizing his words. Judging from this, Georgia guessed – and hoped – his words were as tender as his touch.

R.J. spoke for nearly a minute and by the time he stood up, the monitor sped up again, this time the rhythm remained faster, stronger.

Georgia's eyes closed. Please, please, please, she muttered under her breath. *Please, Lord, bring her back to us.* "Keep trying, honey," she encouraged her baby sister. "Please keep trying."

"Come on, sis," Seth rooted with a passion usually reserved for football games. "You're nearly there. You can do it."

"Of course she can do it," R.J.'s tone implied they'd all lost their minds. "Savannah, get busy an' show 'em I know ya better than they think."

The monitor quickened and Leah positioned herself closer to Savannah's left side, "Someone get the nurse."

R.J. took the initiative, pushed the call button by the bed, "My daughter's awake. Get in here now."

"Daddy," Georgia frowned.

"What?" he snapped, evidently sensing an impending lecture.

"She's not awake yet."

Leah lifted Savannah's left hand, secured her own around the wrist, "No, but she's close."

The hold seemed restrictive to Georgia who suspected why her sister-in-law took the step but R.J. objected to it, pointing at the firm grip, "That ain't no rattlesnake you're holding, girl. Let up."

Leah watched the monitor then Savannah, "I can't because when she wakes up she'll reach–"

Georgia noticed Savannah's throat worked as if trying to swallow. A sputtering cough jarred Savannah awake, her eyes flew open in instant terror.

Leah tightened her grasp on Savannah's left wrist that frantically pulled against the unyielding hold. "It's okay, Savannah," she assured. "The nurses are coming to remove the breathing tube. Try to calm down."

Georgia saw Savannah's wild vision lock on Leah. It took no genius to discern the gist of her expression. *No,* you *take it out – and quick.*

"The nurses are coming," Leah's calm, soothing voice reiterated, "but try to calm down until they get here."

The statement failed to penetrate the panic. Tendons in Savannah's neck stood out in thick cords while she battled Leah's hold. Georgia figured if Leah loosened her grasp one ounce, Savannah would yank free, grab the tube and take care of business herself. Thankfully her sister-in-law tightened her hand as Savannah's frenzied vision darted to her older sister with a plea for help.

Georgia heard her struggling against the ventilator, heard the heart monitor racing in a Morse Code of panic. It concerned her the stress might trigger another heart attack. "Please calm down, honey." She tried using the same gentle tone Leah had, "You'll be okay."

The fight escalated as Savannah surrendered her left hand to Leah then tried lifting her right arm.

Leah nodded to Ennis, "Hold her right arm still, protect the incision." Leah kept her voice even while speaking to Savannah, "I know you're scared but settle down. The nurse is coming." She glanced at Georgia in amazement, "She's so strong even after all that's happened."

She beamed a proud smile, "That's my sister."

Nurses rushed in and at their request, everyone left the room. Georgia wished they'd have allowed Leah to stay. Savannah looked frightened out of her mind and having a familiar face, one that was a nurse, would have helped.

After a few minutes, the nurses exited the room and allowed them back inside. Savannah showed the strain of the previous few minutes. A shadow of her former powerhouse self, her eyelids slipped down, as if just holding them open proved too difficult. Georgia understood the massive fight depleted her energy but she appeared on the verge of a relapse into unconsciousness. She looked to Leah, hoping for an answer.

"The nurses gave her morphine for her ribs and the incision," her sister-in-law replied. "She'll be groggy but she'll be fine."

That was good to know, Georgia thought, because her sister looked a universe away from being *fine*. Besides her droopy eyelids, her complexion blanched and her body rested ragdoll limp in the bed.

Georgia and Ennis claimed the two nearest positions beside the bed. Savannah tried for a smile as Ennis kissed her. Her words rasped out lethargic and tired, "I made it."

Ennis kissed her again, this time letting his lips linger on her forehead, "Thank God you did."

And Georgia had. Standing in the hallway while the nurses removed the ventilator, she bowed her head to praise and thank Him for her sister's return.

R.J. piped up from the foot of the bed, "I told you she was tougher than a one-eared alley cat."

Georgia noticed how pleased he was, as though his gene pool professed unique rights to the survival instinct. She supposed with all his *quoting chapter and verse* in her youth, Savannah *had*, by necessity, developed an iron will and steel backbone. "Daddy, what did you say to Savannah earlier? She sure responded to whatever you said."

"Yeah," Seth added. "I'd like to hear that too."

R.J. smiled, winked at his youngest girl, "That's between me and my baby."

Savannah seemed to understand what he meant. Her voice still hoarse, she tried unsuccessfully to clear her throat to say, "Thank you, Daddy."

He patted her feet, "Don't get into anymore trouble, ya hear me? You're takin' years off my life."

"Sorry," she said, not happy with the way she sounded. She gave another try at clearing her throat then gave up.

Georgia noticed it took every ounce of effort to speak. The conversation exhausted her and Georgia thought about telling her sister to rest but the excitement of seeing her awake and talking delighted her too much.

Mama beamed with joy, "It's great to have you back, darlin'. The girls have been champing at the bit to see you."

The slow, even sound of the heart monitor increased in frequency when Mama mentioned the girls. Savannah's watery gaze lifted to her sister, "You mean Anna is..."

"Anna's fine," Georgia assured. "Jeffrey dropped her by my church. A deacon looked after her until I got there." She watched her little sister thumb the tears away with a relieved sigh.

"Thank God," Savannah reply emerged as a forced whisper. "I tried so hard to catch her, to protect her. I worried he killed her."

"Well, she's doing fine," was Mama's decisive input. "She's as lively as ever."

And with that, Savannah relaxed. Oh yes, Georgia thought. Mama Rutherford accomplished a feat reminiscent of their mother Charlene. She settled Savannah with only a few words.

Ennis swept his sweetheart's hair back, gave her another kiss. He began reciting a Cliff Notes version of Duke Shelton's participation in her rescue, finishing with, "I'm so grateful that Georgia, Lily and Aurora realized you were using sign language."

Savannah came wide awake, croaking, "Lily?"

So much for a halcyon moment, Georgia harrumphed. Thanks, Ennis, thanks a lot…

Fright replaced Savannah's tranquility, "Did she see me–"

"No," Georgia slanted Ennis a *shut up* glance, "she didn't see you or what happened. She saw John imitating your movements and that's when she gleefully showed him how to say *hi* in sign language. Duke said Aurora learned signing as a child because her mother was deaf. Aurora read your message, told Duke and the rest is history."

"And Jeffrey?"

"Bastard got away," R.J. blurted.

"Daddy," Georgia admonished. Had they not discussed this subject for the last three days? Had they not all agreed to postpone telling Savannah that Holland still walked the streets? The woman just woke up, Georgia's expression said, was he nuts? Judging by all the other faces present, they wondered the same.

"She needs to know." He directed his next words at Savannah,

promising, "But don't you worry. Your daddy's here an' I'll plug the son
of a bitch if he shows up again."

26

July 7

Savannah jerked awake when a hand touched her arm. The hand was warm. A far cry from Jeffrey's incessantly cold ones. This hand was also the color of milk chocolate. Definitely not Jeffrey. Thank the Lord, she breathed a sigh of relief.

Images of Jeffrey still crept in during sleep, throwing her back in the fray with the killer. Morphine relieved the pain but fell considerably short of banishing the persistent, horrific nightmares plaguing her. Those would afflict her regularly for months if history repeated itself (which it had a bad habit of doing lately).

"Settle down, Missus. It's just me," her friend Abel said. His deep voice along with his gently patting her arm relaxed the rigid muscles prepared to battle Jeffrey. Abel continued, "You was kicking and moaning so I woke you up. You were all tied up in a knot."

She eased back to the bed, thanking Abel who, without realizing it, saved her from another encounter with Jeffrey. The killer held the golf club, swinging it into her sternum until the bone cracked. A sharp, debilitating pain shot through her chest, stole her breath. He swung it again, this time the heavy club shattered her calf upon impact, the leg exploding into a pink mist of blood and bone. He swung back again, this time aiming for her head. Then dear, sweet Abel saved her by waking her up.

Unaware of his heroic act, Abel nodded toward a bowl sitting on her tray table, "They brought your lunch earlier. Nice looking meal too. Tomato soup."

Savannah nearly gagged. After what she'd been through, the staff thought a bowl of red liquid was appropriate? "You hungry?" she asked.

He shrugged so she offered, "Help yourself to the soup if you like. I'm not touching it."

Abel's smile wilted, "No, Missus, that won't do. Boss and your sister told me to watch you eat, make sure you get nourished."

"I'll make a deal with you. You eat that red stuff the staff brought me and I'll ask Georgia for chicken noodle soup later. It'll be a cold day in the netherworld before I desire anything red and runny again."

"You want chicken noodle soup," the burly black man repeated as if she traded a bag of gold for dirt. "Really?"

"I'd eat rocks before touching a meal that reminded me of what Holland did. I saw more red stuff than I ever want to again."

The description struck a chord with him. He nodded, "Yes, ma'am, I'm sure that's true." He checked his watch, "Lemme run downstairs and get you a bowl of chicken soup. Then we can eat lunch together."

After Abel left she settled back, imagining Georgia's expression about hers and Abel's soup arrangement. Once she ate a bite or two, she'd call her sister and see how the girls were faring. She missed them so dearly the ache to see them grew almost unbearable. Her biggest concern was Anna. Her reaction at the house shouldn't have shocked her but it had. To have her baby draw back from her – then *run* from her – broke her heart in a particular way she couldn't describe.

Her mind slipped back to other memories. They came and went, faded and refocused, like surreal indistinct dreams. She lost enough blood she dropped into a semi-conscious state where she heard men's voices but couldn't respond to her name. She felt hands at her ankles and wrists, removing the bindings. A blanket covered her from toes to shoulders. They kept calling her name, their voices wavering in and out. She tried to speak. She think she managed a weak groan.

She barely remembered someone removing the needle from her neck. A hand on her jaw turned her head aside, bracing it much like Jeffrey had. She must have lifted her hand to push the person away because she received gentle admonitions to stay very still. Then two large, pleasantly warm hands scooped up her cold left one, stroked it in a repetitive motion that soothed her. At the time she dreamed it was Ennis's hands holding hers, and his voice telling her to relax, that she was safe.

Savannah recalled feeling the needle slide out and a steady pressure replace it – just before she lost total consciousness. She remembered reaching for Ennis, calling his name, before the world collapsed, sending her into a vast black hole.

A faint knock on the door pulled her from the memory. She turned to see Peter Thompson peeking around the door.

She beamed, "Mr. Thompson, come in."

The older gentleman, dressed in pressed khakis and a dapper blue dress shirt, nudged the door open with his cane. The scent of Old Spice drifted in with him as he shuffled inside holding a gold vase filled with purple roses, "It is a delight to see you awake and smiling." He placed the flowers beside the arrangements from the police department and Dunwoody Baptist. "So many pretty flowers for such a beautiful girl."

Heat rushed to her cheeks. Mr. Thompson the kind man – and an expert liar. Her hair needed washing and a comb run through it. Until that day, he'd not seen her without a stitch of makeup. During their acquaintance, he'd certainly seen her dressed in classier outfits than a flimsy hospital gown, especially a hospital gown with more wires coming from beneath than a full blown entertainment system. She looked like utter crap but thanked him anyway.

He made his way to her bedside, clasped her hand, "You're looking much, much better today. You've got rosy cheeks again."

"Cherished friends tend to bring out the color."

Peter seemed embarrassed by the compliment. He pointed to the flowers, "Those are from me *and* Bob. He'll clean my clock if I don't tell you that. He probably will anyway since I took off without him. I wanted time alone with you."

She unsuccessfully tried clearing the hoarseness from her voice. Her throat still felt sore from the breathing tube, an unpleasant side effect the nurses promised would subside. "Thank you for the flowers – and tell Bob thanks. Purple is my favorite."

A thoughtful smile curved his mouth, "Georgia told me. She must know you very well."

She noticed his vision settled on the bandage at her neck. He quickly shifted back to her gaze, patted her hand again, "I won't stay long. You've been through a lot and I don't want to tire you out."

"You're fine, Mr. Thompson," she reassured, softly tightening her grasp around his. "Stay as long as you like."

He returned the little squeeze, "I'll stay long enough to rest for the trip downstairs. And how many times do I have to tell you, young lady? Call me Peter."

Of anyone, Savannah appreciated his effort to come see her. Her mother suffered severe arthritis in her knees and ankles for years, preventing her from doing certain tasks, whether necessary or recreational. His playful admonition went against her grain. Elders deserved respect and that meant Mr. or Mrs., sir or ma'am. Mr. Thompson, not Peter. But he'd insisted for months she address him as such, "I'll try to remember from now on."

"Thank you. Now, how are you feeling?"

"I'm alive so it can't be all bad," she said, putting a positive spin on a situation she felt nothing but negative about. Since Jeffrey Holland still drew breath, the same innate fear thrummed through her in a low-level current. She'd never be safe, that fear warned. Her children wouldn't either, not until the man ceased to exist.

Peter centered on her with a paternal frown. The man saw through her the way her grandfather used to, as if he waited for her to confess the truth. She cast her eyes down, afraid he'd read every horror haunting her.

"You have a good attitude. That's what you need." He leaned closer, "But I also see worries buzzing in there like a hive of bees. It's understandable, even expected for what happened to you. No one suffers trauma without bearing scars, dear girl. I'm not speaking of physical scars either." Now he patted her hand to emphasize each word, "Let's try again. How are you feeling?"

"Scared to death," she blurted. The admission eased some tension that mounted since waking from the coma. The paranoia festered, added to it was the inability to protect her children, Georgia or herself. A cop unable to protect those she loved. How ridiculous. How... *Useless.*

She felt useless despite her daddy's pep talk the other day. She heard him whispering in her ear before she regained consciousness. The words sharpened and became clearer the closer she drifted to the surface. He told her how he admired her strength. That she possessed her mother's fortitude and will to live. He told her that losing her would finish him off. For the first time in her life, her daddy said the word please. Please come back to him and the family, he'd said. He spoke of Lily and Anna then Ennis, Georgia and Seth and how they all needed her. He made her sound courageous, resilient and strong and she knew it wasn't true, at least not anymore. She teetered on the verge of tears more often than not. She feared every noise (like the last time Jeffrey attacked her), winced at every touch, awoke shaking and in cold sweats from the nightmares. That wasn't a courageous person. In her opinion, that was a coward.

Now that she'd confessed her innermost worries to Peter, his quiet concern encouraged her to pour out her feelings which she did, "I'm scared for my children, for Georgia, for me." Tears slid from her eyes, "I can't keep anyone safe anymore."

Peter's frail grasp tightened a degree, "Now, now. Remember you managed to save yourself and, according to Georgia, it's not the first time either. Even told me at one point you also saved her life. You are brave, Savannah. Brave and strong."

In several ways Peter Thompson reminded her of Grandpa Prince, a man she confided in many times. And once her tears began sliding hot and fast from her eyes, they didn't stop, "I don't feel brave or strong. I'm tired. Tired of looking over my shoulder for Jeffrey Holland day and night. Tired of the nightmares and the dread that he'll appear and finish the job on me or worse, hurt my family. I'm tired of being me."

Peter stripped a Kleenex from the box beside her, dabbed her tears, "You're only beginning this journey of healing. You *will* heal, Savannah. You've done it before and you know it takes time. You're tired but you'll carry on for yourself and your family. Those precious girls bring a sparkle to your eyes." He smiled when her vision lifted to his, "See? There it is. Your girls and your husband will help you mend physically and emotionally and you'll always have Georgia looking out for you," he rose from his chair to place a soft kiss to her cheek, "and you've got me and Bob."

"I'm so grateful for all of you. That's what makes this worse. My fear is that something awful will happen to you. Jeffrey targets anyone I'm close to."

He winked at her, "Don't you worry about anything. Concentrate on healing. Let us worry about Mr. Holland."

She laughed a humorless laugh, "Peter, you do *not* know what he's capable of." She went on to explain the murders Jeffrey and his stepbrother Cole Jordan committed in the state of Washington before moving to Atlanta where they resumed their murdering rampage and reset their victim count. Nine dead women and, "I was supposed to be number ten. That's what Jeffrey wants. That's what he'll get."

Peter's spoke thoughtfully, "My dear girl, he is a man. A wicked man. But he is flesh and bone. Someday he will meet a person who will show him that his bones break as easily as yours, that his flesh can also be severed. When that day comes, you will have no more reason to think of him or worry about his intentions. Concentrate on your family and live your life as best you can."

His statement came through loud and clear. It hadn't exactly calmed her fears because she knew how shifty Jeffrey was. Still, she smiled at her friend and thanked him.

"You need rest. I'll go and let you sleep. I look forward to seeing you at Georgia's shop again. You brighten the place up."

Savannah reached for him, "Please stay, Mr. Thompson." She quickly corrected herself, "I mean, *Peter*." She felt safe with him and told him as much.

Peter's chest broadened with pride. He patted her hand, "Then I will stay – but only if you promise to stop worrying."

"I can try," was as far as she went. She marveled at how alike Peter and Grandpa Prince were. Peter's doting compassion along with the desire to offer advice sent her back to childhood when her grandfather sat her on his knee to provide such life lectures in his own soft-spoken, considerate way.

Peter shook his head with a good-natured sigh, "You realize Bob's taking credit for saving your life. Telling anyone who will listen – or put up with him."

She playfully swatted his arm, "Be nice to Bob. He's cranky but he's your brother."

Amusement shone in his eyes, "Did I ask for Oscar the Grouch? He's the oldest so he thinks he knows more."

"That goes with being an older sibling, believe me," she chuckled then cringed at the tiny twinge in her throat. "Seth and Georgia have a field day with me."

"But he's taking this hero business to a whole new level. Now his ego's as inflated as his head. Says if he wasn't deaf, you wouldn't have learned sign language. He's a sneaky one, my brother."

She shrugged her left shoulder then wished she hadn't, "He's right about that. I learned sign language – or learned *at* it – because of him."

The door opened. A cheery nurse walked in with gauze, scissors and medical tape. Savannah's pulse jumped in her throat. Images of Jeffrey flashed in her mind. His hand grasping her jaw, turning her head, bracing it. The repeated cold swipe of alcohol over and over as he rubbed the pad along the side of her throat. The prick of that enormous needle and the feeling of him advancing it into her jugular vein...

Mr. Thompson patted her hand, reassuring her, "The nurse is changing your bandage. That's all."

Savannah lightened her grasp on Peter's hand. In the throes of the flashback, she'd gripped it tight, as though holding on for dear life before swirling into an abyss. Yes, in her heart she knew the nurse wouldn't hurt her. But after the nightmare of Jeffrey Holland, she cowered at any medical professional carrying sharp instruments. Trying to calm her heart, she forced a smile at the nurse who seemed at ease with her nervous patient.

Going about her business, the nurse asked, "How are you feeling, Mrs. Rutherford?"

Like I've had half my blood drained out. "Okay. My shoulder aches." God, she wanted to be normal. Not fearful, snarky or leery of every human on the planet.

The nurse reached toward Savannah's throat which inspired another subdued panic attack. Calm down, she told herself. Calm down.

"Soon as I'm finished here, I'll get your pain meds." Her gloved hand turned Savannah's head by the chin then recoiled when the patient wrenched away.

Savannah apologized then politely requested, "I'll turn my head if you ask. It's nothing against you. It's because I still see…" *Jeffrey instead of you.*

She tried again, "I'm not comfortable with…" *Anyone touching me there yet.*

Savannah sighed, frustrated with herself, "I'm so sorry. It's just I'm not…" Normal yet, she nearly said. *I'm not normal yet. I still have visions of Jeffrey, of what he did to me. No one can possibly understand the immense physical, mental and emotional trauma. Even to me it is inconceivable and I was the victim. My body will heal but my mind will take longer – much, much longer. Please bear with me and I'll try to do better. I'll try to… get normal again.*

Confused, the nurse glanced at Peter who seemed to read Savannah's mind, "Still having flashbacks, I think."

She regarded Savannah with a new understanding – and more empathy, "I'm sorry. I don't know all the details of what happened. If you'll turn toward your friend, I'll make this as quick as possible."

Savannah did. She focused on the painting behind Peter. It enchanted her for days. The artist's angle was from the base of a massive towering tree. Clusters of gold leaves covered its gracefully stretched branches and through those saffron leaves shined the bluest of blue skies.

To Savannah it looked as if the tree reached up to God, perhaps in thanks for its splendor.

She jumped at the first touch on her neck then felt Peter's hand tighten around hers. She repeated the same thing over and over to herself. This is a nurse, not Jeffrey... The small bandage stripped away and she relaxed. The hands returned and she tensed, holding her breath. The nurse softly wiped the skin, cleaning the wound. Savannah swallowed hard, narrowed her vision at the painting to concentrate on the artist's attention to detail and the single brilliant ray of sunlight shining between two branches of that magnificent tree. But Jeffrey invaded the pretty scene as he hovered over her, an alcohol swab in one hand, that giant needle in the other. She was going to lose it, no matter how hard she fought to remain calm. The nurse said she'd hurry. This was not hurrying. This was hell.

"Breathe, dear girl," Peter squeezed her hand. "It's okay."

Savannah shifted her vision to Peter's concerned frown. She drew a breath until her ribs protested. The nurse pressed new gauze into place, followed it with two strips of tape, securing the bandage.

"All done," the nurse said, stripping off the gloves. "I'll be back with your pain meds."

Savannah heaved an irritated sigh, "I'm such a head case right now."

"Stop worrying. People understand it takes time to heal both here," he pointed to her shoulder then her head, "and here. Your biggest goal today is to get that pain medication. It's important you feel good when Georgia brings the girls today."

Jeffrey immediately disappeared from her mind. Images of her two sweet, beautiful girls replaced him. Their laughs, smiles and vivacious spirits. It would be so wonderful to see them. A drop of doubt trickled in about Anna, regressing to memories at the house. *That's not Mama* echoed in her consciousness and her dreams at night. How would her daughters react to seeing her? She wasn't sure about much except one thing. She couldn't bear another rejection, not from either of them.

"Anna was scared," Peter picked up on her concern. The man's ability to read her thoughts kind of unnerved her, like when Georgia did it (only her sister's knack was annoying). Peter continued, "Strange man, strange house, strange everything. She wasn't used to seeing you like that. Georgia said she mentioned seeing you so she did recognize you. She was just scared, Savannah. Relax. The visit will go well today."

She closed her eyes, praying he was right.

27

July 7

Shortly after Peter left, Abel strolled in holding a tray. He'd scored two bowls of chicken soup and appeared rather proud of the fact. He placed both on the tray table, rolled it right up to her, shook out a napkin, tucked it beneath her chin and handed her a spoon, "There you go, Missus. Eat hardy."

Her jaw dropped, "You think I'm twins or something? I can't eat that much soup by myself." She pushed one bowl toward him, "Pull up a chair, big boy. You're helping me."

He shook his head with a firm, "No, ma'am. Boss told me two bowls for you. He called earlier, told me he was coming to see you today. Then he insisted on two chicken soups for you. Know what he said?"

"God only knows." She stared hopelessly at the bowls, reasonably sure Duke Shelton lost his ever-loving mind. How in the realm of reality could she consume and digest two whole bowls of anything right now? It was an insurmountable feat and a ridiculous expectation.

"He said, 'Abel, be sure she eats both. Watch her.' So that's what I'm gonna do. I'm gonna watch you eat all your chicken soup while I eat the tomato soup." He fit his bulky frame in the chair Peter vacated earlier, equipped his own napkin and spoon then prepared to dig in.

"Duke Shelton is a bully," was her mild complaint. "An *optimistic* bully but still, a bully."

He pointed to her spoon, his tone slightly more authoritative than before, "Boss said eat. He'll check on you, you know. He's like that."

"Yes, I remember." Besides being a bully, the man was an obsessive control freak. Forget the fact he was a professional dominant and women came to him for training as submissives. Forget the fact that she vowed never to sign a bona fide, all inclusive contract with him for said training despite his continual solicitations to do so. Yes, years ago she'd gone undercover with him *pretending* to be his submissive but it fell far short of the real thing. Despite it all, Duke considered her one of "his girls". That meant checking up on her (in person *and* going through back channels) and keeping track of who she interacted with. His habits and style soared into the realm of unequivocal tyranny but, he said, he kept account of the women he cared about.

He'd treated her like royalty – kissing her hand, charming and pampering her by having food and drink served to her. Residing in his home (as she had while undercover) meant everything was done for her, including bathing, which unsettled her into a constant state of embarrassment.

No matter his Southern upbringing or genial nature, her initial meeting with Mr. Shelton not only flustered but thoroughly dumbfounded her. She'd been investigating the murders of several women. Murders that Jeffrey Holland and his stepbrother Cole Jordan committed but tried pinning them on Shelton. Her introduction to the rich dominant started agreeably enough with a warm, lingering kiss to her hand, an offered seat and pleasant tone and smile. Then something happened. With that same pleasant tone and smile, Duke Shelton unloaded on her with not only her most personal information but past and present problems that were privy to only family or close friends – or so she thought. Her tumultuous relationship with Toby Jackson years earlier. Her father's drinking problem. Her *own* battle with the bottle. And finally her diagnosis and treatments for breast cancer. Shelton divulged this knowledge the way a person won a boxing match. With a constant, steady barrage of strategic blows intended to rock their opponent on their heels. It worked too. Since then she'd never questioned his intelligence, skills or resources. She'd also never known him to lose a fight or an argument, probably because the man was smarter and more powerful than most people walking the planet. Sometimes that was good, other times not so much.

A perfect example: her lunch. He'd assumed control of her meals again, the way he'd done during her undercover assignment. Back then he dictated not only what she ate but also how much. By the end of the operation, she wanted to tear her hair out.

Appraising the two full bowls of chicken soup, she heaved a begrudging sigh then plunged the spoon in and began eating. Duke. He was a charming, well-meaning man and a good friend. But he was also a bully.

28

July 7

The last several days I've stuck by the TV like an old lady glued to her soap operas, waiting for updates on my detective. Days ago I learned that Atlanta Police Detective Savannah Prince (condition not released) resided at Kaiser-Lee hospital under police protection. I remember my days at Columbia – a hospital across town – "condition not released" meant one of two things. Someone in authority strangled the information flow or things didn't look too rosy for the patient. I expect it is the latter.

While Savannah loses the battle for survival and soon will meet her cherished Lord, I am on the run. Sort of. I found a motel, if one could call it that, near Piedmont Park that rents by the week or month. The hovel with a moldy toilet and lumpy, smelly bed attracts its share of druggies and prostitutes and an occasional misinformed tourist. One might find this place listed in Frommer's Travel Guide under "enter at your own risk". It serves my purpose since most of its residents' activities do not include watching television – and that is beneficial to me. With all its advantageous information, the media also has its drawbacks. They managed to splash my name and mug-shot to the whole city, forcing me to change certain aspects of my appearance to get around town. So I will continue living in my hovel listening to the grunts of adulterous husbands humping tramps with names like Heidi Hole and Cherry Pie.

I'm living off the money Tonya fronted me, plus what I found in the house. In light of my current residence, I safeguard the money by keeping it with me and this afternoon, I use a small chunk for a cab ride to Kaiser-Lee. A small park sits across from the hospital. I locate a shaded area with a bench to watch the front entrance. The insufferable, searing heat has set in for the day. People wander into the park in twos and threes so I won't stay long for fear of being recognized.

The six floor hospital is not massive like Atlanta Medical or Emory. It is about the size of Columbia, my old stomping grounds as a surgeon. The difference between Kaiser-Lee and the other hospitals – it serves only the rich. The place is wildly upscale. They have no public emergency room. Regular citizens cannot just walk in, take a seat and demand treatment.

No, unless a person has thousand dollar bills in his wallet and considers it pocket change, he stands no chance of admittance and if he should push the issue, their security force is supposedly top notch and fierce. I cannot – and will not – try to breach the medical fortress to finish my job. The security roadblock frustrates me but I've waited for Savannah before. If she survives, it is a matter of time before she returns home.

Since seeing the news, my biggest quandary was why the ambulance transported Savannah to Kaiser-Lee. The place is too exclusive for her paycheck and unless she has a gold mine in her pocket, the woman should have been transported to another hospital.

I sit, sweating in this furnace called Atlanta, trying to calculate my next move, observing a door I dare not enter without fear of being recognized and arrested. It is maddening. So close yet so far. I require less than one minute in her room to slice her throat and walk out but there are police officers guarding her door (as the TV said) because I see a patrol car parked beside the building. Between them and the hospital's rent-a-cop security guards, I wouldn't make it past the elevators. As unpleasant as the Atlanta summer heat is, I'd rather swelter and wait than take my chances and end up dead.

I shake my head. If I'd just slit her throat before leaving the house, I could have left this miserable city behind with the satisfaction of having conquered Savannah Prince.

An odd sight across the way catches my attention. A black limousine glides into a wide, sweeping turn toward the entrance. This intrigues me. A limo at a hospital. Who would be so pretentious?

Then I find out. Dressed in a dark suit and tie, a giant of a black man exits the driver's side. He opens the back door and Duke Shelton climbs out.

I recognize this man because my stepbrother Cole was once an Atlanta detective. He worked with Savannah and Ennis on what the media labeled the "Ravine Murders". The joke was on Atlanta. While my stepbrother and I preyed on the city, torturing and killing women, Cole also busied himself framing Duke Shelton for the murders. I'm quite sure if Savannah hadn't been assigned the case, Mr. Shelton would have spent his remaining life behind bars for crimes he hadn't committed.

Shelton is a recluse for the most part so to see him at this hospital means one thing. He's here to see Savannah. I hadn't realized the two were close. I assumed their association ended when she cleared his name of the murders. Shelton's presence also might answer a few nagging questions. Duke Shelton possessed vast amounts of money and perhaps he sent the goons to the house to save Savannah and then ordered her taken to Kaiser-Lee. I assume this but let's face it, two and two equal four, right?

Shelton steps away from the door, buttons his gray suit coat, smoothes his burgundy tie. His hair looks shorter and grayer than I remember. This is the one area that age betrays both him and Savannah. If memory serves me, the two are close in age with him about three years older. In the five years I've been away, maturity crept into my detective's dark mane, giving it a sparkle of silver here and there. Each silver hair represents a name, I've heard. I wonder how many have "Jeffrey" on them.

Shelton points to the interior and Black Guy reaches in to retrieve something. What emerges drops my jaw. Brimming with blue, pink and white flowers of various kinds, the flower arrangement is so large the guy takes great pains to remove it without destroying a single bloom.

Shelton and his driver stroll into the hospital with the air of arrogance found in such people who can throw money around like confetti. My vision narrows at the millionaire. Yes, he's the one who spoiled my whole plan. Those weren't cops piling out of those black SUVs at Tonya's house. Those were armed soldiers. Cole said Shelton employed ex-special forces soldiers as bodyguards. Minutes before they arrived, I caught Savannah signing to the camera. I couldn't imagine what she signed until I remembered the package good ol' Paul Smith delivered. It had Tonya's address stamped in bold, black lettering. When Savannah pulled on the entry table, it fell right in front of her. Later, while lying on the bed, her hand formed the "1130" for the house number. The rest I did not recognize but could imagine "Muirfield" coming across the internet loud and clear and everyone on the receiving end scrambling to call the cops.

By the time I noticed her efforts, I wondered how accurate her signing really was. Her movements weakened to a lethargic struggle to move her shaking fingers correctly, as if questioning how to position her hands to form the needed letters. Whether her plea for help was correct or not, I needed to hurry.

I gripped the scalpel, the blade poised at her right breast. I prepared to sink the razor sharp metal into the flesh. My index finger brushed the plump, velvet skin as she uttered a quiet complaint that her chest hurt and the pain was getting worse. I explained why. As hypovolemic shock set in, her heart fought to pump the remainder of blood to the rest of her body. "Your heart," I told her, "is basically suffocating from lack of adequate oxygen." Then I added if she thought her chest hurt now just wait until I cut off her beautiful breasts.

I placed the blade beneath her nipple, saw her eyes open. They looked vacant, as if unaware of her surroundings. But they focused ever-so-slightly when I pressed on the blade a degree. "Five long years I waited for this moment." I pressed again, this time firm enough to draw a line of blood.

"So… c-cold…" she trembled. "C-can't… breathe…" It took great effort for her to speak, forcing her to choose her words carefully, "Chest… hurts…"

Her complaints fell on deaf ears. I'd heard the same complaints from nearly every woman I killed. She would welcome death shortly, I told her. Whether she begged or not, she would greet the Grim Reaper on her knees with thanks. "What do you want me to do?" I asked. "Tell me. What does the great Savannah Prince want me to do for her?"

She just stared at me. I lifted the scalpel smeared with her blood. Her eyes remained unblinking. Her lips parted, moved as if she spoke under her breath.

"Are you praying to your God again? Why? He has failed you, Savannah. You worship a god who doesn't care if you suffer or die."

Still her lips continued moving, her eyes staring straight at me.

My frustration spilled over, "You should ask me for mercy, not some imaginary being. I'm in charge of when you die, not Him. Now, tell me what you want."

"J-Jeffrey," she whispered. "Please…" She squeezed her eyes tight to concentrate on forming her words, "I want..."

I allowed myself a delusionary thought. Could she be that desperate yet? She fast approached the point of no return. Had this strong and mighty creature finally reached her limit to beg for her life? I leaned down, "What, Savannah?"

Her short ragged breaths panted against my ear. By now she sensed her life slipping away. Her pallid skin glistened with sweat. I saw her heart struggling in its frantic race to stay beating.

"Please what?" I prodded. "What do you want me to do?"

When she finally spoke, the words trembled on desperate gasps of air, "I want you to... go... to... hell."

A fury swirled inside me. It started as disbelief. The woman was dying and she not only refused to beg for her life, she told me to go to hell. I'd dreamed of her pleading to live, if not for herself, for her husband and children. I fantasized of smiling into those piteous eyes and saying no. No, I will not spare your life. You won the last two battles but this one is mine. This is *my* victory.

That fantasy crumbled before me. Savannah's last words – or what I assumed to be her last – were uttered upon a benign whisper. Her eyes, though, told a different story. Defiance flickered in the once emptiness staring back at me. A brief narrowing of her vision punctuated her contempt. She cringed and moaned one last time then the lids slipped down over the blue pools. The inner struggle raged on after she lost consciousness. Her chest rose and fell in quick bursts, her lungs strained for breath. I placed my hand between her breasts. The skin felt moist, cool. Her heart pounded hard and fast, drumming against my palm.

I clenched my teeth, heard her hatred echo in my brain. I shook her by the shoulder, "Wake up, Savannah. We're not finished."

The lack of a reaction heightened my anger. I waited five years for this, I told her. I grabbed her wounded shoulder, shook her harder. Still no reaction. My wrath built to a level I hadn't experienced before. I wanted – needed – her to live long enough for me to finish, to repay her for that reprehensible statement. I shook with rage, wanting to hurt someone, blame someone, curse someone. I glance upward, shook my fist at her God as if He actually existed, "How dare you cheat me! She's mine–"

A car door slammed shut. The sound snapped me from my ravings. I drew the drape aside to see two black SUVs pull into the driveway. Behind them: an ambulance. There were no flashing lights, no sirens. Just a quiet approach for the emergency vehicle and a leisure stop in back of the shiny black Cadillacs.

Eight men piled out of the cars in military precision, each one armed with a 9mm handgun.

Instead of my usual calm, collected manner, I rushed down the stairs to the back door. I raced across the lush lawn, jumped the fence to escape into the dense growth of trees near the lake. My panic peaked, my senses sharpened when I saw flashlight beams sweep the surrounding area, heard voices behind me in the distance. They weren't cops. I knew this by the way they shouted orders – orders to shoot me on sight. These men spoke and moved with military precision. I'd felt similar panic once before. When Savannah escaped the cabin and stole Cole's car to rescue Georgia. I'd driven my car down the road to find Cole shot with his own gun – not dead but certainly neutralized as a threat. I helped him to the car and we left before the police arrived.

Several days ago I ran for my life again, scrambling through the inky blackness of night and traversing the overgrowth of trees along Lake Windward until my lungs burned white hot and my legs denied another step. I'd hoped the paramedics rushed in to find her dead. I needed relief from my obsession. The way one feels when a large, festering thorn is plucked from the skin. Except my thorn lodged in my brain five long, agonizing years, irritating me and all too happy to remind me that she'd won not once, but twice. I didn't think I could stand a third defeat.

Yet here I sit across from the damn hospital, planning what to do next. I'm clueless to her condition. Is she improving, digressing or staying the same? I only know that she breathes, whether by herself or with a machine. The five year-old thorn still festers, still aches and nettles in my brain, nagging for relief. Shelton's flower arrangement disheartens me. It says there might be hope for her. My fist tightens, I stare balefully at the medical fortress, wanting so desperately to end this agony once and for all. I'm going insane over this woman. She will not die. By sheer determination or luck, she lives a charmed existence.

29

July 7

The nurse finished giving Savannah a pain shot just as Duke Shelton breezed in with Cyrus. The morphine worked well and surprisingly fast. Savannah looked forward to the day she could breathe without her ribs aching – but for now she'd accept drawing a decent breath without requiring morphine to do so. The ribs and her shoulder worked in concert. If one hurt, the other joined in. So upon seeing her friends enter the room, Savannah wished the morphine quickly took effect because she wanted to enjoy Duke Shelton's company.

The nurse's eyes bugged at the flower arrangement Cyrus hefted to the window sill, "Someone's really special."

Duke winked at the patient, "She's worth every petal."

From the couch, Abel wondered aloud, "Hope my name's on that card too."

Duke frowned good-naturedly, "Abel, you are the *last* person I'd forget on a flower bouquet for Savannah. Your name is second after mine. Satisfied?"

Abel beamed.

Savannah sat slack-jawed at the sheer size and bulk of the arrangement. Large pink stargazer lilies, blue irises and other flowers burgeoned from the basket. Despite the arrangement's enormity, big ol' Cyrus acted as if it weighed no heavier than a feather. Before setting it down, he peeked around the arrangement with a cheery greeting, "Evenin', ma'am. How are you feeling?"

The pain hadn't receded yet however she returned his cheer as best she could, "I'm alive, Cyrus, and thankful for it."

Savannah took note of Mr. Shelton's attire. Gray suit, burgundy tie and spit-shined shoes. Very debonair. The ZZ Top song "Sharp Dressed Man" came to mind and yes, she could see Duke Shelton playing the part. *Gold watch, diamond ring, I ain't missin' not a single thing...* Duke was classy, attractive and possessed the finest taste in everything from food, drink, clothes, jewelry and cars. A woman's dream. *They come runnin' just as fast as they can, 'cause every girl crazy 'bout a Sharp Dressed Man...* Especially if the girl was married to Ennis Rutherford, who happened to be the only Sharp Dressed Man Savannah wanted.

Duke leaned down, placed a kiss on her cheek, "My dear, it is a pleasure beyond words to see you among the living."

She cocked an eyebrow, "I understand you're to thank for that too. Ennis said forensics couldn't trace the video feed and the two techs didn't know sign language. He also said you sent Abel and Cyrus over to guard the girls. Thank you."

Duke folded his tall, brawny frame in the chair beside the bed.

His hand clasped hers, "I protect those who hold a special place in my life. I do regret the incident with little Anna. Georgia said Holland levered the window open somehow. I'm thankful he didn't hurt the child."

Hearing Duke address Georgia by her given name instead of his pet name *Beauty* threw her momentarily. Then she remembered years earlier when he explained that in public, he reverted to proper names for privacy's sake. On the phone or in his home, however, Georgia was *Beauty* no matter what.

She replied, "I'm pretty sure Anna was too much for him to handle."

"Anna's like her mother," he winked again.

She felt herself blush, "Georgia said Aurora translated my signing. I wasn't sure if I got half the letters right. I wasn't exactly in tip-top shape mentally."

"You signed perfectly. I'm sure Georgia explained Aurora learned as a child because her mother was deaf. You spoke, she listened and interpreted your message to me. I sent a team to the address along with a private ambulance. We were grateful you were still alive."

Just barely, according to her family. But alive was alive, she thought, including all the gripes and ailments of her thirty-something year-old body.

Abel looked up from his Men's Journal magazine, "Boss sent eight men after you. When they found that fella gone, Boss assigned me as your new best friend."

Savannah feigned shock, "Imagine that. Duke taking control again, kinda like with my servings of soup."

Abel's pearly whites gleamed, "I'm stickin' to you like glue till we kill that fella."

"Abel," Duke smirked, "remember you're talking to a cop."

He waved it off, "Missus understands me."

"Yes, she does," Savannah replied, "and she never heard a word." Her good hand twisted an imaginary lock on her lips then threw away the key.

Duke peered into both bowls that once brimmed with chicken soup. She ate all of one and a quarter of the other. His tone indicated slight disappointment, "You did well but you can do better."

Her eyes bugged. How, exactly, could she do better?

He ignored her unspoken question, "I asked the doctors if my chef could prepare your meals. They would comply with your prescribed diet while you're here but," he lowered his voice, "the cuisine is much tastier than hospital food. You require enticing nourishment to replenish your body and heal."

She did a mental eye roll. Really? He expected her to believe that, "You *asked* someone's permission to do something?"

He took her ribbing in stride, "It has been known to happen."

"Like snow in the Sahara Desert."

Duke chuckled, "It is good to hear your sense of humor – and see your smile."

"I won't be smiling if you dictate my food the way you did when

I was undercover."

"I will refrain from dictating. I will strongly *suggest*."

"Is Abel my tattletale if I don't clean my plate?"

One brow rose. He volleyed back with his own teasing banter, "Consider him a culinary coach, cheering you on. I remember your favorite meals so you will feast to your heart's content."

That was the problem, she frowned. His chef's capability far outstretched the boundaries of Savannah's waistline. "You buying my new wardrobe when I'm too fat to fit in my jeans?"

"It would give me great pleasure to do so."

"No leather," she hinted.

"I would dare not ask you to wear it."

Savannah enjoyed talking and joking with Duke. When they met years earlier she'd called him a pervert. Not to his face, of course, but her rigid stance on the alternative lifestyle sparked a surprising and improbable camaraderie between them after she cleared him of murder allegations. Now she proudly called him a friend.

The morphine softened the pain's edges, gradually freeing her movement. The ribs eased to a duller ache but now with a stronger rush of relief sweeping across her consciousness, even that was tolerable. The morphine rolled in as warm and mellow as a rippling tide. Her mind welcomed the peace, her body the reprieve from pain. For a moment her eyes grew heavy to savor the overall serenity. She risked a tiny smile thinking *God bless whoever invented morphine.*

The corners of Duke's mouth lifted, "There's the expression I was hoping for." His hand caressed her cheek. To an outsider the gesture might have appeared inappropriate. To Savannah it represented a flash of the past, when she worked undercover with Duke. He meant the simple action as platonic, a way of expressing friendly affection and nothing more. During her assignment years ago, Ennis grossly misinterpreted Duke's actions and dove headlong into the deep end of jealousy and anger. Savannah understood his point of view – she wouldn't cotton to another woman touching him in an affectionate way but she'd trust him to remain faithful to their vows. Ennis, unfortunately, hadn't trusted her. He stunned her with accusations that she'd broken the undercover assignment's contract and slept with Duke. They'd had a blistering argument and a brief separation, one that nearly destroyed their marriage.

Yes, she acknowledged fate and genetics blessed Duke Shelton. Any woman with eyes and a brain had to. Tall and muscular with refined, good looks, it was no wonder women fell at his feet. For some cockeyed reason Ennis assumed she had too. It hadn't helped that her assignment required long hours together with the dominant. Because of Ennis's lack of trust and the outright accusations of infidelity, the marriage hit an abysmal state that seemed to veer inevitably toward divorce. They reconciled but it took a long time to reestablish the trust between them.

Duke, however, still felt the raw sting of Ennis's unwarranted indictment and avoided him whenever possible. A pensiveness settled over him, "When is Ennis due to arrive?"

"Later tonight. Duke, you don't have to schedule your visits around him. He appreciates what you did for me, for the girls."

"It is best I stay my distance. There have been far too many harsh words exchanged over a misconception. I refuse to be the catalyst for additional stress. You, my dear, do not need or deserve it and need to remain calm."

There was an underlying meaning in that statement, she thought. Not just confronting the tension between him and Ennis, but something else.

"I heard you're scheduled for tests tomorrow."

Ah. There it was. He wanted answers but opted not to pry so she volunteered, "They're checking my heart and kidneys for damage. I'm not worried. They ran a couple yesterday too. That's what hospitals do, right?"

In a rare occurrence, Duke Shelton broke eye contact first. That bothered her. "Something you want to confess, Mr. Shelton?" she asked. *Because you look mighty guilty to me.*

He promptly recovered, met her vision again, "Nothing to confess, Mrs. Rutherford. Only that you have my best wishes on the results of those upcoming tests. You've won the biggest battle – you survived Holland. If anything else should arise, we'll address it accordingly. Agreed?"

"Agreed." *Liar, liar, pants on fire. You just won't tell me what's going on.* But no one else had either. She refused to spoil his visit with accusations or nagging. She'd deal with whatever happened, she always had.

With the ribs and shoulder finally under control, Savannah mentioned his spiffy attire, "You're gussied up today. Headed to church or a meeting with the board of directors?" She knew the answer was neither. Since she'd known him, Duke never professed to being religious in any respect nevertheless he stocked his library with Bibles and religious tomes for live-in submissives. As for "the board of directors", there wasn't one. Duke inherited his money but found ways to reinvest with great success.

Duke gifted her a sly grin, "I *gussied up* for a lady friend who is near and dear to me."

She lifted a brow, "I see. So do I know her?"

"You see her in the mirror every morning."

Savannah's face burned with embarrassment, teasing, "You are quite the charmer, I'll say that for you." She stared in awe at the enormous arrangement that dwarfed everyone else's. "You run Buckhead out of flowers for that exquisite piece of floral art?"

He chuckled at that, "I left nothing in my wake. I ordered anything with a stem brought here."

"Thank you for them. They're beautiful."

"A mere token of my household's feelings for you. These are from my girls, Cyrus, Abel and me of course. We all hold you in high regard." Duke leaned onto his knees, pointed to three other bouquets, "Who sent those arrangements?"

She labeled the sender of each bouquet. Her colleagues sent a vase of orange and red lilies and fuchsia carnations. It sat on the far left. Dunwoody Baptist's came next with lavender lilies and magenta carnations, and to its right sat the Thompson brothers' gift of purple roses. In Savannah's opinion, the bouquet cost too much for two financially strapped men relying on retirement and Social Security checks. It was an extravagant yet greatly appreciated gift. "The one on the right is from Peter and Bob Thompson, the two older gentlemen who frequent the bakery."

His voice softened, "Georgia mentioned how close you and the Thompson brothers have become."

"They're both good friends."

"How close are you?"

The personal question roused her curiosity. It appeared that Duke Shelton, for whatever reason, didn't approve of the brothers. "Pretty close. Peter treats Lily and Anna like granddaughters."

"And you like a daughter, I presume."

Again she nodded. Duke's eyes searched hers with an intimate, nearly invasive precision – a trick that always unnerved her. His stares intruded on a person's inner thoughts, as though he saw past the eyes into the mind. Finally she capitulated, "What's the problem with our friendship?"

"I would only advise that you be careful around them."

Now that worried her. For some reason he'd had the two Mr. Thompsons investigated. Duke's resources included crack investigators and they apparently discovered information he disapproved of. The two elderly men hadn't struck her as problematic, squirrely or just plain unacceptable. To her they presented the epitome of chivalrous, Southern gentlemen (except when Bob whacked the table with his fist). "Why should I be careful around them?"

For the first time since she'd known him, Duke Shelton hesitated. He reclaimed her hand, lightly caressed it, "I've debated a while about telling you this. We've been through a lot together and I consider *us* incredibly close too, wouldn't you agree?"

When she replied yes, he gave her hand a small squeeze, "I had my men look into the Thompsons." He lifted one hand in a "stop" gesture to prevent any complaints or arguments, "I also feel close to Lily and Anna so I dug into the two men's backgrounds to protect you all, to ensure their presence isn't of a dubious nature."

In a way it surprised Savannah that Duke trolled into her friend's histories. He normally reserved that step for people entering his home or living with him, to guarantee he uncovered every detail possible about them and prove he or she wasn't *dubious*, as he called it. In the past, Georgia told her about Duke's obsession with certain women. He'd been enamored with Georgia since she was in her early twenties – and he'd done the same background on plenty of people she encountered. Savannah realized he also included *her* in the list of women he safeguarded but investigating two old men? C'mon... "What's wrong with the Thompson brothers?" She threw the question out there fast and blunt, with no resentment or anger. Then an unexpected, appalling thought hit her, "Please don't tell me they're child molesters."

An easy smile curved his lips, "No, my dear, they are not. But I do think you should be aware of their past. My intention is to inform, not to upset you. Please keep that in mind."

"I'll keep it in mind," she agreed.

"They grew up in Miami, then later moved to Charlotte and here to Atlanta, the last move occurred three years ago."

"So far so good."

His hand tightened a degree. Uh-oh, she thought, here it comes... The two older men meant the world to her, Peter especially. Hearing disparaging news about him would be like learning a dear, trusted relative pillaged for a living.

Duke forged on using his customary straightforward approach, "They have a questionable history in Charlotte."

"Questionable how?"

"Let's say when they wanted something done, it got done. They knew the right people to make it happen."

"A lot like you."

"Only my record with law enforcement is less..." he contemplated his answer until, "colorful."

"Colorful? You mean gray as in parking tickets, yellow as in theft or crimson as in murder?" Theft was bad enough but not knowing the circumstances, she wouldn't judge. After all, many people had run-ins with law enforcement in various ways, including traffic tickets. Savannah knew the notion of murder was utterly ridiculous but she threw it in for a joke anyway.

Savannah noticed Duke actually struggling to phrase his reply. This concerned her but she still made light of the situation, "You're acting as if they are the Corleone brothers making people offers they can't refuse."

"To answer your question, their history leans to the color of apples, at least from what I conclude from my men."

Okay, so pillaging didn't sound so bad after all... Not like murder – or *was* it murder? Frowning, she shook her head, "Okay, wait. Murder was crimson, not apple color, whatever that is. And if you say it was murder, I'm gonna call you crazy." Just the thought spurred a subdued fit of laughter. Peter Thompson, a killer? How absurd! And Bob, the grumpy deaf fellow who always demanded extra sugar for his coffee? What might happen, she wanted so desperately to ask. If she fouled up his order would Bob Thompson give her lead poisoning with a .45? In a way, Duke left the impression they were heinous, bloodthirsty villains. Heinous, bloodthirsty villains did not call to check on others during times of crisis. Georgia told her Peter called several times for updates on Savannah's status. Peter's visit earlier that day was simply a joy for her. The man couldn't look dangerous if he tried. Duke had the wrong guys, she convinced herself. Peter and Bob valued friendship like gold. They were normal older men, not trigger-happy geriatrics. Savannah immediately ceased laughing when pain reverberated through her body in shockwaves. Apparently, her injured ribs failed to see the humor.

Judging by his expression, so did Duke, "I understand your

reluctance to believe this information but two men died and the Thompsons were suspected. Whether the deaths were accidental or intentional, I do not know. That's why I say be careful around them – just to be safe."

She reclaimed her left hand, cradled her ribs that still carried a serious grudge then her incision joined in, clarifying in great detail how bad an idea laughing really was. The pain returned full force while she cringed her way through the worst before it mercifully surrendered to the morphine again. The incision held on to the bitter end, and she lifted her hand to the bandage, rubbing it to relieve the ache. It intensified instead. "Your investigators are mistaken," she said. "Those two sweet older gentlemen?"

"Yes, those two sweet older gentlemen." Duke curled his fingers around her left hand, pulled it away from the covered incision with a curt, "Stop that, Savannah. If you'd rather not know about the Thompsons, tell me."

Oh, right. Drop a nuke in my life then walk away? Hell, no. "Just tell me," she tugged, wanting to rub the wound.

He refused to release her hand, "Details are hard to come by. Bob was attacked twenty years ago in Charlotte. That attack left him deaf and five days later the two men responsible ended up dead."

"They could've jumped the wrong person five days later. Doesn't mean the Thompsons bumped 'em off."

"No, it does not. The police questioned several people including Peter and Bob but made no arrest in the deaths. However three men associated with the Thompsons were seen with the victims shortly before they were murdered. As I said, they have many influential contacts in Charlotte and rumor was Peter and Bob frequently used them."

"Rumors?" she snorted her skepticism.

Duke pursed his lips. After a moment he continued, "I see you still retain that annoying stubborn streak. Savannah, rumors tend to have a thread of truth in such cases, you know that. When you investigated me for murdering those women, you found proof I not only knew them but they trained as my submissives."

"But you didn't kill them and I find it difficult to believe the Thompsons are guilty of murder in any respect." She tugged on her hand to no avail.

"I'm merely giving you information, not trying to sway you. But you should also know their given names are Pietro and Roberto Thomasin, not Peter and Bob Thompson. They changed their last name ten years ago." His grasp tightened a degree, "*Stop resisting me, Savannah. I'll not allow you to irritate those stitches.*"

She slumped in the bed, conceding the battle, "Okay, okay. You win. I'll try to leave it alone." The name change threw her temporarily. It wasn't that big a leap from Thomasin to Thompson, not like *Corleone* or *Gotti* to Thompson. So maybe they wanted a new start in a new city. What was wrong with that? Logic dictated if someone really wanted to find them, they could. Charlotte was less than three hundred miles from Atlanta, plus a couple letters difference in a person's name didn't spell *running from the law* or *splitting from the mob*. "Not that I believe what you're saying – nor am I condoning anything – but don't you think I'd go after someone who attacked Georgia or Seth? I'd certainly want revenge."

"As would anyone. However I'm fairly sure you would take the law enforcement route. In my wildest imaginings I cannot see you going rogue or asking a friend or colleague to enact revenge on your behalf."

She pointedly cleared her throat. Had he forgotten a particularly ugly Sunday morning clash years ago? After she and Duke met, he invited her and Georgia over for Saturday brunch. During that meal, Georgia ended up suffering a life threatening allergic reaction to seafood "someone" slipped into the food. At the time Savannah blamed Duke. Once the hospital released Georgia to go home, Savannah drove to Buckhead, barged into Duke's mansion fully intending to break his neck. That was until Cyrus and Abel restrained her and physically removed her from the property. A most unpleasant memory considering Duke was innocent of that charge too. His live-in submissive/wife poisoned Georgia out of jealousy. Any way you sliced it, Savannah's current expression said, her actions fit right in with *going rogue.*

Duke caught her meaning, "I shall rephrase. I cannot see you going rogue *now.* You've matured in your actions and thinking. Savannah, these may be assumptions about the Thompsons but the circumstances seem far too coincidental, at least to me. I've known this information since you formed a friendship. I've also kept track of their movements. Their records are clean here in Atlanta and they've made no overt attempt to contact anyone in Charlotte. They did, after all, change their names so I'm guessing they wanted a fresh start. With that said, it doesn't mean they don't have connections here and I will continue to monitor them as long as you associate with them. And since I've assigned Abel as your security, you have extra protection against Holland and any other possible threats."

Savannah's hand raced to her shoulder for a brief rub. Duke's deadpan expression caused her hand to drop in her lap like a rock. "Please don't remind me about Jeffrey," she said.

"Don't you worry none, Missus," Abel piped up from the couch. "Abel's on the job. I'll keep you safe."

Duke rose from his seat, "Indeed he will. I have a feeling about Holland. Between the police's efforts and my men actively searching for him, his luck will run out this time. When it does," he bent to kiss her cheek, "you will live peacefully again."

30

July 7

When I return to my bench later that afternoon, I see the same mountainous black guy that accompanied Duke Shelton, only this time he escorts Georgia, Lily and Anna inside the hospital.

The sight demoralizes me. Savannah is clearly improving since the female trio appears joyous enough to sing. I sneer when Georgia leads the chorus:

Angels watching over me,

all night, all day,

Angels watching over me, my Lord…

Lily is the only one joining in. Anna busies herself sucking her thumb while clutching a stuffed cat to her chest. Yes, I agree. Savannah's Lord – whoever or wherever He might be – employs many angels to protect His lovely, stubborn, evidently immortal child.

I stare at the cheery group, my hands curling into fists. This is not how it ends. Savannah will not win again. Her Lord may have saved her but I am as determined to kill her as she is to survive.

Suit coat slung over his arm, Black Guy follows behind Georgia and Lily (Georgia carries Anna on her hip). I spy a 9mm automatic in the bodyguard's shoulder holster. He surveys their surroundings, ever vigilant in his job.

Wearing jeans and a grass green pullover, Georgia seems comfortable in the unrelenting heat. The girls dressed pretty for Mama, Lily opted for jeans and a pink top, and Anna wears red and white polka dot leggings and a red and white top with bright flowers on it. The vibrant attire won't faze Savannah. The mere sight of her cubs will kick her recovery into high gear, a fact that makes me clench my teeth until my jaw aches as I watch them saunter to the entrance.

I need another way to Savannah. A way no one expects. One that keeps me in her conscious thought day and night. A way to nudge those angels watching over her and remind them Jeffrey Holland never gives up.

I look around, searching for alternatives but see none. Until... A young boy in red shorts and black t-shirt pedals his bike along the running path. He heads in my direction. The slight breeze tousles his mop of wavy brown hair. He is enjoying his trek judging by his expression. Not in any hurry, just out for a leisurely Friday afternoon ride. I estimate the boy's age around seven years old. He's old enough to remember simple instructions and young enough to jump at the offer of extra money.

While at the rathole motel, I penned a note with hopes of getting it to my detective despite the ironclad security surrounding her. I remove the note from my pocket, along with my wallet. From the latter I withdraw a crisp twenty dollar bill.

The boy doesn't see me until I step directly onto the path to block his passage. He slows to a stop, plants his feet on either side of the bike.

I smile at him, introduce myself as Thomas. As expected he seems leery at first. I quickly follow with a proposal. I need a favor, I say, and will pay twenty dollars for five minutes of his time.

The boy cocks his head when I show him the money, but I notice his feet are ready to about-face and hightail it away from this bold stranger asking for a "favor". He asks, "What kinda favor?"

I show him the folded note with Savannah's name on it. "I need you to go into that hospital and ask where this lady's room is. All you have to do is deliver this note to her or a police officer standing outside her room. Would you do that for me?"

He stares at the note, skeptical of the proposition. He studies my face, probably trying to decide if I'm dangerous or just lazy. He leans onto the handlebars of the mountain bike. I take this as a sign of interest. Apparently I do not pose the threat he initially feared. No, I'm not a pervert, just a desperate man needing to pluck a nasty, festering thorn from my brain.

He weighs the offer then shrugs, "Can I see the note?"

"Sure," I willingly hand it over, wait for him to read it.

He frowns afterward, "This is it? Why don't you give it to her yourself?"

My mouth turns down, "Sadly, we had a falling out. I'm trying to connect with her again."

He gives it another brief glance then folds it, looks at the name, "Savannah Prince. That's who I ask for?"

"The one and only." I extend my hand, "Deal?"

He gives it one enthusiastic shake, "Deal."

I hand the twenty to him and thank him. He repositions the bike, puts foot to pedal to embark on his task. He traverses the busy street like a pro, approaches the entrance and walks in.

I risk trusting this boy to deliver my message. He seems honest enough and though I've misjudged a few people in the past, I'm confident this young man will follow through.

Walking briskly, I relocate a safe distance from the entrance. The police will surely ask the boy questions and probably follow him outside to find this mystery man Junior mentions. They will want answers and a youngster faced with uniforms and badges tends to give them.

Several minutes pass when he steps from behind the sliding doors, grabs his bike. Trailing him – a cop. The boy points across the street to my bench. The officer listens to whatever he says then relays the information via the radio clipped to his shoulder epaulet.

I'm on the radar again so I casually ease my way down the street, heading toward my hovel. I stop for one brief moment and turn toward the hospital and wink. My detective is about to get a wake-up call...

31

July 7

Cyrus, Georgia and the girls rode the elevator to the fourth floor. Lily held Georgia's hand and Anna rode her aunt's hip, clinging to her and her brand new toy kitty, a present from Dane and Georgia to quell the requests for a feline friend. Georgia doubted her sister would mind the addition to the family. Ennis certainly hadn't. The purchase proved successful since the girl's tune changed from "Anna want kitty-cat" to "look at Cookie". Georgia suspected a batch of homemade chocolate chip cookies (Anna's favorite) inspired the name.

The elevator door slid back, revealing a veritable beehive of activity. Nurses passed by, took the time to greet the adults and give the girls a sweet hello. A few visitors lingered around the nearby waiting room. Upon sight of them, Anna cuddled Cookie closer, leaned into Georgia, tucking herself safe and tight in the embrace. In contrast, Lily explored the surroundings, looking everywhere, entranced by the nurses' scripted ballet of movements from room to room. The difference in the girls amazed Georgia. Savannah's oldest was the boldest and her youngest the introvert but no less aware.

Captain Josh Hunter assigned two seasoned uniform officers, not fresh-from-the-farm rookies to protect Savannah. They flanked her sister's room located straight ahead. Gun belts spanned their hips, dipped beneath two pot bellies but the firepower of their Glocks set a person's mind at ease. Georgia remembered the days when Savannah wore the same equipment, only instead of a Glock she carried a .38 revolver as she did now. The cumbersome, heavy gun belt bruised her hips for months, if not years, until her promotion to detective. She'd done her time in uniform, spending her days and nights risking her life for others, including fellow cops. Now it was time for reciprocation.

Lily spotted the two officers then tugged at her aunt's hand, urging her along, "C'mon, Aunt Georgia." She pointed to the two uniforms ahead, "Mama's room is right there."

"Are you sure?" Cyrus teased.

Lily rolled her eyes in youthful frustration, sighing, "Those are the police. Mama's the police too. I'm going to be one too when I grow up."

Georgia wasn't surprised by the announcement but it did have an off-key ring to it, "But Mama said you want to be a professional golfer. You know how much she loves that idea. Plus, golf is something you do together. Isn't it more fun playing golf with her than standing in one of those hot uniforms?"

It took Lily all of a second to nod. Georgia reinforced the importance of the choice, "After she's home and feels better, you can play golf together again because she enjoys it too." She dipped to one knee, "Before we go see her, I want to talk to you both."

Lily huffed, crossed her arms. She reminded Georgia of Savannah in her younger years. Always impatient. Places to go, people to see.

Georgia eased into the subject, "Daddy told you that Mama has boo-boos, didn't he?" The same boo-boos that sent Anna fleeing from her mother, refusing to acknowledge her in any way. Georgia worried herself into chronic insomnia about Anna's upcoming reaction to her mama. There were positive changes in Savannah's appearance. Overall it improved except for the exhaustion and pain. Her voice almost returned to normal. It cracked on occasion but at least she sounded like Savannah again. The blood that the child most certainly remembered had been cleaned away, the wounds repaired and stitched but would Anna remember the chaos at the house? Georgia said a silent prayer that Anna greeted her mama with open arms with her usual giggling glee.

Lily anxiously glanced down the hall then turned back to her aunt, "Daddy said she got hurt."

"She did, honey. When you see her," Georgia touched Lily's right shoulder and side, "be careful here and here."

"Aunt Georgia, is Mama gonna be okay?"

She gave the girl a one-armed hug, "Yes, she'll be fine with time but right now we need to take care of her the way she takes care of you and Anna. Help her dress, maybe even help her eat for a while." Because her sister was anything but ambidextrous. She'd probably poke her eye out trying to feed herself left-handed.

The last part confused Lily. Georgia tried to explain by pointing to the girl's left hand, "Have you tried eating with this hand? Your left one?"

Lily nodded. Her aunt took a guess, "It was hard, wasn't it? Holding your fork and trying to eat that way."

Again the child nodded so Georgia concluded, "Well, Mama has to use her left hand for a few weeks. That's why we might need to help her hold her fork now and then."

Instead of childlike acquiescence, Georgia saw genuine maturity in the youngster when she nodded, "I can do that."

Georgia smiled, "I know you can and will, sweetie. Okay then," she rose to her feet, "let's go see Mama." They passed the nurse's desk with Lily guiding the way, still towing Georgia by the hand.

Savannah's room faced West. Every evening the sun bathed the room in bright light despite the closed drapes, a bright light that would soon began flagging like Savannah's energy. A long recovery awaited her sister, a woman possessing minimal patience when it involved residing in a medical facility or her health in general. Her fussy nature reared up the day before, saying she wanted to go home. She missed her family, her home and her bed.

Lily tugged Georgia toward the room. With no complaints and a little smile, Georgia dutifully kept up.

Amused at the sight, the two officers offered warm greetings to her and the girls then stepped aside.

She reached to push the door open but Lily beat her to it. Abel's usual roost sat empty, making Georgia wonder what took him away from guard duty. Once the hubbub died down, she'd ask Savannah.

"Mama!" Lily tore loose from Georgia's grasp, charged straight to her mother's bedside.

Georgia hadn't seen such wild enthusiasm from the child since Christmas morning. If Lily's reaction heartened a soul, Savannah's brought tears to one's eyes. Upon sight of her children, an instant transformation took place in her sister. Savannah's eyes brightened, the persistent veil of discomfort suddenly vanished, erasing a good five years from her features. A genuine blissful smile that Georgia had not seen in many days stretched across Savannah's face. Her sister's beauty shined in the company of her babies, her youthful joy returned and for the first time all week, Georgia safely assumed Jeffrey Holland was the last thing on Savannah's mind.

"How are my girls?" Savannah's gleeful tone matched her daughter's.

Forget morphine, Georgia mused. The kids were the best pain remedy thus far. Delight brightened Savannah's expression as she eagerly listened to Lily's rapid-fire updates of the last few days. That and the resulting chuckle were signs of true healing.

Industrious Lily pulled the nearby chair closer to the bed and used it as a stepping stone to her mother's side. She climbed into the chair knees first then stood, leaning toward the bed to cross over.

Savannah reached to help then thought better of it as a flash of pain wrinkled her brow.

Georgia steadied Lily on the trek across, "Remember to be careful. Mama's still hurt."

Lily paused to see the sling cradling her mother's right arm. She gingerly crawled next to Savannah's left side, settled in, "What happened?"

Savannah draped her arm across her girl's shoulders, pulled her closer, "I ran across the wrong person, sweetheart, but I'll be fine now."

"Was it that man?"

Savannah glanced at Georgia, "Yes, it was." Her eyes closed as she dropped a lingering kiss to her daughter's hair, "But Mama won that fight so don't worry. Everything will be okay now. I've got my girls with me."

Lily vowed, "Aunt Georgia says we need to take care of you so that's what we're gonna do. She says I can help you eat."

Savannah glanced sidelong at her sister, "'Fraid I'll poke my eye out, aren't you?"

Georgia shrugged with a self-conscious smile.

Savannah took it in stride, "I'm not very adept doing anything left-handed, that's a fact." She chanced a peek at Anna. Georgia felt the tension pouring off her sister. She tried hiding it behind the upbeat conversation while probably bracing herself for further rejection from Anna. At least one of her kids accepted her, her expression seemed to say.

Georgia could see visions haunting Savannah from days before when Anna refused to even look at her. It broke Georgia's heart to remember Anna's wailing "that's not Mama" and running from the room.   To make matters worse, she felt Anna pulling back from Savannah already.   Her rounded brown eyes centered on the noisy IV machine and the tangle of wires and tubes attached to her mother.

"Hi, baby," Savannah greeted.   "That's a pretty kitty-cat you've got."

Georgia prayed Anna acknowledged her mother.   *Please let the child reach for her,* she prayed.   *Don't let her break Savannah's heart again.*

Anna drew against Georgia, pressing into her.   Her fingers tightened on the toy cat then she stuffed its ear in her mouth and began chewing.   So far this wasn't going well at all, Georgia bemoaned.   "Let's show Mama your new kitty."

She shook her head, turned from Savannah.

Georgia tugged the kitty's ear out of Anna's mouth, "She wants to see your kitty.   Didn't you name it Cookie?"

"No," the girl answered.

A shroud of sadness fell over Savannah's once buoyant features. Georgia scrambled to salvage her sister's mood before it crumbled to pieces, "Hon, it's the new surroundings plus the machines and their sounds.   It's all new to her."

Savannah pulled Lily closer, disagreeing, "She remembers what happened, that's what's wrong."

Any other time Georgia's explanation might have reached the common sense part of her sister's brain but a child's rejection hit a mother's heart so wholly it canceled out everything but the pain of that rebuff.

Savannah's chin trembled, tears welled in her eyes. She always worried about two things. One, that she'd be a lousy mother and two, her kids might end up hating her. Georgia saw it written in her devastated appearance. In her mind Anna hated her and until the child proved otherwise, Savannah would believe it forever.

"Where'd she get the kitty?" Savannah asked. Changing the subject seemed to temporarily stem the tide of tears.

"Dane and I thought it might suffice for the time being. Hon, she needs time, that's all. You'll be home soon and things will be back to normal. Don't give up."

Savannah slowly lost the battle. She blinked back tears, refusing to further the subject, "That was clever of you and Dane. Thank you both."

Georgia patted her leg, held her hand there, assuring, "She'll come around."

"Hey, Tiny Toes and Tadpole are here," Abel's cheerfulness echoed through the room. Georgia turned to see him pointing at Lily with a mile wide smile, "You look might happy, Tiny. You tell your mama how big your Lego house is now?"

His prompt brought forth a gushing description of the enormity of the Lego abode he'd helped construct. Lily spread her arms, giving her mother a generous exaggeration of the house's actual size. Savannah sounded appropriately impressed but Georgia noticed her gaze shifted to

Anna who shied away from Abel's deep, gregarious voice.

The second Abel swiveled to greet Anna, she threw her arm around Georgia's neck, scrambling to hide from him. Abel was undeterred, "You playing hide-and-seek with me, Tadpole?" He angled around Georgia's shoulder for a peek-a-boo at Anna. The child wound tighter around her aunt's neck, her eyes as big as saucers.

"Anna, honey, please stop strangling me," Georgia pleaded, trying to pry that small but amazingly powerful arm free before she turned blue.

Meanwhile the child's face flushed fire engine red. She fought her aunt while keeping her distance from Abel who ultimately stepped away. It was too late. Anna burst out in a screaming cry that made Georgia's ears ring. "It's okay, sweetie," she tried to calm her down. "Abel's not going to hurt you."

Kitty gripped tight in her fist, Anna's tear-streaked face turned to Savannah, both arms reaching for her as she cried, "Mama."

With a trembling smile, Savannah let the tears spill down her cheeks. She stretched her left arm, inviting the child to her, "Come here, my precious baby."

Finally, Georgia expelled a relieved sigh. With that one word and singular action, Anna mended her mother's heart.

Georgia swiped her own tears blurring her vision then placed the reaching child next to Lily. The toddler's wailing wound down a notch when Savannah cuddled her closer, spoke softly to her.

Georgia marveled at the scene. Who would have guessed? The answer to her prayer came in the form a man who looked more intimidating than he actually was – at least with friends.

Abel looked positively confounded at Anna's reaction. Georgia tried to salve his feelings, hoping her explanation consoled him better than it had her sister, "She's confused by the surroundings, Abel. Don't take it personally."

"Abel's a friend," Savannah told her youngest who squeezed tighter between her and Lily, Cookie clutched to her chest. The crying subsided to sniffles once she settled next to Mama who added, "And look what he brought. Yummy chocolate pudding."

Georgia nearly laughed. Earlier, her sister sounded more chipper about being boiled in oil than conforming to Duke's enforced nutrition regimen. When in the company of her children, however, eating became a celebratory occasion. Or, Georgia figured, she'd try to pawn off a meal or two on the kids. It would not work, according to the giant bowl of chocolate pudding Abel sat on the hospital tray table. He rolled it right up to Savannah and the girls, opened the bowl and sank a silver spoon deep into the sweet, creamy dessert.

He tapped his watch, "Eat up, Missus. Boss'll be calling in an hour wanting to know your progress."

The girls sat eagerly eyeballing the dish brimming with pudding while their mother's stared stupefied at the sheer volume of food. Georgia admitted there was enough to feed three of her sister – which meant Duke realized her girls would also be present.

"Abel," Savannah whined the name. "Your boss has lost his mind if he believes I can consume this much chocolate pudding."

He poked three more spoons in, winked at her, "There's enough for four appetites he said. You, Tiny, Tadpole and Miss Georgia."

Lily grabbed a spoon, scooped a big serving into her mouth. "This is *good*," she announced then dug in for more.

Using her thumb, Savannah swept the corner of Lily's mouth, "You happen to bring napkins along with dessert? My kid forgot her manners. Lily, slow down. There's enough for all of us, even Aunt Georgia. Hint, hint…"

"Don't drag me into this," Georgia warned good-naturedly. "I had a filling lunch."

"There's always room for pudding," she reminded.

"That's Jello-O, not pudding, but nice try. I will feed Anna though. She's eyeing that stuff the way you ogle peach pie." She planted herself in the chair, spooned up a small serving for Anna.

Abel passed out napkins, pointed to the bowl, "Join the party, Missus."

Savannah gave a half-hearted salute, "Yessir. Don't want to upset Mr. Shelton, do we?"

Lily's brow sank, "Is he the man with all the ladies?"

"That's him," Georgia answered while feeding Anna another bite. "I'm surprised you remember him. You've only seen him a couple of times." And those times really creeped Lily out, Savannah said. His stiff posture and manner of speaking caused the child to withdraw in his presence – a true feat considering Lily's outgoing nature. Duke tried to be kid friendly but couldn't quite manage. Every year he sent both girls a Christmas gift. This past year Anna received a set of children's books and Lily received a Barbie doll. A Barbie doll that due to its outrageous popularity, no family member could track one down locally or on the internet – and if they *had*, a bank loan would have been necessary to purchase it. Still, with all his efforts, Duke fell short of charming little Lily like he had dozens of full grown women.

"Mr. Shelton's the reason we're eating chocolate pudding and not slabs of green Jell-O, kiddo," Savannah reminded. "He's trying to help Mama get well."

"He's weird," she shoved the spoon in the bowl, scooped up a bite and held it to Savannah's lips.

Savannah ate the bite, thanked her then reciprocated the gesture, "He's not used to kids but he tries. He got you that Barbie doll for Christmas, remember? The one that no one else could find? I mean, not even *Santa* could score one, at least not in time."

Lily's frown deepened with utmost disapproval, "Mama, he's okay but he's not better than Santa."

Savannah admitted, "Maybe not but he's a first-rate guardian angel."

Georgia gave Anna another bite of pudding, amused at the conversation. For a woman who claimed no patience – and vowed never to have children – Savannah impressed her sister. Earlier Georgia saw the tiny flinch when Lily accidentally laid a hand on her mother's injured shoulder but Savannah hadn't complained. Though invisible to the youngsters, the underlying current of pain was evident to a halfway observant adult.

Georgia saw Anna staring at the IV machine as if it bared long, sharp teeth and growled at her. The whirring noise did resemble a growl, she supposed. The girl scooted against her mother, away from it. Savannah glanced at her, saw the child's wide eyes switch to the IV taped on top of Mama's left hand. Savannah assured her it was okay but Anna in true form, shied from it.

"You may have to hold her again," Savannah forewarned Georgia. "The IV is scaring her."

"Be glad it's temporary," a wicked gleam sparkled in the older sister's eyes, "unlike someone's fear of flushing toilets."

"Who was that?" Savannah asked on a chuckle.

Oh, so Baby Sister thought that was *funny*… Yeah, Georgia smirked, funny until she found out it was, "You. You used to be afraid of flushing toilets."

Savannah's subdued laughter instantly stopped and reversed into a denial, "I did not."

Lily giggled, "Mama was scared of the throne."

"*I was not*," she defended, "and stop using Daddy's term for toilet."

Georgia teased, "Lily, every time someone flushed, your mama would cry and cry and hide if she could. I found her under her bed several times. Grandpa found her in the closet and I believe Grandma found her in the–"

"You've made your point," Savannah interrupted. The razzing

chafed her good humor, especially when Georgia nearly revealed their mother found little Savannah curled up in the clothes hamper beneath all the dirty socks and shirts – just to avoid hearing a toilet flush.

Georgia winked at her, "So you *do* remember…"

Savannah returned the mischievous smile, "I remember. But you just wait, sister. Wait till you have rug monkeys of your own. I've got stories banked to tell your babies too."

Georgia backed off the subject. Yes, her sister probably recalled a few embarrassing moments of hers as well. She decided not to push the issue past, "You girls should know your mother's never been scared of much in life–"

"But she was scared of the throne!" Lily shrieked herself into hysterics. The laughter inspired Anna to join in, much to their mother's chagrin.

"Thanks, sis," Savannah sighed. "Thanks a lot."

Abel, clearly trying to hide his own laughter, volunteered, "That's okay you were scared of the john, Missus. My mama said I screamed like a girl every time I saw jelly."

Another round of hilarity ensued with Savannah chancing her own chuckle. Georgia barely heard the knock on the door over the laughing. A uniform officer stepped in, waved Georgia over. He extended a folded piece of paper to her, his voice low, secretive, "Some kid dropped this off for Detective Prince. Said a guy paid him to do it. Take a look."

Her brow furrowed at his ominous tone. The hair on the back of her neck prickled. The last time a person delivered something, Jeffrey paid him to do it. Thanks to the TV coverage, the whole city knew Savannah's location so why wouldn't Jeffrey? The piece of paper in her hand opened another Pandora's Box, her gut feeling forewarned. Had he at some point entered the hospital to see the security detail outside Savannah's room then enlisted a boy's help to deliver this note? Had Jeffrey actually breached the front lines of Kaiser-Lee's security guards and stood right down the hall from her sister's room? If the cops and Abel weren't present, it would be easy for him to slip on a doctor's coat, breeze past the nurse's station and into Savannah's room to finish what he started.

Georgia shook off the chill scraping her spine, whispered to Abel with a covert motion to join her.

The uniform repeated what he told Georgia. Abel sobered upon hearing the news, his jolly demeanor disappeared and his vision narrowed at the note. Georgia recognized the block lettering from the note delivered at the house. Savannah's name stood out in the same blue ink and bold block letters. She took a deep breath and unfolded the note. The author wrote a simple one line message but the meaning spoke volumes. *I'm waiting for you...*

32

July 12

I can fool anyone into believing I'm harmless. Just look at young Lily who happily accepted my stuffed pony without the slightest hesitation. Better yet, remember baby Anna retreating to me instead of her own mother. Oh yes, I can be charming when I choose to be and right now it is imperative.

I hitch a ride from Piedmont Park to Dunwoody with a college girl from Georgia Tech. The university is near the park so finding a ride wasn't that difficult. In a way, this girl reminds me of a young Sally Field. In her early twenties, sweet face, short mousy brown hair. She is dressed casually in tight jeans and a baseball jersey. The Braves, of course. She's headed to the game later, she says. Am I?

No, I reply, I'm meeting an old friend, wanting to catch up with her. That deflates her somewhat. For some reason, her smile lingers and I wonder what pleases her so. A moment passes when she confesses, "I know who you look like now. Mc-What's-His-Name on that hospital show."

I return her grin, "I hope that's a compliment." She continues staring at me until I calmly point to the road. Eyes ahead please, I silently convey. I have unfinished business and I'd like to arrive in one piece.

She obediently shifts her vision forward, "I don't watch the show but I think he's cute."

"Ah, so you think I'm cute, do you?" *I tease. This woman is easy to flirt with and I find the light banter a nice change of pace – for now.*

She certainly is not shy, "Yeah, but I mean it in a good way. Not puppy cute but George Clooney cute."

I thank her. In that time my mind wanders to my goal. To pluck that pesky festering five year thorn. To finally get relief. I'm not done with you, my lovely detective. And no amount of police security will protect you, not today…

"What street did you say again?" *College Girl asks.*

"Tilly Mill Road. Just let me off at the intersection on Coldstream."

"The intersection? But aren't you visiting–"

"She spends her free time outside tending her flowers. I want to make sure I surprise her."

"Oh. Okay."

Savannah's house sits in the middle of the block. It will be a generous walk from the intersection but it will also give me time to think. I need to see the strength of police protection, how many officers and where they are before I do anything. "Actually, why don't you drive by *first? I'll see if she's home."*

"*If she's not, I can ditch the game and we could go to dinner together."*

"*Sure, why not?" I lie, knowing Savannah will be home with her cubs along with those extra badges guarding her.*

My driver turns from Mt. Vernon Road onto Tilly Mill Road. When I drove Tonya's Volvo, I came the shorter route to the house, down Peachtree Industrial Boulevard. The route from Mt. Vernon Road is an endless trial and stretches for literally miles until arriving at Savannah's place. On our ridiculously long trek we pass the intersecting street Holland Court. The irony is not lost on me. The name is a reminder for my detective, and I'm curious if I pop into her mind every time she passes by the sign. I smile at that thought as we, at long last, reach the four thousand block.

Tilly Mill Road is a picturesque avenue with plentiful tall, leafy trees making it perfect for families and block parties. I envision neighborhood barbecues where husbands gather to talk football and drink beer while wives swap recipes and gossip. Oaks, pines and mature magnolias dwarf the homes and driveways. Flower gardens brighten each yard (apparently Savannah prefers hibiscus). Dunwoody is a little slice of suburban utopia and worlds apart from her previous residence. The beauty of the neighborhood escaped me on my previous visits but this place truly suits my detective and her family.

"*What address is it?" Nosy Rosie inquires while surveying the larger homes.*

"Just keep driving. I'll know it when I see it." We approach the house and without any reaction, I cut my vision toward it. I catch a glimpse of her place through the tangle of trees. I quite like the white one story home with the sprawling Southern front porch. It's classy but not pretentious. Her Charger is parked at the garage. The absence of Ennis's truck tells me he is busy searching for the bastard who tried to kill his wife. But the green Chevy Tahoe snugged behind the Charger gives me pause. Older sister is still looking out for baby sis, probably cooking, cleaning and babysitting. Along with the police officers I have yet another obstacle to overcome today. Georgia.

"Wow," College Girl points at Savannah's place. "Look at the cop cars. Hope nothing bad happened."

Not yet, friend, but it will… *I see two police units parked at the curb. A calling card to me – enter if you dare. Well, thanks but I do not dare, at least not through the front. For when we pass by, I see two officers sitting in chairs on her porch, looking more like lazy relatives after a Sunday church service rather than a Wednesday afternoon guard duty assignment.*

I wave my driver along since she slowed to gawk at the activity around Savannah's house. I don't need the attention drawn to me. My face sports several days' growth, gifting me with a halfway decent mustache and beard. I prefer to use the word "rugged" but truthfully the damn thing itches like mad and I hate the way I look. I contend with the discomfort to avoid being readily recognized but once Savannah is dead, I will put a razor to this mess and get free of it too. I point forward, "Her place is up ahead."

We pass a few cars parked at the curb, one at the neighbor's house, another two doors down. Despite the extra vehicles, the neighborhood is quiet – no kids playing outside, no adults mowing lawns or roaming about. I only see the two cops on Savannah's porch.

College Girl drives until I choose a suitable house with a car in the driveway, "Looks like she's there." Then remind, "Coldstream is coming up, just let me off there."

"Okay. If you really don't want dinner with me, that is," she hints, sounding almost disheartened.

"I would if I hadn't promised my friend I'd visit the next time I was in town. You see, we share quite a history together. We've known each other five long years and each time we meet, we play a game. So far she's beaten me every time but this time," I wink, "I feel lucky."

She turns onto Coldstream Drive, pulls over, "What kind of game? Chess or something?"

I consider the comparison, "Something like that." I get out, thank her for the ride.

"Anytime. You and your friend have fun."

"Oh, we will," I beam. "We will."

After she drives away and is out of sight, I stroll down the street until the porch comes into view. The two cops still lounge in the white wicker chairs, enjoying their coffee.

I ease between the properties, staying in the shadow of the neighbor's numerous trees. The cops continue their conversation, *oblivious to my presence.*

I hear a child's laugh so I tiptoe toward Savannah's backyard. An eight foot wood picket fence blocks my view except when I focus between the slats. There they are. Mama's little cubs and a surprising bonus – Mama herself relaxes at a patio set with a ceramic cup brimming with coffee. A sling cradles her right arm. The bruise from the jugular cannulation is still visible on her neck. Savannah slumps a bit in the chair, telling me her strength dwindles quickly. By her features, she struggles to keep a cheerful, smiling façade for her girls. This would be easy. So very easy to pluck my festering thorn.

I notice little Lily has taken after her mother in yet another unexpected way. In her hands she holds a golf club made for a young girl her size. The club – a wedge, I believe – cost a chunk of change, judging from the shiny metal shaft and club head. No cheap purchase for Savannah's girl.

Lily takes a practice swing which is eerily reminiscent of Savannah's technique. The sight makes my leg ache.

She steps up and with intense concentration, assesses the white golf ball before her. Savannah told her to line up three in a row, so she could take three good practice swings with the club. Lily swings back – but not too far – then clobbers the ball that soars in an arc toward a large orange "Homer" Home Depot bucket sitting in the middle of the yard. It misses to the right by a mile. The girl huffs, "Mama, I need help."

Savannah slowly rises, makes her way to the child, "Remember what I said about rocking a baby?"

Lily nods. Mama asks for a demonstration. The girl lays the club aside, extends her arms palms up, elbows slightly bent as if cradling a tiny baby away from her body.

Savannah watches her hands and arms swing together in a rocking motion. Left, right, left, right. Using her left arm, Mama mimics the motion only in a smoother, more fluid arc. Lily imitates her, slowing her movements, refining them.

Mama nods with approval, "Try it with your club."

The girl grabs the wedge, assumes her stance. I remember when I stood, ready to splinter Savannah's legs with Mr. Thatcher's driver. Left hand over right... Feet apart... *For Lily, the stance comes naturally with practice, at least more practice than I had.*

"Now," Mama steps back, saying softly, "rock the baby and don't swing so hard. Keep your eye on the ball during your swing."

Lily follows her mother's directions. The club lifts half as high as before then strikes the ball. It sails – nearly floats – through the air, landing within a foot of the bucket. Savannah patted her daughter's back, a genuine smile brightening her features, "Great shot, sweetheart. You're doing wonderful."

The praise straightens Lily's posture and encourages her to try again. The ball bounces off the bucket just short of going in. Savannah cheers her on. Try again, *she says.* You're so close.

Her last shot hits the rim but falls inside. Lily shrieks with delight, her little fist thrusting in the air as a sign of triumph. Mama joins her with her own subdued fist pump and glowing praise.

Savannah returns to the table and I see the exhaustion set in again. Keeping her spirits aloft cost her so much energy she sits back with a sigh and a muted groan. Anything for her children, I tell myself. She proved that at the house. She'll do anything for her girls, even sacrifice her own health and life for them. Her brave face doesn't surprise me in the least.

"When are we going golfing again?" Lily asks.

"It'll be a while for me, honey, but I'll take you when you want to go. You're doing so well. Daddy will be impressed. You need to show him how good you are when he gets home."

Lily giggled, "I will." She places another ball on the ground, swings. It lands squarely in the bucket. "I get an ice cream," the child sings.

This is news to Savannah, "Did Daddy promise you ice cream if you made that shot?"

"Yep."

I hear Mama's relaxed, whimsical laugh, "You've made that shot twice now. Does that mean he's buying you two?"

With an earnest nod, Lily begins collecting the stray balls in the yard. At this rate Ennis will be plenty poor by the time his oldest daughter finishes practicing. She takes the sport as seriously as her mother once did. It seems little Lily aspires to be like Mama in every way possible and so far she's doing a five-star job.

Lily wanders closer to the fence – to me. I weigh the risk of climbing the fence and scooping Lily into my arms to keep Mama under control. Even if she alerts the cops out front, by the time they arrive, I'll have sliced Savannah's throat and voila, no more thorn to fester and ache.

The back door screen opens, Georgia leans out, calls Savannah and the girls.

"What is it?" Savannah asks.

"You've got a phone call," her sister answers.

"I'll take it out here."

"I need to change your bandage and the girls have had enough sun for now." Her placidity jumps a notch to assertive, even parental, "Come on, girls. All three of you. Inside now."

To me her voice sounds insistent but normal. Savannah, however, seems to sense something awry. Confused, she capitulates, dragging out the word, "Okay."

A large black man steps out the back door – Savannah calls him Abel. Abel helps her to her feet then scoops Anna into his arms. Lily follows behind Mama, leaving Abel bringing up the rear.

Moments later I hear the screen door close followed by the inner wooden door. I hear the distinct sound of a deadbolt sliding into place. Georgia suspects something. I do not know how but hers is no reaction to mere paranoia. Being the protective sister, she likely will not tell Savannah of her suspicions. Whatever was happening, it too confuses me. Things move with flawless precision, calling her and the kids inside and locking the doors behind them. I can hear the cops still chatting and laughing on the front porch. They are not alarmed so why did I detect a hint of edginess in Georgia's tone?

"Hey," a man summons from behind me. "What're you doing?"

I can only hope it's a neighbor or just some passer-by. I slowly turn, trying not to appear as panicked as I truly am. Why am I peeking through the fence, the person will ask. I can only hope he hasn't called the police since two officers stand guard less than a hundred feet away. Unless the mystery man is a cop I did not initially see…

When I face the guy, my pulse stampedes. "The" guy is actually two men, one standing with arms crossed, the other with his hands behind him. They want answers. There are no uniforms, badges or guns. I hear those two officers still on the porch, jawing about the job. The two men I face are older, in their mid-thirties and wear jeans and tank tops, the latter exposing the fact they and steroids are intimately involved. Together their broad shoulders span most of the width I require to flee. These are not Duke Shelton's militaristic squad of commandos, nor do they fit the image of Savannah's neighbors who evoke thoughts of eight to five jobs, briefcases and business meetings. No, these are bone-breaking street thugs.

In that span of time, noise erupts inside the house. I hear a TV blaring a kid's show, the volume so loud I can clearly hear music and nearly discern words. I think I hear an exchange between Georgia and Savannah but cannot distinguish what they're saying.

In front of me, the men step forward. "You belong here?" one asks.

He knows the answer. The smirk on his face says so. I remain silent.

The second guy (Number Two I call him) joins in, "You were watching through that fence. That's wrong, man. Really wrong."

I try to step past the pair but am shoved back. My back collides with Savannah's sturdy, unforgiving fence. A fist buries in my stomach so hard the urge to puke flirts with me. "Who the hell are you?" I heave the words, giving in to the urge to retch.

Fingers clench in my hair, yank me straight. Number One's hand wraps around my throat, squeezing down on my windpipe. "We're the neighborhood watch, asshole. Welcome to the block."

The face scowling into mine remains unblinking. My rising tide of panic swells to a tsunami. I want away from them, to run and never look back. These men exude evil. They exude death. They reinforce that fact by admitting they know who I am, why I'm there.

The next punch buckles my knees while the hand around my throat holds me upright. Number Two brandishes a metal pipe from behind his back. I throw a punch into Number One's stomach but he barely flinches. Number Two converges, swings the pipe Atlanta Braves-style and the instant it connects with my right knee, Number One clamps a hand over my mouth to muffle the yelp. Another swing and the hand presses so hard, I feel splinters from Savannah's fence bury in the back of my scalp. Number Two strikes once more, the pipe's end sinking so deep into my stomach, it feels entombed there.

"Not so much fun is it, asshole? Being ambushed and having the shit beat outta ya," Number Two taunts. His and his buddy's repeated attacks leave me incapable of speaking beyond groaning.

"Just wait till we sharpen our knives," Number One chimes in. "We'll do more than carve a number into you, buddy."

Another punch drives me into the fence, making it sway an inch or two from the sheer power Number One used. "Answer when you're asked a question." He punctuates the last five words with their own individual punch, "Are... you... having... fun... yet?" Then he nods an unspoken instruction to his companion who aims at my left knee. His technique puts Babe Ruth to shame. This blow will crush my knee, cripple me from any chance of escaping these two madmen.

Believe me, it is no less painful being struck with a pipe than a golf driver. Number One's hand clamps over my mouth, reducing my earsplitting cry down to a negligible whimper. He releases me, allowing my body to crumple in the grass. I am close to shedding tears for the first time in my life.

"Oh yeah," an idea occurs to Number Two. "Now I remember. Fractured ribs too."

I extend a trembling hand, a silent plea for mercy. Savannah also did this. Like me, she tried fending off the attack. And like me, she realized the futility of it but instinct demands a person try.

The foot rears back and I can do nothing to stop it. For an instant I feel the terror that surely engulfed Savannah when my foot did the same. When the force of the kick lands, my scream would raise the dead – if I could actually scream. Tears squeeze from my eyes. Oh yes, now I understand the pain I inflicted on her. Especially when that large, heavy foot swings back again – just like mine had.

I plead with them while my shaking hand lifts in a feeble attempt to deflect the blow or at least cushion it somehow. The foot buries into my already busted ribs. I cry out again, hoping someone nearby comes to my aid. I don't even care if it's the cops on the porch. I just want away from these two. At this point I want to survive this any way possible, even in prison. Anywhere these men can't find me.

My breaths are short, agonizing attempts to draw air. Again the irony is not lost on me. I see the parallel between my situation and Savannah's several days ago. I want to live, and these men are determined that I will not. I also want to know who these men are. How did they recognize me, realize what I was up to – who the hell did they answer to? My fractured ribs force me to use small, excruciating breaths to express myself. A breath for each word and I clench my teeth against the pain, "Who... are... you?"

I can't bear this level of pain for long. I will need a hospital and quick. But when they grab me and drag my broken, aching body along the neighbor's lawn, the truth dawns on me. I won't ever see a hospital.

"Let's just say we're real good friends with Peter and Bob Thompson and they're not happy about how you treated their lady friend."

I glance at Savannah's front porch. Abel has joined the cops who rise to their feet upon seeing the men dragging me to a nearby car. The three stand, staring at me. I want them to intervene. I want to cry for help. My broken ribs prevent anything past a sick whisper now. I try to convey my wishes through my expression. Please help me. Stop these men.

The trio watch the scene unfold then nod to the two thugs carting off their victim. When they smile, I know. I know there's no help for me anywhere, not even from the people sworn to protect and serve. But then I hunted one of their own, didn't I? Tracked her down and tried my best (oh, how I tried) to kill her.

One officer points a finger gun at me, pulls the imaginary trigger. The Thin Blue Line. They protect one another with a fierce spirit and I crossed the line, trampled and mangled it. Now I paid the price. For a fleeting instant, I wonder how Georgia learned of my presence. The cops stayed on the porch. The neighborhood was quiet. In the fervor to pluck my nettling thorn, had I missed these two animals hiding nearby? Or perhaps the cops weren't as engrossed in their chitchat as I thought. Perhaps they alerted Georgia after making a call to the two Mr. Thompsons.

Whatever the case, they weren't about to help me. I halfway expected them to open the car door for these two, then give them a full blown escort to my final destination.

I'm surprised when both cops pick up their coffee cups, turn to the front door and they, along with Abel, leisurely saunter inside. The front door shuts and locks, leaving me to assume neither Savannah nor her children will ever learn of my presence or of my fate.

33

July 13

Savannah awoke worried about her sister. Every day Georgia came over to cook, clean and tend to her sister and the girls. She made meals, straightened things, did laundry and babysat while helping Savannah with various needs like showering. She took time out to check in at the bakery to ensure the business ran smoothly in her absence. Savannah wasn't sure how her sister shouldered so much responsibility without cracking – until yesterday when Georgia's behavior showed such stalwart workaholics were *not* immune to stress's effects on the mind.

Savannah planned an early morning call to her sister. *For the love of God,* she'd say, *please stay home and rest because yesterday scared the bejesus outta me.* Everything seemed fine until that afternoon when Georgia called her and the girls inside – no, *ordered* them inside. She had a phone call waiting, Georgia said, but when Savannah asked for the phone, her older sister shrugged, saying it was a solicitation. Then why had she sounded so urgent about the call? She wanted to ask Georgia that question but her sister barged past her to the TV, cranked up the volume to a cringing level, then immediately headed toward the laundry room.

"Don't go anywhere," Georgia had said, "I need to tell you something."

"How about telling me you're making an appointment for hearing aids," Savannah suggested but her sister hadn't heard her.

Meanwhile, Abel vacated the premises, opting to stand outside with the two uniform officers. What the hell was going on, she wondered at the time.

"Where's your extra detergent?" Georgia had shouted over Sesame Street's Elmo and Cookie Monster who debated over how many cookies were in Elmo's plate.

She raised her voice to be heard, "Where it always is. In the cabinet above the machine." Georgia knew all this so why ask about the detergent's location? It didn't make sense.

Savannah went to lower the TV's blaring racket but her sister now stood in the living room doorway shaking her head, "I turned it up for the girls. Cookie Monster is Anna's favorite."

"Anna can come into the living room to watch the show. Right now outer space can hear Cookie Monster." She reached for the remote but retreated upon viewing Georgia's stern frown and pronounced shake of the head.

Her sister hated noise. Georgia savored peace and quiet and her peculiar behavior struck Savannah as more than odd. It troubled her to the point she struggled to drift to sleep that night. The weirdest part – as quickly as the craziness started, it ended. All it took was Abel and the two officers to walk in and request a refill on their coffee. Georgia calmly closed the utility room doors, muffling the wash cycle's churning. She headed to the TV, ran the volume down to a tolerable level then fetched the coffee pot to fill the officers' mugs. The world went insane for ten minutes then returned to normal. Savannah looked to her sister, praying some screw hadn't come loose.

Then Georgia's cell phone rang. It was Peter Thompson. "Yes, Mr. Thompson, she's feeling better today... Oh? That's great news," Georgia gushed. "So the traps worked. Yes, they *can* kill your flowers overnight... But you say the garden is now pest-free? I'm absolutely *thrilled* to hear that..."

Savannah listened to her sister fuss over gardens and traps for another minute until the call ended. "He gardens too?" she asked Georgia.

The cheerful grin on Georgia's face inspired her own while the older sibling nodded, "Has for years. Wireworms got into his gladiolus so he set traps for them."

"You two'll be talking flowers and fertilizer at the shop now. Trading tips and giving advice." Curiosity got the best of her, "So how do you trap a worm?"

Georgia shrugged, "I didn't ask. Anyway, he's so happy his garden is pest-free, he said he had to let me know. He also said he'd call you later this evening. Give you time to rest."

Savannah nodded then asked, "You still want to change my

bandage?"

Georgia laughed with such ease, it scared her. Her older sister traversed the scale of emotion from grim fanaticism to boisterous laughter in the blink of an eye and that worried Savannah because in some circles, those mood fluctuations required medication…

"Of course, I'll change your bandage, sweetie. Give me one minute to make a call."

"Telling Dane about Mr. Thompson's worms?"

Georgia laughed again, "Telling Dane when to heat our supper."

She started to dash from the room with not only Savannah questioning her sister's rational mind (if she still had one) but both her girls gaping in disbelief at Aunt Georgia's off-the-wall actions and flip-flopping mood.

"You feeling okay?" Savannah wanted to know before she made a call of her own to Dane saying *get Georgia to a doctor fast.*

Georgia swiveled to her and Savannah swore the smile on her face was the most beautiful thing she'd ever seen. A movie star smile. She stepped closer, kissed Savannah's cheek, "I feel perfect, little one. Absolutely one-hundred percent perfect."

Drawing herself from the memory, Savannah yawned. Mental note: Call Georgia, tell her to take a spa day or something. Today, *she* would manage the household by herself. It would be a challenge but her sister really needed a break.

First order of business. Get up, get dressed and go feed the security detail. By that time, her husband and kids would be awake and ready for their breakfast. The officers assigned to watch her house were young and sweet-natured for having such crappy duty. Protection detail rated lowest among a cop's dream assignment but the two toughed it out with smiles – and cake, coffee and a meal or two that she or Georgia prepared. It always paid to feed the guys protecting you, she thought.

She awaited the day she could sleep and shower without a sling. Being a side sleeper and not a back sleeper posed its own obstacles. Actually *sleeping*, for one. Getting comfortable for another.

And showering? Forget it. She did fine until needing her back and good arm washed. That's where Georgia came in if Ennis wasn't home. Nothing made her feel more like a baby than having her sister bathe her – any part of her.

The sling not only cramped her style and self-esteem but also her neck that felt stiffer than steel. As if she required any more complications, the simplest tasks such as dressing herself or eating became hopeless and comical. The graceless effort of left-handed eating roused giggles from her girls along with comparisons to Anna's clumsy attempts to feed herself. Ennis and Lily tried assisting her with certain meals but Savannah hated feeling anymore babyish than she already did.

She credited Georgia with preserving a sliver of her eroding ego. Her sister, thank God, prepared thoughtful dishes geared toward the poor unfortunate human unable to cut her own steak. Georgia cooked easily handled meals such as fried chicken bites, quesadillas, pot pies and casseroles. Thanks to Duke's amazingly talented chef and Georgia, Savannah packed on six pounds so far and needed to stop the madness.

Her pants were already hard enough to button.

She sat on the bed with jeans in hand (ready to see if they still fit). She intended to accomplish one clear-cut goal that morning. Dress herself without any help.

Left foot, right foot, pull 'em up past the ankles. Now came the fun part. Ennis or Lily gladly helped her with these everyday tasks however a five o'clock wake up call seemed rather cruel. She'd just have to manage.

She stood, pulled up the jeans, battling serious twinges in her right side as her left hand awkwardly strained to operate the zipper and fasten the top button. Southpaws, she sighed. How the hell did they get along in life anyway?

Blouses presented the biggest challenge and where Lily felt most competent. Savannah's helpful girl needed a break *and* her sleep though. Temporarily ditching the sling, she carefully slipped her wounded wing through the blouse's armhole. So far so good. The left arm, not the right one, usually caused the problem when she reached her left hand back to slip on the blouse. She curbed a groan behind pursed lips. Stretching the arm pulled the stitches on the right side, inflamed the dull ache in her ribs. She would not wake Ennis to help her dress. *I can do this myself.* After fighting the maroon blouse (which now matched the color of her cheeks from all the wrestling), she spent the next three minutes buttoning six maddeningly tiny buttons, one-handed of course, and having a devil of a time doing it. Now for the sling. Again, once the stretching with the left arm concluded, the groan averted, then she slid her arm through and sighed. She was halfway done. To the bathroom she went to run a brush through her hair then arm herself with a potentially dangerous implement. A toothbrush. Left-handed tooth brushing, she discovered, required tedious accuracy, sort of like juggling nitroglycerin – one slip could turn disastrous. Upon completion, she winked in the mirror, congratulating herself. She hadn't knocked out any teeth, hadn't accidentally swallowed the toothbrush or dropped it. The day was looking up already.

Before leaving the bedroom, she stopped by the dresser for her wedding ring. Finally, something her right hand could legally do (according to the doctors). Slip on her cherished ring. While easing it on her left hand, her vision wandered to the appointment card beside her jewelry box. She sneered. An attending cardiologist at Kaiser-Lee wanted another test. According to the experts, she suffered a heart attack due to the stress and blood loss. He classified it as *mild* whatever that meant. To her a heart attack was a heart attack and damn it, she hadn't had one, she argued at the doctor. She would *know* if she'd had one.

Except he'd produced the results to prove it. He translated the electrocardiogram and echocardiogram results into straightforward terms until the glaring truth hit home. She'd suffered a heart attack. At her age. With her normally excellent health. Great, she thought at the time. Just freakin' wonderful.

With all their concern, tests and follow up appointments, she hated to tell the doctors but until Jeffrey Holland ceased to exist, heart damage was the least of her worries.

Oh fiddle-dee-dee, she bolstered herself in the dresser's mirror. I'll worry about that tomorrow. Scarlet O'Hara may have been a flighty broad but she had the right idea. Focus on now – and right now Savannah had kids, a husband and two cops to feed.

Muted light from the living room spilled into the hall, along with an occasional flash from the TV. She walked in to see her guard detail lounging in hers and Ennis's recliners, their attention riveted to a rerun of Law & Order, the sound turned low. They'd shed their duty belts but kept them close by. When the girls awoke, the officers would re-equip the belts for safety's sake.

Both in their mid-twenties, Maurice Mitchell and Troy Jones hung out together off duty since they still claimed their bachelorhood. Guard duty – according to them – was easy money. It was if boredom didn't kill you, she wanted to say but hadn't. Boredom never stood a chance. The two clean-cut, sturdy cops aggravated and teased each other like brothers, she noticed.

They greeted her with wide grins, "Mornin', Detective."

Savannah stopped, curious about the blatantly large smiles, "Mornin'. Everything okay?"

"All quiet, even outside," Jones said. "It's going to be a beautiful day. Perfect for a walk in the park."

What an optimist. Savannah told him as much while reminding herself for *normal* people, yeah, a perfect day for a walk in the park. For targets of a psychopath on the loose, not so much.

The officers traded humorous glances. Mitchell tossed in his two cents, "Just wait, Detective. Just wait."

She regarded them with a generous dose of cynicism, "Okay."   .

Jones switched off the TV, "Your private security fella took off around eleven last night."

And this was supposed to be good news? Duke specifically instructed Abel to stay around the clock. Good ol' reliable Abel, the rock (and teddy bear) of the Shelton security force bailed on her at her most vulnerable time. Everyone around her needed a check up from the neck up. Even Duke Shelton. After Georgia's little mental hiccup with the TV and washer, Duke called to check on her and see how she was feeling. Once the chitchat concluded, he apologized for intruding on her relationship with Peter and Bob Thompson. He had no right to judge them or taint their image with her, he'd said. His call confused her. What happened to the people in her life, she wondered, because Duke Shelton *never* apologized for being meddlesome.

Savannah spent several minutes assuring him he hadn't tainted anything and not to worry. No, Peter and Bob Thompson – or whatever their names were – held a special place in her *mildly* damaged heart.

She sighed, still puzzled and surprised that Abel split when he did. She thanked the uniforms for not following his lead, "I'm happy you guys didn't abandon ship. You hungry?"

"How about a Pop-Tart?" Mitchell asked. "Those are mighty tasty, especially the cherry ones."

His partner nudged him, "Stop eatin' her out of house and home. Maybe the kids want those."

Savannah waved it off, "No, Lily likes Cocoa Puffs and Anna prefers eggs. Believe it or not, Ennis eats the Pop-Tarts and he doesn't mind sharing. Jones, what about you?"

The young cop thought a minute then stood, "You got anymore instant oatmeal? I can make it, save you the trouble."

She motioned him to sit, "You're keeping me and my family safe, the least I can do is cook breakfast for you – such as it is."

They both thanked her. Mitchell pointed to the dining table, "Brought your paper in. You might want to take a look."

Savannah veered to the table, yawning, "Why? The mayor cutting more overtime?" She flopped it open, turned it over to view the headlines.

Above the fold read *Serial Killer Found Dead.* Well, it wasn't *her* serial killer, she frowned at the headline. Jeffrey's little hiding place eluded law enforcement and Duke's men. He seemed to appear or disappear at will, which only supported her theory he possessed an evil immortality like those horror movie villains.

She looked at the headline again, thinking how wonderful life would be without the threat of Jeffrey lurking around every corner. Serial killer found dead, she harrumphed. That headline could have meant anywhere in this big ol' U.S. of A. For that matter, anywhere in the freakin' *world...*

For the sake of curiosity, she referenced the dateline. Atlanta. Not Chicago, New York or Los Angeles but right in her very own city. *Okay, I'll bite. Who was this killer who vacated the planet to make it a better place? And Lord, big favor here. Could we make that name read Jeffrey Holland?*

The cops exchanged whispers. She ignored them while her vision studied the photo. Atlanta uniforms swarmed what appeared to be a ravine. Taken from a considerable distance, the photo showed a blurred set of bare calves and feet. The ravine concealed the rest of the body. She didn't recognize the detectives crouching near the deceased murderer.

She skimmed the article, daring to hope just a little. Her eyes widened upon viewing the name *Jeffrey Holland. Oh. My. God. I'm gonna pass out – or definitely kill someone if...* "Is this a joke?" she accused the uniforms. Because someone *would* lose their teeth while she lost her religion on the culprit.

With a laugh, Jones levered to his feet, joined her in the dining room, "No ma'am. It's no joke." He withdrew a piece of paper from his trouser pocket, handed it to her, "The lead detective's name and number. I got a coupla details from a uniform who worked the scene. He said someone really tore Holland up so bad it looked like a victim's relative got hold of him."

Then bestow a shiny medal and sainthood upon that relative for cleaning up the streets. She took the offered number with a thanks. "What details did you get?"

He shot a covert glance toward the hallway, Savannah figured to ensure no children overheard him. "Whoever did it beat Holland black and blue. Busted his ribs until his side caved in."

Savannah winced on that one – and so did her side. She resisted the urge to cradle the sudden twinge.   Jones continued, "Broken arms and legs, mutilated hands and his throat was cut clean to the bone. There's more but I'll let the detective tell you about it.   It's safe to say Holland didn't go out easy."

She shivered despite herself, "No one's crying over it either." Yes, Jeffrey got a taste of what he dished out to his numerous victims.   She wondered if he begged his torturers to stop – or, perhaps tried crying out to "her" God once or twice.

As Jones predicted, it *was* turning out to be a beautiful day.   A day for a walk in the park.   Jeffrey was finally gone.   Out of her life, her kids' lives and Georgia's too.   If this was a dream, she prayed to never wake up.

"Detective, are you okay?" Mitchell asked.

One more look at the headline.   Another glance at Jeffrey Holland's name and a solid stare at the note in her hand, the one listing the lead detective's name and number.   Everything *appeared* real.   The crisp, rustle of the morning rag.   The note's smooth surface and sharp folds beneath her touch.   Everything *felt* real.

Another pang from her ribs verified that yes indeedy, she stood in the middle of a real life dream come true, not a ghastly nightmare that cruelly teased her with hope.   The usual fatigue that crept in after the ordeal of dressing vanished in an instant.   Replacing it was a spark of excitement she hadn't experienced in over two weeks.   "I'm more than okay," she answered Mitchell.   "This is one of the best days of my life."

Shock surrendered to a smile.   A smile accentuated a giddy un-

Savannah-like giggle that broke the two uniforms into their own laughter. She rushed past the officers toward the master bedroom. Her exhilaration rated as euphoric as Lily's on Christmas morning when she bolted into her parent's bedroom at four o'clock begging them to get up and open Santa's gifts. Whoever killed Jeffrey brought Savannah an early Christmas gift. The best one a person could ask for. Her life. "Ennis, wake up!" she called, not caring if she woke the entire world. She raced to his bedside, put a hand on his shoulder, rocked him to and fro, "Wake up, wake up."

"I'm getting seasick," he mumbled. One eye parted into a slit, "What's got you so riled?"

A large, toothy grin stretched across her face. His eye narrowed, "That smile is scary happy. You win the lotto?"

"I sure did." She presented the headline, holding it for him, "Read."

His eye moved lazily across the headline, "Mmm," then the lid drifted closed.

Savannah waited, remembering it took her a few seconds to process the news too. She did not move but kept the paper displayed for when the truth hit him.

Ennis bolted upright, his hair fanned like an Indian headdress in the back, "You're actually *smiling*." He pointed to the paper, "Because of that?"

She nodded, tapped her finger on Holland's name. He yanked the paper from her grasp, focused strictly on the blurb beneath the picture. Fifteen seconds later he lifted his wide eyes to her, "This isn't a joke, is it?"

She wagged the small slip of paper back and forth, the one the uniform handed her, "Jones gave me the lead detective's name and number. I'm calling him as soon as I calm down."

"At that rate, you'll be too old to *see* a phone, much less dial one. You're too hyped up." Ennis barely got the words out when she threw her good arm around him and planted a long, passionate kiss on his lips.

She parted from the lip-lock with a gleeful, "We're finally free, babe."

He drew her back to him, "Say that again – and start with the kiss."

"Mama, why're ya shouting?" Lily stood at the bedroom door, her balled fists rubbing her eyes.

Savannah hurried to her, dipped to one knee to hug her baby close, "Mama's happy, little one. That's why I'm shouting. The bad man is gone forever."

Lily's eyes widened in a way reminding Savannah of her own reaction, "He's gone? Really?"

Savannah looked at her beautiful girl. She would watch her grow up, attend college, get married and perhaps, some day, Savannah would hold grandbabies in her arms. With Jeffrey gone, anything was possible. "Sweetheart, he will never bother us again. Never."

34

July 29

Savannah looked forward to her usual Saturday shift at Pie In The Sky – this time with abbreviated hours. She missed the laughter and the customers. She missed living her life and this was another step, however small, in reclaiming it.

Her energy returned slower than her eagerness. She noticed fatigue set in sooner after only twenty minutes waiting on customers. Georgia reminded that she should sit down more often. "That's why I scheduled the usual servers," she said. "So you could take your time and not feel rushed."

Well, there were no worries there. Even if she *felt* rushed, getting her body to respond to the impulse seemed tricky. Savannah cursed herself for being so weak and frail. She'd had weeks to recuperate – and go stark raving mad locked up in that house – so it was past time to get back to normal.

When she mentioned returning to the bake shop (before she lost each and every marble), Georgia wheedled a promise from her. Only two hours with frequent breaks then Ennis or Dane could pick her and Lily up to take them home. Savannah reluctantly agreed. Two hours. Feh. That was nothing. She wanted at least half a day but Georgia refused to hear it.

Savannah spent every requisite ten minute break sitting down, watching her sister flit around the kitchen the way a butterfly zipped from flower to flower gathering nectar. Georgia could wear a person out. The woman's oomph rarely gave out. Savannah slumped in the chair, silently grousing on being cheated on the "oomph" DNA end of things. "I tire out faster watching you work than I do actually moving around," she rose from her seat. Somehow it felt more like a "time-out" for a brat than a break for the physically challenged. "I'm getting busy."

Georgia leveled her best authoritarian frown, "Only ten minutes and only if you can hold up."

"Yes, Mama," Savannah capitulated. It was, after all, Georgia's shop. She made the rules, silly as they were…

Lily giggled in the chair beside her mother, "You don't tell Aunt Georgia what you tell Daddy."

"What does she tell your daddy?" Georgia wanted to know.

"To mind his own beeswax."

"Your mother knows better than to say that to me. I'm the older sister," she winked at Savannah. "I own her."

Lily laughed, "I'm gonna tell Anna that. *I'm the older sister. I own you.*"

"She'll hate you if you do," Mama warned good-naturedly. She patted Lily's knee, "C'mon, kid. Let's make Aunt Dictator some money. Go turn on your charm 'cause I'm fresh out."

The bell over the front door jingled, announcing more customers. A quick glance at the clock told her who those customers were. And just in time too. She'd finished her mandatory rest period.

She peeked around the corner to see Peter toddling to his usual table, cane in hand. He eased into the chair with a smiling sigh. Bob occupied the chair beside his brother, signed to him. *Took you long enough, old man.*

Peter waved him off, "Oh, be quiet."

Bob returned the dismissive wave then hammered his fist on the table, the not-so-subtle hint he wanted service now.

Savannah turned to inform Lily that the Thompson brothers had arrived but the youngster seemed to sense it – or heard it considering Bob's pounding not only announced his arrival but also annoyed nearby patrons. The girl ran past her mother with open arms, "Mr. Thompson!"

"There's our girl," Peter bubbled with delight, his own arms spread wide. "Give ol' Peter a hug."

Before interrupting them, Savannah watched the scene unfold. Three weeks had passed since Savannah saw Peter (and later Bob) at the hospital, but a long, lonely month for Lily. The girl dearly missed Peter and it showed in her tight embrace the two shared. Her daughter embraced the older man with an excitement reserved for a cherished grandfather. Lily adored Peter Thompson and anyone saw the feeling was mutual.

Savannah saw Lily greet Bob by signing her customary *Hi Bob* and he reciprocated with his own hello and a rare smile.

"Say," Peter spoke secretively to the youngster, "is your mother around today? We've got a little something for her."

"Sure!" She wheeled on one foot, shouted toward the kitchen, "Mama, Mr. Thompson wants to see you!"

Savannah cringed. The fiercest blush heated her face until she practically broke a sweat. *Dear God*, she rolled her eyes. *The whole world thinks we're from the back hills now. Yeah, the back hills from another planet...*

Georgia, busy rolling out pie dough, laughed, "I've never seen you so red." Then reconsidered, "Well, maybe when Lily asked what Mama and Daddy's bedroom rodeo was but only then."

"Never gonna live that down," she mumbled. Another Ennis-ism their oldest cleverly adopted. Without knowing it, Lily blurted his slang for sex to the whole family in Texas – on Christmas Day, no less. The female relatives sat in stunned, awkward silence. The male relatives roared with laughter. Savannah left the room, leaving Ennis to dig his way out of the mess. "Yeah," she agreed with Georgia, "she had to ask *that* in the middle of Christmas festivities. Thought Mama Rutherford's eyes would drop out of her head before mine. Ennis doesn't believe me when I say kids pick up everything you *don't* want them to learn."

She wiped her left hand on a dishtowel, wishing she could ditch the sling already. The damn thing hurt her neck, plus the fact she flat hated to be feeble.

At least her presence at the bakery represented some form of normality. A return to the sublime routine of life without Jeffrey Holland. Her list of practical tasks, however, shrunk to about two or three. Having a bum arm limited her duties to handling small orders or working the cash register – but she couldn't completely blame her arm for the latter since she never quite got the hang of operating the damn register in the first place.

"Mama!" Lily summoned a second time.

Trekking out of the kitchen she noticed the customers staring at her. They obviously pegged her for "Mama". She uttered a chagrined "sorry" to the masses then focused on Lily, gently reminding, "Honey, don't yell. It's not polite."

"Sorry," she pouted but immediately bounced back. "Mr. Thompson's got something for you. I wanna see what it is."

Savannah met her friend's gaze. A bright beaming smile split Peter's face as he rose from his seat, gave her a gentle embrace, "Dear girl, it is such a delight to see you. We've both missed you."

She returned the hug, her good arm snug around him, and kissed his cheek, "I've missed you too." A fist rapped on the table and Peter eased away from her, "He's such a pest."

She chuckled and turned, signing as best she could, "I've missed you too, Bob."

He nudged her hand away, signed to her – *Save your strength. Remember, I can read lips.* She extended her arm to hug him – a first since their acquaintance. Bob presented an aloof manner that kept most people at a distance – that and his fussy nature, that was. But today she wanted to thank him for his support, kind words and prayers during her recuperation. He'd just have to like it or lump it.

Bob hesitated at her bold move, his eyes a bit wider than normal when they shifted to Peter then back to her. He shrugged at his brother as if asking *what do I do?*

Peter sighed, "She's not gonna break, you idiot. Go ahead."

Bob advanced a step, meeting her halfway for the embrace. He placed one hand on her hip, the other gently across her back – the way his brother had – only Savannah swore this time she hugged a tree, not a frail older man. A big, sturdy redwood, she thought. His stiff manner and the two mechanical pats on her back revealed Bob Thompson was utterly uncomfortable expressing affection of any kind. His blush also told her he was as bashful around women as he was cranky about his coffee.

"He's a real Don Juan with the ladies, isn't he?" Peter needled. He mumbled under his breath, "Treating her like a plague victim…"

Bob stepped back, glared at him. His hands motioned vehemently at Peter. Savannah read the message – *I don't want to hurt her, you dope.* With Savannah his features softened, his signing smooth, composed – *How are you feeling?*

She started to sign back until he took her hand in his (another first), held it gently then pointed to her lips, mouthing *Speak.*

"He's afraid you'll wear yourself out signing to him," Peter explained. "He's worried about you. Surprised me to learn he had a heart."

Bob scowled at him again then brightened when Savannah kissed his cheek, "Both of you are so thoughtful – *and* entertaining." She answered Bob's question, "I'm feeling better and stronger every day."

Bob patted her back with more ease this time. *Excellent news,* he signed then followed up with *I'll take my usual please.*

She lifted one brow, "Extra sugar?"

Of course.

Peter took her hand, volleyed his brother's scowl back to him, "Let us talk before you saddle her with work. Impatient, impatient. He was a week early when he was born too." Looking back at Savannah, he inquired, "How are you honestly doing?"

"I'm healing in many ways, Mr. Thompson. Physically and emotionally. The knowledge that Jeffrey Holland is dead is better medicine than half the stuff they gave me in the hospital."

"From what I understand he suffered quite a while before he died. I consider that, what do they say – karma."

"I'm certainly not shedding any tears over it. I really wish I knew who killed him." She lowered her voice to a whisper, "It may sound horrible but I'd like to thank them."

He shrugged, "Perhaps it's better this way. He had plenty of people wanting him dead. One of them got lucky."

"Well, whoever it was I owe them a debt of gratitude."

Bob rapped his knuckles on the table hard enough to startle the customers. Savannah felt Lily recoil against her while Bob signed, his movement stern, purposeful.

Peter's expression softened toward his brother, "He's right. You owe nothing to anyone."

Savannah smiled a little. These two men were true blessings to her and her family and she was proud to call the two Mr. Thompsons (or Thomasins) friends.

The reference to Thomasin reminded her of Duke. She presumed his men killed Holland. He outright vowed that if his men found him, they would kill him. When Jeffrey turned up dead however, her good friend denied any involvement in making the world (especially hers) a safer place. She decided Peter Thompson (Thomasin) was correct. Lots of people wanted Holland dead, one just got lucky.

Bob leaned forward to see the new waitress headed for their table. She balanced a serving tray in one hand – on it, Savannah recognized Bob and Peter's orders. She reckoned Bob would fuss about it too. He preferred Savannah or Georgia to serve his coffee and pie and grumbled if someone else tried. If anyone might crack his granite surface, Amy Williams could. She was a sweet girl of twenty-four with an alluring, almost shy smile. Her friendly nature won many patrons' approval the last three weeks and showed so much promise that Georgia rescheduled her shift to Saturday, their busiest day.

Upon Amy's arrival, Peter straightened a degree, his voice lilting, "Oh, who's this young lady?"

Savannah introduced them, seeing Bob's steel door slam shut – and lock tight – despite Amy's polite greeting. Peter, on the other hand, appeared enchanted with her cute face and long dark tresses. Savannah guessed Amy's shapely figure hadn't hurt her appeal either. Savannah got a kick out of seeing Peter smile and smooth his hair while greeting Ms. Williams. He edged closer to Savannah, bobbed his brow, "She's a keeper."

She smiled knowingly, "I believe she is, Mr. Thompson." For many reasons, she mused to herself.

Amy handled the tray with expert dexterity, slid it onto the table where Bob stared at it, sulking. Savannah heard him sigh with resignation (and a tad of disgust), as if the girl served him a cup of mud. He signed his displeasure to Savannah – *Is the coffee fresh?*

"Yes, Bob, the coffee's fresh," Savannah assured.

He nodded toward the pie. How about the pie? This question was implied since he went on a sudden signing strike, refusing to do anything past crossing his arms.

"The pie came out of the oven," she checked her watch, "twenty minutes ago." She patted his arm, "Amy knows what she's doing, Bob. Give her a chance."

Amy smirked at the exchange while placing the brothers' orders on the table. Savannah could tell by Bob's expression he was not happy to be served by anyone other than her or her sister. Bob Thompson and the concept of change mixed as well as foil and a microwave. Emphasizing his disgruntlement, he stabbed his index finger next to the coffee cup.

Savannah deduced his complaint in an instant, "Amy, can you

bring Bob two extra sugars? He's picky about that."

A bashful smile curved the young lady's mouth while she reached in her apron pocket, "Georgia told me."

Peter shook his head, "My brother the malcontent." He warned Bob, "Stop being so finicky. The poor girl's trying to earn a buck."

Savannah watched Bob break his strike and sign to his brother who shook his head, rolled his eyes, "Friendly? Who would accuse *you* of being friendly? I said, 'Stop being so *fin-ick-y.*'" Peter waved Savannah closer, cupped his hand around his mouth to block Bob's eavesdropping, "He should work in a complaint department. Would fit right in."

Bob banged the table, signing to Savannah. *What did he say?*

She chuckled, "Leave me out of this. I've got my own sibling to deal with." She hitched her thumb toward the kitchen.

Amy wrote the bill and stripped it off the order pad. Savannah confiscated it, her hand gently pushing Peter's away. He thumped the floor with his cane, "No, ma'am. You're not pulling this trick on me again. That's my bill and I'll pay it."

"No, sir," she replied. "You're my friends and today is my first day back and I insist." She pointed to his cane, winking, "Bob's habits are rubbing off on you. His fist and the table, your cane and the floor."

"Difference is I still have my manners." He bent toward her and kissed her cheek, thanking her for "picking up the tab".

Bob knocked twice on the table to gain Peter's attention. He followed up with a universal and well-exercised hand gesture – *hurry up.*

"He's been waiting all week for this," Peter said. "Most people value the notion of patience. Okay, okay," he waved at his brooding brother. He reached in his pocket, withdrew a long, flat black velvet box.

Like any woman, Savannah immediately recognized it as a bracelet or watch jewelry box. Stunned, she shook her head, tried to keep her jaw from plummeting to the floor, "Mr. Thompson, no…"

"Yes," he countered kindly. He took her hand, turned it palm up and placed the box in it the way he handed Lily her Saturday treat money. "Don't argue with these old men, Mrs. Rutherford. It's your first day back and we get *our* way too, at least with this. Now," he nodded to it, "open it."

"C'mon, Mama," Lily prodded, eyeing the gift. "I wanna see what you got."

Savannah felt enormous guilt accepting the gift, whatever it was. They spent a chunk of money for her rose bouquet at the hospital and now this… "You two shouldn't have–"

"You stall like my daughter used to," Peter shook his head.

Bob blew out a breath, signing – *Open. The. Box.*

She handed the box to Lily who gleefully accepted custody of it. She held it for Savannah who removed the lid. This time her jaw did plummet, awe-struck, "It's gorgeous." She gathered the silver braided charm bracelet in her hand, lifting it to view a pink crystal heart dangling from the middle. Across the heart was a silver ribbon engraved *Survivor.*

"Peter…" her voice caught, forcing her to swallow back the rising emotion. Don't cry, she berated herself. *This present is from two special friends who care about you. Why are you ruining the moment by tearing up?*

She lifted the heart to the light, noting the different facets and how they sparkled. The two Mr. Thompsons went whole hog with their flowers *and* presents, "You and Bob spent a small fortune–"

Bob knocked on the table, this time gently. She turned as he signed – *A good friend is worth it.* He emphasized – *You are worth it.*

Peter nodded, "Finally, he speaks sense. We wanted to find a little gift for you. This represents survival in many ways, not just what you recently went through. According to Georgia, that pink heart also represents another kind of survival, one my precious daughter never saw." He clasped her hand in his arthritic grasp, "My dear girl, take care of yourself as well as you care for your family. Always keep abundant hope, preserve your youthful spirit and frequently exercise your beautiful laugh. Above all, remember you have many people who love you," he winked, "and me and Bob – ornery as he is – stand at the front of that line."

Lily tugged on Savannah's blouse, "Can I see it?"

Savannah nodded, handed the bracelet to her then wrapped each brother in a one-armed hug, "The two Mr. Thompsons are, and always will be, our treasured friends. You are true blessings in our lives. Thank you both."

"What's that word?" Lily pointed to the silver ribbon stretched across the pink heart.

Peter leaned down to Lily, placed a hand on her shoulder, his voice gentle as his touch, "Lily, that word is *survivor.* It takes a lot of strength and courage to be a survivor. It means your mother is very brave and that she protects the people she loves with all her heart. I bet someday she'll tell you her life story and when she does, you'll understand how brave and strong she is. Your mother is a true survivor."

J.L. Lemon lives in Texas surrounded by a loving and supportive family, two adorable and devoted puppies, and hordes of garden gnomes.

Before 2002, J.L. Lemon wrote opinions and product reviews for an online consumer guide. When fellow reviewers cited the author's knack for humor, she decided to return to writing fiction. Along with the standalone title Second Chances, she's published 11 books in the Savannah Stories Series.